Who
Is to
Blame?

Who
Is to
Blame?

A Russian Riddle

JANE MARLOW

RIVER GROVE
BOOKS

Published by River Grove Books
Austin, TX
www.rivergrovebooks.com

Distributed by River Grove Books

Design and composition by Greenleaf Book Group
Cover design by Greenleaf Book Group
Cover image: Casther and lazy clouds, 2016. Used under license from Shutterstock.com
Interior Images: MATULEE, lazy clouds and Forest Foxy, 2016. Used under license from Shutterstock.com
Note to Reader and Author photos: Amelia Anne Photography, Bozeman, MT.

From *Riddles of the Russian People*, collected by D. Sadovniko, translated by Ann Bigelow. Copyright ©1986 by Ann C. Bigelow. Published in 1986 by The Overlook Press, New York, NY. www.overlookpress.com. All rights reserved. Used with permission.

Cataloging-in-Publication data is available.

Print ISBN: 978-1-63299-104-1

eBook ISBN: 978-1-63299-105-8

First Edition

NOTE TO READER

ONE HUNDRED AND seventy years ago, political activist Alexander Herzen wrote the original *Who Is to Blame?*—a satire depicting the coarseness and pettiness of the Russian landed gentry. Herzen, himself the son of a rich Russian landowner, is credited with spawning the political climate that led to the emancipation of the serfs in 1861. As a tribute to that accomplishment, this book is dedicated to Alexander Herzen, a courageous activist and writer whose works have been translated into multiple languages.

Nobility

MAXIMOV FAMILY

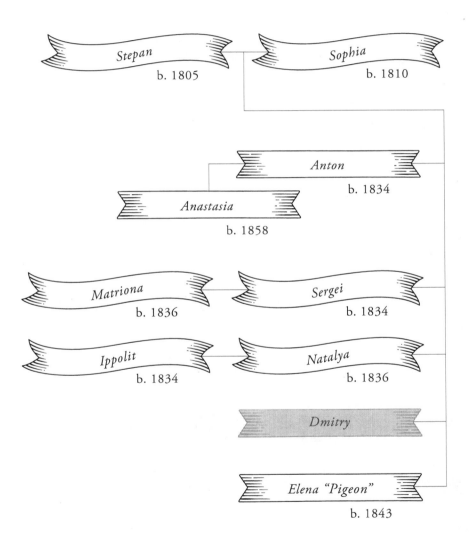

Stepan
b. 1805

Sophia
b. 1810

Anton
b. 1834

Anastasia
b. 1858

Matriona
b. 1836

Sergei
b. 1834

Ippolit
b. 1834

Natalya
b. 1836

Dmitry

Elena "Pigeon"
b. 1843

Peasants (Serfs)

ANAFREV FAMILY

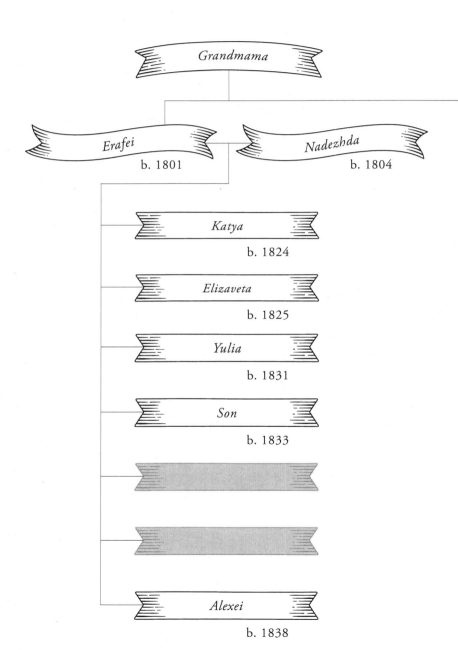

Grandmama

Erafei
b. 1801

Nadezhda
b. 1804

Katya
b. 1824

Elizaveta
b. 1825

Yulia
b. 1831

Son
b. 1833

Alexei
b. 1838

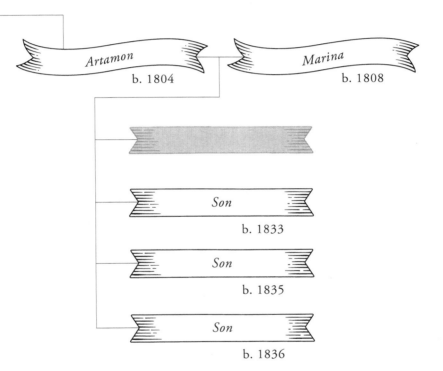

Artamon
b. 1804

Marina
b. 1808

Son
b. 1833

Son
b. 1835

Son
b. 1836

Peasants (Serfs)

VORONTSOV FAMILY

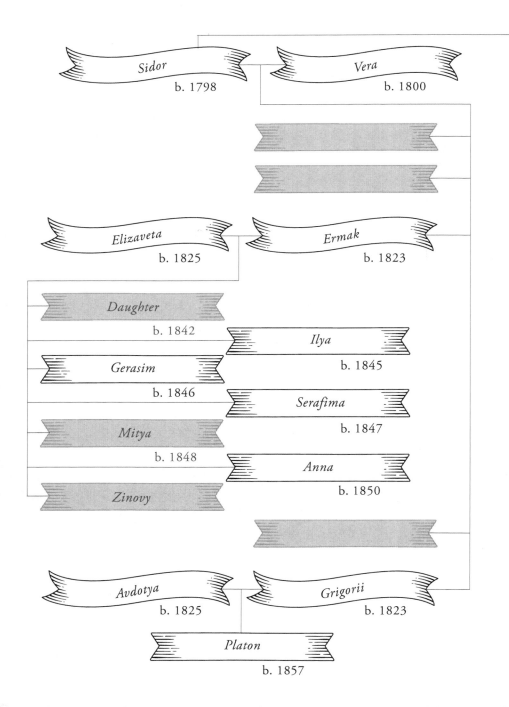

Sidor
b. 1798

Vera
b. 1800

Elizaveta
b. 1825

Ermak
b. 1823

Daughter
b. 1842

Ilya
b. 1845

Gerasim
b. 1846

Serafima
b. 1847

Mitya
b. 1848

Anna
b. 1850

Zinovy

Avdotya
b. 1825

Grigorii
b. 1823

Platon
b. 1857

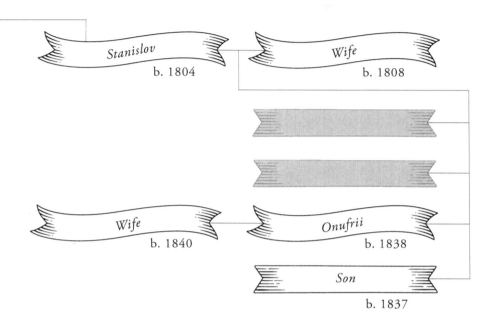

Stanislov
b. 1804

Wife
b. 1808

Wife
b. 1840

Onufrii
b. 1838

Son
b. 1837

Locales &
Supporting Characters

LOCALES

Petrovo (estate)—the agricultural land, buildings, and house owned by the Maximov family

Petrovo (village)—small village comprised of peasants located on the estate of Petrovo

Sukhanovo—district capital

SUPPORTING CHARACTERS

Peasants (Serfs) in the Village of Petrovo

Feodor Zhemchuzhnikov—lifelong friend of Elizaveta

Nikifor Zhemchuzhnikov—Feodor's father

Anisia Zhemchuzhnikov—Feodor's mother and Elizaveta's godmother

Evdokim Seleznyov—tavern owner; Zhanna's father

Illarion Loktev—the village rumormonger

Maximov Servants (Serfs) on the Estate of Petrovo

Cockeyes—distillery overseer

Dasha—housegirl

Gennady—butler

Matriusha—nanny

Yegorka—stableman

Maximov Employees

August Wilhelm Roeglin—estate steward

Hilda Behrens—tutor

Nobility

Rusakov family—good friends of the Maximovs; live on a nearby estate

    Vladimir—husband

    Yustina—wife

    Victor—son

Valeryan Kirillovich Shelgunov—Stepan's cousin from Moscow

    Leonora—wife

    Rodya—son

    Sonya—daughter

    Nadya—daughter

A.A. Gabrichevsky—wealthy owner of estate neighboring Petrovo

Ippolit Filippovich Gabrichevsky—nephew of A.A. Gabrichevsky; husband of Natalya Maximova

Filip Ilyich Gabrichevsky—father of Ippolit Filippovich Gabrichevsky

Others

Alexander Nikolayevich Romanov (Alexander II)—Tsar of Russia 1855–1881; son of Tsar Nicholas I

Father Diakonov—Petrovo's priest

Varlaam Gorbunov—holy beggar

Veniamin Savelyevich Pichshenko—tax farm's chief inspector

Vaska the goat

European Russia

PART

One

Elizaveta

1840

What won't feed you without a beating?
Grain.

THE GIRLS FROZE. Their grain flails halted in mid-air, as their heads cocked toward the approaching jeers and raucous clanging. Elizaveta and her seven girl-friends flung aside their flails and dashed to the slouching wood gate at the road's edge. A mocking throng was clustered around a horse-drawn cart, behind which a tethered, barefoot woman plodded through gummy road mud. The aggrieved crowd had stripped her naked above the waist and sheared off her long hair, leaving short spikes like the head of a thistle. From the roadside, scolding neighbors pounded blackened pots with soup spoons and oven prongs. Others pelted the woman with garbage and blistering insults.

Petrovo's village assembly had found Grusha Prokofieva guilty of illicit sexual penetration and sentenced her with public shaming. While the all-male assembly pointed condemning fingers at the unchaste woman, it sympathized with the wronged husband and ignored the male co-fornicator.

Long before Elizaveta understood the meaning of "unchaste," her parents and the Church had pounded into her that such women threatened the moral sinews of the family and, by extension, the entire village. Of like mind with her neighbors, she usually regarded promiscuous women with self-righteous scorn. But not today. Over the past few months, Elizaveta had discovered the heady throes of her sweetheart's warm body pressing against hers. She had come to understand temptation.

Watching the adulteress dodge apple cores and chicken bones, Elizaveta resolved to grant no favors beyond kissing prior to her wedding vows. She was new to the business of kissing, but her older sister Katya, with her one year of romantic experience, had warned her that all boys wanted more.

Elizaveta wasn't certain of the details of "more" when they involved a man and a woman, but she'd been familiar with the various acts of propagation for livestock and fowl since before she reached the age of reckoning. And living in a one-room hut, she was privy to the nighttime noises of her parents as well as those of her aunt and uncle. However, she had never actually witnessed "more."

Desires, she vowed, would be bridled until that blessed day she became a bride. But a familiar dread instantly lodged itself in her chest. So many obstacles stood between today and her wedding day. *Well, really only one obstacle,* she tried to reassure herself. But it was such a huge one. And when it eventually reared its head, she'd have to go toe to toe with her father, Heaven forgive and protect her.

As the taunting mob sought retribution farther down the mucky road, the girls traipsed back to the threshing barn and picked up their wooden flails. In the unvarying cycle of the seasons, few rhythms were more familiar to teenage girls than the timeless *thwack* against a mound of rye. A flail had been thrust into each girl's hands as soon as she was strong enough to handle the unwieldy device, even before her height matched the handle's length.

The eight budding young women chattered like swallows while they freed the precious grain from its dry husks. Tongues flitted with anticipation over the upcoming winter parties—parties that would include boys.

First, the girls settled on a fair compensation for the once-a-week use of the Widow Shabanova's single-room hut for the parties. They'd give the old hunchback a couple of *kopeks* plus supply their own firewood. And they'd turn her frostbitten vegetable plants into the dormant garden soil. But knowing Shabanova, they predicted she'd balk, "Too stingy!" If all else failed, the girls would concede to helping the childless widow maneuver the ice-bound road to the Divine Liturgy every Sunday. But that was as far as they'd give in to her excessive demands.

The buzzing conversation shifted to which boys would attend. Zhanna Seleznyova was adamant that runty Demian Osokin be excluded.

The lone dissenting voice belonged to Elizaveta, her chin jutting forward. "We agreed village boys between fifteen and eighteen were welcome."

Zhanna pitched an impatient glance at Elizaveta. "Demian's too puny."

Elizaveta halted her flail. "So you're saying appearance is all that matters? A shiny new kopek is worth more than an old one? Our little wooden church is less holy than a big stone one in Moscow?"

Zhanna huffed a sigh of condescending tolerance. "What I'm saying is, weak boys can't work as hard as strong boys. Therefore, nobody wants to marry one. So why invite him?"

True to her nature, Elizaveta dug in her heels. "Demian's the right age, so it's only fair to invite him."

Zhanna flipped her flail end for end and plunged its handle into a mound of rye. "Have you failed to notice? He has red hair." Zhanna smirked. The irrefutable fact was certain to bring the discussion to a swift conclusion.

Elizaveta acknowledged that people with red hair were, as a rule, untrustworthy. "But Demian has never done anything to make us believe he's devious or dishonest."

Zhanna stood her ground with mulish obstinacy, as did Elizaveta. Work stopped as the other girls joined the heated debate. After many contentious glares and much foot-stomping, the majority concluded no harm would come if redheaded Demian were admitted into their circle.

Humiliated by her defeat, Zhanna went after her adversary's tender spot: She ambushed Elizaveta's dearest friend since childhood. "Based on age, Feodor Zhemchuzhnikov definitely won't be invited."

Elizaveta's breath was knocked from her as solidly as if she'd been ramrodded by the end of the flail. "What?"

"Zhanna's right," said Marfa, whose family's grain they were threshing. "He's only fourteen."

"As you yourself pointed out, boys have to be at least fifteen." Zhanna's deep dimples dug into her cheeks. "The knife cuts both ways, Elizaveta."

Elizaveta's chest billowed. "Feodor turns fifteen in January, and we'll still have parties then. So he should be invited."

"No. They have to be fifteen before the first party." Zhanna leveled her longlashed eyes at Elizaveta. "You'll turn fifteen in October, so these will be your first winter parties. You need to understand how we do things."

"You're being unfair!"

"I'm completely fair. Besides, Feodor's even scrawnier than Demian." Zhanna's mouth puckered at the tartness of her own words. "Everybody thinks Feodor is a milksop. Except you and your sister."

Elizaveta's free hand grabbed the rough homespun of her skirt and balled it inside a tight fist of rage. She looked to her older sister for backing, but Katya merely gaped at Zhanna.

Marfa made a tiny offering of support on Feodor's behalf. "Oh, Zhanna, Feodor's just, well, a little boring. And as romantic as a turnip. But that doesn't mean he shouldn't be invited. But only after his birthday." Using the tip of her flail's handle, Marfa drew a line across the dusty planks, staking out an uncrossable boundary.

The girls, with the exception of Zhanna, eventually agreed Feodor could attend the parties after he turned fifteen in January. But not before.

Work resumed, and the discussion switched to which party games should be played and which ones were too risqué. But Elizaveta heard little of it as she pounded the grain in righteous rage.

The gall of that Zhanna! In fact, the gall of all those girls to belittle Feodor. Her Feodor! But then again, none of the girls realized how deeply their comments slashed her heart. Not even Elizaveta's beloved but chicken-hearted sister Katya knew that he was *her* Feodor, in that extra-special way. Several times, Elizaveta had come within a hair's width of confiding in Katya, but the risk was just too great.

Indeed, anyone with a functional set of eyes could see Feodor was tall and lanky like a scarecrow, with arms so long his fingers dangled to his knees and feet that stretched out farther than his shadow in late afternoon. His limp hair wasn't a desirable brown or black or even a disagreeable red or an uncommon blond. Rather, the nondescript color lay somewhere between mouse and mud puddle.

But Feodor was as caring and loyal a friend as anyone could want. Plus, he worked harder than any of the other village boys. Why did the girls judge him solely on his appearance when there was so much more?

As Elizaveta gave the grain a good trouncing, she slid a disappointed look toward Katya. The two sisters and Feodor had been fast friends since they sucked their cloth pacifiers. But Katya, true to form, had stood as mute as a fence post while Zhanna spouted her cruel words. Elizaveta sighed. Katya always allowed herself to be blown about like chaff in the wind.

Elizaveta rested her flail while she swatted gnats and stretched her shoulders. Her muscles were weary from the endless threshing and knotted with pent-up rage at Zhanna. She wiped the sweaty grime from her forehead onto her sleeve.

Inhaling deeply, she lifted the far tip of her flail to shoulder level once more, then bent forward at the waist to sling the swingle down in an arc to strike the grain heads. The swingle, a flat stick almost as long as her arm, was attached to the end of the wooden handle with a leather thong.

Zhanna, tightening the knot of her kerchief under her chin, rekindled the topic of Prokofieva's public shaming. "About time that slut got what she deserves." She picked up a broom and began gathering the loose straw and chaff, which would be fed to livestock during the coming winter.

"Must you always be so critical?" Elizaveta asked. "Have you never made a mistake?"

"Mistake?" Zhanna flicked her pretty head. "Prokofieva's *sin* was hardly a *mistake*."

"Have you nothing but meanness inside you?"

The other girls ceased their threshing. Their wary eyes shifted between Elizaveta and Zhanna.

"You're defending everyone today, aren't you?" Zhanna sneered. "First those little weasels, Demian and Feodor. And now the slut Prokofieva."

Elizaveta could think of nothing that would bring more pleasure than shoving her fist into Zhanna's smug mouth. "You've been a snob since the day your mother pushed you from her body!"

"And you think you know everything! You always have to open your big mouth, don't you?" Zhanna gave a mighty sweep with her broom, hurling a cloud of chaff at Elizaveta.

Elizaveta wiped the powdery grit from her eyes, then bent forward to spit her words. "Ever wonder what people say about you, batting your eyelashes at every boy in the village? Following in Prokofieva's footsteps, perhaps?"

Zhanna's jaw dropped as she groped for a comeback.

"Liza!" Katya hissed. "Leave off, will you?"

Ignoring her sister, Elizaveta angled her head at a cocky slant. "When you and Arkhip slipped away from the circle dances last summer, exactly how much *fun* did you have?"

"At least I have a boyfriend! All you have is that pathetic little toad Feodor!"

Elizaveta's insides blazed with fury and hurt. She seized the flail's handle with both hands and swung it in a shoulder-high horizontal arc in Zhanna's direction. She meant the action to be merely one of intimidation. But her hands were clammy with emotion, and the handle, after years of being clasped, was as smooth as river stones. The flail slid from her grip, whirled though the air past Zhanna's head, and slammed into the barn wall.

Crack! The dry wood of the swingle fell to the ground in two pieces.

"You could have killed me!" Zhanna screeched.

Elizaveta stomped across the floorboards, snatched up the flail, and shook it at Zhanna. What remained of the swingle flopped like the broken neck of a goose. "Next time, I'll take better aim." She stalked from the barn, her head high, her body rigid with anger.

But hidden behind the growl and the strut was the waver of anxiety. The flail's near miss was the least of Elizaveta's concerns. To her way of thinking, a miss was a miss, whether it was by the width of a hand or the length of a field.

Her real problems waited at home. First, there was the broken swingle. All of the family's possessions—everything from the hut, barn, and sheds to the totality of their contents—were handmade with sweat, labor, and time. Worldly goods were few and precious, and were to be treated accordingly. A fierce tongue-lashing awaited anyone who was careless.

Second, when word of her foolhardy behavior reached her family, her father would be furious. His reprimands were swift and unsympathetic.

Third, Zhanna's parents would pound on the Anafrevs' door this evening, livid that their daughter had almost been beheaded. Elizaveta would have to swallow her pride and ask forgiveness from Zhanna's parents and, worst of all, from Zhanna.

If she didn't apologize, she wouldn't be welcome in the circle of her friends. When winter descended, the girls would huddle in the warmth of the massive clay stove to sew and embroider and gossip. And she'd be excluded. In the village of Petrovo—a cluster of only fifty-one families—being ostracized was unbearable punishment.

The heat of anger flushed her face—anger at that arrogant dimwit and anger at herself. She dropped her head back and beseeched the Blessed Virgin in Heaven to help her rein in her unruly tongue. Why couldn't she follow her grandmama's advice? The wise old woman had told her over and over: "The word is like a sparrow; you can't catch it once it has flown."

CHAPTER 2

Maximov

1840

What creature is this?
It feeds all the people
and gives light in the church.

A bee.

AS WAS HIS habit, Count Stepan Stepanovich Maximov woke during the soft interlude between night and day. The old manor house creaked under the sun's first rays, as if stretching after a night's slumber.

As he tossed aside the coverlet, his sleep-fogged eyes settled on the bedside pedestal table and its pewter candlesnuffer. Memories of bygone evenings with his wife washed over him: smoke swirling about the pillows, his fingers loosening the tasseled cord, her dressing gown gliding to the floor.

Stepan rose and, in the muted light, gazed across the bedsheets at the graceful curve of his wife's spine. *What happens to your soul,* he wondered, *when the most precious person in your life turns a cold back toward you?*

With a heavy tread, he moved to the paned window and nudged it open. In streamed the dewy essence of roses and new-mown hay. The bouquet's ripeness carried tender memories of limbs entwined like grapevines. Of two people lost in a paradise of touching, holding, relishing. Of a time when the simple presence of one another evoked unfathomable bliss.

His forehead slumped against the cool glass. Like a candle snuffed, the easy flow of miraculous days and enchanting nights had ended abruptly with Dmitry.

BENEATH THE PORTE-COCHERE, Stepan dropped a ruble onto the grimy creases of Father Diakonov's outstretched palm. As his jagged fingernails closed over it, the priest muttered his customary "May God be with you." His voice reeked of last night's vodka and his hunger for the silver coin.

The mouth of the wolf and the eye of the priest—never satisfied. Stepan was certain the expression found its consummate example in Diakonov. And yet how gladly he'd slip a hundred-ruble note into the grasping hand if the priest could successfully petition God to give his wife back to him.

Stepan nodded the priest's dismissal and pushed open the mahogany door. The aroma of freshly baked pies rolled over him. Like a bird dog, he trailed the scent across the foyer, through the dining room, and into the kitchen.

Ever wary, he stepped behind his wife and encircled her waist with his arms. "Mmmm. Poppy seed pie. My favorite."

Sophia pivoted to face him. "That is why I had the cook make several."

She's smiling just like old times, he thought. *A good omen.*

"Father Diakonov blessed the beehives?" she asked.

"Yes, he sprinkled his holy water, the same as every year. The peasants will be lapping up honey, and the church will be ablaze with beeswax candles." Stepan placed his lips close to his wife's ear. "Join me for some pie while it's warm?"

"Just a quick bite. I told the nanny I expect her help sorting through the attic trunks. They are overflowing with clothes the children have outgrown. Shall we eat on the terrace, or would you prefer the dining room?"

"Let's stay right here."

"In the kitchen?" Half of Sophia's face slid upward in lopsided confusion. "Whatever for?"

Stepan pulled out a chair for her. "Why not? Here's a perfectly good table we never use."

Sophia's head angled in baffled amusement as she took the proffered seat. "Perfectly good, you say?" With an air of purpose, she laid the flat of her hand on the blackened circle left behind by a scalding pot, then rocked the square table on its uneven legs.

Stepan's grin was broad. "Point well made." He settled himself on a chair, its desiccated wood moaning with age. His finger traced one of many random etchings left behind by knives. "A tribute to the table's decades of service, wouldn't you agree?" His eyes crinkled in merriment, and he took it as another good omen when hers did the same.

He reached under the timeworn boards and clasped her hand. She didn't pull away. An especially good omen. "In regard to your question, we're eating in the kitchen for two very good reasons. First, thousands of families throughout the Motherland are celebrating the Feast of the Honey Savior by enjoying their poppy seed pies at their little tables beside the stove. It makes you and I part of the larger whole."

Sophia playfully lifted a skeptical eyebrow. "And your second reason?"

"This room smells too good to leave."

The cook and the butler worked in tandem to present slices of pie on china plates along with linen napkins, silver forks, and tall glasses of lemonade. A lusty racket heralded the arrival of the Maximovs' three children followed by their trudging nanny, Matriusha.

Natalya sidled up to her father, her brown eyes inspecting his plate. Stepan lifted the four-year-old onto his lap and was rewarded by the deepening of her angelic dimples. As he slid a tidbit of pie off his fork and into her mouth, the twin boys stood gracelessly beside the table, their antsy feet buffing the floorboards.

Matriusha's fleshy fingers drummed her round abdomen. "All right, you can each have one slice."

The boys scrambled onto the two remaining chairs while the butler presented their pie and tableware.

"Stop gobbling your food like a couple of hounds," Matriusha scolded.

"In a hurry," Anton said. "Going with Yegorka to get a baby goat."

Their mother's eyebrows plunged. "Get. A. Goat?" Each word was coated with vexation.

Stepan intervened, explaining he had given the twins permission to purchase a goat. The servants had put the notion in the boys' heads that goblins inhabited the stable's rafters. The evil spirits resembled polecats and ran along the backs of the horses after dark, working the poor animals into a frenzy. But the night creatures gave wide berth to any stable that smelled of billy goat.

Sophia shook her head. "You will have to postpone your goat. I am paying a visit to Yustina Rusakova this afternoon. You boys will go with me and spend time with Victor."

"Not that namby-pamby!" Distaste shot from Anton's mouth. "Do we have to?"

"Yes, you have to. Vladimir and Yustina Rusakov are your father's and my closest friends. I want the two of you to be friends with their son."

"But Mama," Sergei mewled, "Victor's no fun."

"That's the end of it," Stepan ordered. "You'll do as your mother says."

"Just going to the village for our goat. Back in plenty of time to go with you." Anton's head bobbed with assurance.

"Please, Mama?" Sergei bleated, sounding like a goat himself.

Stepan's teeth clinched. Sergei's whine grated on his nerves like an axle that needed greasing.

The kitchen, with three servants, three children, and his wife all within arm's reach, suddenly felt overstuffed to Stepan. "Pour me a little more lemonade to wash down the pie," he instructed the butler before turning to Sophia. "I'm headed to the stable to check the horses' hooves and the harnesses for the trip to Nizhny Novgorod."

Anton added an enticement to his appeal. "Mother, if Sergei and me go to the village, we'll hire a peasant girl to pick beautiful meadow flowers you can take to Madame Rusakova."

"Sergei and I," Sophia corrected. "That is very chivalrous of you, Antoshka."

Chivalrous? Was it possible, Stepan wondered, *for a six-year-old boy to be chivalrous?*

Anton's lips curled into a cherub's smile while his eyes continued to petition his mother. Sophia shrugged a sigh. "Oh, run along. Get your goat. But be back in time for our visit. And do not return smelling like a couple of billies."

Anton patted her arm. "Count on me to get the best flowers."

After the twins tore from the table, Sophia chirped a singsong. "Natalya, my darling little one, would you like to go to the attic with Mama and Matriusha and look in the big chests? We might find clothes you wore as a baby."

The small head bobbed, bouncing the silken tresses with copper highlights acquired from her mother.

"Off you go, sweetie!" Sophia nodded for the nanny to take Natalya upstairs. "I will be up directly."

While Matriusha's tremendous girth followed the little girl out of the kitchen, Sophia slid her empty plate from her as though the painstaking movement required the totality of her concentration. With the same precision, she folded her napkin and placed it beside her plate.

A chilly wave rolled over Stepan.

Sophia's full lips thinned as she turned toward him. "So you are going to the Fair?"

The singsong voice had disappeared, replaced by one with a bitter edge. Two little lines appeared between her eyebrows. Stepan instantly recognized these as troublesome omens.

"Yes, I'm going." Of course he was going. Every August, he and Vladimir Rusakov indulged themselves with a "three-week airing" at the great marketplace at Nizhny Novgorod.

"I am astounded you would even consider the trip." Her chin tilted upward. Another worrisome omen. Stepan's shoulders tensed. "Why?"

"After what happened last year." She pushed back from the table, the feet of her chair screeching against the floorboards.

He followed her into the foyer, caught off guard by the change in both the subject and her disposition. She was halfway up the stairs when he called, "Sophia, stop."

She did an about-face. Cocking her head in one direction and her hip at the opposite angle, she was the portrait of long-suffering exasperation.

He climbed the steps, stopping two treads below her. He tempered his urge to shout *What is it this time?* and settled instead for a calm "What has upset you?"

"You know perfectly well that Fair is to blame for Dmitry's death."

When Stepan returned from last year's trip, his serf Yegorka brought back a case of the measles. Yegorka shared his malady with only one person—pregnant Sophia.

Following her near-term miscarriage, Stepan had ached as his wife wept her inconsolable grief into her pillow. Sophia's face, at first puffy with tears, became gaunt after weeks of barely eating. She lived day and night in a baggy housecoat.

As the year passed, her anguish had eased somewhat. She had abandoned her robe in favor of black widow's weeds and kept her head covered with a black knit cap. Now, on occasion, she was the warm, affectionate woman Stepan had married. More often than not, though, she secluded herself emotionally from her husband.

She cast her eyes downward in defiance. "You deem it acceptable to leave me here, drowning in memories of what happened exactly one year ago?"

"You seem so much better, more like yourself." His hands curled, driving his fingernails into his palms. *Mother of God, why can't she put the past behind her!*

"If I seem better, it is largely due to the comfort Antoshka offers me."

"Anton?" Could she hear the sarcasm in his voice? He certainly could.

"Why, yes. He spends time with me. He listens to me. Which is more than I can say for his father."

How unjust! He battled to find a benevolent tone. "I've spent untold hours holding you, trying to console you, even when you acted as though you wished I was on the far side of the world."

"Is that how you perceive yourself?" One eyebrow rose in a spiked arch. "What I see is you bestowing your superficial attention on me, all the while in a hurry to get me out of the way so you can tend to your crops and your distillery and your horses. Anton is patient. He never brushes aside my sorrow."

Slashing curses threatened to erupt. He brought to bear the whole of his self-discipline, but his words still burst forth pinched and caustic. "He's a child, Sophia. Do you really think he understands any of this?"

"A child he may be, but he shows me more compassion than does my husband." She gathered her skirts to continue up the stairs.

Stepan caught her arm as she reached for the balustrade. She halted and stared over the banister into empty space. He had always admired her profile, as flawless as a creamy cameo. Today, the outline of her face was every bit as hard and cold as the engraving.

A stinging remark begged for release, but going tit for tat would merely fan her malice. He pressed himself to slow his words, soften their timbre. "If I haven't shown my heart's ceaseless concern for you, that's a failing on my part." The backs of his fingers stroked her unyielding lower arm. "Perhaps we need to spend more time together. Talk on the terrace like we used to. Or have Yegorka drive the two of us about the countryside."

She swiveled an icy glare toward him. Snarled words spewed from between her taut lips. "You seem to have mistaken me for a torn harness or a broken-down fence that you can patch up." She shook off his hand. "Understand, Stepan, that a mother can never fully put aside the death of her child."

CHAPTER 3

Elizaveta

1840

Who offers everyone his hand?
A door.

ELIZAVETA SCOURED THE length of the dirt road to the left, probing each homestead, including her own. Her eyes pivoted to the right, down the narrow road that stretched past another string of thatch-topped huts to the far edge of the village, where the tile roof and bell tower of the small wooden Church of Saints Peter and Paul overlooked the low-slung huts.

Seeing no one, she squeezed through one of the countless gaps in the Widow Shabanova's battered fence and sprinted to the equally decrepit barn. The door's wooden hinges heaved their familiar rasp as she slipped into the dimness.

Her heart quivered while her eyes strained to see through the shadows. Shards of dusty sunshine wedged their way between the barn's shrunken boards. Since the death of Shabanova's husband five years earlier, no one except field mice had used what remained of the structure. It was the ideal hideaway for young lovers. Except for its location.

Halfway between the two ends of the pocket-sized village, the rutted road forked around the sole public water well and its neighboring steam bathhouse. The thoroughly tromped patch of ground was generously dignified as the "village square." It was with good reason that Elizaveta's heart bounded about her chest every time she slipped into the barn—the widow's homestead was within spitting distance of that center hub.

She eased her back down the stall's rough-hewn boards and settled into the straw Feodor had supplied for warmth and cushioning against the dirt floor. As her heart calmed, her lips grew pouty. Damn Zhanna and her ridicule of Feodor! And the same went for the other girls, following the snob's lead like a bunch of witless sheep. Yet not one of them had a suitor who, in addition to sweating in the fields, squeezed in time to earn extra rubles.

Only three men in the village of Petrovo had a source of income beyond what they reaped from the land. One was the priest. Another was Zhanna's father, who owned the tavern, the village's one and only business. The third was Feodor's father.

Like all serfs on Count Maximov's estate of Petrovo, Nikifor Zhemchuzhnikov's primary function was to till the Count's fields. But occasionally, the Count would pay Nikifor to supply cartage to the district capital, Sukhanovo. With increasing frequency, Nikifor relinquished the reins to his eldest son, Feodor.

Feodor must have made a very fine impression on the Count, because out of the whole village—the *whole entire* village—whom had he chosen to travel with him to the upcoming Great Fair in Nizhny Novgorod? Her Feodor!

No family worked as hard as the Zhemchuzhnikovs. And someday she'd be part of that family, if everything went as planned.

"Please," she whispered into the dank air as she brought her knees up to her chin and snugged her skirt's folds about her calves.

But even the stars in Elizaveta's love-struck eyes couldn't blot out the images of what would happen if her secret were to be discovered. Her father would rant that God would punish her spiritual debauchery. Her neighbors would castigate her, just as they had the adulteress Prokofieva. Count Maximov would be within his right to have her flogged. And the priest would proclaim she was halfway down the road to Hell.

She bit her lower lip. Her father, the village, the Count, and God had one thing in common: Their righteousness was unyielding.

Not that any of this predicament was her fault, she reasoned. Who could have ever imagined that things would turn out the way they had? But then again, it should have been as clear as daylight from the very beginning. Even when she and Feodor had crawled about on all fours, they were as inseparable as cold from winter. Some of their earliest memories were of each other's face.

Through the years, Elizaveta, Katya, and Feodor had gathered mushrooms in the shaded summer woods, pummeled each other with snowballs during the endless months of ice and frozen breath, and put their heads together year-round to hatch all manner of childhood pranks. But somewhere along the way, Elizaveta and Feodor had tumbled into that unique closeness that allows room for only two people. Games of hide-and-seek among the cemetery's tombstones gave way to tickle-and-kiss in the fragrant meadow grass.

Elizaveta and Feodor's lifelong friendship had the blessing of both sets of parents, who were themselves the best of friends, even serving as godparents for each other's children. Both families assumed that Elizaveta and Feodor were merely childhood chums whose affection had remained steadfast during the peak-and-valley turbulence of adolescence.

But Elizaveta knew the day was approaching when those blessings would shatter.

She dropped her forehead onto the rough homespun covering her knees. Every time she thought about the calm assurance of Feodor's arms and words, she was convinced that Heaven had cast a gilded net of good fortune over her. Except for that one loose thread that could unravel her entire future.

Marriage between the children of godparents was considered tantamount to spiritual incest and was unequivocally forbidden.

WHEN FEODOR DROPPED onto the hay beside her, Elizaveta curled under his extended arm. He listened while she poured out the saga of her clash with Zhanna, even though the tale was already common knowledge among Petrovo's 450 residents.

"Be careful how far you raise Zhanna's hackles," Feodor warned. "Her teeth are like fangs, and she's always looking for an excuse to use them."

She curled her lip in distain. "She's selfish and vain and deserves to have that yapping tongue yanked out of her mouth."

"Make sure you don't cut yourself with your own sharp tongue."

That's what she loved about him, had always loved about him: his serene good sense. Plus, he knew her as well as she knew herself and understood how hard it was for her to choke back words that screamed for release. She relaxed into a smile as she gazed into eyes the color of weathered acorns.

Having exhausted the topic of haughty Zhanna, they explored Feodor's upcoming trip to the Great Fair with Count Maximov. How long would it take? Might there be bandits along the way? Where would Feodor sleep? But above all, how wonderful that he had been handpicked to go along. Perhaps this was a test. Perhaps the Count had bigger plans in mind for Feodor.

Swelled with pride, Elizaveta smiled into those familiar eyes. Feodor placed two fingers under her chin and raised her lips to his, and they dropped into their favorite pastime.

In the distance, the church bell pealed five steady strokes. But Elizaveta's ears became alert to another noise, fainter but closer, and very familiar. And very dangerous.

The plaintive creak of the barn door.

CHAPTER 4

Elizaveta

1840

What can't be measured or weighed,
but everyone has it?

Speech.

FEAR FLOODED ELIZAVETA'S chest, shoving her heart into her throat. *Holy Mother of God, help us!*

Entering the barn were two sets of footsteps, followed by a girl's titter of laughter and a long silence. Elizaveta and Feodor bolted to crouched positions facing the noise, hidden from view by the boards of the stall.

"Don't do that."

Elizaveta gasped. Zhanna!

Next they heard high-pitched giggling, followed by silence.

"Stop," came Zhanna's voice, "or I'll leave."

Another stretch of quiet.

"That puts an end to it! I'm going home." Footsteps padded the dirt.

Heavier footfalls scuffed after her. Elizaveta suspected they belonged to Zhanna's boyfriend, Arkhip Melnikov.

"Don't go." It was more of a whine than a request.

Elizaveta narrowed her eyes in furious disbelief. That wasn't Arkhip's voice. It belonged to mealy-mouthed Pavel Vorobev.

Katya's boyfriend!

The scoundrel, Elizaveta fumed. Pavel was far and away the most handsome boy in Petrovo. But Elizaveta long ago recognized that he was all feathers and no meat, a weak-willed simpleton who hid behind a peacock-proud swagger. And now he had proven himself disreputable as well.

"Come on, let's go to the hay and talk," he urged.

"Only if you promise to behave."

The footsteps drew closer. Elizaveta's mouth went as dry as rye chaff. She turned to Feodor. In panicked silence, they weighed their limited options. Which was worse—waiting until they were caught or gaining the upper hand by confronting the interlopers?

Feodor's anxious eyes ticked upward. Elizaveta nodded. They forced their legs to straighten and raised their heads above the rough planks of the stall.

Zhanna and Pavel froze as if roped from behind. Zhanna's coquettish smile slid away. Pavel's cheeks glowed raspberry red. For a paralyzed eternity, the two girls locked eyes.

Zhanna broke the tightly stretched silence with a voice as sweet as honey. "Well, well. You two are much closer friends than I realized."

"As are the two of you." Elizaveta cringed at the squeak in her voice.

Zhanna threw back her head and sniggered. "What a sight this is. Mild-mannered Feodor Zhemchuzhnikov and sassy-mouthed Elizaveta Anafreva, having a little tryst in the Widow Shabanova's barn."

"What a sight *this* is. Zhanna the flirt with my sister's two-faced suitor." Elizaveta shot Pavel a look of disgust. His Adam's apple leapt.

Zhanna raised an innocent eyebrow and shoulder. "We weren't the ones lying in the hay."

Elizaveta saw no point in denying it. "Only because we beat you to it." Feodor's foot tapped her ankle in warning. But instead of holding her tongue, she bellowed, "How many other suitors have you stolen?"

"You smug little sinner!"

"You just take whatever you want, don't you!"

"Shut up, both of you," Pavel growled, "or the whole village will know our business." His raspberry cheeks were now drained of color.

"Let the village know." Zhanna's words were defiant but hushed. "These two are the ones who are depraved, not us." Her lips curved into a dimpled sneer. "Oh, my. The village will feast on this juicy scandal."

"I don't think so." Feodor's voice was unruffled.

Zhanna snorted. "Pardon?"

"You can't write in the chimney with charcoal."

"What's that supposed to mean?"

"How will you point your finger at us without involving Pavel? And based on what he just said, he wants to keep word of his tomcatting away from Katya's ears."

Zhanna flung a fierce look at Pavel. He retreated behind lowered eyelids.

Feodor continued, "And what about the damage to your own reputation,

Zhanna? Everyone thinks you're Arkhip's girl, yet you're sneaking around with other boys. Fathers don't choose unfaithful flirts for their sons to marry."

Zhanna's menacing eyes scuttled between Feodor and Elizaveta. Pavel studied his shuffling feet. The only sounds Elizaveta heard were the furious, scared gusts of her own breathing.

Zhanna's eyes settled on Elizaveta's and bored into them. After a small eternity, Zhanna gave a slow, measured nod that Elizaveta interpreted as *All right. If we keep this debacle between ourselves, we'll all be better off.*

Elizaveta's single nod implied her silent agreement.

Zhanna turned on her heel. With a whipped dog's slouch, Pavel followed her from the barn.

The whole episode had taken less time than to unhitch a horse from a wagon. But Elizaveta shuddered at the fearful consequences that may be lying in wait. The brief encounter could well be the first step toward the unveiling she'd been dreading.

CHAPTER 5

Maximov

1840

What can't a person live without?

A name.

TRAILED BY TWO serfs, Stepan threaded his way through the jostling crowds. He wound past bowed peasants bearing backpacks as they repaired boots and cut hair. He swerved around the two-wheeled carts of shaggy tradesmen who shoed horses and salvaged crippled wagons. He shook his head at the working girls who offered their services without benefit of backpack or cart.

Stepan's initial trip to the annual Great Fair with Vladimir Rusakov had occurred eight years ago, shortly after Vladimir had married Yustina and moved from St. Petersburg to an estate located close to Stepan's, where Yustina had been raised. When Yustina's parents died, the property had passed into her and Vladimir's hands.

A fervor had stirred in Stepan's veins the first moment he stepped onto the immense triangle of sandy soil at the confluence of the Volga and Oka Rivers. The pulsating horde of 100,000 included merchants, retailers, wholesalers, manufacturers, traders, vendors, agents, brokers, speculators, and bankers.

Despite the irks and rankles of the trek—torn harnesses, kidney-bruising dirt roads, post houses replete with lice and bedbugs—the vivacity of the ancient marketplace lured him back time and again. For centuries, fairs had played a vital role in the Empire's commerce. But the summer market at the old fortress city of Nizhny Novgorod was the queen of them all. St. Petersburg was said to be Russia's head and Moscow its heart. But Nizhny Novgorod, as Stepan had witnessed, was its wallet.

Notwithstanding last year's calamitous incident with the measles, Yegorka once again accompanied his master. Stepan usually brought along two serfs, the second being Nikifor Zhemchuzhnikov. However, this year Nikifor had asked the Count to take his consumptive-looking eldest son instead. The gaunt teenager gave the impression of having been patched together in an awkward, slapdash manner—all elbows and knees. Against his better judgment, Stepan had agreed to Zhemchuzhnikov's request—and had been berating himself ever since. The scrawny kid, whose given name Stepan couldn't remember, would be useless if the wagon came to be mired in the ruts, potholes, and muck of Russia's notoriously poor roads.

Stepan wove through throbbing swarms of flea-infested peasants as they ogled sackcloth, hats, and cheap jewelry. The air was fragrant with a potpourri of pastries, teas, spices, and tobacco. He paused at a booth of traders from central Asia and purchased some Turkish tobacco and a sack of his favorite nuts. He looked around for his serfs. Yegorka and young Zhemchuzhnikov were gawking at the shoddy stalls' arrays of dried fruit, rugs, rice, and semiprecious stones.

"Carry these." Stepan handed the tobacco and pistachios to the spindly boy. The youngster seemed like a lost lamb among the teeming throngs of hucksters, pickpockets, and unscrupulous dealers. Stepan added, "Hold them close and watch for thieves."

A nearby vendor hawked, "Hot, hot! Sweet, flaky *pirozhki*. With sausage. With Kiev jam. Melts in your mouth!"

"Buy yourselves something to eat." Stepan handed a paper ruble to Yegorka. "Meet me back here in two hours."

When Stepan crossed the threshold of the majestic main arcade, he entered a world devoid of tawdry, badgering peddlers. Inside the vast building, merchants passed the time in calm repose in front of their shops, retailing their commodities and amassing orders for next year. Bearded Persians in turbans rested cross-legged, smoking hookahs next to their piles of carpets. The Armenians enjoyed a leisurely but lucrative business in caviar from Astrakhan. Chinamen languidly waited for purchasers to browse their tea, porcelain, and silks. The slow pace belied the hundreds of thousands of rubles that changed hands over a few succinct words.

Stepan's attention was snared by elaborately painted, brass-plated chests of exceptional Siberian craftsmanship. Remembering that Sophia mentioned the need for more storage trunks, he purchased one.

In front of a shop displaying Tatar dresses and dressing gowns, his fingertips caressed the downy softness of a fringed cashmere shawl with red, yellow, and bronze flowers. Stepan preferred to avoid dealing with Tatars, as they tended to hard-sell their overpriced merchandise. But his mind's eye pictured the shawl draped over Sophia's slender shoulders, the cinnamon background underscoring the amber in her hair. He handed over the rubles.

Oh, Sophia, his heart pleaded. *Please accept these gifts as they are intended— tokens of my love—and not as a mere ploy to quell your anger.*

Later, when he met up with his two serfs, he told them where to find the trunk and instructed them to return to the inn. He handed the shawl to the boy. "Don't get it dirty. Tell the innkeeper to have a samovar of tea ready when we return this evening, around ten o'clock. Listen up, both of you: I expect the carriage and the wagon to be ready to return here at half past eight tomorrow morning. And no hangovers."

The bone-thin boy earnestly repeated his master's instructions. "Samovar ready at ten tonight. Return tomorrow at half past eight."

The kid's attention to detail appealed to Stepan. He searched again for the boy's name, but it continued to elude him.

"I ASSUME YOUR harvest was as abysmal as mine. I dare say, Stepan, I'm almost convinced you're correct."

After going their separate ways their first day at the Fair, Stepan and Vladimir met up for the evening meal at Nikita Egorov's, which catered to the culinary tastes of the Fair's powerful tea, textile, and other wholesalers. Joining the two men was A.A. Gabrichevsky, a neighbor of theirs who happened to be at the Fair and who also happened to be among the wealthiest of the wealthy.

A.A. Gabrichevsky's bluster and self-importance were justified by his five thousand male serfs, known as "souls," who were scattered in two dozen villages on three different estates. Gabrichevsky's mansion and buildings on the primary estate were serviced by hundreds of household serfs, from carpenters to footmen, gardeners to stable boys, cooks to musicians.

The three estate owners were finishing their after-dinner cordials when Gabrichevsky deigned that Stepan might in fact be correct.

"In what way?" Stepan asked.

"Your praise for potatoes. Russia leads the world in rye production, but this overdependence on one grain will be our ruin. We must diversify. Potatoes are the answer."

Stepan nodded. "That's why I intend to have my serfs plant them next spring, although they'll undoubtedly raise Cain about it. Whenever my steward mentions it to them, they fall to their knees, insisting the potato is the forbidden fruit

Adam and Eve ate. Hence, whoever eats a potato disobeys God and will never see Heaven."

An exasperated breath streamed between Vladimir's lips. "Where do they come up with such nonsense?"

"Ignorant people invent stories to excite their fears all the further," Gabrichevsky opined in his vainglorious voice. "The peasants' horizons are so narrow and their outlook so constrained, they'll believe any story any fool dreams up."

Vladimir waved a dismissive hand. "Why can't they use their brains? Can't they see the value of what we're telling them?"

"Use their brains?" Gabrichevsky threw back his graying head and brayed. "It would be like asking a fish to use its legs."

Stepan asked the pervasive Russian question, "So what's to be done?"

"Peasants aren't as stupid as they look. But they definitely are lazy." Vladimir retrieved a pipe and tobacco pouch from his pocket. "Contrary to appearances, serfs don't do all that much work. Subtract Sundays and holidays from the work year. Then subtract the three days a week they till the fields allotted to them. That leaves only one hundred thirty-five days they actually work for us."

"I see an altogether different kettle of fish." Even as Stepan said this, he knew Gabrichevsky would rebuke him. "The culprit is drunkenness, which leads to idleness, sloppy work, thievery, fighting, and a general decline in morality. When it comes right down to it, the serfs' biggest problem is vodka."

Gabrichevsky stroked his muttonchops. "I've overseen serfs ten, maybe fifteen years longer than either of you. And I can assure you that peasants, by their very nature, are childlike and require constant direction. Drunkenness, laziness, and all other misbehavior must be nipped, or it will spread like fire in a hay shed." Gabrichevsky gave a derisive snort. "Two of my peasants were caught in the act of fornication. I had them both flogged and forced them to sit for two days in repentance with their heads half shaved."

Holding the bowl of his pipe, Vladimir pointed the stem at his two dinner companions. "The other day, I discovered that one of my unmarried house servants is pregnant. Banished her to the dairy. Filthy work, as we all know."

Like Vladimir and Gabrichevsky, Stepan's agricultural magazines purported that iron discipline was mandatory. Though rarely used on his estate of Petrovo, birch switches, whips, and the dreaded knout were ever-present threats. Fines were of limited use, because peasants rarely had any money. Incarceration was a poor option, since an imprisoned serf was an unproductive serf.

Notwithstanding their occasional oppressive measures, Stepan and his two dinner companions saw themselves as benefactors who took care of those less fortunate. Why, they would no more turn out a serf to fend for himself than they would a young pup. Countless times they'd discussed the question of who benefited the most from serfdom. The answer never varied: the serf, of course.

Gabrichevsky pulled a silk handkerchief from his breast pocket and mopped his pendulous jowls. "As their *pomeshchiks*, do what I do. Look after their marriages."

Stepan cocked his head in question.

"I have my steward make a list of all the girls who are at least sixteen and all the boys at least eighteen. I tell them to find themselves mates within a month or I'll do it for them. Before I implemented that policy, six or seven years would pass before the peasants got the notion to get married. Meanwhile, I lost six or seven years of offspring and future laborers. Once married, they fornicate like frogs. Children are wealth to the family, wealth to the village, and wealth to me." Gabrichevsky's fleshy palm slapped the white tablecloth. "Works like a charm."

The huge sums of money Stepan had seen exchange hands that afternoon, combined with the satiating geniality of the dinner's wine, prompted him to muse over his prosperity. Or rather, the deficit thereof. The more he contemplated Gabrichevsky's suggestion, the more he found it to be a champion idea.

The discussion segued into Gabrichevsky's recent trip to Paris. The windbag recounted how he had gorged himself on oysters and champagne. Then he described how certain Russian nobles (whom he declined to name, out of respect for their privacy) had sunk into a sexual mania with the city's beautiful courtesans.

Stepan lost interest and stared at his half-empty cup of Turkish coffee. The day's events had caught up with him, and his eyelids were growing heavy. He planned to spend tomorrow strolling along the massive wharves, where a seemingly endless stream of boats and barges would unload mountains of domestic and international goods—be it fine Chinese silk or bales of dusty cashmere wool, chests of tea or bars of iron, scented soaps or dried fish.

As he tugged at the confines of his frock coat, he remembered the homesick look of the Zhemchuzhnikov boy and felt his own wistful nostalgia. The best part of the three-week airing was when the reins slapped the horses, setting Stepan en route to Petrovo, where he felt at one with the timeless collage of fields and meadows.

Where each morning, Matriusha insisted the children say their morning prayers "just like the cock does when he crows."

Where, in the evenings, he and the children piled onto the divan for fairy tales about snow maidens and enchanted fish.

Where Anton couldn't get enough of *Emelya and the Magic Pike*, whooping with delight whenever his father's voice boomed, "By the pike's command; by my own request!"

Where he and the woman he loved would slip between their cool French linens and, with natural openness, reach out to one another.

Or at least, they *used* to reach out to each another. Would his marriage ever return to what it had been? At age thirty-five, Stepan was beginning to feel, for all practical purposes, like a widower.

TIRED AND OVERSTUFFED, Stepan and Vladimir returned to the three-story, family-operated inn where they kept a standing annual reservation. The innkeeper's wife instantly appeared beside Stepan. "Count Maximov." She wrung her hands. "Count Maximov."

"Yes?"

"Count Maximov." She bowed. "We've had some problems."

"What problems? Out with it."

"Please come with me. My husband will explain."

"Explain what?" Stepan asked as he and Vladimir trailed after the woman.

"Your servant. My husband is patching him up."

CHAPTER 6

Maximov

1840

With what food
the more you eat,
the more is left?

Nuts.

IN A KITCHEN redolent of fried onions, the innkeeper hovered over the Zhemchuzhnikov boy. Perched on a stool, with a bloody rag pressed to his nose, the teenager had the ashen look of a burnt log that would disintegrate in a stiff breeze.

The innkeeper's voice was wary. "We've never had thieves. You come here every year. You know we run a reputable inn."

Vladimir murmured, "Oh, no," sharing Stepan's assumption.

"And I've never traveled with a serf who steals." Fists clenched, Stepan took a step toward the boy.

The wife's fleshy arm shot between him and the youngster. "Oh, no, sir. It's not that. Not that at all."

Zhemchuzhnikov lowered the crimsoned rag. "I didn't mean to ruin your things. I took good care of them until . . . until . . ."

Front teeth tugging repeatedly at his lower lip, Zhemchuzhnikov described the evening's events.

He had taken the purchases upstairs toward Stepan's room, but when he reached the door, he heard muffled noises inside. Since it was nowhere near ten o'clock, he assumed whoever was inside wasn't the Count. He put his ear to the door. He heard whispers along with drawers opening and closing. Flickering candlelight passed across the space beneath the door.

"I thought maybe it was thieves, but I didn't know," the boy explained. "I was scared and didn't know what to do. So I flattened myself in the next doorway. A man and a woman came out of your room carrying sacks and walked down the hall away from me. They never saw me in the doorway."

Stepan nodded. That was easy to imagine. The kid was as skinny as a pipe cleaner.

With the liberal use of his hands, the boy recounted how he had run up behind the couple, thrown the shawl over the man's head, and swiftly tied the ends around his neck. The woman began hitting him. He pitched the loose tobacco in her face. She yelped and clawed at her eyes. Then he flung the pistachios across the wood floor. The man, blinded by the shawl, slipped on the scattered nuts and rammed into a tall clock. The hallway vibrated as man and clock crashed to the floor.

The Zhemchuzhnikov boy picked at a patch on his trousers. "I'm so sorry. The shawl is dirty. And the nuts and the tobacco are gone. I'm terribly sorry." His head hung down as if he deserved the guillotine.

The innkeeper likewise apologized in earnest, explaining the woman was a recently hired maid and the man was her accomplice. But Stepan brushed aside the apologies as he studied the malnourished string bean. The lad—*What was his name?*—couldn't scare off so much as a goose, so he had used the resources he had at hand. Incredible pluck for a serf. A champion response, by anyone's measure.

Earlier on the trip, Zhemchuzhnikov had shown some degree of inquisitiveness, good sense, and dependability. Stepan suspected these traits, if properly developed, could one day be assets to the estate. Too bad the kid looked as though he could be snapped in half with one hand. Perhaps he'd give young Zhemchuzhnikov a chance to prove that what he lacked in brawn, he made up in intellect.

CHAPTER 7

Elizaveta

1840

What goes about in the entryway
but won't come into the hut?
A door.

AT THE RAT-A-TAT-TAT, the girls jumped to their feet and pinched their cheeks to give them color. After three months of planning, discussing, and bickering, the first winter party was finally underway.

The boys arrived in a huddled group and as ill at ease as fish nosing about a baited hook. In synchrony, they doffed their coats and, with November's cold clinging to the rough sheepskin, handed them to the girls to hang on wooden pegs. Likewise in unison, the fellows stomped the chill from their feet and cupped their hands over their mouths and blew on them.

The hostesses tucked their skirts under them as they settled on the rough-sawn benches and stools that formed one crescent of a circle. Their guests established a united front on the far side of the circle, passing a bottle of vodka from one hand to the next. Behind the curtain in a corner, the Widow Shabanova snored like a bear in hibernation.

Conversation was stilted, despite the young people having known each other the entirety of their lives. The youngest girl, Avdotya, was congratulated on her fifteenth birthday. Then followed speculations regarding when the river would be frozen solid enough to use as a roadway for carriages and wagons. The girls smoothed their skirts while the boys continued to blow on their already warmed hands.

The conversational ice was broken with a tried-and-true party favorite—riddles. The brainteasers included rhyme and lyrical rhythm along with wordplay.

What eats hay without a mouth
but with three teeth?

Several voices shouted, "A pitchfork."

"Listen to this one," said a fellow named Ermak.

> What looks under everyone's feet
> and under all the girls' skirts?

One of the lads answered, "A threshold."

The next riddle came from Ermak's younger brother, Grigorii.

> When do you open up the shaggy one
> and stick in the naked one?

The girls gave a mortified shriek as their cheeks crimsoned.

"What's wrong?" Grigorii's expression was as innocent as a newborn babe's. "You can't figure out the answer is 'When putting on a mitten'?"

The girls protested, but without much conviction, that the riddles were too disgraceful, and coaxed the boys into practicing some new steps for next summer's circle dances on the village square. Tongues loosened as feet shuffled and kicked across the hard-packed earth floor. The taller boys had to duck under the beams of the smoke-blackened roof.

Elizaveta was attending the party for one reason—to ward off any suspicion about her and Feodor. She cared not a fig about dancing and, in fact, used the circle dances to cast a critiquing eye on her peers' clothes.

At first glance, the billowing, swishing skirts appeared indistinguishable not only from one another but also from those worn by generations of maternal ancestors. But to a discerning eye, each garment was a singular article of beauty. The homespun linen was painstakingly embroidered with plants, animals, and goddesses that symbolized the girl's future as a wife and mother. As a safeguard against evil, cord gathered the folds of each blouse about the wrists and the neck.

The upturned corners of Elizaveta's lips bordered on a gloat. With an artist's hand, she had designed her skirt's tree-of-life motif, replete with peacocks and other showy birds. It was far and away the most elaborate at the party. And there were plenty more embroidered linens of equal quality tucked away in her bridal trunk, linens she would present to the Zhemchuzhnikovs on her wedding day.

Her eyes skimmed over the boys' drab, birds-of-a-feather clothes. Their homespun garb never varied—a white, long-sleeved tunic, the hem of which fell outside the trousers about the hips. Gathered with a sash, the shirt accentuated the broadening shoulders and narrow waist of a boy approaching manhood.

When the dancing drew to a close, seats were retaken and laughter tumbled across the room. Candles and oil being precious commodities, the room's paltry light came from burning splinters—long, slender, dry sticks that hung from the rafters. They put forth a feeble bead of light accompanied by a copious amount of smoke.

Elizaveta had been sharing a short bench with Marfa, but during the dancing, the girl had felt ill and gone home. The vacant spot was taken now by Illarion Loktev, who for the past year had hovered about Elizaveta, as irksome as a mosquito. Illarion gave her a gape-toothed smile. She tightened her lips in a quick grin while trying to avoid looking at his pasty face in the throes of an eruption of pimples.

The boys drained the last of the vodka and headed for the tub of *kvass*, a home-brewed beverage that accompanied the peasants' every meal.

"We should have brought more bottles, boys!" Grigorii ladled the amber drink down his gullet and gave a discontented belch. "Vodka certainly tastes better than this piss water."

"Grigorii, be nice," scolded Zhanna, the self-appointed leader. "Avdotya made the kvass."

"Avdotya? Well, that figures." Grigorii took his seat on the bench next to the girl in question. "Ever heard of adding honey, Avdotya? Or maybe thyme for flavor? Or mint?"

Elizaveta bristled. Avdotya Sharovatova was as meek as Grigorii was surly. The two had become an item last summer, and the romance had continued on and off through the autumn. Elizaveta was certain Avdotya could attract someone better than the loudmouth Vorontsov boy. The small-boned girl possessed a certain appeal, even if her frightened expression had the appearance of a wide-eyed fledgling about to take its first leap from the nest.

As always, Elizaveta spoke her mind. "Grigorii, we should be thanking her for bringing the kvass, not criticizing her."

"I'm just teasing." To prove it, he jabbed his elbow into his girlfriend's ribs. "We all know Avdotya isn't as fragile as she looks. These skinny arms can do damn near a half day's honest work." He picked up her elfin hand and lifted it to her quivering chin. Then he spread his fingers and watched her hand fall to her lap like a wounded bird.

Avdotya turned as pale as bleached linen.

Elizaveta boiled with fury at Grigorii's poisonous wisecrack. When a father scanned the village for a daughter-in-law, he looked for someone who was strong enough and clever enough to juggle fieldwork, a kitchen garden, cleaning, laundry, preparation of food, spinning of fiber, weaving of cloth, and sewing of clothing, not to mention caring for children, cattle, sheep, pigs, and assorted fowl.

Red-headed Demian Osokin said, "There's no reason to hurt her feelings."

"She's my girl. I can say what I want." Grigorii's hand encircled Avdotya's thin upper arm and bore down. "It's not like everyone doesn't know she's as useless as tits on a boar hog when it comes to swinging a sickle."

Avdotya cast her eyes downward, and a teardrop fell onto her homespun skirt.

Demian leaned forward on his bench. "If she's your girl, why can't you show her some respect?"

"Ha! Look who's talking. You're not much bigger than she is, Little Red."

Demian's nostrils flared. "Does it make you feel bigger when you belittle other people?"

The malevolent mirth in Grigorii's eyes was replaced by pure aggression. "Listen, you little pipsqueak, don't tell me what to do."

Undersized Demian was no match for muscled Grigorii, but Constantin Sipko took up the fight. "I'll tell you what to do. You apologize to her."

Grigorii spat with great skill just beyond the tips of his shoes. "Go fuck yourself."

"I said, apologize."

The knuckles of Constantin's clenched fists blanched white while Grigorii's face heated to fuming red.

"Back off, Sipko." Grigorii's older brother Ermak gave an admonitory crack of his knuckles.

"Why should I? We've all had enough of your brother's bluster."

"Go fuck your mother," Grigorii retorted in a variation of his previous directive.

"Pipe down," Zhanna hissed. "You'll wake Shabanova."

Grigorii bolted to his feet and pointed a menacing finger across the circle at Constantin. "He's the one who needs to pipe down."

"Me? You're the obnoxious bragger who picks on girls." Constantin's leg bounced up and down until he sprang to his feet, toppling his stool backward. Uttering an oath, he started across the room toward Grigorii.

Ermak leapt up, grabbed Constantin's shoulder, and flung him around. "You touch my brother, you'll wonder where your teeth went."

Constantin shook off Ermak's hand. "You watch yourself, Vorontsov, or—"

"That's enough!" Zhanna's hands went to her hips. "We're here to have a good time. If you three don't want to behave, leave!"

Constantin, Grigorii, and Ermak each waited to take his cue from the other two. The remainder in the room held their breath. No one doubted the two brothers were itching for a scuffle. Their noses had been broken in so many scraps, no one could remember their original shape.

"Ah, piss on it." Grigorii sat down and tapped Avdotya's shoulder with his. "Shit, sweetie, you know I was just joking with you."

"There," Ermak said. "You happy, Sipko? He apologized."

Constantin glared in disbelief at one Vorontsov, then the other. "That was no apology."

"It's as good as you're going to get," Grigorii called from across the circle. "Like Zhanna said, if you don't like it, leave."

Constantin looked around the room for the group's response. Finding no encouragement to escalate the brawl further, he pulled on his jacket, cinched its belt with an implacable yank, and stormed from the hut.

While the plank door quivered, the teenagers fidgeted in their seats, the silence broken only by Avdotya's sniveling.

Elizaveta assured Avdotya, "I think your kvass tastes fine." She glanced at Grigorii and into eyes as black and ominous as a snake's, eyes that had borne the same meanness as far back as she could remember. As a kid, he'd been a dyed-in-the-wool brat, smirking whenever he succeeded at tripping her as she left the church.

To this day, her stomach curdled as she remembered ten-year-old Grigorii throwing rocks at barn swallows and stunning one. She had been horrified when he yanked out the creature's wing feathers, stomped on its feet, then snickered as it floundered about until it died.

He was absolutely the meanest boy in the village. Everyone thought so.

And his brother Ermak was cut from the same cloth.

One of the boys lightened the mood with "Hey! Zhanna wants to play Mares!"

Zhanna gave a saucy lift to her chin. "I said no such thing."

The boy's beckoning arm coaxed enthusiasm back into the group. "All right, girls! To the center of the circle. Mares, splendid mares! Come and buy them, fellows."

The potential buyers circled the girls, their thumbs and forefingers stroking their chins as they contemplated each mare from top to bottom. Any kind of touching, such as examining their teeth for wear or picking up their feet to inspect their soles, was off limits.

The first buyer was Grigorii. He chose Avdotya, who had ceased sniffling. He led her to a bench and pulled her onto his lap. Spots of color spread on Avdotya's cheeks as she teetered precariously on Grigorii's knee.

Arkhip Melnikov made the second selection. When he grabbed Zhanna's hand, she pawed at the ground and brayed like a disgruntled donkey, but she ended up on his lap all the same.

The next purchase was Pavel's. Katya pranced like a young colt to his lap, slid a daring arm around his neck, and whispered in his ear.

Elizaveta flashed a look at Zhanna, whose return glare ordered, *Keep your mouth shut if you know what's good for you.*

Illarion made his choice by pulling Elizaveta toward his lap. She thwarted his plan, however, slipping onto the bench next to him and staring straight ahead. She pulled her hand free and tucked it between her skirt and the bench.

Illarion leaned over and brushed her ear with the prickles of a patchy beard sprouting amid a constellation of pustules. "Now you're mine."

Elizaveta didn't think she could bear any more hand-holding, lap-sitting, or earlobe-tickling. She wanted to go home, wrap her sheepskin blanket around her, and pretend it was Feodor's arms.

Illarion looped his arm through hers. "I'm supposed to shear our sheep tomorrow. Want to help me?"

Shear their sheep? The itchy, smelly job should have been done at least a month ago to allow time for the wool to regrow before bitter winds swept in from the north. But then again, the procrastination was hardly surprising. The entire village knew that the Loktev men were as lazy as bears in winter.

"You're just now getting around to the second shearing?" she asked.

He nodded.

"That's just plain cruel. You'll be lucky if the naked animals don't die during winter's first storm."

"Come on," he coaxed, "we'll have fun together."

Elizaveta's face scrunched in disgust not only at the greasy, dusty work but also at helping Illarion. "No." She freed her arm from his and replaced her hand beneath her thigh. "I'm not going to shear your sheep. Get that through your head."

"Remember, I bought you. You're mine."

She hoped he was teasing, but his tone contained no trace of it.

Illarion continued, "And you have time. All your rye is threshed. And most of your other autumn work is done."

"How do you know that?"

"I watched you from the road."

Her eyes widened. "You've been watching me?" Elizaveta's thin patience evaporated, along with her perpetual pledge to control her words. "At least we had grain to thresh."

"What do you mean?" His voice cracked as he shrank back from her.

Sitting as tall as she could, she leaned ever so slightly over him. "I mean, everyone knows the Loktevs always harvest more weeds than grain."

Illarion turned as red as the waddle on a turkey cock. The angles of his jaw were working furiously.

Suddenly the door banged open and six fathers stormed into the hut. Constantin Sipko's father, his face livid, dragged his son by the hair. "Shabanova! Get out here!"

The widow emerged from behind the curtain with eyes bleary from sleep and age. The fathers, beside themselves with outrage, ranted that they had been leaving the tavern next door when they heard a noise behind Shabanova's hut. There they'd found Marfa and Constantin under a sheepskin blanket—a rendezvous that was premeditated. Marfa wasn't at all sick, and Constantin had used his argument with Grigorii as a handy pretext to leave the party.

The fathers lambasted Shabanova. If she couldn't properly chaperone the young people, they would forbid their daughters to ever again rent the hut.

The old woman, who clearly needed the compensation, vowed that such brazen depravity would never happen again. She crossed herself three times to affirm the solemnity of her promise.

The party was over. The boys bolted from the hut. The girls tidied the room, puttering about as they relived the entire evening. They dissected it piece by piece, analyzed the various implications of the slightest innuendo, and speculated about the potential consequences of every conversation. Elizaveta was the only female who had no desire to drag out the party beyond its natural demise.

When at last the girls tumbled from Shabanova's hut, acrid wood smoke hung in the still night air. The two Anafreva sisters' felt boots crunched the brittle frost. Elizaveta's gloved fingers rubbed her earlobe, scouring away any lingering traces of Illarion's bristles. No more parties for her. She'd sit at home spinning thread with her mother and little sister Yulia rather than endure such foolishness again.

"Who's that?" In the dim light of the cold stars, Katya pointed at a slight figure running down the road toward them.

"Liza!" a thin, reedy voice gasped. "Liza!"

"Avdotya?" Elizaveta called. "What is it? What's wrong?"

Avdotya panted white fog when she reached the sisters. "I heard him say it."

"What are you talking about?" Katya asked.

"He said . . . he said . . ."

Elizaveta shook Avdotya's shoulders, not hard, but enough to fill Avdotya's eyes with alarm. "Who said what?"

"Illarion Loktev. He said you wanted to make a bed in the rye with him."

"What!" Elizaveta yelped as if stung by a wasp.

"That's what he said. 'Make a bed in the rye.'"

"The filthy, lying pig!" Elizaveta backhanded the air, slapping aside Illarion's ridiculous claim.

Avdotya flinched and stumbled backward.

"You're sure it was Illarion?" Katya asked.

"Oh, yes. I was almost home, walking past the Karpovs' house. A group of boys were talking. One of them was Illarion. The Karpovs and the Loktevs are second cousins, you know."

"Second cousins?" Katya was doubtful. "I thought they were first cousins."

"Oh, no. They're second cousins, because Sasha Karpov and—"

Their drivel was stretching Elizaveta's nerves to the breaking point. "What difference does it make how they're kin to that brainless little maggot!"

But Katya hungered for every detail. "Who else was there? How many boys did he tell?"

"It doesn't matter!" Elizaveta snapped. "By tomorrow his rubbish will have spread through the whole village."

Avdotya drew back as if to disappear inside her sheepskin coat. Elizaveta felt sorry for the anxious girl. How horrible it must be to live like a frightened rabbit.

Elizaveta drew a deep breath of frosty air and calmed her tone. "Thank you, Avdotya, for telling me."

"Th . . . there's more." The meek-as-a-lamb girl looked as if she were about to faint dead away.

"More?"

"He said that after he left the party, he . . . he . . ." Avdotya seemed incapable of taking the story further.

"He what?" Elizaveta's prompt elicited more quivering. "Tell me straight out, Avdotya. What?"

"He tarred your gate."

"Tarred our gate!"

Avdotya tucked her chin between cringing shoulders.

Katya, accustomed to her sister's outbursts, advised, "Settle down, Liza. Everyone knows he's a shameless liar. Remember when he made up that tale about Marfa's sister being engaged to Savva Osokin?"

Avdotya gave Katya a knowing nod. "I knew that story wasn't true, because Savva's brother is married to my uncle's goddaughter and he told me, while we were at their baby's christening, that Illarion's tale was nothing but a pack of lies."

"Who told you?" Katya dug deeper into the tale. "Savva's brother? Or your uncle?"

Elizaveta felt as though she were about to fly apart into little pieces. Her reputation was being ripped to shreds while Avdotya and Katya were babbling about trivia! She calmed herself long enough to reach out to fainthearted Avdotya and put a gloved hand on Avodtya's shoulder. "You're a true friend for telling me."

Elizaveta dashed toward home, her mind racing as fast as her legs. People in this village were always ready to believe rumors, even from scum like Illarion Loktev. She'd be labeled as a girl of loose morals. As Feodor had pointed out to Zhanna, fathers, including Nikifor Zhemchuzhnikov, didn't allow their sons to marry such girls. And even if the villagers didn't believe Illarion's lies, they always kept these little tidbits of hearsay tucked in the far reaches of their memories, to be retrieved whenever a second whispered morsel added credence to the first.

Fury ripping through her, Elizaveta drew up to her gate. The tip of her finger touched the black splotch and instantly jerked back as if it had brushed a hot flame. She shifted her gaze toward the weak glimmer in the sole window's rippled glass. The wavering light outlined something dark. Elizaveta's breath caught. Not content to merely defile the gate, that half-wit son of a dog also smeared the window with dung.

As she stepped through the despoiled gate, she cursed her behavior. Everything had been fine for her this evening until she made that cutting remark about Illarion's family. Feodor, her grandmother, her parents—they had all warned her that if she didn't curb her reckless tongue, it would become her enemy. And now it had.

CHAPTER 8

Elizaveta

1840

On what slender sapling
do our lives swing?

Ears of grain.

ADVENT'S SNOW LAY hard upon the ground as Elizaveta, the sole female in a gathering of full beards and broad backs tough as jerky, teetered on an unsteady stool in a shadowed corner. She twitched with impatience, as though her skin were crawling with sheep lice.

Her father, as *bolshak*, or patriarch, of the Anafrev household, had called the meeting of the village assembly, which was composed of his fifty fellow bolshaks. At stake were the reputation of his daughter and the honor of his household. The deceitful little rumormonger Loktev must publicly retract his blatant lies and be reprimanded.

Elizaveta and the bolshaks were clustered in Evdokim Seleznyov's tavern, a bedraggled square structure of thick hand-hewn beams and a hipped roof of thatch that melded with Petrovo's other squatty, single-room *izbas*. Seleznyov had good reason for keeping it indistinguishable from the other huts: Imperial law required that all drinking establishments be licensed. To the bureaucrats' knowledge, this particular izba was merely a private residence that was kept open all hours of the day and night purely in the spirit of fellowship.

The meeting's start was jagged as bolshaks wandered one by one into the tavern and cursed the eternal uncertainties of farming. The men relived the drought and hail that had ravaged the rye crop. Then they chronicled last spring when the sun disappeared for weeks, rotting the roots of the rye and allowing only half the oats and millet to be sowed into the cold, soggy soil. The men's faces were grim as they questioned what they had done to incite Mother Nature's wrath two years in a row.

Last year's harvest had been paltry, but this year's was tragic. On this snow-blown afternoon, two-thirds of a year lay ahead before the next crop would be harvested.

Yet the family granaries would be bone-chilling vacuums by Easter. Without grain, there'd be no bread. And no gruel, porridge, kasha, mash, thick soup, or stew. No pancakes, fritters, pies, or kvass. Even the Eucharist required grain.

As each man began detailing his household's woes, Erafei Anafrev reminded the bolshaks why he had called the meeting. By now, Elizaveta was ready to burst like an overripe melon.

When told to give her account of the story, she offered a silent prayer to the Holy Mother of God to help curb her tongue. Her description of Illarion's unwanted advances concluded with her eyes downcast and her manner demure. "Finally I had no choice but to push him away with my words. He tried to get even by humiliating me. Never, ever would I suggest anything immoral to a boy until after the sacrament of marriage."

Erafei sprang to his feet and swept his hand toward his fellow bolshaks. "In smearing my gate, Illarion Loktev smeared my daughter's reputation and did her unspeakable harm. All of you know my Liza is a good girl."

Illarion's father leapt up. "Ha! Her tongue never stops wagging, like a puppy dog's tail. *Make a bed in the rye.* No one doubts she would say such a thing!"

Erafei went after the Loktev bolshak with both fists. The other men restrained both fathers and persuaded them to sit back down.

The bolshaks found Illarion guilty of attempting to ruin a marriageable girl's reputation. The following morning, an azure sky and mild weather that hovered around freezing lured several dozen villagers to the square to listen to Illarion apologize to Elizaveta. A piece of tarred string was tied around his neck as an admonishment to refrain from such behavior.

"If it happens again," the bolshaks warned Illarion, "you'll be flogged."

Elizaveta practically skipped home, basking in her victory and encircled by the other twelve members of her family: the matriarch, Grandmama Anafreva; her two sons, Elizaveta's father and her Uncle Artamon, each of whom had a wife; the girls in the family, Elizaveta's two sisters, Katya and nine-year-old Yulia; and five small boys whose continual horseplay the household withstood.

At their izba, coats and scarves were lopped onto pegs, ruffling the cobwebs higher up on the plank wall. Everyone made straight for the hand-hewn table. The adults and older children settled onto wooden stools and backless benches, the seats slick and dark from years of use. Four of the young boys jostled each other for standing room beside the table while Elizaveta's youngest cousin crawled about on the wood planking, a luxury that had been laid a couple of years ago to cover the bare ground.

Wooden spoons were dipped into bowls of thin gruel as the family rehashed Illarion's well-deserved public shaming.

"Yes, justice has been served."

"But will it be enough to keep the liar's tongue quiet?"

"Deceit is in his blood."

"True, but next time, he'll pick another victim."

"He's learned to never annoy the Anafrevs again."

When the topic was finally wrung dry, Nadezhda instructed her daughters, "Katya, Liza, after you clear the table, get working on the flax. We need plenty of good linen so Katya can finish her trousseau. Won't be long before a matchmaker comes calling." She gave her eldest daughter a tender, knowing smile.

Grandmother Anafreva stopped gumming her pickle. "Matchmaker? She's too young for a matchmaker."

Katya's eyes bulged. "But I'm sixteen. Legal age."

Her father shook his head. "Legal don't matter. Your grandmama is right. Many things you need to learn before you become a wife."

Katya's hands flapped about wildly. "But, Papa, I'm a good spinner. I can embroider and weave. I cook and bake bread and tend the garden. I harvest grain and take care of livestock and babies." Her list of skills was so lengthy, she ran out of breath.

Elizaveta leaned forward to listen. She couldn't recall the last time Katya stood up for herself. If, indeed, she ever had.

"You and the Vorobev boy made plans?"

"No, Papa, but—"

"Good. Because his family hasn't spoke to me about it."

"But Papa, Pavel and I are friends."

"Friends you can stay. Nothing more. You're not ready to be a wife and mother."

"But Papa," Katya's voice quivered, "Pavel is a good person. He works like a horse—"

"It's not Pavel Vorobev I'm talking about! It's you I'm talking about." Her father's hand sliced through the air. "It's settled. Not a word more about it."

Katya's eyes filled with anguish as the knuckle of her thumb pressed against her front teeth.

Erafei finished off his miserly portion of cooked groats and tossed his spoon into his empty wooden bowl. "Nadezhda, get me more *kasha*."

His wife's response was flat. "There is no more."

Erafei backhanded the empty bowl across the table. "Not enough food for a man to live on!"

"No need to bark at me!" Nadezhda's voice flared with the trilogy of fatigue, anger, and fear. "There's simply none to be had."

Grain wasn't the only crop to suffer from the previous spring's ill-tempered weather. The Anafrevs' ravaged garden had produced only a couple hundred heads of cabbage, twenty-five pounds of flax oil, and a lean supply of cucumbers, onions, beets, turnips, carrots, and radishes. Almost all had been eaten.

Erafei's bulky fingers combed through the curls of his beard. "Don't have enough to get through the winter."

No one responded to the already known fact.

Erafei swallowed hard. "Have to sell the cow."

Erafei's brother Artamon put an abrupt halt to picking his teeth with a wooden splinter. "Sell the cow?"

"No choice." Erafei rubbed three fingers together, signaling the need for money.

"Makes no sense at all," Uncle Artamon said. "Everyone's in the same fix. You wouldn't get half what she's worth."

"We can't afford to feed her."

"This is the worst time to sell her. Might as well just give her away." Artamon flung the wooden splinter onto the floor in disgust.

"We'll get nine rubles if we sell her now, before she gets skinnier."

"First, we need to slaughter the shoats and sow. Piglets are quicker and easier to replace than calves. So are geese and chickens."

"All that goes without saying. But the pigs and the poultry will go into our bellies." Erafei's forefinger thumped the scarred boards of the table. "What we need is rubles to buy grain. And buy it now before the price of rye goes higher."

"For the love of Christ, Erafei, can't you wait and see how things go before you sell the cow?"

"See how things go? Maybe rubles will fall from the sky? Or sheaves of grain might drop from Heaven?"

"The answer is simple."

All eyes turned toward the brittle voice of Grandmama Anafreva, the only female in the family with enough clout to put forth her opinion.

"Borrow the rubles. Then you won't have to sell the cow. Evdokim Seleznyov always has money to loan." To the villagers, the tavern owner was a man of inestimable wealth—a bottomless well of vodka and rubles.

No one in Petrovo was able to accumulate a disproportionate amount of resources, including rubles. Except Evdokim Seleznyov. Even his roosters seemed to lay eggs. Because Seleznyov had a knack for making money in a moneyless society, the Anafrevs, like all of the villagers, viewed him with suspicion. Perhaps he was aided by supernatural forces. Or maybe he used unethical practices that didn't place the mutual benefit of the community as the first and foremost concern.

Erafei vetoed his mother's suggestion. "I'd sooner tear out my beard than borrow from that snake in the grass!"

The matriarch leveled her milky eyes at her eldest son. "What good is your honor on an empty belly?"

"But Mother," Nadezhda said, "the rubles would have to be paid back. With interest. Ten rubles borrowed today means twelve rubles owed next month. And more after that."

"We'll repay with the help of the Blessed Virgin, using next year's crop." Grandmama Anafreva's blue-veined hands pushed against the table to help her rise. Bent like a shepherd's crook, she shuffled across the floorboards toward the warm, clay stove, a structure so ponderous it occupied a fifth of the izba. She eased onto a short, homemade bench and snugged her shawl around her shoulders.

Uncle Artamon's wife, Marina, asked, "But what if we have another bad year?"

"God is merciful. He won't let things get worse, so they are bound to get better. Yulia, be a good girl and bring me my yarn." A bony forefinger crept from under Grandmama Anafrava's shawl and pointed to one of the many crude boards fastened to the walls as shelving. It was her signal that she had given her final contribution to the conversation and if they were sensible, they'd heed her words of wisdom.

Uncle Artamon summed up his sentiments with "As far as I'm concerned, Evdokim Seleznyov can use his rubles to wipe his ass."

CHAPTER 9

Maximov

1840

What do you call a hundred brothers
jammed into one little hut to spend
the night?
Grain inside the husk.

THE GIFTS STEPAN had purchased at the Fair in August had been received
with tepid enthusiasm before Sophia relegated the Siberian-crafted trunk to the
attic and the cashmere shawl to the bottom drawer of her bureau. As the daylight
shortened and the days grew brisk, he had waited for her to wear the shawl. But
it never appeared.

Although Stepan had been stung by his wife's rebuff, the affront was a minor
bruise compared with the heartache inflicted by her volatile temperament
throughout the autumn.

Bottomless melancholy, sweetness and light, lizardlike cold: Sophia's perilous
mood swings had everyone, both family and servants, walking on tiptoes. Everyone, that is, except Anton.

When her pouty lips could be enticed to smile, it was usually in response to
Anton's antics. She'd tousle her son's generous head of hair or playfully pinch
his cheek, and he'd grin benevolently before slipping out from under her hand.
Anton was a boy's boy with little interest in activities that didn't involve speed,
skill, or daring, a fact that left Stepan perplexed by the long walks Anton took
with his mother and by the boy's occasional emergence from behind the closed
door of the master bedroom.

At his wits' end, Stepan secured the advice of the physician from A.A.
Gabrichevsky's estate. He diagnosed Sophia as having been seized by hypochondriac affections. Perhaps time would free her from them. Perhaps not.

Heartsick and lonely, Stepan felt as bereaved as though the singular love of
his life had died. But she wasn't deceased, as her ill humor reminded him daily.

On the verge of emotional collapse himself, he vowed to beat back the resentful despondency that had overtaken him. He had a family to raise, and by God, he intended to do a first-rate job of it!

Although not normally an introspective man, Stepan recognized his deep-seated need for a meaningful life. His innate ardor and buoyancy had to be channeled into something worthwhile. Plus, he required a refuge from Sophia's hostile gloom.

His solution was to fling his substantial energies into his agrarian pursuits. He had always reveled in the creation of grain through the combination of soil and water. Hoping the twins would come to appreciate the adage *Russia lives close to Her soil*, he began hauling the six-year-olds about the estate. Vaska, the boys' goat, trailed along with them.

Other than their mops of curly black hair, the twins were poles apart. Sergei's playtime consisted of arranging and rearranging his toy soldiers into various formations. Although his face lit up around horses, he was leery and kept his feet planted on the ground, his legs wrapped around a stick affixed to a wooden-headed stallion.

As a counterbalance to his brother, Anton was a precocious little fellow with no fear of wandering alone on the paths that crisscrossed the dense birch woods of the estate. He doggedly pushed the limits of the swing hanging from the stout limb of an oak and was quite at home in the rough-and-tumble world of the peasant children in the village across the river. When the weather turned foul, he lingered in the estate's distillery, mesmerized by its serpentine coils and delighting in the company of the serf who oversaw the steam-driven apparatus. As a toddler, Anton had been captivated by the young man's wayward eyes that refused to point in the same direction. The child had dubbed the serf "Cockeyes." The moniker became so affectionately entrenched in the family, they could barely remember the serf's real name.

Anton never tired of Cockeyes's endless supply of riddles, most of which leaned toward the crude.

> I bend.
> If you break me,
> I have something shaggy.
> In what's shaggy, it's sleek,
> and in what's sleek, it's sweet.
> What am I?

Although the answer—a nut tree—was innocuous, Stepan told the serf to use discretion around the twins. The term *discretion* befuddled Cockeyes, so Stepan directed, "No dirty jokes."

Stepan doted on all aspects of the estate's agricultural production, but it was the distillery that laid claim to his burning aspirations. How could it not? The monetary advantages of distilling vodka were as numerous and interdependent as sheaves of grain in a shock.

The first and most obvious benefit was the considerable income derived from the sale of the end product.

Second, that which went into the production—Petrovo's serf labor, rye, and wood—was, for all practical purposes, free.

Third, a by-product of vodka's production was *barda*, which provided fodder for Stepan's cattle.

Fourth, transportation costs were substantially reduced by avoiding shipment of grain to distant markets.

However, one factor far outweighed all the others combined. Since the mid-1700s, Russian law had placed a protective barrier around the business of making vodka and other liquor. The right to produce alcoholic beverages belonged to one narrow sector of Russia's population—the nobility.

Stepan made full use of that perquisite. He couldn't afford to be nonchalant about Petrovo's profitability. His money was invested with a banker in Moscow, where he intended it to stay, so his children would inherit some liquidity in addition to land. But for too many years, his living expenses had consumed all of Petrovo's revenue, forcing him to tap his Moscow accounts.

Petrovo was a trifling amount of land compared with the estates owned by the bloated rich such as A.A. Gabrichevsky, but the parcel lay in Tambov province, the center of Russia's vast heartland of grain fields. The black earth would grow nearly anything, and grow it bigger and faster than anywhere else in the Empire. Deep in his soul, Stepan knew he could accomplish great things with the bounty he had inherited. He read everything he could lay his hands on regarding crop production and livestock husbandry in addition to studying Swiss, German, and English agronomy.

While Stepan envisioned himself as a disciple of progressive agrarian thought, he knew his neighbors viewed him as an eccentric. His fellow landowners were Russian nobility of the old stamp who knew no life other than inheriting rubles, making more rubles, and then spending those rubles. To them, grain cultivation was a bothersome chore quite below their status. Most refused to even talk about it, particularly if the discussion involved the topic of smelly fertilizer.

But the Maximovs weren't anywhere near the stature of Tambov's Gabrichevskys, Golitsyns, and Gagarins, families that were continually bolstered by wealth that never ran out. Stepan's limited resources required that he make full use of the little patch of earth God had granted him.

Like most pomeshchiks in Russia's Black Earth region, he allocated a portion of his tillable land to his serfs, so they could raise grain for themselves and sell any excess. His income came from the remainder of the cultivation, which was farmed by those same serfs with their equipment and horses.

As the linden trees shivered in December's wind, Stepan hunched over his old, sprawling mahogany desk and sifted through the estate's financial books. When he calculated the amount of grain raised by his serfs on land he had allocated to them, and then compared the resulting figure with the amount of grain the serfs raised on land retained by his estate, something seemed amiss. He took up the issue with his steward.

Several years earlier, Stepan had hired as his steward a thirty-five-year-old, ruddy-faced German named August Wilhelm Roeglin. It was a choice that Stepan had come to both applaud and to regret.

Roeglin was a competent, complacent man of few words, whose girth increased proportionately with his age. Having worked on Russian estates for half his life, the German not only had a comprehensive knowledge of agriculture, but also spoke and thought in Russian. Stepan had presumed these to be champion traits, but instead they'd proven to be stumbling blocks in his plans to modernize Petrovo's feudal agricultural methods. Through seven growing seasons, Stepan had buttonholed Roeglin at least monthly to discuss ways to increase the estate's productivity. At the end of these conversations, the bull-necked steward invariably stymied any progress with "Russian grain does not grow according to a foreign system."

In response to his boss's question about the disparity between grain yields, the steward shook his heavy head. "All my life I've heard serfs complain that they can't get a good stand of grain, because the pomeshchiks keep the best land for themselves. And estate owners tell me the serfs produce more grain for themselves than they do for the estate. It's all fanciful thinking. Your fields and the peasants' fields are so intermingled that a disparity in yields is physically impossible."

"Rather than the soil, could the problem lie elsewhere?" Stepan asked. "Do the serfs work their fields during better weather than they do mine?"

Roeglin twirled the ends of his graying moustache. "Easily solved by insisting half the peasants work your estate fields while the other half work their own field allotments. Then switch the next day."

Stepan coerced Roeglin into making four commitments to be implemented the following spring. First, require the peasants to change over to the new alternating system. Second, plant a tall, productive plant, such as hemp, around the periphery of the fields to protect the rye and other grains from wind damage. Third, dig ditches in the low-lying fields to drain off excess rain and prevent waterlogged roots.

The fourth commitment was, technically, a compromise. Yes, this spring Roeglin would ensure that the peasants planted potatoes on the land retained by the estate. But the steward advised against forcing the peasants to grow the root vegetable on their land allocations, saying, "It would be best to wait."

"Why? I can demand the serfs plant whatever I want, be it potatoes or clover or even catnip, for that matter."

Roeglin peered at his boss from under shaggy eyebrows. "This winter, the peasants' bellies will be empty for the second year in a row. Next spring, they'll want to plant all the rye they can. Make them plant potatoes on their allotments the following year, after they've gotten used to handling the tubers on the land they till for you."

"But it's all my land!"

Roeglin held up a warning forefinger. "More than one estate owner has suffered his peasants' wrath. Remember Boris Khanykov? When his peasants got riled, they cut off his nose."

Roeglin's hand sliced like a meat cleaver in front of his own broad snout, halting further discussion.

CHAPTER 10

Elizaveta

1840–1841

What is lumpy, spongy, and holey,

humpbacked and raw,

sour and sweet,

tasty and lovely,

round and light,

soft and hard and crisp,

black and white,

and to all people dear?

A loaf of bread.

THE DAY AFTER Christmas, Evdokim Seleznyov announced, "It's not the stomach that drinks; it's the wallet," and bolted the tavern shut.

On New Year's Eve, each bolshak placed a few grains of rye in the snow. The next morning, eager eyes searched for a covering of ice on the grains, a sure sign that bread would be plentiful the following year. The kernels, however, were unglazed.

Faces darkened with worry.

From the hard lessons of experience, Elizaveta's family—like every village family—knew the spiraling consequences of crop failure. Households would ration not only bread and other grain-based foods but also the oils obtained from grain. Eventually, there'd be none. Thatch would be removed from the roofs of the barns and sheds and fed to the livestock. When the animals grew emaciated, they'd be sold at deplorably low prices in order to buy a little grain at exorbitantly high prices. Families would exist with no meat and pitifully few eggs. Epidemic diseases would attack the weakened bodies. The young, the old, and the sick would die.

For two weeks in late January, Elizaveta's entire family suffered with fevers, clogged noses, and raging throats. They burrowed into the loose straw of their sleeping benches, which were wooden planks that rested on legs like low tables or attached partway up the walls like wide shelves. Scattered around the perimeter of the single-room izba, each sleeping bench contained two people—more in the case of the smaller children.

It was the water that got the Anafrevs back on their feet. As part of the Christmas observance every year, Father Diakonov bestowed a blessing on the river on the holy day of Epiphany. Each village family took home some of the consecrated river water to wash themselves and sprinkle on their livestock. The remainder was stored in the root cellar. During their illness, the Anafrevs retrieved their stash and scrubbed themselves. They praised God when, shortly thereafter, their bodies healed.

Within a few days, however, Elizaveta suffered a relapse. This time, the holy water didn't do the trick. Chilled with sweats, she spent the dim winter hours under piles of sheepskin blankets, too weak and achy to leave her sleeping bench. A rash spread across her upper chest and back, and eventually to her neck, underarms, belly, and inner thighs.

Every medicinal herb her mother, grandmother, and aunt had on hand was rubbed on her, put in steaming water to be inhaled, or given to her to drink. Her throat screamed with each swallow of broth, and the weight melted off her slender frame until her skin sagged in folds. Her young cousins giggled and said that her cheeks were redder than apples but the rest of her face was as white as the underbelly of a fish.

The Anafrevs prostrated themselves before the izba's sacred icon corner. Above the light of a solitary sheep-tallow candle, the Kazan Icon of the Mother of God was draped in a ritual cloth meticulously embroidered by the women of the family. As the household's judge and protector, the Virgin gazed impassively at the Anafrevs as they uttered anguished prayers for Elizaveta's recovery. When their prayers had no effect, the family plea-bargained with the Virgin.

As the endless, comfortless winter dragged on, the villagers canceled their traditional pre-Lenten Maslenitsa dancing, games, and bonfires. Clothes hung slack on wasted bodies. The few remaining livestock bawled nonstop and were mere skeletons covered with skin.

The frost was at its cruelest and the men's spirits were at their lowest when Seleznyov reopened the tavern for a meeting of the village assembly.

THE DAY AFTER the meeting, Elizaveta's mother cornered her husband while he ate his morning meal—a single egg and a dollop of kasha thickened with nettles and tree bark, all of which he shared with Artamon. Elizaveta, curled in a shivering ball under her sheepskins with her eyelids clamped shut, wished everyone would speak more softly. Their agitated words pummeled her throbbing head, causing nauseating bile to gather in her throat.

"The meeting was a long one, eh?" Receiving no answer from Erafei, Nadezhda prodded further. Her technique was blunt. "Anyone found guilty of anything? Wasn't Sasha Novikov supposed to tell his side of the story?" The new daughter-in-law in the Novikov family had presented charges that the bolshak had sexually abused her. In the close living quarters of the izbas, such abhorrent incidents, although not common, certainly weren't unheard of.

Erafei's response was thick with last night's vodka. "That clucking tongue of yours. Why don't you mind your own business for a change?"

"Why should I?" Nadezhda challenged. "In Petrovo, each of us knows the others the same as she knows the fingers on her own hand. Now tell us about Novikov."

"Novikov's troubles are between him, God, and the assembly."

His wife gave an exaggerated shrug. "Keep it to yourself, if that's what you want. I'll hear all about it from the women at the well." She delved into a different topic. "Was there talk of potatoes at the meeting?"

"There's always talk of potatoes."

"So?"

"So what?"

"So what was said?"

"Woman, I am trying to fill an empty stomach! A man is entitled to a few moments of peace in his own house. What else is there to eat?"

"Nothing except garlic and pickles." After muttering something about "a bulky old mule," she declared, "I have a right to know if I'll be expected to handle the Devil's root. Was Maximov's flea-brained steward at the meeting?"

"Yes, the blockhead was there."

Nadezhda planted her fist on her cocked hip, put her other palm on the table, and leaned into her extended arm, so she could cast intimidating eyes down on her husband. "What. Did. He. Say."

Erafei's fist smacked the table. "Just as well there isn't anything to eat! Your nagging's given me a bellyache." His head dropped forward, and his fingertips traced the creases in his forehead. "Might as well tell you. All of you sit down and keep your mouths shut."

Erafei recounted how the steward Roeglin had announced that Count Maximov was willing to have several loads of grain shipped into Petrovo. The grain would be dispensed among the peasants according to need. The Count would also loan rubles to replace livestock and poultry that had died or been sold. Repayment for the grain and animals would occur following the harvest.

Around Seleznyov's tables, the hollow-eyed bolshaks had breathed a united sigh of relief. They crossed themselves and thanked God in Heaven for His generosity and Count Maximov for his fatherly mercy. After a desperate winter, they would be able to feed their families—not well, not even adequately, but they could at least nourish hungry bellies. And there would be seed for next year's crop.

Roeglin asked if the peasants thought the offer was fair and generous. The men agreed the Count's benevolence was exceeded only by God's and the Tsar's. As with every discussion, every gathering, every undertaking, and every decision, the agreement was solidified with a drink, this one courtesy of Roeglin.

The men hoisted an assortment of cups, glasses, and mugs—some wood, some earthenware, some glazed, some not—and bawled out toasts to Count Maximov, Roeglin, and next year's crop. Elbows thrust sideways at shoulder level, the men blew across the top of the vodka to drive away the devil that waited to leap into their open mouths. The clear liquid was tossed back with a flick of their wrists. Thick, calloused hands slammed the assorted vessels onto the table, hoping for a refill. Roeglin obliged.

While the bottle was being passed a second time, Maximov's steward said, "There are conditions the Count insists all of you agree to."

The men stopped praising Maximov and God and waited for the other shoe to drop.

"In exchange for the Count's help during these dire times, he expects two things from you. Without any complaints. First, each family will plant potatoes this spring."

By now, the liquor had sped from the men's hungry stomachs up to their heads. Curses rose to fill the air like flies from a carcass.

Roeglin lifted a stout hand for the men to hold their quarrelsome tongues. "This is a bone we have fought over for the last time. The Count demands that potatoes be planted on the land he reserved for himself. On the land allotted to you, you can plant whatever you please."

"We won't touch the vile Devil's root!"

"I'd sooner rip out my liver than dig those cursed things out of the ground!"

"Maximov can keep his loan!"

"You have no choice in the matter." Roeglin remained unruffled. "With or without the loan, the Count requires you to harvest potatoes this year. If the crop proves valuable, you'll plant more next year. Under the conditions of the loan, you'll make a pledge cast in stone this evening to plant the potatoes without complaint and without disturbance."

Feodor's father, Nikifor, asked, "You said the Count expects two things. What's the second?"

"Count Maximov feels you've been slow in getting your children married. He wants every girl sixteen and older and every boy who is at least eighteen to be married before the spring planting begins. Whoever doesn't secure a mate will be assigned one."

"Impossible!" The men spat their contempt on Seleznyov's plank floor.

Months were required to arrange matches and plan weddings. The men knew their womenfolk would have a fit when they heard matches would be made and weddings held in such a short amount of time. Rumbles crisscrossed the room. Had Maximov lost his mind? Everyone knew October was the divinely ordained month for young people to marry—when food, money, time, and congenial weather were plentiful.

Roeglin again put forth his open palm. "I remind you, the conditions of the loan are that you do the Count's bidding without complaint. And without disturbance."

TWO DAYS LATER, their hangovers assuaged, the bolshaks again hunkered around Seleznyov's tables. Their plan was to appeal to their pomeshchik's compassion. Members of the Zhemchuzhnikov clan were the only ones in the village who could read and write, so a letter was dictated for Nikifor to put on paper.

> *Your Majesty, Count S.S. Maximov, from all the village,*
> *Your generosity is appreciated beyond words. May God bestow His goodness on you in recognition of your kindness. However, the bolshaks of Petrovo speak with one voice as we beg you to show your fatherly mercy and do not make us plant the evil potato. Also, there is not enough time for marriages to take place before planting begins. We beg you to reconsider this also.*

August Roeglin reported back to the men that the Count intended to proceed with the potatoes. As for the weddings, he'd take it under consideration.

Rumors flew along Petrovo's single road that the shipment of grain was supposedly on its way. However, weeks crawled by with no sign of the rye. Speculation ran rampant. Perhaps Maximov had reneged on his promise. Perhaps the grain was tied up in some bureaucratic snarl.

Hope left the peasants when the spring mud arrived and Russia's unpaved roads became quagmires.

The last of the Anafrevs' flour was mixed with mashed acorns—more acorns than rye. Three hens supplied the thirteen Anafrevs with animal protein. In the abbreviated daylight of early spring, the three fowl never produced more than a solitary egg between them.

The story was the same in every izba. Savage hunger twisted stomachs into painful knots. Anemic bodies and sluggish minds hoarded their waning strength atop sleeping benches. The meager supplies of food were concealed from the feral eyes of neighbors. Visits from friends and relatives were presumed to be hostile acts by those looking for handouts. Families resorted to eating squirrels, which was prohibited by the Orthodox Church. Nevertheless, the villagers fell like hungry wolves on the forbidden meat.

CHAPTER 11

Elizaveta

1841

What hovers about your nose
but dodges your hands?

Smell.

"GLORY BE TO God!"

Shortly after Easter, the peasants crossed themselves and flung their bodies flat against Mother Earth. Maximov's grain shipment had arrived.

The aroma of freshly baked bread clung to the village, like lovers unwilling to release their hold after a long separation. With each turn and slap of the supple dough, the women's fingers and hearts sang their gratitude. Men lifted full bowls above their heads and proclaimed, "Thanks be to Mother Rye and Mother Kasha."

The bread and kasha acted like a tonic on Elizaveta. As her strength returned, the Anafrevs thanked the Virgin of Kazan as well as Elizaveta's robust constitution.

During St. Thomas Week, the second week after Easter, the earliest shoots of spring vegetation pushed through the damp, dormant ground. The earth had rested beneath the snow and was now ready to nourish those who tilled it. Men prodded the soil with sticks, their fingers, and the toes of their boots, hoping the fields were dry enough to accept their impatient ploughs. For the twentieth time, the women checked their cucumber, radish, and flax seeds for reassurance they had made it through the winter, safe from the greedy eyes of mice.

In an unparalleled display of feet-dragging, the villagers managed to stave off the mandatory spring weddings. Once the fieldwork began, even Maximov couldn't justify proceeding with the ceremonies. Although the Count still required that every adult and nigh-to-adult enter the state of holy matrimony, at least the nuptials would occur in autumn, exactly as tradition dictated.

The first Saturday in May, Petrovo's men made their all-important first trek to the fields. Each man carried his oat seed in bags purposely left unfastened so the soil wouldn't "tie up the seed."

The villagers' preoccupation with this annual ritual gave Elizaveta and Feodor an opportunity to meet privately for the first time since the previous autumn. After the debacle in the Widow Shabanova's barn, they chose a new hideaway—a secluded glade beside the river, beyond the eastern edge of the village. The grassy recess was carved into the bottom of a cliff, atop which sat the Holy Trinity Women's Community.

The age-old orphanage lay where Petrovo's inelegant road shrank to twin ruts that crossed the vast blackland prairies. The village's collective memory had misplaced how or why the two-story white stucco buildings came to be perched on a bluff overlooking an insignificant river on the outskirts of an inconspicuous village. The peasants had little contact with the cloister of nuns and the orphans they sheltered, and all parties were content with that arrangement.

The young lovers' hour rushed by. Feodor returned to the village along an animal path beside the river. Elizaveta climbed the cliff, gave the orphanage a wide berth, and then turned onto the potholed road toward the village.

Even as she basked in the afterglow of Feodor's embraces, a furrow crept between her eyebrows. Last autumn and now again today, he had been determined to fondle her breasts, and he persistently tried to raise her skirt. Perhaps, Elizaveta reasoned, if she gave in regarding her breasts, he would be content and stop trying to get beneath her skirt.

Worries about wandering hands melted away as luscious sunshine spilled across her shoulders, a delightful contrast to the cool air that fanned her face and neck. She was as content as a turtle sunning itself, and she vowed to never again take for granted even God's simplest gifts.

After months of sickness and near starvation in the fetid, airless izba, she saw tired, tumbledown Petrovo with fresh eyes. The village's very banality was like the open arms of an old friend.

Up ahead was a wind-beaten izba, followed by a bedraggled gate, then a dilapidated fence, and another sagging izba. Each of the one- and two-acre homesteads was an undistinguished version of the same theme: an izba plus a half dozen or so decaying barns and sheds that housed wooden tools and farm implements, poultry and livestock, horse harnesses and wagons, smoked meats, and preserved vegetables. Only the occasional homestead had the luxury of its own steam bathhouse.

Loud cracks and rumblings drew Elizaveta's gaze to ice breaking free in the river, another part of Petrovo she had failed to appreciate before her illness. The meager waterway was navigable only by small craft and of no consequence to anyone who didn't live along its banks. It was spanned by a plank bridge, which led on the far bank to a long lane shaded by a double colonnade of linden trees.

The lane's sole destination was the snow-white portico of the Count's house. Tall, sun-filled windows overlooked the manor's lawn as it sloped to the water's edge. Behind the estate house stood a tidy assortment of barns, workshops, and carriage houses, all constructed of the same red brick as the house.

Elizaveta watched smoke the color of morning mist drift from two of the house's four chimneys. The pristine wreaths whirled above the tile roof and spun into slender tendrils before melding with the crystal-blue sky, providing a stark contrast to the village side of the river, where blackened chimneys poked out of grimy thatched roofs and belched gray smoke.

Elizaveta had no formal education and possessed a view of the world that extended no farther than the fields surrounding the village. However, she understood that the scene before her underscored, in some imprecise way, the disparity between substance and subsistence, between wealth and poverty, between the elites and the masses. And the young woman also knew that, just as surely as the wind held dominance over the flame, Count Maximov held absolute control over his entire estate, even the smoke.

A hand tapped her shoulder. She jumped the length of a broom handle.

"Hello, Elizaveta."

Her face puckered with revulsion. "Illarion! How long have you been following me?"

"Since you came out of the orphanage."

Her hands curled into fists. The deceitful blockhead always reeked of trouble, no matter the circumstances. But his appearance just after she'd left Feodor made the sweat on her back turn cold. "What do you want?"

"I want to talk. Will you talk to me?"

"Get away from me." She resumed walking, her strides long and brisk.

He moved alongside her. "Don't stay mad. Stop and talk to me."

"Leave me alone!"

He grabbed her upper arms and yanked her to a halt, facing him. "Won't you listen to me?"

"Let go of me!" She looked up and down the road, hoping someone would witness the scene, but as luck would have it, no one was in sight. She thrust her fists upward between his two arms and threw off his hands.

He fell back a pace and held both arms out to his sides. "I won't touch you. You have my word."

She resumed walking, swinging her arms, propelling her body faster.

"Don't you understand?" He fell in with her swift pace. "I made up that story about the bed of rye to make you see that's what I wanted you to do with me."

Elizaveta reeled. Certainly he didn't think she'd be willing to . . . The thought was so loathsome, she couldn't finish it. "First of all, you didn't *make up a story,*" she snarled. "You told a bald-faced lie. And second, you're cracked in the head if you think I'd ever want to do such a thing with you."

Illarion stopped walking and seized both of her shoulders, already going back on his word. He spun her toward him. His pimpled cheeks were blistering red. "Give me a chance."

"Give you a chance?" Words sprang from Elizaveta's lips faster than a frog's tongue after a cricket. "I never want to talk to you."

"Elizaveta—"

"You have the brains of a turkey and the sensitivity of an ox."

"Don't be mean to me." He bared his teeth like a wolf. "You'll regret it."

"I don't want to be seen anywhere near you. The whole town knows you're born of weak stock." She brought both hands between his arms and shoved his chest.

As she started to run home, she heard him spit.

CHAPTER 12

Elizaveta

1841

They cut me.
They bind me.
They beat me mercilessly.
They break me on the wheel.
I'll go through fire and water,
and my end will be a knife and teeth.
What am I?

Grain.

"DON'T YOU HAVE a calf for sale? We have a young bull."

The parents of Pavel Vorobev, Katya's suitor, were dressed in their best wool clothes when they called upon Erafei one evening in late May. They were in search of a match for Pavel.

Erafei's shoulders drooped as he consented to an October wedding. With Maximov's marriage dictate, what choice did he have?

As an elated Katya showed her future mother-in-law her trousseau of embroidered linens, Elizaveta stood off to one side, uncharacteristically mute. It would have taken a prophet, she brooded, to predict such an unlikely sequence of events. The Count's mandate, combined with both Katya and Pavel being the stipulated ages—if only such dazzling good fortune would fall so freely into her own lap. If only. If only . . .

As the summer days lengthened, Elizaveta kept an attentive ear for scandalous tales stemming from the blabbermouth Illarion. But no rumors surfaced.

On July 9, the day following the Feast of the Kazan Icon of the Mother of God, the villagers picked up their scythes and began reaping the grain. In a furious race against time, the serfs called upon every morsel of their grit as they labored with quiet stamina using the same type of handmade, wooden implements that had been wielded for centuries. Under the broiling sun, they first harvested the golden fields of winter rye, followed immediately by the spring grains of barley, oats, and buckwheat. There was no leeway, not if the grain was to fully mature yet be harvested before an early frost.

Without so much as a day's break following the harvest, the bone-weary peasants hitched up their horses and ploughed the fallow fields, then sowed the winter rye that would be harvested next summer. During the annual six-week Time of Suffering, the villagers' bodies were laid waste by ruthless labor, poor nutrition, and scant sleep.

On a sweltering morning in mid-August, Elizaveta lay on her pallet of loose hay, hoping against hope that she'd cross paths with Feodor today. She hadn't spoken more than a superficial greeting to him since June. First the fieldwork had kept them apart; then he had again accompanied Count Maximov to the Great Fair. But yesterday, she had heard that Feodor was back home.

The earliest songbirds had yet to welcome the morning when her father said grace at the table. Elizaveta swung her legs over the edge of her sleeping bench. Under the sallow light thrown by a single burning splinter, she ran a forefinger over the calluses on her palm. With the same finger, she stroked the lizard skin of her sunburned cheek. What an awful sight she must be!

She shuffled from the izba, numbly chewing a piece of pork lard, the best possible source of long-lasting energy during the Time of Suffering. The sun flamed on the horizon, filling the eastern sky with streaks of yellow and orange. Elizaveta trudged down the dusty road, the checkered imprints of her woven sandals blending with scores of others. In the spongy air, her shirt was already clinging to her skin.

She was swatting away a humming cloud of mosquitoes when footsteps ran up behind her. She spun about, suddenly wide awake, a smile unfurling ear to ear. She planted a hand on each of Feodor's shoulders and gave him three sisterly kisses on alternating cheeks as villagers passed around them. Feodor told her how much he had missed her by holding her gaze for an extra heartbeat.

Heading toward their fields, they walked easily together, as well they should. They'd been doing it the whole of their lives. Their shoulders were less than a hand's width apart, yet not once did they brush against one another. They were like two neighboring strands in a spider web, never touching but never swaying asunder.

Over the ardent clamor of roosters, Feodor described his trip to the Great Fair, concluding with a breathy "Oh, Liza. Both trips, last year's and this year's, showed me how very large the world is. And our village is so very small. Did you know that some people have skin the color of tallow? And eyes that look like this?" His fingers stretched the outer corners of his eyelids.

"And their churches—they're nothing like ours." He stopped walking, dropped to his haunches, and, using a twig and the dirt road, scratched silhouettes of a Tatar mosque and a Chinese pagoda roof. His eyes grew distant with thought. "Liza, do you think all those foreign people will burn in Hell, even though they've never heard about our loving God?"

Although the question caught her unawares, she wasn't surprised by it. Feodor was always turning over some long-held belief to see how the other side looked. Lacking an answer, she tried to appear exasperated, even as his soft smile rippled through her. "Why must you view life different than everyone in Petrovo? And ask questions no one else asks? Why do I put up with you?"

His acorn-hued eyes bowed into mirthful crescents. "Because I brought you a present from the Fair."

He fumbled in the rear waist of his trousers and brought forth a handheld mirror. She seized its smooth wooden handle and simultaneously examined both the gift and her image in it. She scowled at her cracked lips, cheeks burned to the color of raw beef, and eyes rimmed red like a radish and underscored with dark circles. It was the way all women looked during the Time of Suffering.

"Of course, it's for both you and Katya. Your whole family actually."

"Thank you, Feodor. It's a very generous gift." Her smile turned devilish. "I'll show you my gratitude another time."

That evening, her father and Uncle Artamon denounced the mirror as an instrument of vanity and waste. All the females, even Grandmama, huddled around it and examined their hair, eyes, teeth, and necks. When the women finally relinquished control of the mirror, several small hands seized the handle. The five boys stuck out their tongues at themselves and propped two-fingered devil horns above each other's heads. Only after the mirror had been hung on a wooden peg did the Anafrevs drop dog-tired onto their sleeping benches.

Elizaveta's deadened sleep was penetrated by fervent pounding on the frame of the izba's sole window. "Nadezhda!" Feodor's mother hissed through the open window. "Get up. It's important."

Elizaveta's eyes flew open.

Receiving no response, Anisia Zhemchuzhnikova raised her voice. "Nadezhda! It's about your daughter."

Elizaveta grew cold and weak, as though all the blood had drained from her body. Anisia had found out about her and Feodor!

CHAPTER 13

Elizaveta

1841

Sunset, sunset star,
a pretty maid
was walking through the village
shedding tears.
The moon saw them;
the sun hid them.
What are they?

Dewdrops.

NADEZHDA CRAWLED DOWN from her sleeping bench above the stove, scuffed across the floorboards in her nightshirt, and swiveled the wooden latch on the door.

Elizaveta's chest was so full of dread, she was afraid to breathe.

Anisia's voice was fast and low. Elizaveta heard the word *secret* and grew light-headed.

Just as she knew her mother would do, Nadezhda brought her husband into the conversation. While Erafei lit a splinter hanging from a rafter, Elizaveta crossed herself. She begged the Virgin Mother of God to help her say the right words, words that would convince her father that she should marry Feodor.

Wait. Elizaveta arched her neck. *What did Anisia just say? What does "with child" have to do with anything?*

"Elizaveta, get over here." Her mother's tone was as sharp as salt on the tongue.

The three adults and the teenager took seats around the table. Elizaveta heard the rustling of straw as the other children crept to the edge of their sleeping benches to eavesdrop.

Nadezhda started to speak to her troublesome second daughter, but the words wouldn't come. On the third attempt, she shook her head and sputtered, "With child?"

"Who's with child?" Elizaveta asked.

"You."

"Me? Of course I'm not with child."

"Everyone thinks so."

"Everybody thinks I'm with child?" None of this made sense.

"Were," Anisia cut in.

"Were?"

"Thinks you *were* with child."

Her mother's explanation came in short bursts. "Illarion Loktev. Said you gave birth. In secret."

Elizaveta's fears dissolved. This had nothing to do with Feodor. "Another of that liar's stories." Elizaveta rolled her eyes. "No one will believe him. Given the chance, he'd blacken his own mother's name."

"But they do believe him." Anisia explained that in this evening's darkness, Illarion mutilated a rooster—an important fertility symbol—and hung the bloody carcass on the Anafrevs' gate. Padraga Karpova—the Zhemchuzhnikovs' neighbor and Anisia's second cousin—caught him in the act and chastised him. Illarion told Karpova that Elizaveta had secretly given birth and disposed of the baby. Karpova rushed straightaway to tell Anisia—immediately after she shared the news with her own family plus anyone she encountered along the way.

"Disposed? How did I supposedly dispose of a baby?"

"Don't know. Maybe buried it. Or threw it in the river."

Elizaveta drew back. Anisia sounded as if she believed that her goddaughter would not only debase herself with an immoral sexual act, but also kill her own baby. "How ridiculous," Elizaveta scoffed, "to think a secret birth could occur in a village that knows no secrets."

Anisia planted both palms on the table and leaned forward. "Illarion said this happened last winter and spring. Remember, Liza? When you were home with the fever and rash."

Suddenly it all made sense. She had been housebound for months, first by influenza, then by that evil illness. Elizaveta's long absence from public view lent credence to Illarion's story.

Elizaveta tucked a clump of hair behind her ear. "And who's the father?"

"Illarion says he doesn't know, but it isn't him."

"What are we going to do?" her mother wailed.

Erafei said he knew exactly what he was going to do. He'd make sure the assembly flogged Illarion Loktev to within a breath of his life.

Aunt Marina joined the foursome at the table. "I've often said all the Loktev men should have been drowned at birth. It would have saved us all a lot of trouble."

Nadezhda nodded her agreement. "But it's too late now."

Anisia's fingers drummed the battered tabletop. "The assembly will want proof that Elizaveta was truly sick last winter and not merely hiding her condition." She turned to Elizaveta. "Who saw you during that time? Where did you go? To church?"

She shook her head. Elizaveta had missed each Sunday service plus the feasts of several saints as well as Shrovetide and Easter.

Anisia recollected, "I visited several times. But as her godmother my word won't carry any weight. Who else visited while you were sick?"

Silent faces implored Elizaveta to come forth with names in order to save her own soul, but she raised her open hands helplessly. No one had visited the family during that difficult time. When food became scarce, neighborly visitations had ceased. Furthermore, the family was self-sufficient. No handymen or peddlers ever came to the izba. The Anafrevs milked, raised, preserved, and stored everything they put in their bellies, and they grew, wove, and stitched whatever they placed on their backs.

Elizaveta's desperate eyes roved around the table. In the dim light, the faces of those she loved most, the people who would do anything they could for her, looked pinched and drained of hope. The heavy silence lasted so long, the crickets in a dark corner of the izba commenced chirping.

At last, Elizaveta saw a ray of hope. "What if I cast rye kernels into the river?" Everyone knew that if a maiden tossed rye kernels into the river and the kernels floated, she was a virgin.

Following the Divine Liturgy the next morning, a handpicked group of women assembled at the river's edge. Without hesitation, Elizaveta flung the rye kernels in an arc as if sowing grain. The Anafreva women breathed a collective sigh of relief as they watched the seeds bounce atop the shimmering waves. It was proof positive of her virtue.

The only Anafrev to attend that evening's church service was Erafei. He used the opportunity to call an assembly meeting so the bolshaks could once again dole out justice to the worthless Loktev boy.

When Erafei returned home, his bulky frame burst into the izba. His anger filled the room. Elizaveta looked up from her mending as he marched straight toward her. He wrapped his paw-like hand around her upper arm and yanked her to her feet. The trousers and needle dropped to the floor.

Erafei's fingernails dug into his daughter's skin. "I never for a moment believed you said those things about the rye field to that little Loktev scoundrel. And of course, I know his latest rumor is nothing but a lie. But you'd better assure me what I heard tonight isn't true either." Menacing breaths hissed from his nostrils. "You look me square in the face right now and tell me what Zhanna Seleznyova is saying about you is just another lie!"

Elizaveta's veins turned cold.

"Tell me now!" Erafei kicked Elizaveta's mending across the room. "Is it true or not about you and Feodor?"

Elizaveta's eyelids closed, and her mouth filled with a sick taste. He released her arm. She heard him stomp over to the table and pound it over and over.

"What's this about?" Nadezhda moved to stand next to Elizaveta.

Elizaveta opened her eyes to see her father's pointing, outstretched arm. "That girl, your daughter, has been lying in a field of rye with her cousin! Feodor!"

Everyone above the age of eight gasped.

Elizaveta blurted, "He's not my cousin," as if it made a kopek's worth of difference.

"He's the same thing as your cousin."

Elizaveta blinked her eyes, trying to stop the room from swaying. Everything was out of focus. After an eternity of keeping her secret hidden, the ice she'd been walking on had finally cracked, and she was going under.

"How do you know all of this?" Aunt Marina asked.

"Everybody knows it. Thanks to Seleznyov's tart of a daughter."

Elizaveta's shoulders slumped forward as she silently filled in the story's gaps. According to reputable gossip, Zhanna was in a rage because, due to the Count's mandate, she was being forced to marry Arkhip Melnikov while Katya got the most handsome prize (if you could call Pavel a prize). Elizaveta easily pictured Zhanna's poisonous tongue lashing out with complete inappropriateness at anyone who happened to provide a target. The sister of Pavel's future wife offered an easy mark.

"So it's true?" Nadezhda asked quietly.

Elizaveta gave a single nod. "But not the part about the field of rye. We haven't . . . we haven't . . ."

Erafei's voice was restrained, like an angry bull subdued only because of the ring through its nose. "How long have the two of you been carrying on?"

Elizaveta hesitated. She couldn't very well respond, *Forever*. Nor could she demean the relationship by saying *Only a short time*. She gave an indefinite "A while."

Not a word was spoken while the family digested this piece of information. Erafei paced the room. "You know what you have to do now."

He meant, of course, that she needed to stop seeing Feodor. But that's not what she needed to do. She straightened her shoulders. "Yes. I have to marry him."

"What!" a medley of voices rang out.

"I love him, and he loves me."

Her mother buried her face in her hands. Erafei strode across the floor and towered over Elizaveta. "Marry? How can you talk about marrying your own kin?"

"He's not kin."

"In the eyes of God, he is."

Elizaveta knew she needed to start talking, fast. Time and again she had rehearsed the words. But now that the moment had arrived, her arguments sounded as forceful as cooked noodles.

"Papa, please hear what I have to say—"

"No! You listen to me. The purpose of marriage is to increase productivity. And you can't have productivity if you have imbecile children. And imbecile children is what happens if you marry your own kin."

"But the Anafrevs aren't truly kin to the Zhemchuzhnikovs."

"Maybe not by blood, but they're family just the same."

"Papa, you know what a fine person Feodor is. He's Nikifor's son, for goodness' sake. There's no better family in all of Petrovo. Feodor works hard. He'll take good care of me."

"I'd rather carve out my own liver than allow my daughter to marry the son of her godmother." He resumed his pacing. "Spiritual debauchery!"

"But Papa—"

"This goes against God and the Church. The Devil flays people like you!"

"Feodor and I didn't intend for things to turn out this way. It just happened—"

"You'd better get down on your knees and beg God's forgiveness!"

"Papa—"

"Enough! I've heard enough!"

"Please listen!"

"No more!" Palms outward, Erafei's crisscrossed hands flew apart as they sliced the air. "End it now! If I hear you're still carrying on with him, I'll snap his skinny little neck in half!" Erafei's bearlike shoulders heaved with anger.

Elizaveta feared he was about to backhand her.

His voice dropped to a terrifying growl. "Do you understand? Stay away from him."

She nodded, knowing full well her father was demanding the impossible.

Erafei stormed to the izba's door and jerked it open. He announced to the room in general, "I'm going right now to apologize to Nikifor Zhemchuzhnikov for my daughter's shameless misbehavior." The door slammed behind him, only to reopen before it stopped quivering. He shouted to his wife, "And you'd better go do the same with Anisia."

Elizaveta sank onto a stool and stared at the dusty plank floor, where all her beautiful dreams lay like scattered lint.

CHAPTER 14

Elizaveta

1841

What can't be locked up in a trunk?
Light.

ELIZAVETA'S FUTURE WAS in tatters, ripped to shreds by a father who supposedly loved her but didn't care a fig about her happiness. Of course, she acknowledged, it wasn't only her father. Her mother was of like mind, as were Feodor's parents. And silently behind them stood the entire village. And behind the village, the Church. It was a battle she never could have won.

She and Feodor sat, shoulders touching, beside the river in the secluded cove below the orphanage's cliff. Their doleful eyes watched the water's insatiable quest to round the next bend.

Elizaveta had the sensation of being swept away by a current, unable to regain her footing. She was powerless to control her own future. It hadn't always been that way. Throughout her childhood, her family had needled her endlessly about her stubborn willfulness. Now, though, she was helpless to direct her own fate.

Feodor asked, "What about living together without marriage?"

Elizaveta's body jerked as if hit by a bullet.

"You think it's wrong?" he asked.

"Of course it's wrong. Horribly wrong."

"If two people love each other, they should be married in the eyes of the Church and in the eyes of the community. But we're forbidden to." Feodor paused, measuring his words. "Who benefits by our living apart? No one. And who would be injured by our living together?"

She spun to face him. Was he was merely talking nonsense to escape for a few moments from their bottomless gloom? "It's sinful!"

"Calm down, Liza." He took her hand in his. "I'm only daydreaming. Think about it. Without our parents' consent and the sanction of the Church, we'd have to live on our own, just the two of us."

"How could we do that?"

"We couldn't. No izba. No barns. No livestock. No plough. No wagon, pots, table, loom, or spinning wheel. Plus, the village would discredit our relationship and wouldn't allot us any land to till. Not to mention our children would forever be labeled as bastards."

Yes, Elizaveta understood the foolhardiness of living outside the laws of the Church and the dictates of the community. Under normal circumstances, newly wedded couples needed very little other than clothing. The groom's family provided an established household, and the pomeshchik provided arable land. Lacking the support of a family and a village, a peasant would perish like an abandoned child.

Since living together was out of the question, Elizaveta and Feodor considered the idea of running away. But without a passport authorized by the Count, they would be fugitives. No village would take them in, and no one in the city would hire them. Eventually they'd be caught and returned to Maximov. The Count would probably flog her and send him to the Army.

Elizaveta's heart plummeted like a stone sinking into the black waters of a well. She dropped her head against his shoulder while the river slapped against its shore.

WHEN ELIZAVETA RETURNED home, she found her mother's eyes were ringed with the red of tears.

"Mama, what is it?"

"Ask your father. He's in the barn."

"Why won't you tell me? Is someone hurt?" Receiving a shake of her mother's head, Elizaveta came up with a more likely scenario. "Did I do something wrong?"

"No, no, you did nothing wrong. It's that harebrained Maximov who did something wrong."

"Count Maximov? Mama, tell me. Please." Receiving no response, Elizaveta redirected her appeal. "Aunt Marina? Please. Why won't you tell me? Why do I have to ask Papa?"

"Because your father made the decision," Aunt Marina said. "It's his decision to make."

"You have to understand," Nadezhda said. "Your father had no choice. No choice at all."

"No choice about what?" Elizaveta bit back her scream, *Stop talking in circles!*

Aunt Marina and Nadezhda looked sideways at one another in a momentary silent conversation.

Nadezhda's open hands floundered in front of her shoulders. "Liza, you must understand—we have to do what Maximov demands."

Elizaveta bit down on her tongue while her mother stumbled over words that just wouldn't come.

Aunt Marina took over. "When is your birthday, Liza?"

"Next month."

"How old will you be?"

"Sixteen."

Mouths grim, the two women stared at her.

It hit Elizaveta like a thunderbolt. Sixteen! She had been so completely absorbed with her dilemmas about Illarion and Feodor, she'd overlooked that the Count postponed the wedding deadline from last spring until this October. Her name would be included among the marriageable girls!

Her head swayed from side to side. "No." Her throat quivered with terror. "No."

Both women stood as still as time itself.

"Who?" The question was more a rush of air than a word.

Her mother delivered the blow. "Your father struck an agreement with Sidor Vorontsov."

Her aunt nailed Elizaveta's coffin shut with a single word. "Ermak."

Elizaveta knees refused to hold her up. She staggered to a bench and sank into a heap like a sack of grain.

How could she have been in Feodor's arms only a few moments ago and now be betrothed to vile Ermak Vorontsov? Heavenly Creator, let it not be so!

Grief and fear and nausea swelled up in her. She put her head between her knees.

Aunt Marina explained the wretched twist of fate. "There's no one left. Everyone else has a match. Ermak's in the same situation as you. He'll turn eighteen next week."

Elizaveta wiped away scalding tears. "But, Mama, you know Ermak. He's always been mean. Hideously mean."

"It's not the choice your father would have made, but there is no alternative. You must accept that."

"Ermak's cruel!"

Through her blurred vision, Elizaveta saw despair in her mother's eyes before she turned away to stir a pot of soup. "Talk to your father, but it won't do any good. They drank to the agreement."

"You want me to be miserable the rest of my life?"

"They struck an honest-man's agreement. That's the end of it." The large wooden spoon kept going round and round, beating the sides of the ceramic pot.

"I'm not chattel. I'm a person. I have feelings."

Her mother continued churning the cabbage.

Elizaveta slid off the bench, clutching her writhing stomach. Her knees sank to the floor, and she collapsed against her trunk.

Her aunt placed a hand on her shoulder. "Don't blame your mother or your father, Liza. It's out of their hands. And you'll learn to live with Ermak and have his children. You'll grow used to him. It may not seem possible to you now, but you'll manage."

Elizaveta buried her face in the crook of one arm while her other hand traveled along the rough wood of the trunk her father had made for her when she was a child. Inside were ceremonial towels, some as long as six feet, embroidered with the thread of her dreams. The towels had been woven and stitched to bind her to Feodor in marriage, to hang from the overhead beams to pull on as she labored to deliver Feodor's children, and later, to wrap around their babies as swaddling.

Elizaveta pounded the top of the trunk. All of her dreams were going to the Vorontsovs.

She frantically searched for a glimmer of hope in any of the options she and Feodor had discussed at the river. But she was shackled by the impermeable isolation of Petrovo and by the choiceless oppression of serfdom. There was no hope.

CHAPTER 15

Maximov

1843

What always has its back to the wall
and its face to the room?

An icon.

STEPAN'S HEART LATCHED on to vibrant hope during the spectacularly beautiful spring of 1843 when Sophia seemed on the verge of her former self. It was as if the burst of the sun's rays had melted away the final sharp icicles surrounding Dmitry's death.

Stepan and Sophia spent teatime in easy companionship at the small iron table on the terrace, keeping a watchful eye on the children as they played vulture-and-chickens or climbed the flowering black alder tree. At night, the symphony of the river's icy rush of melted snow filtered through the windowpanes, enticing husband and wife to entangle about each other between the fragrant sheets.

Sophia's mood was so congenial, she was elated when Stepan's cousin, Valeryan Kirillovich Shelgunov, along with his wife and three children, stayed at Petrovo for a few days in May. The Shelgunovs were traveling by carriage from their residence in Moscow for a visit with Valeryan's in-laws in Orenburg. Petrovo offered a much-needed respite on their six-week journey.

Stepan's close relationship with his cousin stemmed partially from the winters the two boys attended boarding school together in Moscow. But sealing their friendship were the three summers Valeryan had lived with the Maximovs on the Petrovo estate during the rebuilding of his parents' Moscow home. The mansion had been destroyed by the fire that engulfed the city in 1812 following the invasion of Napoleon's troops.

Stepan was fond of Valeryan's wife, Leonora, an affable, cultured woman whose family owned large mining and smelting concerns in the Ural Mountains. The Shelgunovs had two daughters—one equal in age to the nine-year-old

Maximov twins and the other still a toddler. Their boy, Rodya, was a sprouting eleven-year-old.

On the second day of the Shelgunovs' visit, the three boys coaxed their fathers into hollowing out the trunk of a large poplar and turning it into a canoe. During breaks from shipbuilding, Rodya taught Anton and Sergei the art of juggling. They started with spoons, then progressed to croquet balls, tapered candles, and finally goose eggs.

Stepan was delighted by Anton's polished-to-perfection manners, especially toward his cousin Sonya. The boy had a knack for treating the opposite sex with deference, perhaps learned during all the mollycoddling he'd been forced to bestow on his mother. Without coaxing or coercion, Anton rose whenever Sonya entered the room, and he held her chair at the dinner table. He inquired as to her favorite foods and assured her that the cook would prepare them specifically to her liking.

Anton offered Sonya and Rodya a tour of the distillery, and Valeryan and Stepan tagged along. Stepan remained in the background while Anton traced the grain, water, and yeast through the purifying and concentrating processes until they emerged, coalesced, and metamorphosed as alcohol.

"Quality vodka should look exactly like spring water." Anton put a small amount of the concentrated liquor in a glass bottle and shook it. "See how the bubbles quickly burst? A sign of purity. If we were to set it afire, it would burn with a blue flame, leaving nothing but pure water."

Stepan chuckled when Anton cajoled Sonya into taking the smallest taste of vodka diluted considerably with water. The boy could maneuver his way with anyone, intuitively knowing how to hitch an engaging smile on to just the right words. When Sonya's little mouth puckered at the alcohol's bite, Anton told her the next time he would add some flavorings.

"Perhaps during your next visit, Father's peaches will be in season. You'll like that. Gives the vodka a wonderful smell. Or mint leaves, but only a smidgeon or the taste is too strong."

Later that day, Anton discovered that young Nadya had never heard the story of *The Little Humpbacked Horse*, and Sonya hadn't read it in years, so he gave an after-dinner reading. Sergei and Rodya had no patience to listen to a tale far below their level of maturity, so they retired to Sergei's bedroom to put sheets over their heads and run about acting like ghosts.

The next evening, Vladimir, Yustina, and Victor Rusakov joined the two families for dinner. As the sun threw purple rays across the fields, the three men had the urge to break out the cards.

"Care to join us?" Valeryan asked the boys.

Anton jumped at the opportunity, while Sergei and Rodya opted to resume the previous night's ghoulish activities, dragging Victor upstairs with them. Anton took to whist like a duck to water, eventually assuming the role of scorekeeper.

"In the future," he insisted at the end of the evening, "let's place bets with kopeks instead of dried beans."

ON THE DAY following the Shelgunovs' departure, heavy clouds rubbed their gray bellies against the top of Petrovo's forest, dumping rain over the countryside and thwarting Stepan's plans to check the wattle fences the peasants had supposedly repaired. He came upon Sophia in the entry hall. She was kneeling beside one of her many tall ferns, poking her forefinger in the soil. The stormy afternoon light seeped through the cantilevered shutters, highlighting her beauty.

Sophia swiped her hands together to brush off the traces of dirt. When she started to rise, Stepan placed a hand on her shoulder and dropped to his haunches beside her. "Stay with me."

Her bewildered eyes widened to meet his.

He placed his forefinger under her chin. "I want to tell you how much I love you."

Her face softened from puzzled to tender. "I love you, too." Her words were no louder than an autumn leaf gliding to the ground.

Scooting his back against the wall, he opened an arm for her to curl into. With her head against his chest, he slid off her tidy, black knit cap and let her silken waves flow over her shoulders. In silence, they listened to the rain tap the window and watched gray shadows swirl around the furniture.

He chuckled. "What would the servants say if they saw us hidden away behind these fronds?"

Her laugh was full-bodied.

Fearful that the Shelgunovs' departure might unravel Sophia's good spirits, Stepan had masterminded what he considered to be a champion plan. Now was as good a time as any to begin implementation.

"During Valeryan's visit, I found it to be rather awkward to have the children doubled up in the beds. While it may be acceptable now, in only a couple of years, Rodya and Sonya will expect their own rooms. That's a bit indecorous, don't you agree—not offering respectable sleeping accommodations?"

He felt her nod against his chest.

"What if we turned the children's playroom into a bedroom? And we might consider converting part of the attic into an additional bedroom. There's already a dormer, and we could put a grate in the floor to let heat rise." Stepan gave a quick shake of his head to dislodge the silly notions. "Never mind my harebrained ideas. The amount of time and work it would require on your part . . . I shouldn't have mentioned it."

Sophia straightened and leaned back against the wall, resting her shoulder against his. "Why, it wouldn't be that much work for me. I have the servants' help. And I know I can count on you." Her fingers picked nonchalantly at the piping on her skirt. "But what about the cost?"

"This place hasn't had a thing done to it in decades. Certainly we can justify spending a few rubles. And while we're at it, we could consider replacing some of the furniture."

Sophia was drawn to the idea like a flock of rooks to a freshly harvested grain field. Eyes bright and mind alert, she strolled about the house for weeks, scurrying back and forth to her desk to jot down her thoughts. She and Yustina Rusakova took Yegorka and Feodor Zhemchuzhnikov along on two shopping expeditions to the provincial capital. Both times, the wagon and the carriage returned home filled to capacity.

Of all Sophia's purchases, the only ones that perturbed Stepan were the icons. Petrovo's smoky-eyed Our Lady of Jerusalem was joined by St. George the Victory-Bearer, St. Juliana, the Vladimir Virgin, and the Kiev Virgin.

Autumn was a jumble of canvas drop cloths, the invasive odor of paint and wallpaper glue, and the pounding of serf-carpenters who had been borrowed, for a fee, from A.A. Gabrichevsky. Stepan gritted his teeth as he dipped into his investment accounts. But it was worth every ruble if Sophia remained at peace with herself.

In the study, she created a small nook for her writing desk by having a wrought-iron trellis erected, then adding a climbing ivy. The living plant was extended by a trompe l'oeil border of ivy around the top of the room. She changed out Stepan's dark mahogany desk for an understated birch secretary with glass doors above, claw feet below, and in between, velvet-lined pigeonholes and tiny drawers.

Stepan selected a single item for himself—a cushioned armchair with ottoman, upholstered in deep India-red brocade.

The nuns' orphanage became the recipient of the stodgy poplar-veneer barrel chairs and the ponderous leather sofa that Stepan's parents had received as a wedding present. Taking their place in the parlor were a new Empire divan, matching chairs, and an oval pedestal table. The heavy drapery was replaced with Belgian lace.

Stepan encouraged Sophia to dispose of the old, poorly done Maximov family portrait that hung by a velvet tie at the head of the stairs. She refused, insisting the Napoleon-era painting looked charmingly clumsy only because it was too old to be modern but not old enough to be considered antique. Someday, their children would cherish the painting of ancestral women in raised-waist dresses and men sporting nipped frock coats.

At Sophia's urging, Stepan agreed to change bedrooms, leaving the one in which he had slept for almost forty years in favor of the master bedroom across the hall. In honor of their new, expansive room, Sophia ordered a huge bed of Karelian birch that she covered with a quilt of cornflower-blue blossoms embedded in a deep eggplant background.

In this bed, Elena Stepanovna Maximova was born in December.

CHAPTER 16

Maximov

1844–1845

What's easiest of all?

To see others' flaws.

STEPAN'S HOPES HAD been misplaced. The renovated house, the birth of a healthy baby . . . Nothing could keep his wife's spirits buoyed. Although Sophia stayed on a relatively even keel during spring and summer, each winter invariably plunged her into mood swings as raw and tumultuous as the season itself.

With time and effort, he learned to accept her good days and tolerate her bad ones. Rather than pounding his head against this reality like a demented woodpecker, he walled off his pain deep inside himself, where it was rarely examined.

Stepan wished he were the sole casualty of Sophia's inner turmoil. But the rest of the family were also victims—even Anton. On days when she was immersed in her bleak world of spiritual torment, she pressured Anton to kneel beside her in front of the Icon of Our Lady of Jerusalem, clutching him to her side during her morbid fits of crying. When bedridden with headaches, she'd wail for him to apply cool compresses to her forehead.

On the twins' tenth birthday in 1844, as Sophia was climbing out of her winter despondency, she decided the time had arrived to place the children's education in the hands of a private teacher. She searched far and wide for an experienced tutor who could teach algebra, geometry, history, geography, and French, plus impart some instruction in drawing, dancing, and appreciation of European art and music.

Sophia selected Hilda Behrens, a German spinster whose father had served as a diplomat to Russia when she was a child. After taking her degree at the University of Dorpat, she had spent eight years tutoring the children of Russian gentry on various country estates. The short woman was as solid as a peasant and as round as a cabbage. She had an erect bearing, a tight bun of brown hair, and stalwart arms that seemed to be permanently folded across her ample bosom.

Hilda spent six hours a day by the Maximov children's sides, working like (and somewhat resembling) a draught horse. Her first year of tutoring had quite dissimilar effects on the three children. Natalya lavished her new ability to speak French on her parents, her brothers, the servants, the barn cats, and anyone who could be forced to listen. Anton developed a fascination with history and devoured books such as *The Legend of How the Soldier Saved Peter the Great*. Stepan couldn't tell that Hilda had much influence on Sergei except the boy now routinely used his slate to draw pictures of soldiers mounted on horses. A budding artist he was not.

Hilda's structured regimen included instilling etiquette while sharing the family's midday meal. On the Tuesday prior to the start of the seven weeks of Lent, the cook prepared the most splendid Shrovetide *blini*. The family was smothering their pancakes with butter and sour cream as Hilda issued her copious instructions. It seemed to Stepan they all began with the same two words.

Do not—
    Come to the table without your hands and face washed and your hair combed
    Make noises with your tongue, mouth, lips, or breath when eating or drinking
    Foul the tablecloth
    Foul the napkin all over, but only at one corner
    Use your knife to convey food to your mouth
    Stuff your mouth full
    Scratch your head, clean your nails, or worst of all, pick your nose in the company of others.

Just as the last of the blini was being mopped off their plates, the herdsman appeared at the dining room door, his cap clasped in front of him, a broad smile across his face. He announced that one of the mares had just given birth to a fine-looking colt.

"Champion news!" Stepan's open palm thumped the tabletop. "I'll come to the barn directly."

Sophia set her fork on her plate with a disturbing clatter. Her ramrod-stiff body swiveled toward eight-year-old Natalya. "This is why, as young girls, we learn to subjugate our own will to the will of others. Quite essential if we expect even a semblance of happiness in our lives."

A chill rippled through the air. Natalya stopped chewing and wrinkled her forehead at her mother.

"What are you saying?" Apprehension stiffened Stepan's back.

"I'm saying a woman's wishes are always secondary to a man's, and she'd best become accustomed to it early on." Sophia's lips, full and inviting moments ago, were now pressed in a thin, horizontal line.

He stared at her, confused. "What are you referring to?"

Sophia threw her words like daggers, castigating him for leaving the family on such an important holy day in favor of tromping about the barn. "Your priorities are entirely out of order!"

Fury surged through him. "Would you stop indulging yourself with self-pity! The whole family is tired of listening to you anguish over something God fated to transpire five and a half years ago!"

Her eyes became storm clouds. "You're saying I wear my emotions on my sleeve?"

"On your sleeve? No! I'm saying you flaunt your wounds like jewelry." Stepan flung his crumpled napkin onto the table. "My God, there is no peace with you!"

Her hand flew to the base of her throat as if he had just rammed the butter knife into it.

He barked at the twins, "The three of us are going hunting for a few days. Be ready to leave for the lodge in three hours."

Two years previously, Stepan had ordered a primitive, one-room cabin be built in Petrovo's woods, so he and the twins could have overnight hunting expeditions. The family charitably referred tongue-in-cheek to the structure as their "lodge."

Stepan stormed to the barn and ordered Yegorka to gather their supplies and bring their breakfast and supper every day. "And find Feodor Zhemchuzhnikov. Tell him to hightail it to the lodge, clean it up, and stock it with firewood."

On his way back to the house, Stepan crossed paths with Roeglin. "I'm going to the lodge for a few days. When I get back, you and I will make some changes in the way this place is farmed."

"Oh? Anything in particular you have in mind?" Roeglin wiped a drip from his red nose onto the back of his glove.

"To start with, the three-field system. The average yield of crops in Russia falls below every major European producer."

Roeglin's German accent thickened, as always when he became pig-headed. "You think the culprit is the three-field system?"

"A full third of our land is always out of production. In France, the ratio is one to seven, and in Germany, it's one to sixteen."

Roeglin's face had the unyielding look of wood. "The peasants understand that with Russia's stingy growing season, the three-crop rotation works the best. Try to change them and you'll be climbing up a greased pole."

"But think about it, damn it! It makes perfect sense to leave the field fallow the first year, then put winter rye on it the second year and plant spring grain the third year, with the fourth year being clover."

"If that's what you want, that's what we'll try. But"—the steward's heavy head swung elegantly from side to side—"you're asking too much of the peasants' simple understanding of farming."

Stepan took a step back and studied his robust steward, from the few hairs that remained atop his head down to his work-worn boots. The steward was competent, hardworking, conscientious, and honest. But his mind was closed as tightly as a walnut shell.

Stepan thrust his words through gritted teeth. "We'll settle this when I return."

THE LODGE WAS a man's retreat, a low-slung, rustic affair with log walls and a slate floor. The room smelled of must and mothballs, and its furnishings were limited to a couple of beds, a wooden table with mismatched chairs, and a gun case that stood empty fifty weeks a year.

Before sunup on their first morning at the lodge, Stepan stoked the fire in the small woodstove to warm the room before the boys arose, then went out into the brittle air to relieve himself. He turned up the collar of his coat while his eyes scanned a semicircle.

The forest was deep in winter repose, like a charcoal sketch. Not a speck of color was manifest. Whites—the thickly drifted snow, the cold brilliance of the stars, the plume of his breath—contrasted with blacks—the spidery branches of dormant trees, the hard straight lines of the lodge, the predawn sky.

In this moment of quietude, he reflected on the magnificent woman he had taken as his wife a dozen years ago. Sophia hadn't possessed the nervous disposition and excesses of passion of other gentry women. Rather than indulging herself with migraines and smelling salts, Sophia had nurtured a merry, level-headed approach to life. During those early years, he'd counted his blessings that he had found a steadfast spouse to stand beside him as they faced the world with singleness of mind and purpose.

Between then and now, how had the woman he loved drifted so far beyond the reach of reason? He closed his eyes and shook his head at the finality of it. He no longer had the stamina to keep blowing on cold embers.

Back inside the lodge, Stepan woke the boys. As they readied themselves for the outdoors, Sergei made a whiny fuss, insisting he wear his lightweight hunting coat with the blue lapel.

"It's the middle of February," Stepan asserted. "Save the fancy coat for fall or spring." He gave another weary shake of his head.

They tramped through the morning's hushed landscape, with the sun lying on the snow like a glaze. Stepan spotted a hare, its ears pressed back, running across the windblown snow of a glade. As quick as a finger snap, he heard a gun being cocked, then the blast of its shot. The hare turned a somersault and dropped lifeless.

"Champion shot!" He gave a manly pat to Anton's shoulder. He glanced at Sergei, whose shoulders were hunched protectively about his ears while his feet shuffled against the cold.

All three heads swung toward the sound of breaking twigs.

Stepan motioned for the boys to ready their guns, and they moved toward a thicket, where Stepan saw that his presumed prey was actually three peasants. One carried an ax, one had a hatchet, and one stood beside a hand-pulled wooden sled, the size a child would use.

"Halt!" Stepan's bellow cracked the air's ice crystals. "Show yourselves."

The three men stopped in their tracks and guardedly turned. Stepan squinted into the blinding glare of the snow. "Lower your scarves."

The men tugged the mufflers from their faces. Stepan recognized two Loktevs and a member of the Karpov clan. "I'm sure you realize you're chopping down estate trees."

The peasants waggled their heads and bowed low.

"No, sir."

"It was a mistake, Master."

"We would never do that."

Yesterday's ire resurfaced in Stepan's blood. "Rubbish! You're stealing from me, and you can count on being punished."

The men extended their arms sideways, their ax and hatchet still in hand. "Oh, no, Master, we wouldn't steal. We were just walking."

"Don't lie to me. Given a chance, you peasants would cheat God Himself."

"We'll go back to the village now."

"The hell you will." Stepan motioned for the twins to stay put. He strode forward, stopping halfway between the boys and the peasants. "How stupid do you believe me to be? Do you think I don't know you steal my timber? That you gradually widen your strips of fields into mine? That you purposely take longer to plough my land than yours?"

The peasants mumbled their denial, more white breath than words.

The serfs' duplicity infuriated Stepan, particularly as he remembered last Easter when a procession of filth-crusted peasants passed under the portico of the estate house. How piously they'd removed their caps, bowed, and bestowed on the family the red-painted eggs. And oh, yes, last summer when the bell had cracked upon taking a tumble from the church tower and he shipped it to Moscow to be melted down and remolded. How the villagers had called him "our little Father" and rejoiced at his "great generosity of spirit." That monstrous clanger cost him a small fortune.

"Your juvenile displays of rebellion, your little work slowdowns—they're your spineless way of retaliating against my order that you plant potatoes. And for pressing your children to marry. You're too dumb to see these things are for your own good."

The three men muttered among themselves.

Prudence told him to drop the matter and let Roeglin handle this slight infraction. But his indignation erupted against all the injustices he had recently received—Sophia's malevolence, Roeglin's obstinacy, Sergei's insipidness, Mother Nature's capriciousness, and now his peasants' covert defiance.

"Wait until this spring. I'll see to it that potatoes sprout up all over your kitchen gardens. Plus, I intend for you to toss aside your old, worthless wooden ploughs and use metal ones, like the rest of Europe does. And anyone who goes against my bidding will feel the knout across his back and have his nostrils slit."

Tension cut through the air as the peasants swapped looks with one another. Their shoulders squared. The man with the ax tightened his grip, as did the one with the hatchet. They swung the handles against their gloved palms. *Thap. Thap. Thap.* The third peasant picked up a broken tree branch the diameter of his forearm. He angled the branch so its end dug into the snow, then came down on its middle with his boot. *Crack.* The man raised his club, its jagged end a golden yellow in the sun.

The starch left Stepan as he weighed the vulnerability of himself and the boys. Surely, he reassured himself, the peasants wouldn't be such idiots as to escalate this incident into violence. On the other hand, in the isolation of the woods, their wolfish tendencies could take control. His muscles drew taut as he recalled Roeglin's tale about Khanykov's peasants slicing off his nose.

Stepan's mind grappled for his next move. He was armed, and he was within his right to shoot the peasants. But he was the type of man who used physical force only as a last resort. To take a person's life over a few sticks of firewood was contemptible. Plus, the villagers would retaliate by steering their cloaked rebelliousness down a more bloodthirsty path.

Over the hammering of his heart, Stepan heard the crunch of boots on snow behind him. He was standing between the twins and the peasants—a dangerous spot, knowing Sergei. The boy could easily panic, fire, and rip a hole through his father by mistake.

"Osip Karpov? Is that you?" Anton's voice was as sprightly as if he were calling his favorite dog.

The peasants cocked their heads.

Stepan's eyes flicked toward Anton, who was sauntering past him. The barrel of the boy's shotgun rested harmlessly on his shoulder as he stopped half a dozen steps ahead.

"Tell your son I found that slingshot I told him about." Anton's stance was jaunty, all of his weight on one leg with the other one out front, its knee bent lazily. "I'll bring it to Vasya later in the week and give him some pointers on how to use it."

The intruders partially eased down their weapons.

"And I have some glass marbles for him, too. Even some the color of oxblood."

After murmuring among themselves, Karpov gave a single nod of his head, grabbed the sled's rope, and turned away. The others followed him. Stepan and Anton returned to Sergei.

Through the fog of a long sigh of relief, Stepan looked at the twins. Sergei's eyes were gullible, showing no inkling of the danger they'd been in. In contrast, Anton's narrowed eyes shrieked that he was fully aware his father had created a foolhardy predicament that he'd been unable to control.

Stepan felt an invisible wall descend between himself and Anton.

CHAPTER 17

Elizaveta

1847

What is not baked,
not boiled,
has not been on a plate,
not sliced by a knife,
but is eaten by everyone?

Breast milk.

THE HOT AIR of August was breathing down Elizaveta's neck as she trudged home with two-month-old Serafima in her arms. The nursing baby had lain under a shade tree while her mother and extended family harvested buckwheat by hand in the blistering fields. Because Serafima hadn't felt well the past couple of days, Vera Vorontsova had sent her daughter-in-law home early. That way, Elizaveta could get the evening meal on the table for the eleven other family members.

As she neared her twenty-second birthday, Elizaveta felt crushed beneath a massive load. If she continued to have babies at this rate, she could easily have a dozen more. She truly loved Ilya, Gerasim, and Serafima with all her heart. But she didn't want any more mouths to feed, any more temper tantrums, or any more backaches from carrying two small children at the same time.

She knew these emotions were immoral and crazy. What a family, any family, dreaded most was infertility. Running a close second were crop failure and barren livestock, these being a form of infertility in their own regard. Nevertheless, she wished Ermak would leave her alone at night. After Serafima's birth, he had refused to wait the compulsory forty days for the impurities to leave her body before he climbed on top of her.

At the Vorontsov izba, Elizaveta placed her daughter in the cradle hanging from a roof beam. Serafima began howling, thick yellow mucus bubbling from her nose.

Elizaveta's eyes, burning from a day of sun and wind, listlessly rotated toward the icon in the corner. Every day during her first year in the Vorontsov izba, she had knelt, forehead to the floor, and begged St. Nicholas the Wonderworker to free her from her marriage. And she had pleaded to the dried willow branches behind the icon to please intervene with the Savior on her behalf to somehow bring her and Feodor together.

One year into her marriage, she had experienced a harrowing birthing that lasted all day and into the night and almost cost Elizaveta her life. The tiny baby was born weak and refused to suckle.

"Oh, Elizaveta, why did you have a girl?" Ermak blamed her not only for the baby's fragility but also its gender. A daughter was something you had while waiting for a son. She was useless goods, a transitory guest in the izba until she became another family's laborer.

Elizaveta had again appealed to St. Nicholas as she prayed, heartsick and sobbing, for the frail newborn. Her daughter had lived three days.

Today, Elizaveta turned her back on the corner icon and poured milk into a shallow pot. Serafima was getting little nourishment from her mother. Elizaveta's breasts were quick to dry up, just as they had been with her two sons.

Her mother-in-law was the first family member to return from the fields. When Vera saw the milk, she stomped her foot to put an end to it. "It's Friday," she said by way of explanation. All Wednesdays and Fridays were fast days, devoid of meat or dairy products.

Elizaveta knew she should bite her tongue, having learned long ago the futility of locking horns with her in-laws. But her instincts as a mother couldn't be squelched. "Look at her face. It's flushed with fever. She's eaten almost nothing for two days." For emphasis, Elizaveta used the hem of her apron to first wipe the baby's snotty nose, then remove the crusty matter from eyes flaming red with field dust. "If she'll swallow the milk, I have to give it to her."

"Feed her kasha."

"She won't eat it."

"Dilute it with more water."

"She simply won't eat it."

"Then boil some beets and mash them with hempseed oil."

"Mother, if I could nurse her, she'd be drinking milk. My milk. Therefore, I believe the Church condones babies drinking milk on fast days. Especially sick babies."

"The Holy Church condones no such thing. God would sooner pardon a murderer than someone who violates the fast." Vera removed the pot from the stove and poured the milk back into the crockery jar. "Take it back to the root cellar."

"Mother—"

"Beets. With hempseed oil."

While wrestling to get two mouthfuls of the purplish concoction into her daughter, Elizaveta thought of a string of querulous remarks she'd love to shout at her mother-in-law. But she was struck by the blurry sensation of being in the Widow Shabanova's barn and Feodor tapping her ankle with his foot, cautioning her to hush her fiery words toward Zhanna. So she heeded the imaginary warning and merely glowered at Vera. During her six years with the Vorontsovs, she had at last mastered the skill of swallowing back her words. It was a matter of survival.

Ermak held his wife responsible for every misfortune that befell the Vorontsov izba, and he meted out punishment accordingly. His discipline had started a few weeks into their marriage with a slap across her face, an action that caused him no more concern than if she had been a mosquito.

During their first couple of years together, Ermak came into full beard and his stormy eruptions grew increasingly terrifying. A hideous beast would emerge and pummel Elizaveta in fits of white rage. Ermak drank little vodka compared with his brother Grigorii and his Uncle Stanislav, and his frenzied fits of temper were tied equally to sobriety and inebriation. He lashed out at anything that aggravated him, as borne out by the fate of the kitten that clawed his hand and ended up with its head cleaved by a hatchet.

At one point, Elizaveta's father sought retribution from the assembly for his daughter's excessive beatings. But Erafei's fellow bolshaks discredited his use of the word *excessive* and reminded him that wife-beating was perfectly legal and natural. "Remember the wisdom our fathers passed to each of us: '*A wife isn't a jug. She won't crack if you hit her a few.*'"

As the sun was about to set, Ermak and Grigorii arrived home, followed by Grigorii's cowering wife, Avdotya. A few moments later, Sidor, the bolshak, and Sidor's hard-drinking younger brother, Stanislav, stomped through the door. Bringing up the rear were Stanislav's downtrodden wife and two sprouting boys. Dusty and tired, all of them expectantly headed straight for the table.

Elizaveta sulked as she sat with her two boys on a bench along the wall, spooning kasha into one-year-old Gerasim's hungry mouth. She vowed that snow would fall in August before she'd join the conversation or even look at her in-laws. But short of stuffing wool into her ears, she couldn't block out their words. Nor did she want to. The supper topic was Illarion Loktev, the person she disliked most in the world—after her husband, of course.

Earlier this year, Illarion had spread false rumors that a neighbor was stealing from the Loktevs' kitchen garden. At the assembly meeting, the bolshaks had found Illarion guilty of soiling an innocent person's good name. The bolshaks were fed up with Illarion's slanderous lies. His punishment was conscription into the Army, a virtual life sentence since he faced twenty-five years of ruthless treatment and shameful living conditions. Rare was the soldier who ever made it back to his village.

Hoping the Army would reject him for health reasons, Illarion had filled his ears with lye and rubbed it over his scrotum. True to plan, the recruitment officer disallowed him for the pus oozing from his swollen ears as well as for his damaged sac, which was reputedly the size of a head of cabbage and the color of an eggplant. His ears and, supposedly, his sac returned to normal after many months, but the incident had left Illarion half deaf and, it was speculated, sterile.

At tonight's supper table, the Vorontsov men described Illarion's private parts and his reproductive shortcomings in language as graphically vile as possible.

Why? Elizaveta brooded as she wiped kasha from Gerasim's chin. Why couldn't she be safely tucked away in the Zhemchuzhnikovs' izba? Why couldn't she live with a sensitive, polite, spiritual family rather than with these coarse, inconsiderate boors who had the manners of cockroaches?

She routinely silenced pointless frets such as these, as they served only to deepen her anguish. As did chance encounters with Feodor, be it leaving a church service, drawing water from the well, or walking toward the fields. Whenever their paths crossed, she nodded a silent greeting while her stomach twisted in on itself and her wooden smile felt more like a grimace.

Having exhausted the topic of Illarion's carnal woes, Elizaveta's father-in-law moved along to another subject. According to reliable gossip, the village of Gorenki had been struck by horse thieves. Anxious questions were hurled from all directions.

"Did they catch the evil scoundrels?"

"Are all the horses gone?"

"Were the thieves Ukrainians?"

"Were they Tatars?"

"Cossacks?"

"Gypsies?"

Elizaveta sat with feigned indifference, but she took in every word. Whenever a village was preyed upon by marauding gangs of horse thieves, Petrovo's peasants sent up prayers of gratitude that they weren't the victims. The horse ploughed the fields. The horse hauled the hay and grain. The horse provided transportation to the district capital. The horse had offspring that could be sold. In short, a family could not survive without a draft animal. The loss of all the horses resulted in a village that couldn't sustain itself.

The Vorontsovs determined that horse theft wasn't surprising this year. It always increased during times of dearth. The grain crop had been devastated by a baneful combination of drought and a late-season hailstorm. It would be a bleak and hungry winter for the second year in a row.

Elizaveta regarded her three children, then scanned the faces around the table. She had the sensation she was sinking in a vat of tar. Avdotya was bound to have a baby sooner or later. And it wouldn't be too many years before Uncle Stanislav's two boys took wives. How many additional hungry, crying creatures could fit in the already crowded izba? How many more spoons could dip into the meager common pot?

Her dreary thoughts were interrupted by her mother-in-law. "Since you once again don't have any milk, you'd better get Serafima on gruel. We'll have to sell the cow before long."

Elizaveta turned heavy eyes toward Vera. Then she swung her head toward Ermak as he declared to her and Avdotya, "On the way home from the fields, Papa said we might have to sell some of the things in your trunks."

Elizaveta yelped, "What!"

"Papa said we might have to sell some of your things," Ermak clarified through repetition.

Elizaveta's hand went to her cheek in disbelief. "We've had hard times before and never touched my things." She looked to Avdotya for support, but the submissive woman focused her gaze on the chunk of bread in her hand.

"But now we're behind in our taxes," her father-in-law explained. "Plus, we still owe the rubles we borrowed from Maximov to buy that old nag."

"Still owe the Count for money you borrowed before Ermak and I were married?"

Sidor outlined the chronology of their indebtedness. "No, Maximov got his rubles years ago. We paid him with rubles we borrowed from Seleznyov at the tavern."

Elizaveta couldn't come anywhere near deciphering the amount of interest on a six-year-old loan. But she knew it was far, far, far more than the original amount borrowed.

"But why do you need to sell my things? I thought you were selling the cow." Elizaveta's lower lip jutted out.

"Have to sell the cow plus your things," Sidor replied. "Can't be helped. We need twenty silver rubles for taxes and a partial payment on the loan. And don't forget—we'll have to buy grain because of this year's puny crop."

Elizaveta was staggered not only by the amount owed but by the fact that the Vorontsov men would pilfer a woman's untouchable trousseau. As a peasant woman, Elizaveta had virtually no property rights. Her trunk and its contents were the only possessions she could claim as her own.

"Some of those items were passed down to me from my grandparents. They'll be given to Serafima when she's old enough."

Ermak cracked his knuckles, his ill temper surfacing. "Most of what's in your trunk are linens and clothes you decorated too fancy to be practical."

"You can't sell my things. I won't let—"

An ominous shadow fell over Ermak's face. "Enough."

"You can rot in the grave before I'll let you touch my trunk!"

Ermak leapt up and came at her.

She cringed as his open hand sailed toward her cheek, then hit its mark. Gerasim howled.

Ermak screamed at his son to shut up and received an ear-splitting screech in return. Then Gerasim's older brother started wailing. Like a maddened bull, Ermak moved toward Ilya.

Elizaveta sprung up and, with the palm of her hand, shoved the back of her husband's head. This wasn't the first time she had deflected his fury from one of the children onto herself. When Ermak was in one of his blind rages, he didn't care whom he battered.

Now, neck veins bulging, he turned livid eyes on her.

She kept his anger centered on her and away from the boys. "Why don't you pick on someone your own size rather than a little child?"

Ermak wrapped one of her braids around his hand and dragged her from the izba and into the Vorontsovs' bathhouse, his favorite location for administering the discipline necessary to curb her willful behavior.

CHAPTER 18

Elizaveta

1847

I'll poke and poke
into a golden holder,
thrash around in there,
then come back out.
What am I?

A fire poker.

"MY OWN WIFE!" Pacing the floor, Grigorii raised his arms toward Heaven. "Tell me it isn't true!"

The hut resonated with shame, sin, and betrayal. The children—Uncle Stanislav's two adolescents and Elizaveta's three youngsters—had been scurried to an aunt's izba.

Avdotya sat folded in half on a bench, her face buried in her skirt. Sidor sat at the table, his elbows propped on the boards, his head cradled in the upturned palms of his hands. Stanislav was on a stool with his back against the rough-hewn wall, his legs stretched out defiantly, his ankles crossed. Stanislav's wife lay sobbing on her sleeping bench. Slouched on various other benches were the remaining adults—Ermak, Elizaveta, Vera—all pale with disbelief.

The family had been at a wedding reception when, halfway through the afternoon, Avdotya left the celebration with a sore throat. A short while later, Grigorii entered a shouting match with three Novikovs. He threatened to carve up the Novikovs' livers for dog meat. The Novikovs countered they'd gut Grigorii like a fish.

Outnumbered, Grigorii looked around for Ermak's backing, but his brother was nowhere in sight. Grigorii had no misgivings about leaving the reception early, the bride's parents having underestimated the amount of vodka needed to consecrate the sacred union of their daughter and her new husband. So Grigorii told the Novikovs to fuck themselves and swaggered home.

Soon thereafter, word reached Sidor at the reception that his drunken son and his drunker brother were brawling in the road in front of their izba. Sidor grabbed Ermak and raced home, followed by the Vorontsova women. They found Grigorii wielding a cabbage cleaver. His uncle was armed with a pair of sheep shears. Sidor herded everyone into the izba.

Vera tried to calm her son. "Perhaps you jumped to the wrong conclusion."

"Wrong conclusion? His trousers were around his knees, and he was on top of her!" Blood oozed from Grigorii's nose while he pounded his fist into the palm of his other hand. His face grew a fierce red as he swiveled to glare at his wife. "You whore!" He strode across the floorboards. "How many times has this happened?" He pushed back Avdotya's kerchief and grabbed a fistful of her hair, wrenching it from her braids. Using her hair, he yanked her head up. His calloused hand slapped her face. "Slut!" His hand retraced its path and struck her other cheek. He released her hair, and she fell sideways onto the bench.

Vera tried to intervene. "Grigorii, it might be best if—"

"Shut up, Mother."

In less than an instant, Sidor was on his feet and in front of his son. "None of that talk! Your mother gave birth to you and reared you and shed tears over you." He pulled the front of Grigorii's jacket, so he was nose-to-nose with his son. "I ought to smash your ribs for talking to her like that."

Grigorii straightened to his full height, daring the older man to take his threat to the next step. Sidor released his son's jacket and shoved his chest.

Grigorii yanked off his jacket and flung it across the room. He turned his wrath on everyone, his fierce look shifting from one face to the next. "We can't sit twiddling our thumbs while my wife entices my uncle to lie with her. And stallion that he thinks he is, he takes full advantage of it. Stanislav needs to be driven from our izba! And that little whore needs to be sent back to her parents!"

"What good would that do?" Sidor scoffed. "We need the labor of Stanislav and his sons if we're going to scratch out an existence on this earth. And your wife, despite her loose morals, is a tireless worker. Don't be a fool and cut off your own nose." Sidor retreated back to the table.

Grigorii again seized a clump of his wife's hair and yanked her to her feet. He slammed his fist into Avdotya's abdomen. A retching gasp flew from the fragile woman's mouth. Her body tried to knuckle over at the waist, but Grigorii still gripped her hair. She hung like a rag doll, blood oozing from her scalp.

"What if the bitch has a baby?" he bellowed, although after five years, the family had their suspicions that Avdotya was barren. "Who's the father?" He flung his arm and threw aside his wife like he was casting aside the gutted innards of a fish. She toppled to the floor and coiled, wheezing, onto her side.

Hot rage flamed inside Elizaveta as she recalled the countless times she had caught Stanislav's eyes roving over her own body. And how he took every opportunity to rub against her as he slid past. "Think about it, Grigorii. She's just a small thing. She can't fight off Stanislav."

Grigorii stomped over to Elizaveta and towered over her, his face ugly with hate. "You sanctimonious imbecile. Haven't you seen how she and that shameless old sinner always stand close to one another? How she allows him to touch her when she thinks I'm not watching? I remember what she did with me before we were married. I'm ashamed to call that wench my wife."

Elizaveta yanked her shawl tight around her shoulders and leaned forward. "Avdotya never enticed Stanislav! If you want to cast blame, look at your black-souled, evil pig of an uncle!"

Ermak barreled across the room and shoved his brother aside. He hovered over Elizaveta, his fists convulsing with fury. "This is none of your concern!" His eyes reduced to slits as he raised an arm and pulled back an open palm. "Unless you laid with him, too. Have you?"

She cringed as the hand swiped toward her. The sting exploded across her cheek as her head whirled to one side.

"Have you?"

"No!" Her palm flew to her burning cheek.

He clamped on to her wrist and yanked her hand from her face. With his other hand, he grabbed hold of her little finger and twisted it. Searing pain stormed up her hand. He spiraled the finger yet further.

"Stop!" her gaping mouth rasped.

He bore down tighter on her wrist and wrenched the finger harder.

Awww streamed from her mouth as she slid off the bench, onto her knees.

"Son, that's enough!" Vera shouted from across the room.

But he continued to crank, harder, until the finger gave a loud pop. He pitched her hand into her lap and tromped to the table.

Through tear-clouded eyes, she saw the entire length of her little finger was rotated toward the outside of her hand.

Ermak retreated to the table and dropped onto a bench across from his father.

Throbbing with pain and loathing, Elizaveta crawled across the floor to Avdotya and folded the quivering woman into her arms. Blood oozed from Avdotya's scalp, mingling with her tears as well as blood from a split in her lip. The room's silence was filled by the whimpering of Stanislav's wife on her sleeping bench.

With slow, deliberate strides, Grigorii marched to the stove and wrapped his hand around a poker. Brandishing it, he moved toward his uncle.

"Sidor!" Vera screamed.

Sidor and Ermak leapt up and grabbed Grigorii from behind. He bucked and strained, but his besotted mind and body were no match for the two men. They wrested the poker from him.

Grigorii stood with his chest heaving, the hate from his eyes drilling holes into his uncle. Sidor and Ermak relaxed their grip on him.

Spittle shone on Grigorii's lips. "The two of you arranged to leave the wedding early, didn't you? So you could fornicate while the rest of us were at the wedding, oblivious to your depravity."

"An appropriate word, Grigorii." Half of Stanislav's mouth rose in a one-sided sneer. "You've been pretty *oblivious* to the actions of your little wife."

"You drunken old cud . . ."

"Ha! The pot calling the kettle black. You're so drunk right now, you couldn't get your cock up if you wanted to."

"Enough foul talk!" Sidor stood with his two sons in a semicircle around his seated brother. "Listen to me." His forefinger jabbed at Stanislav. "I expect you, from this day forth, to never again damage the name Vorontsov. Keep your hands off women other than your wife."

"The day that happens, hens'll start to crow." Grigorii spat at Stanislav but instead hit the wall beside his uncle's head. The wronged husband then turned toward his wife, who was still huddled on the floor with Elizaveta. His eyes were as cold and bright as a midwinter moon. He gave a low, vile laugh. "Do you know what I am going to do to you?"

Avdotya buried her head in her sister-in-law's arms.

A chill coursed along Elizaveta's backbone, as if someone had chucked a handful of snow down her blouse.

Grigorii's lips thinned, their corners curled up. "I'm not going to beat you, even though I should. But what I will do is see to it that you and I are no longer man and wife."

A communal gasp resounded through the room.

"Grigorii, think about what you're saying," his mother stammered. "There's marriage, but no divorce."

"I'm saying she's filthy trash, and she damaged the Vorontsov name." Grigorii was enjoying the stir he had created.

Vera tried one of the peasants' favorite sayings. "A wife is not a glove. You cannot remove her from your hand."

"Wait and see, Mother. Wait and see."

Sidor slammed the heel of his hand against the wall boards. "I forbid you! God unites—no one separates. You go against my wishes, I'll see to it the Army takes you!"

Tears, anger, and threats continued through the night and for several days. Eventually, Grigorii abandoned his plan to send Avdotya back to her parents, but he and Stanislav kept their distance from one another. Elizaveta and Avdotya bonded as true sisters, vowing before God to do everything in their power to protect one another from their brutish husbands.

CHAPTER 19

Maximov

1848

When is a fool smart?
When he keeps still.

"IDLENESS OF THE mind, like idleness of the body, is the mother of all evils," Hilda Behrens lectured her three pupils. "Work is a simple, immutable responsibility of the fulfillment of one's debt in life."

Stepan suspected that, after three years at Petrovo, the tutor was targeting her comments toward Anton. The boy had a mind like a sponge that effortlessly absorbed a host of diverse topics. His face already held promise of being lean and angular, and he held himself as straight as a fireplace poker, poised and confident far beyond his almost fourteen years.

But Stepan also detected a worrisome trait in his son: the vice of sloth. Intellectual exertion was unknown to him. Anton paid no attention to the orchard, the cattle, the fields, or anything outdoors except hunting and horses. He loved cards, billiards, socializing, reading, sleeping late, and exchanging riddles with Cockeyes in the distillery.

A strict taskmaster, Hilda seldom cracked a smile as she administered her schooling. The tutor entered the study promptly at nine o'clock five mornings a week, and woe to anyone who was late. The children feared, respected, and liked her, their attitudes depending on whether they had completed their lessons to her satisfaction.

But a different persona emerged during dance lessons. The beefy tutor tinkled with laughter and was as light on her feet as a nubile sixteen-year-old. She believed dancing to be the most enchanting of all human amusements. "It banishes melancholia, cheers the evening hours, and rouses a mixture of delightful sensations," she instructed. "When diligently practiced, it increases strength and suppleness."

Natalya plunged into the subject. Sergei eventually mastered the steps with something approaching elegance. Anton, however, claimed the field of study as his forte from the very first time he put his arm around Hilda's ample waist. While Hilda hummed the music, he had a pleasing command of her, sidestepping the potted palms, gliding with finesse past the Kiev Virgin, and circumnavigating the Queen Anne lowboy. The children learned the polka, the waltz, the cotillion, the schottish, and the minuet, but Anton's métier was the mazurka, its intricate steps requiring both grace and agility.

The fields were soaking up the final vestiges of snow when Hilda approached her employer with her idea.

The family was clustered in the study. Stepan was in his red brocade chair, sketching a diagram of his planned expansion of the apple orchard. In the chair next to him, Sophia crocheted a doily. Across the room, Natalya thumbed through the *Magazine of Women's and Men's Fashions*. In the cushioned window seat, Anton was engrossed in the Russian translation of *Robinson Crusoe*. Sergei, swaddled in an afghan, dozed by a roaring fire. Baby Elena had already been put to bed.

"Excuse me, Count, I wonder if I might speak briefly with you." Hilda's voice was hushed as she pulled a straight-backed chair beside his armchair. She licked her lips. "Sergei, Anton, and Natalya have all become quite skilled at dancing. Quite skilled, I must say."

An awkward silence stretched, which Stepan eventually filled with "I'm sure that skill is a tribute to your expert instruction."

Her tongue again flitted over her upper lip. "But the ability to perform the steps, even as brilliantly as Anton does, isn't sufficient in and of itself."

Another pause.

"What are you suggesting, Hilda?"

She licked her lips once more before rephrasing her statement. "The mere ability to perform the steps isn't sufficient. Those skills must be accompanied by the social graces necessary to conduct one's self fittingly during an evening of social discourse." Her tongue glided over her lips a fourth time.

"I couldn't agree more." *What was this normally direct woman circuitously hinting at?*

"I think it would behoove the children to practice going to a ball before they actually attend one in actuality."

A practice ball? Before they actually attend one in actuality? Huh? Stepan blinked and waited for her to continue.

"With your permission, Count, I would like to designate a Saturday evening for the Maximov Ball."

"I beg your pardon?"

"We could move the furniture out of the parlor to make room for a family ball. You and the Countess and the three children. And myself, of course, as their tutor."

Sophia, who was eavesdropping from her seat on the opposite side of Stepan, slanted her upper body across the arm of her husband's chair. "Such a wonderful idea! I remember how petrified I was at my first evening party. I would have loved the chance for a dress rehearsal."

"Oh, yes." Hilda bent her head toward Sophia to keep their voices from carrying across the room to the youngsters. "Practice makes perfect. Don't you agree, Monsieur?"

"Yes, practice makes perfect sense." *What in Heaven's name were the women proposing? A dress rehearsal for the family?*

Once the fundamental idea had been forced past her lips, Hilda bubbled forth with a fountain of inspirations. "The children could dress up, so they have the feel of being prim and proper for an entire evening. Dancing in a full skirt with a train is a world apart from trouncing about the parlor in a house dress."

Sophia leaned closer to Hilda so the two women were face-to-face in front of Stepan's nose. "I have a lovely old taffeta gown that could be taken in for Natalya."

"The boys would wear waistcoats and polished boots."

"And we might allow Natalya to use a touch of powder." Sophia kept tethering her animated voice back down to a whisper.

Stepan's face contracted into a labyrinth of bewilderment. Why would three children and three adults want to play dress-up and force their servants to do likewise for an evening at home among themselves? "Don't you think a twelve-year-old is a little young for long dresses and powder?"

Both women turned and gazed at him, their side-by-side cheeks a hand's length from his own.

"Why, no." Sophia looked at him as if potatoes had suddenly sprouted from his ears. "At this very moment, she's browsing fashion magazines."

Stepan's question having been adequately dispensed, Hilda burst forth with another morsel of her scheme. "We'll need the finest beeswax candles, not lamps, to ensure the light is most becoming to the complexion."

"And we could borrow some of Gabrichevsky's serf musicians. Would that be acceptable to you?" Sophia asked Stepan, as if his opinion mattered.

"Whaaa . . . ?" warbled from the oval of Stepan's mouth, like the nonsensical sputter of a baby. Nothing about this outlandish affair was the least bit logical.

Hilda's head bobbed up and down in synchrony with Sophia's. "Holding a polite conversation while an orchestra is playing is a capability that can be honed only through repetition."

"And Natalya can practice writing invitations. Let's see, invitations to a ball should be issued at least ten days in advance. Is that correct?" Sophia tapped her chin with her crochet hook. It had been so long since she had hosted, or even attended, a formal ball, the rules of social conduct eluded her.

"At least ten days but no more than two weeks." Hilda's tongue passed over her lower lip. "But, Madame, I'm a little concerned about the small number of us. I wonder if there's someone else on the estate who might be skilled at dancing and could join us. You understand, don't you, my concern that the children have a range of different partners?"

"I agree. But I don't know of anyone else who would be appropriate." Sophia rubbed her forehead as if doing so might make a well-cultured individual materialize at Petrovo. "Perhaps Vladimir and Yustina Rusakov could be persuaded to come. Too bad Victor is away at boarding school."

"I believe August Roeglin can dance." Hilda's lip-licking picked up in earnest.

Stepan came to life, guffawing at the image of his bulky, reticent steward waltzing about the parlor. "August Roeglin? He's as light on his feet as a hibernating bear."

The lip-licking ceased as apprehension wormed across Hilda's brow. "But I do believe he mentioned that he used to dance in his younger days."

"Ask him if you want, but I can't feature he'll agree to come."

"Perhaps you'd inquire of Monsieur Roeglin?" Hilda asked.

"Me?" Under no circumstances would he involve himself in any of this nonsense.

"Of course." Enthusiasm glittered in Sophia's eyes. "He'll be glad to."

CHAPTER 20

Maximov

1848

Where did a horse neigh,
so the whole world heard?

In the ark.

STEPAN'S FINGERS RHYTHMICALLY drummed the blotter on his desk. The sound reverberated through his study like the onerous beat of an army drum. His head was a dense thicket of worries. Mother Nature had trounced the previous two years' crops with the worst of her temper—late frosts, hail, drought—reducing the fields to wastelands. Both years, Stepan had plunged deeply into his Moscow investment accounts. Besides tending to Petrovo's ongoing expenses, he also bore the cost of purchasing grain for the famished peasants. Now this spring's weather was off to an equally combative start. Could Petrovo survive three years of dearth?

His thoughts jumped to the Church of Saints Peter and Paul. He was the descendent of the noble who had built the church, and the current owner of the estate. Consequently, its upkeep fell to him. Eight years ago, hail had shattered several colored glass windows. A couple of years later, the bell took its tumble. Now Sophia was pestering him that the icons, including the gilding, had deteriorated from merely dingy to outright shabby. And the wall plaster was in need of renovation. He didn't dare dip further into his plundered nest egg. Especially with the looming threat of cholera.

Military recruitment had been canceled last year when the disease erupted along the Caspian coast and raged northward up the Volga into the heart of Russia. The epidemic had exploded this spring and was headed this direction. Only God knew how much devastation the Vomiting Death would leave in its wake.

As Stepan slapped shut his account ledger, his gaze lighted on the recent letter from his sister in Moscow, updating him on their father. Some years back, the once intellectual and highly respected man had started his gradual descent toward disorientation. Three years ago, the widower's malady of the brain had required that Stepan's sister take him into her home. During Stepan's last trip to Moscow, he had been sickened by the claw marks left by his father's fingernails on the door as he fought to escape the prison of his daughter's house. According to this recent letter, the argumentative invalid could no longer tend to his dietary or toilet needs.

Burdened by the same old torments and no new solutions, Stepan sought some much-needed fresh June air. As he passed the parlor, Hilda's deportment lessons were in full swing. He stood to one side of the double doorway and peeped in. His clenched jaw loosened into a half-smile at the unintended comedy.

"Etiquette is the underpinning of society. It protects us from disagreeable, under-bred people who refuse to take the trouble to be civil. Natalya, while sitting, you can either place one hand cupped in the other, in your lap, or you can play with your fan. But whatever you do, do it with quiet gracefulness and without affectation."

"But I don't have a fan. I need a fan." Natalya appeared as if she were about to cry for want of a fan. "I must go to Sukhanovo to buy a fan."

"Natalya, please stop squawking like a disgruntled goose." Hilda turned her attention to the twins' bowing. "Put one foot in the second position and the other in the third position. Good. Keep your head in a direct line with your body, and allow your torso to gently fall frontward. I said *gently*, Sergei. Don't flop over like a pillow standing on end."

Hilda clapped her hands twice. "Enough practice. Go ready yourselves for tonight's test." Natalya pirouetted from the room while the boys made a mad dash.

The house was quiet except for Matriusha's heavy footfalls on the stairs. Stepan speculated about Sophia's frame of mind at tonight's ball. She had been sunshine itself at breakfast while she prattled about Natalya's new hairstyle. But by now he knew Sophia could delude a person into believing everything was in order, then turn the tables in a blink of an eye.

Stepan headed for the stable. The herdsman had told him that his premier mare, Zhelannyi, was being cantankerous with the stud. The mare had been bred by the stallion last month but had not gotten with foal. She was in heat again but was unwilling to accept the stallion. A barren mare equated to expense-with-out-income. Stepan's brow furrowed. *One more financial headache.*

As he strode past the distillery, he heard laughter. He peeked in the solitary, dust-caked window. Anton was roosting on a stack of firewood. Cockeyes sat cross-legged on the ground, his lips grinning around a dried stem of rye as he told a riddle.

What twists the legs,
rubs with the belly;
'e'll rise it up
and poke it in?

Anton whooped and called him a shameful old willy-nilly.

Cockeyes removed the straw from his mouth with mock indignation. "Shameful? What's shameful about weaving?"

Stepan detected a slur in the serf's words.

Anton chortled. "You think you're so clever. Try this one. What are there none of on earth?" Unable to wait for Cockeyes to take a stab at the answer, Anton blurted out, "Bird tits!"

"Good day, gentlemen," Stepan announced as he entered the shed.

The serf jumped to his feet, grabbed the cap off his head, and assumed a hang-dog appearance. "Good day, Count."

Anton remained sprawled on the firewood. "Hello, Father. We were waiting for the fermentation vat to cool so it can be cleaned out."

As if to verify Anton's statement, Cockeyes lifted his foot and tapped the vat with the toe of his boot. Stepan didn't like the way he swayed unbalanced on one foot. He had a gnawing suspicion that sooner or later, he'd catch the serf sampling the distillery's products.

Anton continued, "He was telling me about the new still you're proposing. Sounds like it will do a first-rate job."

Stepan eyed his son. Anton's intent to deceive was unmistakable. Although the serf might have mentioned the proposed still, their conversation had long since gravitated from that topic. Anton could charm the birds out of the trees. But right now, Stepan wanted to smack the engaging smile off that winsome face. How could the boy look so sincere while being so disingenuous? Hadn't he taught his children that a half-truth was the same as a whole lie? The young rascal needed an unsparing disciplinarian. And starting today, that's what he'd receive.

"I'm going to the stables. Zhelannyi is being belligerent with the stallion. Get your brother. It's time the two of you learned something about horse breeding."

On his way to the barn, Stepan mulled over the necessity of having someone trained and ready to take over the distillery when Cockeyes pushed his luck too far. He knew who that person would be.

Feodor Zhemchuzhnikov had been unfailingly dependable while providing cartage services, mainly day jaunts but also a few overnight trips. And he did an exemplary job when called upon for the occasional odd task that required some intellect. This coming autumn would be a good time to expand the young man's duties. Unlike Stepan's other servants who lived in the serfs' cottages behind the estate house and produced passels of children Stepan had to contend with, Zhem-chuzhnikov could continue to live in the village and till his fields. In the autumn and winter when the distillery was in operation, Stepan would toss a couple of rubles his way.

A champion idea! But his smile faded as he thought about Zhemchuzhnikov's lack of children. Why wasn't he married? True, the mandatory marriage edict turned out to be more troublesome than beneficial, and Stepan had allowed it to seek its own natural demise. Nonetheless, Zhemchuzhnikov was being inexcus-ably lackadaisical about taking a bride.

The twins arrived in the stables, and Sergei straight off crinkled his nose. Ste-pan rolled his eyes. He found horse dung to be one of the most relaxing of all scents. What was wrong with his son?

The stallion likewise sniffed the air, but he honed in on an odor that he found quite appealing and eased across the large stall toward the mare's side. She was a large horse, sixteen hands high, and of a deep chestnut color. With obvious bad humor, she glared at the stud, her neck arched. As he neared, she snorted and pawed the dirt. The stallion stood his ground, biding his time until she calmed herself. When he took a courageous step toward her, she lowered her head and shook her mane. When he braved another step, she curled her lip and stretched her neck to bite at him. Again he waited with sincere and longing desire.

The herdsman rested his arms atop the gate and one foot on the bottom board. "The patience of Job." He snickered, sounding somewhat like a horse himself.

Stepan nodded, thinking how many times he had undergone the stallion's emotions while lying in bed next to Sophia. But he no longer had the stallion's fortitude to wait out strong feelings of antipathy.

Anton elbowed Sergei's ribs. "She's definitely not drawing her handkerchief across her lips, is she?"

Sergei chuckled. "I think she's twisting the handkerchief with her left hoof."

Stepan looked at his sons' conniving grins. "Do you want to tell me what you're talking about?"

Anton pulled a folded piece of paper from his breast pocket and handed it to his father. "Our homework assignment."

Stepan browsed Hilda's precise penmanship.

Handkerchief
drawing across the lips   *Desiring an acquaintance*
drawing across the cheek   *I love you*
drawing through the hands   *I hate you*
folding   *I wish to speak with you*
over the shoulder   *Follow me*
twisting in the left hand   *I wish to be rid of you*
twisting in the right hand   *I love another*

Fan
drawing across the forehead   *We are watched*
drawing across the cheek   *I love you*
drawing across the eyes   *I am sorry*
drawing through the hand   *I hate you*
twirling in left hand   *I love another*
handle to lips   *Kiss me*

The stallion took a step closer and the mare's hind hoof lashed out, striking the side of the pen. When the boards stopped vibrating, Sergei wisecracked, "If she had a fan, I bet she'd draw it across her hoof."

Anton chimed in with "I bet that stallion would like to use that fan to wallop her haughty ass."

Stepan's neck muscles tightened as he pondered what was happening. The answer, of course, was simple. His sons were growing up. Adult men were being forged. And for better or for worse, people like Hilda Behrens and Cockeyes were responsible for much of the molding.

Something nudged his buttocks. He turned to find Vaska nibbling on his trousers. As he swatted away the goat, he remembered Vaska was on the premises only because the servants had planted in the twins the belief that a billy kept goblins at bay.

Stepan had never forbidden the boys to socialize with the serfs or their children. But now, particularly given the easy familiarity between Anton and Cockeyes, he was having second thoughts.

CHAPTER 21

Maximov

1848

What is quicker than thought?

Time.

THE HERDSMAN, WEARING a velvet jacket for the first time in his life, reined the horse to a halt under the porte-cochere at precisely eight o'clock. Natalya, Anton, and Sergei, perfectly turned out in formal attire, had entered the carriage just minutes earlier and now alighted following an excursion around the barns.

The parlor was ablaze with candelabras, their warm hues reflecting off the burnished wood floor. Lining the walls were the lyre-backed dining chairs interspersed among a lush arrangement of Sophia's ferns plus ambrosial bouquets of peonies. The size of the provisional ballroom required the string quartet be seated in the hallway.

Once the guests were stiffly seated on the edge of their chairs, Dasha the house-girl entered the parlor wearing a black dress with a white apron. Lace doilies lined her silver tray and overflowed with egg and meat turnovers, cold veal, and cubes of cheese. Gennady the butler offered beverages. Stepan, Vladimir, and Roeglin opted for sparkling wine, while the women selected sparkling cider. When Anton and Sergei reached for glasses of wine, Hilda wagged a fleshy finger at them.

"This is lessons, not a party." Hilda's matronly appearance had been swept aside by her new powder-gray gown and the lissome ostrich feathers fluttering from her upswept hair. A fan dangled on a golden chain encircling her plump wrist.

A.A. Gabrichevsky's serf musicians began their ensemble with a gay Viennese waltz. Anton initiated the evening by striding over to his sister, bowing, and requesting a dance. Natalya accepted and started to rise.

Hilda tore across the room, the folds of her skirt billowing behind her. "Stop!" Natalya fell back onto her chair.

"Think about what you are doing. Do you know this young man? No. Yet you have agreed to dance with him. If a gentleman presumes to ask you to dance without an introduction, you will, of course, refuse."

Hilda straightened and patted her coiffured hair in case it had become mussed during her lope across the parlor. She tugged at her skirt to lower its waistline, which had crept up her stout German girth while she arched over Natalya.

Natalya fluttered a fan borrowed from her mother. The scent of rosewater wafted far and wide. "I must decline, sir, not having the honor of your acquaintance."

Stepan, brooding over the interminably long evening ahead, tossed the wine to the back of his throat like a peasant swigging vodka. Palms on his knees, he pushed himself up, and walked over to the threesome.

"Mademoiselle Natalya Stepanovna Maximova. My complete pleasure to see you looking so well. Are you acquainted with my son, Anton Stepanovich? No? Then allow me to present him to you."

Introductions completed, Anton guided his sister onto the dance floor.

Hilda's hands flew into the air. "Anton! Please!" The ostrich feathers quivered frantically. "Don't bear down so tightly on her waist. Gently place the open palm of your hand." Hilda gripped Anton's hand, wrenched it from the small of Natalya's back, and planted it in a suitable position. "You don't want to make a disagreeable impression."

August Roeglin strode over to Sophia and bowed. To Stepan's surprise, his steward had voiced no qualms about attending the Maximov Ball. With his new swallow-tailed frock coat, trimmed moustache, oiled hair, and clean fingernails, Roeglin appeared almost dapper.

"Greetings to you, Madame Maximova. Perhaps you remember me? We were introduced by your husband."

"Why, of course, Monsieur Roeglin." Sophia lifted a hand gloved in pale ecru.

Roeglin's fingertips lightly pressed the proffered hand. "Is this waltz spoken for?"

Stepan heaved a sigh of relief. Sophia was in one of her more radiant moods. As he gulped a second glass of sparkling wine, he saw Sergei leaning against the wall, his arms and ankles crossed. Stepan's neck sagged forward. Why did the boy carry about the uninterrupted appearance of uncertainty?

With a jerk of his head, Stepan motioned Sergei to ask Yustina Rusakova to dance. Hunched-shouldered, his son complied.

Stepan promised himself to request the next dance of Natalya, but it turned out to be a minuet. Stepan found its curtsies unbearable, so he beckoned Gennady for a third glass of wine and opted for the next dance, a more pleasurable waltz.

While holding his daughter in his arms, he glanced at the other couple on the dance floor. Sophia clung like a vine to Anton, her tapering fingers raking through the black curls on the back of his collar while she whispered in his ear.

No amount of wine could make the scene palatable. Anton was no longer Sophia's little boy. How could she not realize the inappropriateness of her actions? There were times when looking at his wife repulsed him. And those times were growing in frequency.

Stepan shifted his gaze to his daughter, his heart instantly warming with paternal tenderness. Dancing with a pixie was somewhat awkward, but he was charmed by the grace and lightness of her step. Although she lacked Sophia's sculpted, timeless beauty, she would be an undeniably stunning woman. In only a few short years, she would be dancing in the arms of beaux. And a few short years after that, this parlor would be hosting her wedding reception.

"Stop!" Hilda poked her head between Stepan and his daughter. "Look at your hands, Natalya." Hilda's closed fan rapped Natalya's forearm. "You know perfectly well your thumb should rest upon your forefinger while keeping the other fingers loose. And turn your elbows in slightly, for a more delicate appearance." Hilda rearranged Natalya's arms to her satisfaction.

The tutor turned a critical eye on Stepan. Upon examining him from top to bottom and then to top again, she said in a restrained tone, "Monsieur, those who are tall and slender, such as yourself, benefit by holding their arms a little more forward and farther apart, in order to give their bodies a just proportion. Only a suggestion, Monsieur."

Stepan felt like screaming at her, *"I simply want to dance with my daughter before she dances away in another man's arms."* Instead, he realigned his appendages.

At the conclusion of the waltz, he broke in on Anton and Sophia. Stepan thought he detected a flicker of relief on Anton's face. But maybe it was only his imagination. The sparkling wine was making the finer details of the evening a little blurry.

After a polka with Sophia, followed by one with Hilda, Stepan contented himself with sitting on the sidelines and admiring his children's poise and dignity of carriage. All three of them were incredible. And so soon they'd be incredible to someone other than himself.

Why, only a flicker of an eyelash ago, the twins were bounding down the stairs like gangly borzoi puppies. Now, their voices were at a stage where every sentence spanned three octaves. And this fall, the fourteen-year-olds would leave Petrovo to attend the First St. Petersburg Cadet's College.

His maudlin reflections wandered through a medley of sepia-hued sketches:

Sophia applauding the children's watercolor paintings. Nimble little tykes somersaulting down the front lawn to the river. Hobbyhorses, tops, and wooden dollhouses spilling from the children's playroom and down the hallway.

A glorious whirlwind of happy memories engulfed him. Sleigh rides through the frozen forest. Snow houses turned to ice by pouring water over them. The steamy warmth of a cup of *shiten* with its honey and spices.

How could time have marched so quickly and so unnoticed? Perplexed, Stepan ran a hand through his hair, but his thinning tresses aggrieved him further.

His children were rushing to adulthood. Except Elena. She was a delight. His little Pigeon, as he called her, was the antithesis of her sister. Whereas Natalya's hair was silky and straight, Elena's was a halo of relaxed curls. Although both inherited Sophia's full lips, Natalya's mouth was pouty, and Elena's smile was wide and open. Rather than Natalya's fine features and small bones, Elena had the round face of a muffin. She'd take a tumble and get up and run again, not stopping for the kisses on her skinned knee that her older sister had required. She adored viewing the world from atop Stepan's shoulders, a perspective that had made Natalya scream in fear at age four.

Stepan placed a middle finger at the outside corner of each eye and stretched the skin toward his temples. He mustn't let time's winged chariot make him downhearted, or he'd end up as deep in the doldrums as Sophia. He reached behind him and placed his palm on the windowpane's inviting coolness. No one would notice his absence for a few minutes.

Outside the mahogany door, he tugged his starched collar to give passage for the bracing night air. Only the hoot of an intrusive owl disturbed the stillness. It was exactly what he required: a reprieve from the incessant music . . . the stuffy parlor . . . his bittersweet memories.

"Apparently I'm not the only one who needs a breath of fresh air."

Stepan whirled about.

It was Yustina's voice, but the moonless night hid her.

CHAPTER 22

Maximov

1848

When I was young,
I shined bright.
When I began to age,
I began to fade.
Who am I?

The moon.

AFTER STEPAN'S EYES adjusted to the inky black, he made out Yustina's silhouette leaning against one of the portico's columns.

He moved toward her and chuckled low. "These people throw such ostentatious balls, don't they?"

"They invite only the *crème de la crème*." Yustina's smile was broad and warm, but she remained stationary, her back against the white pillar and her indigo shawl, laced with silver threads, wrapped around her shoulders. "You've danced with every female in the room except me. Should my feelings be hurt?"

Did he detect undertones of flirtation—flirtation that had vanished without a trace twenty years ago after he'd sought mindless, momentary pleasure in the arms of another woman?

"I assumed your dance card was full."

"There was always room on it for you."

He started to contradict her, to remind her how she had spurned him despite his repeated pleas for forgiveness. But he held his tongue. He had come outside to shake off yesterday's memories, not have more piled on top of him.

"Sophia seems happy tonight," Yustina observed.

"Yes, happy tonight. But that could change tomorrow. There's no making her out."

"I apologize for not visiting her more often. Complete selfishness on my part. She can be so . . . well . . . wearying. I know how much I miss the old Sophia. I can only imagine the loneliness you feel."

"Sometimes I miss her so terribly, I think I might lose my mind and end up as daffy as my father." Stepan's head fell back, and he stared sightless at the portico's high ceiling. "I apologize. I shouldn't burden you with this."

Her tone grew tender, intimate. "Please, Stepan, you can say anything to me. It's just plain old Yustina, whom you've known the whole of your life."

Stepan thought Yustina looked neither plain nor old as the bronze candlelight from the parlor window reflected off her dark eyes and lightly rouged cheeks. She was a petite woman with a slim figure and skin as white and smooth as an Easter lily. Hers was an understated beauty, a gracefulness in no way diminished by the sprinkling of gray that wound through her hair.

He was acutely aware he was standing too close to her for cordial conversation. Yet he didn't step back.

"Never forget I'm always here if you need someone to talk to. Trust me"—she rested a delicate, gloved hand on his forearm—"your confidences will go no further."

Her hand lingered but a moment, and he was relieved when the slight pressure was gone. Her touch, even through his shirt and jacket, evoked urges that had lain dormant for years.

"I should have told you long ago," he said, "how much I appreciate the friendship you've continued to offer Sophia, even though she's only the shell of the person we used to know."

Yustina's half-smile contained the palest shade of melancholy. "Who'd have thought that I'd learn to love the mistress of this house when, once upon a time, I assumed that woman would be me." She wrapped her arms around her slender waist, tightening the soft Merino wool across her breasts.

God, he wished that her mouth would stop beaming, that her eyes would stop twinkling. He yearned to reach out to her, slide the gauzy shawl off her shoulders, and unshackle her arms from her waist. Yustina hadn't said a single coquettish word, not a single unprincipled implication, but somehow she looked so receptive. Or was his own ache for happier times shading his perspective?

The two of them had laughed and played and loved through two golden years of courtship. She had been spirited and bewitching; he had been self-assured and ambitious. He hungered to relive those feelings. His fingers curled inward and stroked the moist heels of his hands.

"You mentioned your father a moment ago. How is he?" she asked.

"Worse. Always worse."

"Did he recognize you during your last visit to Moscow?"

Stepan pruned his answer. "His mind is completely washed away. My sister has to keep him under lock and key so he doesn't wander off." Talking about the widower's condition twisted Stepan's stomach into knots as tight as a hangman's noose. All too readily he would choke on images of the old man's fouled diapers and the dried drool pasted to his gray beard.

"I'll send your sister a note to let her know I'm thinking of her."

"You are one of the kindest women I've ever known."

The hem of her silk taffeta gown whispered on the pavers as she pulled away from the pillar. "I'm also your oldest friend," Yustina murmured as the crescent moon came out from behind a cloud.

"A priceless friend." He hesitated, bent forward, and kissed her cheek. The sinews of Stepan's neck tightened. It was still there—the faint scent of lilac.

As he straightened, she grabbed his upper arms. "Speaking of days gone by," she rose onto her toes, and placed her lips next to his ear, "I dare say if your son had asked me to dance twenty-five years ago, you, Stepan Stepanovich Maximov, wouldn't have stood a chance." She dropped away from him, a ghost of a smile flitting about her lips.

He grinned, grateful for the lightened mood. "I assume you mean Anton." He threw back his shoulders. "A chip off the old block."

The giggle of her youth sprang forth as her hand rose and her splayed fingers partially covered the gold choker that circled her willowy neck. Her girlish laughter sounded so splendid, so familiar. It took him back to half a lifetime ago, to the gentle, sunlit springtime of his life.

Stepan offered his arm. Yustina slipped her hand around it, her smile laced with pensive affection, and they went inside.

Hilda, who had doled out her meddlesome intrusions with undiscriminating generosity, diminished her fussing as the evening wore on. As Stepan sat sipping another glass of sparkling wine, he noticed the tutor talking to Roeglin, her face relaxed in a jubilant smile. Apparently she was content with the evening's outcome. When the orchestra began a Strauss waltz, Stepan watched his stout, ruddy-cheeked steward and the plump tutor glide onto the dance floor.

The realization hit him like a brick. Who would have ever suspected? Not that they looked mismatched. Both were sturdy, educated Germans. How many years' difference in age lay between them? Fifteen? Stepan thumped his thick skull with the heel of his hand. *So that's the true purpose of this faux ball.*

Anton slid into the seat next to his father.

Recalling his sons' grown-up conversation in the stable, Stepan continued in like vein, inclining his head toward Anton and flicking his eyes in the direction of Hilda and Roeglin. "What's going on with those two?"

Anton glanced at the robust couple. "Oh, that. They've been chasing each other around for months."

Stepan was stunned an affair had blossomed right under his nose, and he'd been blind to it. Yet his son had sniffed it out.

Hilda turned from Roeglin and clapped her hands twice at eye level. "Everyone! This will be the last selection. Even though the evening is still young, you don't want to be the last to leave the ballroom. Staying too late gives others the impression you don't often have an invitation to a ball and must make the most of it." She faced her dance partner, and his thick arm encircled her thick waist for the final waltz.

Stepan waved Gennady over. He set his empty glass on the butler's tray at the same time his son took a glass of wine. With an accustomed gesture, Anton lifted his glass to Stepan in a toast. "The evening went well, don't you agree?" Anton asked.

Stepan rolled his cufflink between his fingers as Anton quaffed the bubbly liquid like a seasoned veteran.

CHAPTER 23

Maximov

1848

Everything rides on me:
both joy and sorrow.
What am I?

The mail.

THE WINTER FOLLOWING the Maximov ball, Elena scrutinized Vaska's pointed beard as it jutted at her eye level. Her mittened hand grasped the goat's goatee. "Satan's beard."

Her father chuckled. Only a child would notice the similarity. "Don't pull Vaska's hair, Pigeon."

"Why?"

"It hurts." Stepan's fingernails curried the length of the goat's neck with long, slow strokes. "This is what Vaska likes."

Elena stroked the dense winter hair coat. She smiled as Vaska's eyelids lowered blissfully.

The goat had followed them into the moist, aromatic cow barn, and Elena was in the mood to linger. Most children preferred horses since they could be ridden and were more responsive to human contact than plodding bovines or dull sheep. But Elena found delight in all the barns, conversing in equal measure with the various livestock and paying Vaska a bit of special attention.

As they watched the herdsman pour a bucket of milk into a tub, Stepan asked the herdsman, "Whose milk is that?"

"Khitruska's."

The cow in question raised her wide snout into the air and bellowed four times.

"It seems to be a rather small amount," Stepan observed.

"Yes. She's fallen behind today."

"Why, Khitruska?" Elena asked the cow. "Why did you fall behind?"

The herdsman explained, "She's lonely today, but later this afternoon she'll visit the bull, and tomorrow she'll once again be content."

"Good!" Elena shouted to be heard over Khitruska, who was once again bawling her disgruntlement.

The herdsman led the cow out of the barn and promptly returned, pitchfork in hand. The sharp smell of ammonia filled the air as he loaded a wheelbarrow with Khitruska's soiled straw.

Elena's mitten pointed to the pile of muck. "Why do cows poo-poo so much, Papa?"

"Because they eat a lot." He pinched her chin.

"But why?"

"Because they are big, big animals." He patted his coat pocket. "The horsie is waiting for you to give him his sugar. Are you ready to go for your birthday horsie ride?" Elena could have requested a dollhouse, a chalkboard, and any number of toys for her fifth birthday, but she insisted all she wanted was a "long, long horsie ride with Papa."

"Let's give sugar to the cows."

"Cows don't like sugar." He took his daughter's hand.

"But why? You said everybody likes sugar."

THE SUN WAS about to sink into the bare limbs of the birches when Stepan and Elena returned from their ride across the white quilt of snow. The crystalline air had turned the child's cheeks and nose the color of apples, and her hat plastered her hair against her head. After being excused from the dinner table, she led herself to bed. Stepan, also fatigued, slipped first into his fur-collared robe and then into his red armchair.

"Father! Mother! Look what's arrived!" Natalya rushed into the study in a compromise between a gallop and a genteel stroll. "Letters from Sergei and Anton! Read them out loud."

Stepan broke the seal and removed two pieces of paper.

"Wait. Should we get Matriusha? She'll want to hear."

"That's a champion idea, Natalya." Stepan was touched by his daughter's thoughtfulness. Even though Matriusha was a serf, she had worried, wept, and celebrated holidays with two generations of Maximov children. Surely she'd want to hear the boys' newsy tidbits.

"But do hurry!" Sophia urged, looking up from her embroidery work.

Stepan had been relieved that Sophia remained level-headed when the twins had set out three months earlier for the First St. Petersburg Cadet's College. But, of course, they had left during her annual summer buoyancy. Now that she was steadily sinking back into her winter melancholia, the boys' departure after their upcoming holiday visit might precipitate an entirely different scenario.

As Matriusha lumbered into the study, her vigilant eyes gave the door a scathing once-over. The white-haired nanny lifted her apron and rubbed the brass escutcheon. When the shine didn't meet her satisfaction, she blew on the plate and buffed with added vigor. Limping toward a rocking chair, she muttered vague phrases about the housegirls' laxness.

Stepan smoothed the wrinkles from Sergei's onion-thin stationery.

12 November 1848

Dearest family,

I apologize for not writing very often during our first months at the College, but the routine is very strenuous, particularly the drilling and the mathematics, all of which makes me very homesick.

The General inspected us this morning while we stood at stiff attention, hardly daring to breathe. The General asked each of us a question. I gave the correct answer and felt proud as I clicked my heels and saluted. Later our Colonel told me and Anton that we both had a manly bearing during the inspection.

Please visit us this spring. You'd be thrilled by the parade of hundreds of thousands of soldiers and the bright green artillery caissons and the prancing horses. Tsar Nicholas refers to it as "the spectacle of the gods."

I barely get by on the thirty rubles you send me every month. There are so many unexpected expenses here, and I don't want to fall behind the other Cadets. It is assumed that we all purchase gifts for our instructors and, of course, everyone smokes. Cigarettes are quite expensive.

Did you receive a letter from Colonel Prohorov about Anton getting caught after curfew? Also, last week, one of our classmates (a real scalawag) accused Antoshka of cheating in cards. He said Anton turned a 0 into a 9 on the tally sheet. Anton swore he hadn't, so it was Vvedneskii's word against Anton's.

We've heard that next week our regiment will display our maneuvers at the Winter Palace for His Imperial Majesty and then have tea with one of the Grand Dukes. But that rumor has yet to be confirmed.

I must close as I am to meet some pals for skating on the Neva.

Anxious to be home at Christmas,

My love to all of you,

Your son and brother,

Sergei

As his eyes skimmed over the letter again, Stepan felt a swell of irritation that Sergei had tattled on his brother. The Colonel had indeed written to Stepan describing how Anton had been caught past curfew, for which he received demerits and extra chores. The Colonel's letter stated that such minor infractions were not uncommon during one's first year at the military academy and were usually not repeated except by the more incorrigible students.

Stepan unfolded the second letter, a utilitarian piece of paper, its top edge torn from a writing table. He adjusted his eyes from Sergei's fastidious handwriting to Anton's free and easy scrawl.

To all whom I miss on Petrovo,

This letter must be brief as I have to study my French. How I wish Natalya was here to help me!

Another subject I am having trouble with is marching and parading, not that it is difficult but because it is extremely dull and I find my officers to be pompous egoists. Thanks to Hilda's tutoring, history and geography come easily to me, although I don't understand why Hilda didn't teach us about surveying and fortification! I am only jesting, Hilda, so don't get your skirts riled at me. You taught me something far more important, and that is how to dance. I hope I will have more use in life for the mazurka than I will for employing a compass to map roads and streams. Promise you'll tell me all the details of your honeymoon when I am home over Christmas.

I think Sergei is a little more homesick than I am. Of the two of us greenhorns, I guess I am better able to handle the harsh treatment of the officers and the older Cadets. In fact, a couple of the older guys even allow me to pal around with them.

Scraping by on my allowance is a little difficult, but I am able to add to it with my winnings from whist. Don't worry, Mother, I place only modest bets.

I'm eager for Christmas when I can give Mama, Natalya, and Matriusha giant bear hugs. And I hope to get a big kiss from Elena. And Father, I want to hear your thoughts about the effects of the revolutions in France and Germany. Will Russia follow suit with a constitution of its own? And have you bought Cockeyes that new still yet?

Until I see each of you,

Anton

Stepan tucked the letters into the envelope, his thoughts turning dark. First, Anton's last question was an unmistakable jab about his father's relentless desire but perpetual failure to upgrade the distillery. Second, Stepan was convinced that Cockeyes was drinking his profits, but damned if he could catch him at it.

Natalya threw her head back, exposing her long, slender neck. "I can't wait to hear about their classmates. And the ceremonies at the Court. And the latest fashions. And—"

Her father interrupted her. "Do you really think the twins will be able to describe the latest fashions? After all, they're required to wear uniforms."

"Oh, Anton will be able to tell me. I'm certain he notices what the girls are wearing." Natalya smothered a giggle behind her hand.

Sophia rose to retire to the bedroom for her evening prayers. "Poor Sergei. So miserably homesick. Matriusha, tell the cook to prepare jellied suckling pig over the Christmas holidays. You know how Sergei adores that with parsley and slices of lemon."

Stepan's mouth made an oval as he started to say that coddling would only make the boy more homesick when he returned to school. But he kept his thoughts to himself as Sophia and Matriusha shambled from the room.

Natalya took the envelope from Stepan's hand, her face puckered in a pout. "You didn't say anything about my earmuffs."

"Earmuffs?"

She pointed to the braids that circled over her ears.

"Oh, yes. Very fashionable. And quite elegant. A champion idea on your part."

Apparently he had said the right thing, because she dimpled happily before retreating closer to the piled-up fire to read her brothers' words for herself.

As Stepan propped his tired legs on the ottoman, a somber question surfaced. What was this business about Anton cheating at cards? That had to be a lie on the part of the classmate. But why was Anton hanging around scalawags? Then again, Anton's devil-may-care streak was as wide as the steppe. It was only natural he took up with those of a similar mind-set.

A nightingale popped out of the gold clock atop the mantel. Naked branches tapped against the storm windows. Stepan drew his robe tighter, and his head nodded off to one side.

CHAPTER 24

Elizaveta

1850

The dough has been kneaded,
but it isn't rising.
What am I?
A childless marriage.

REMORSE GRIPPED ELIZAVETA'S heart as she held the small bundle in her
arms. How shameful to not want a child. But even when she closed her eyes, Elizaveta couldn't blot out the teardrop-shaped crimson birthmark on the newborn's
cheek. The little girl, whose birth had been brutal, was day-and-night different
from her sister Serafima, who had an angelic appearance even as she slid effortlessly from Elizaveta's womb.

"Were you attacked by a turkey cock?"

Elizaveta's eyes flitted open. "What?"

Stanislav's wife was bent over Elizaveta's sleeping bench, inspecting the tiny
girl. "Attacked by a turkey cock when the baby was inside you. Sometimes that
will cause a mark."

Stanislav stood beside his wife, his small, piglike eyes scrutinizing the infant.
"That wasn't caused by no turkey cock. That's the kiss of the Devil, no doubt
about it. You oughta take care of that baby before it brings disaster on this house."

"Take care of her? Are you . . . are you saying I should drown her?"

"That's one option." Stanislav shuffled like a bear to the table, his wife trailing
a step behind him.

Elizaveta's disgust drilled into Stanislav's retreating back. Although everyone
knew certain children accidentally died due to drowning or suffocation, it was
accepted that those occasional mishaps were in the best interest of the family and
the village. Such was the case when a child was born so deformed, it would be a
perpetual drain on the household and would never contribute to the welfare of

the community. Likewise, a mother might understandably end a starving baby's life when a famine plunged the entire family into destitution.

But to Elizaveta, slaughtering a baby because of a blotch on its face, even if the disfigurement might be the work of the Devil, was unthinkable. She didn't want the little girl dead. She merely wished she hadn't been born.

She would be married nine years this fall, and had given birth six times. After her first child died as a newborn, the next four—Ilya, Gerasim, Serafima, and Mitya—each came a year apart. It was a mystery to her why God would claim the life of a perfect, precious boy like Mitya but allow the birth of a damaged girl.

The straw rustled as Avdotya sat down on the sleeping bench. "The mark might fade with time."

Elizaveta rolled her eyes at the unlikelihood. She whispered for Avdotya's ears only, "I'd give anything to stop having babies. I wish God would strike me barren, so I wouldn't have any more of Ermak's children."

As sudden as a hiccup, Avdotya's tender smile tightened like a wound across her face.

Too late, Elizaveta realized the hurt she had inflicted on her sister-in-law. "Oh Avdotya, I didn't mean to make you feel bad. It must be heartbreaking to not be able to have a baby, especially when everyone our age is having litters of them."

Avdotya's gentle, muted eyes turned to stone. Without a word, she rose to her feet.

Elizaveta grabbed her sister-in-law's delicate hand. "Don't leave. Please forgive how thoughtless I am."

Avdotya pulled her hand free and turned away.

Elizaveta seized the woman's skirt. "I'm so sorry."

Avdotya stood like a statue, eyes pinned on the far wall.

"Is something else wrong? What is it? Sit beside me and tell me."

After a long hesitation, Avodotya lowered herself onto the sleeping bench. Her gosling neck quivered as she answered in a small, beaten whisper. "It's not me. It's Grigorii. He can't make a baby."

Elizaveta's mouth gaped.

"He can't." Avdotya's hand waved evasively at her lap. "He tries, but he can't."

"You mean, he doesn't get . . . big?"

They glanced about the room for eavesdroppers.

"Sometimes. But then he shrinks again. I don't think he's ever actually . . ." She averted her eyes.

"He's never . . . finished?"

Avdotya's "no" was as frail as the bleat of a newly born lamb.

Elizaveta fumed, "He lets everyone think it's your fault there's no children, when in reality he isn't able to . . . able to . . . ?"

Avdotya's head hung as low as though the shame were hers.

ELIZAVETA FELT THE weight of the infant in her arms but paid the baby no heed. Two months of age, and just now being christened with a Christian name! What kind of mother was she?

During the weeks following the little girl's birth, Ermak had been too repulsed by the baby's Satan's stain to even look at his daughter. And Elizaveta, trapped in the despondency that had overtaken her life, lacked the initiative to do more than nurse the baby. The poor child lived from day to day without the protection of the Sacrament of Holy Baptism until Vera put her foot down. "It's your duty as parents," she ordered Ermak and Elizaveta, "to see to it that your child will be welcomed into her Heavenly family should God call for her!"

The christening of her other children had filled Elizaveta's heart with an exultant joy. But today, mournful images flew through her mind like a flock of geese, their squawks smothering Father Diakonov's incantations. Her thoughts harked back to when three back-to-back years of empty bellies—1846, 1847, and 1848—had taken a woefully heavy toll. Grandmama Anafreva had shriveled until at last she died, as did the Widow Shabanova and numerous others, both old and young.

Elizaveta's parents had been forced to sell their horse early in 1848. Her father and Uncle Artamon took turns dragging the plough through the defiant soil. As the younger of the two brothers, Artamon weathered the ordeal, but the battering left Erafei permanently bowed like a top-heavy sunflower. The heat chiseled deep lines in his face that never smoothed out.

That was the first of dozens of recollections that pushed and shoved past the christening's incense and chanting. Each image paused momentarily before scurrying away to make room for the next.

Elizaveta heard with biting clarity August Roeglin announcing that cholera was in Paris and was moving toward Moscow. Then she heard the tremor in her sister Katya's voice. "Mikhalek Karpov told Evstafii Osokin, who then told our Uncle Artamon, that he, Karpov, personally saw cholera flying through the air just beyond the nuns' orphanage."

Elizaveta had no control over the swirling memories. She felt the ground tremble as horse hooves beat toward the square. She saw the lurid glittering of the medals on the breast of the officer's coat, and she heard the crinkling of stiff paper as he unfolded an official document.

Orders of His Majesty and our benefactor, the Emperor of Russia, Nicholas—

All of Russia, including this village, is under quarantine until further notification. This notice shall be posted on all public buildings.

Elizaveta saw in her mind's eye the officer holding the paper over his head and slowly turning in a circle for all to see.

She heard Zhanna's haughty laugh while boasting how her father had negotiated with the Colonel who maintained the cordon around the district capital, Sukhanovo. In exchange for an undisclosed number of rubles, Evdokim Seleznyov was allowed to purchase and haul vodka to Petrovo during the quarantine. Two months later, Zhanna's husband, Arkhip, was the first villager to die of the Vomiting Death.

The haunting images became more searing as Elizaveta recalled the stench of rotten bowels while her mother and young brother Alexei lay prostrate on their benches. She remembered dumping the buckets of vomit and liquid feces on the road in front of the Anafrevs' izba and watching the slurry trickle along the wheel rut until it sank, little by little, into the earth. Elizaveta watched the Anafrev family rejoice when Alexei arose from his sleeping bench and was able to stand on his own unsteady legs, having beaten back the cholera. She saw her mother's agonized face, shrunken and discolored like a dried plum, as Nadezhda took her last breath.

She heard herself praying to the church's Icon of the Blessed Virgin. "Our Lady, please keep Ilya, Gerasim, and Serafima safe. And Feodor. Always Feodor. Our Lady, please honor the requests of your humble servant. Our Lady . . ."

She heard the unremitting mourning of mothers as the Angel of Death culled their children while the contagion loitered in the Russian countryside for two years. She felt soul-lifting relief when the cholera finally left the small village of Petrovo. By some miracle, it had passed over the Vorontsov izba. Her children were safe. As was Feodor.

Frozen in her memory was her father's exclamation, "When a son is born, even the coals rejoice!" as he had congratulated Ermak over the birth of Mitya. Then came her mother-in-law's scream a half year later. Elizaveta's little son lay lifeless on the floor following a tumble from his hanging cradle, his neck twisted like a chicken's. Ermak blamed Elizaveta and beat her accordingly.

She felt the inconsolable tears of countless losses.

Ermak elbowed her ribs. "Hold out Anna so Father Diakonov can sprinkle her with holy water."

She looked blankly at her husband. He repeated his statement.

"Who?" she asked.

"Anna. Father Diakonov named her."

Elizaveta held forth the sleeping bundle. If she understood Ermak correctly, her daughter's name was Anna. But the girl's name held no import for Elizaveta. She was aware of only one thing—drowning in a cauldron of pain and defeat.

CHAPTER 25

Maximov

1852

I sit on a trough
and can't be fed my fill
of priests or scribes
or feasts or villages
or good folk or elders.
What am I?

Death.

STEPAN WAS ACCUSTOMED to Sophia's disconsolate depression during the abbreviated days of autumn and winter. But he actually had feared for her sanity two Decembers ago when she ordered Dasha and another housegirl to exorcise evil spirits by walking through each room shaking a rattle every evening for a week, at which time Sophia declared the spiritual intruders were purged. Feeling despair like none he had ever known, Stepan moved his sleeping quarters across the hall into his childhood bedroom while Sophia remained in the large bed of Karelian birch.

During the past year, Stepan had withstood his wife's pleadings to have Father Diakonov hold nightly family vespers at the estate house. However, he conceded to a service in the parlor on major holidays. On this eve of Lent, Diakonov's somber chants, air heavy with burning beeswax, and wavering light from the red votive holders lured Stepan into his private world of self-commiseration. With his chin resting on his chest, he hoped he appeared deep in prayer, but he didn't really give a damn if he wasn't deceiving anyone.

As if the ringing of the final death toll for his marriage weren't bad enough, his sister had summoned him to Moscow to give his final regards to their dying father. The desiccated old man was bedridden, his room fetid from bedsores. His shriveled mind was vacant except when, for no apparent reason, he became incensed with his visitors and spat on them.

The tentacles of trouble reached farther when Anton brought disgrace to the family and trepidation to Stepan about the boy's future. Late last fall, Stepan had received a letter from the head of the Cadet's College requesting he come immediately to St. Petersburg and take his son home. Permanently.

During those three years, Anton had acquired a list of infractions as long as his arm—tardiness, curfew violation, gambling, and intoxication. But this time, Anton had been caught in an unpardonable situation with the wife of one of his professors, a highly respected Colonel. According to the details Stepan had received upon arriving at the College, Anton and the purportedly beautiful thirty-year-old Arina Andreyevna Borodina were cavorting under the sheets when the Colonel burst upon the scene.

Father and son had sat in alienated silence while the carriage rattled along the roads between St. Petersburg and Petrovo. The boy showed not the least remorse over bedding a married woman thirteen years his senior. Stepan gripped the edge of the corduroy upholstery to keep from striking his raffishly handsome son.

Anger and foreboding had alternated in Stepan's belly as he glanced at the curls, as thick as sheep's wool, tumbling over his son's collar. How could Anton have been so foolhardy, so imprudent, as to wreck his brilliant prospects? The boy had so much going for him—an exceptional mind, the gift of elocution, the sleekness of a thoroughbred. He was head and shoulders above Sergei, Victor Rusakov, and all the other local lads.

Therein lay the problem, Stepan had conjectured. From the day of his birth, Anton was gifted with a robust intellect, personality, and wiliness. And it had turned him into a lazy good-for-naught. If everything came too easily, how would he ever develop the perseverance and strength of character required to succeed in life? Stepan feared his son was a living, breathing manifestation of the old fable about the tsar whose touch turned everything to gold until he died from hunger.

Self-discipline. That's what the boy was lacking, and Stepan had vowed to instill it in him. He'd uproot the gadabout's indolent attitude.

Sophia had been waiting for them in the foyer when they arrived home. Anton gave her an abbreviated greeting, kissed her forehead, and dashed up the stairs to his bedroom. Without so much as a "Hello," she flew into a passion with her husband. "What do you intend to do?"

"What do I intend to do?"

"About his behavior."

Stepan's frayed, travel-worn nerves strained as he calmly addressed his wife. "Every young man must have his fling. With time, he'll train himself to behave with dignity."

"No!" Sophia's open palm slammed the top of the Queen Anne lowboy. "This is not a mere case of temporarily straying down the wrong path! If your son doesn't straighten up his life now, his future will be reduced to rubble."

Stepan was sorely tempted to tear the ever-present little black cap from her pious head. "Let's not overreact to this one incident, reprehensible though it might be."

"Reprehensible?" She shrieked her words like a cat impaled by a pitchfork. "It's far worse than reprehensible! It's nefarious! Such licentiousness! My precious Savior, what this has done to me!"

Sophia was so personally offended by her son's erotic transgression that Stepan felt a needle prick of horror. Those years of long walks, hand-holding, stroking his hair. Was Sophia so demented in her soul as to be in love with her own son? He pushed aside words like *Oedipus* and *incest* to be inspected later. Right now, his wife was standing before him, eyes blazing with maniacal fury, chin thrust forward, expecting a response. He needed to supply one and then escape from her malicious insanity.

"Yes, definitely an atrocious incident. But he's just a young peacock. Give him time to smooth his plumes."

Her forefinger tapped the lowboy. "Wrong, Stepan, he is not simply fanning his tail feathers. It is your responsibility as his father to ensure he settles down. God will not only punish Anton for his actions. He will punish you for failure to correct his errant ways."

"Hell and damnation, Sophia, find it somewhere in yourself to be reasonable!" Stepan stomped from the house. The muscles in his back, already knotted from the carriage's jostling, were strangled with anger.

Behind him, Sophia stuck her head out the door and let loose a screech that would wake the dead. "The faults of your son will be attributed to you as his father!"

It took every morsel of his self-control not to barge back into the house and ask her to what extent Anton's cavorting was the result of her warped neediness and her clutching caresses. *Trace back, Sophia, to the start of his deviant proclivity for older women, and figure out how much of it is due to your malignant influence.*

Instead, aloud to no one but himself, he said, "She's stark raving mad." His thoughts darted to his deranged father, and a cold shudder coursed through him.

His fury searching for a target, Stepan had headed for the distillery. Just as he had hoped, Cockeyes was napping on a chair, a half-empty bottle of vodka on the floor beside him. Stepan shoved the sleeping man's shoulder, and the chair toppled backward. Stunned, Cockeyes struggled to his knees and rubbed his askew eyes as he tried to collect his small amount of God-given wits.

"Count Maximov." Cockeyes had the look of a dog faintly wagging its tail in penitence. "Didn't expect you back today."

Stepan told Cockeyes he was no longer allowed in the distillery or in any of the estate's buildings. He was to live in the village with the field serfs.

The blood drained from Cockeyes's face until it was the color of dirty linen. He wailed like a wounded wolf that he had followed in his father's and his grandfather's footsteps as a manorial servant. His relatives in the village, none of whom he could even recognize, would never claim him as one of their own, and he would be without a roof over his head.

Turning a deaf ear, Stepan restated his demands with perfect impassibility. He could have banished Cockeyes to Siberia, but he determined a more fitting punishment would be for him to live the hell of a rudderless serf, without a family and without a village. To rub salt into the serf's wound, Stepan informed him that, starting this very day, Cockeyes's duties would be taken over by Feodor Zhemchuzhnikov.

Cockeyes damned "that scrawny, grasping bootlicker" to Hell.

Now, three months later, as the priest flapped his censer back and forth, Stepan drifted deeper into the past, to the cholera epidemic that had devastated Russia.

A couple of cousins in Moscow had died of the dreadful disease, as had Sophia's father. Quarantines surrounded Moscow, leaving despondent Sophia unable to return to the city to grieve with her sister. The Maximovs finally made the journey in the summer of 1850. The city was hotter, filthier, and crasser than Stepan remembered it. Making it worse were the mobs of visitors kicking up their heels at the festivities honoring the twenty-fifth anniversary of Nicholas's accession to the throne.

The trip had coincided with the reading of his father-in-law's will, which left Anton and Sergei an undivided interest in their grandfather's Moscow mansion while it meted out his dacha and money among his other grandsons. The inheritance lifted a worry from Stepan's shoulders about his boys' financial future. And the relief was even more heartfelt after the young laggard trounced his opportunity for a military career.

The cholera epidemic had a ruinous effect on Petrovo. An 1850 government-ordered soul census revealed that the two-year contagion had claimed the lives of one out of every five of Petrovo's peasants. Stepan's assets and the estate's productivity both suffered horrendous blows.

But Stepan's financial wounds went still deeper. During the past few years, distillers like himself had found their profits becoming more and more slender. Many landowners had shut down their distilleries, and Stepan daily pondered the same action.

On the other hand, he had finally abandoned the traditional three-field rotation in favor of a four-year cycle. Stepan counted the experiment a success when not only Petrovo's output of rye increased but so did its fodder from the clover and potato tops, which in turn meant more cattle and, subsequently, more manure for fertilizer. The potatoes themselves were turned into vodka.

The potatoes grew so happily, however, they overtaxed the amount his distillery could process. The surplus tubers required burdensome and expensive hauling to molasses or starch factories several days away. Stepan wondered if perhaps instead of shutting down the distillery, he should expand it to make better use of the surplus potatoes.

Christ above! First he couldn't get potatoes grown on his land, and now he had more than he knew what to do with. Every fiber of his being cried out for rest after years of trying to eke more revenue out of Petrovo. One by one, his optimistic ambitions had been snuffed out like candles. Life had evolved into a string of unmet desires.

What he wouldn't give to be able to turn back the clock to those verdant years when his children's biggest problem had been preventing their knuckles from being rapped by Matriusha. Those years of afternoon teas with his wife on the terrace. Those years when he had faith that confidence would always beat failure. All had been peaceful and good. Then the blows had begun to fall.

He'd lost the resiliency of youth and was ready to retreat from life's trials. He was only forty-seven. Why did he feel older than Methuselah? He had led the privileged life of the nobility, a life anyone in Russia would relish. Perhaps the world was lashing out at him, seeking expiation for the easy existence he had taken for granted.

Anton's elbow tapped Stepan's. "It's over."

"Huh?"

"The service is over."

Stepan dropped a ruble into the perpetually upturned palm of the long-haired priest.

PART

Two

CHAPTER 26

Maximov

1855

I saw such a monstrosity:
six legs, two heads, just one tail.
What was it?

A horseback rider.

ELENA WAS SITTING on the floor pavers when Anton led his mare into the stable. He handed the reins to Yegorka and squatted beside his sister.

"What are you doing, Pigeon?"

"Soaping a saddle. Something you've probably never done." Elena flashed a smile, boasting teeth that gleamed like sunlit snow, a matching set to her brother's.

"Ha! I've soaped many a saddle. Father required Sergei and me to take care of our own tack. But he figured once we learned how to do it, the intelligent choice was to hand over the chore to the servants. And if you had any sense, young lady, you'd do the same." Anton chucked her chin.

She stopped massaging glycerin into the saddle just long enough to leap to another subject. "Antoshka! Have you seen Malinka's new calf?"

Two years ago, a nearby estate owner had boasted to Stepan about his recently acquired Russian Swiss cattle. The new breed, a cross of Swiss Brown and German Brown Mountain, produced animals that were excellent milkers yet retained quality beef production. Never one to pass by an opportunity to boost Petrovo's profitability, Stepan purchased a pregnant heifer with the intent of selling the extra milk to wholesalers in Sukhanovo. Elena adored the animal, which she named Malinka. Stepan gave it to his daughter with the stipulation that she accept responsibility for at least half the feeding, the milking, and the mucking of the stall, with the barnkeepers taking care of the remainder.

Anton, however, regarded the cow as just one more example of Stepan's good intentions gone awry. During the spring and autumn when the roads were impassable mud slurries, the milk soured as it sat for weeks in the root cellar.

Anton rallied enthusiasm into his response regarding Malinka's new calf. "A heifer or a bull?"

"A heifer. And she's every bit as pretty as her mother. You must go see her."

"I certainly shall. Before I set off for Gabrichevsky's."

The crisp September weather made Anton eager for the two-day hunt with the young men from the neighboring estates. The snipe, woodcock, ducks, teals, grebes, and geese would all be fair game until he and his colleagues became too soused to safely handle their guns. At that point, the weapons were handed to the servants so the sportsmen could sit around the fire and drink in earnest.

During the four years he'd been home from the Cadet's College, Anton had concluded that the camaraderie of hunting was one of the exceedingly few pleasures offered by country living. While his father delighted in "sitting in nature's lap," Anton found provincial life as stifling as a coffin, day after uneventful day notched on a wooden stick. He wasn't cut out to be rural gentry. He required more verve, more panache than the stagnant countryside had to offer.

On the rare occasions the family journeyed to Moscow, Anton's pulse quickened with exhilaration, as though he were riding on the crest of a wave. But he landed with a thud as soon as he stepped out of the carriage back on the estate of Petrovo.

Not a moment went by that he wasn't beckoned by the Moscow mansion he and his brother had inherited from their maternal grandfather. But for the time being, he was trapped in the middle of Russia's endless grain fields. His only source of income, apart from the paltry allowance his father grudgingly gave him, was the mansion's rent, which he split with Sergei.

But someday . . . someday he'd be part of the gas-lit world where snow fell on troikas carrying mutton-chopped dignitaries. Where windows glimmered with parties vibrating with lively discussions. Where brightly colored hundred-ruble notes cluttered green card tables until the small hours of the morning. At which time powdered, accommodating women took over.

Someday.

He turned his attention back to his sister. Elena was saying something, and her brightness had clouded over. "I asked, when can I go hunting with you?"

"You've been told, you're too young."

"I'll be twelve in December."

Rather than belligerence or sulkiness, Anton saw a face set with genuine determination. Elena possessed far more maturity than he, Sergei, or Natalya could have laid claim to at eleven years of age. One would have assumed that, as the baby of the family, Elena would have been so unbearably spoiled, she would never grow up. But quite the opposite was true. Perhaps the underlying reason was that she spent so much time either in the company of adults or by herself, she had never learned to act like a child.

She passed her hours in the quiet solitude of the woods, locating the homes of foxes and raccoons and chasing skipping grasshoppers. At the pond, she tossed stale bread to the fish and searched the reeds and water lilies for the hiding places of ducks and snails. When she wasn't exploring the countryside, she haunted the barns, working side by side with the serfs. Her indoor recreation, during those few hours she spent inside, centered on billiards, and Anton found her ability to handle a cue almost challenged his own.

For the past year, her pleas to go hunting had been unremitting. But Anton couldn't take her with him and his comrades. There was too little hunting, too many off-color jokes, and too much dedication to inebriation. Perhaps she could tag along with their father sometime when he hunted with his old cronies. But that idea didn't seem plausible either. During the hunt, male pride and passion were at their peak. Anton couldn't imagine Stepan's chums putting up with a girl.

"Please, Antoshka!" she entreated. "Can't you see I'm growing up?"

Anton took her hostage by wrapping an arm around her neck. His finger ran down the slope of her nose. "But I don't want you to grow up. I like you just the way you are."

She retaliated by thrusting her glycerin-saturated rag under his nose.

He released her. "You're certain you want to traipse around the woods and get windblown and dirty and covered with stickers and burs?"

Elena dropped her hands onto her jodhpurs. "I want it more than anything." Her baleful hound dog eyes implored her brother as she leaned on her saddle, its cold leather creaking with its own form of pleading. "I don't want to spend my life like a caged canary."

"I'll talk to Father. Perhaps something can be worked out. But for right now, we'd better get to the table. You know how Father likes to eat on schedule."

Joy spread across her face and she pecked his cheek. "I knew you'd understand. You understand me better than anyone."

But Anton didn't understand. Not at all. He didn't understand why she didn't enjoy playing with dolls and arranging her hair in different styles. Or why she preferred a pair of Tula pistols as a present for her birthday rather than an ivory trinket box or curios to decorate the forsaken top of her dressing stand. Or why she was more at home among straw and manure and animals than she was with giggling girlfriends.

He worried that she was too much of a tomboy and if she didn't outgrow it soon, she'd never find her place in civil society. He loved Elena to distraction, and he admired her gusto for life, which was the antithesis of Natalya's supercilious addle-headedness and Sergei's cautious hesitation. But understand her? Not in the least.

Maybe it was because Anton so thoroughly understood women that he couldn't make sense of Elena. Since he was little, he'd possessed an uncanny grasp of the workings of the female mind. He attributed that sixth sense to the volume of time he had spent with his mother. He'd learned the precise words to calm her, the right way to pat her hand to soothe her miseries, the foolproof way to cuddle her head against his chest to squelch her tears. As Anton grew into a teenager, he instinctually applied those manipulative insights to his female cousins, neighbors, and servants.

He and Elena removed their muddy boots at the back entrance to the house. As they walked through the steamy kitchen, Anton told the cook her meal smelled delicious. He glanced in the tiny mirror that she kept beside the pantry door and ran his fingers through his shock of hair. In the foyer, he found Natalya performing a more elaborate version of the same action in the gilded beveled mirror.

Standing behind her, he studied her reflection. His eyes squinted and his mouth grimaced. Natalya's face and neck were chalky. Her dark eyes stood out like ebony buttons atop a white tablecloth.

"What's wrong with your face?" he asked the ghost.

"Nothing. It's good for it." Natalya's gaze didn't leave her image in the mirror.

"What's good for it?"

"The salt and sour cream."

"The what?"

"The salt and sour cream." She glanced at his image as he cocked his head. "I alternate it with oatmeal and egg white." His expression remained befuddled and bemused. "It's for my complexion, silly. It removes the old skin and nurtures the new skin."

"I'm sure he thinks you're beautiful, with or without nurtured skin."

Natalya examined her profile as she poked some flyaway strands of hair into the braided chignon at the back of her neck. "It's been a year since I've seen him. What if he doesn't find me attractive anymore? What if he doesn't care a straw for me?" A web of wrinkles tortured her forehead.

"Then he's a fool, and you'd be better off with someone who appreciates you for who you are."

Anton was finding it increasingly difficult to appreciate the older of his two sisters, ever since she had become enamored beyond all measure. The previous fall, A.A. Gabrichevsky's nephew and his family happened to be traveling through the province during the time of Gabrichevsky's annual autumn ball. Natalya insisted that during her very first dance with Ippolit Filippovich Gabrichevsky, she'd seen his soul flow through his eyes, and fell hopelessly in love with him.

As Anton held Natalya's dining chair for her, Matriusha waddled into the room and straightened the grouping of dried willow branches behind the Icon of St. George the Victory-Bearer. The old woman looked around the dining room, sniffing her displeasure or pleasure—it was impossible to tell which—before ambling away, hand pressed to her lower back. With Elena being the sole child in need of a nanny, Matriusha had little to occupy her time.

"Is it asking too much for everyone to please settle into your chairs so we can eat?" Stepan leaned back to allow Gennady the butler to distribute the platters of food. Then he bent toward his elder daughter, his upper lip curled in repulsion. "What's on your face?"

"Salt and sour cream."

"In lieu of oatmeal and egg whites." Anton winked at Elena, whose nose was wrinkled like a pug dog's.

"Have you seen Malinka's baby, Papa?" Elena asked.

"Yes, Pigeon, I have. She's a beauty. And Malinka has a good bag."

"I named the heifer Malinka Two."

"Why would you give two cows the same name?" Stepan asked.

"No, Papa, not Malinka *too*. Malinka *Two*." She held up two fingers.

"Oh, Malinka *Two*. You mean like the tsars. Peter the First, Peter the Second, Peter the Third."

"Yes, except I'm not calling her Malinka the Second. I'm calling her Malinka Two."

"Will Mother be joining us for lunch?" asked Natalya, obviously bored with the discussion of bovine names.

"She's upstairs. A headache," Stepan said.

The comment swathed the Maximov table with an asphyxiating silence that was broken only by the tinkling of silverware against china and the nightingale popping out of its house to call out the time.

Eventually Stepan said to the occupants of the table in general, "Remind me when we visit Sergei in St. Petersburg that I need to look for those newfangled clocks that only need winding every eight days. Matriusha said it would help her joints if she didn't have to wind the clocks every day."

Anton questioned, "So you're buying new clocks rather than assigning the chore to another servant?"

Stepan's fork paused above his spiced crab apple. "And exactly what would you have me to do with her?" Stepan glanced about for the nanny and lowered the volume of his growl. "There's damn little that old woman can do around here that's useful. Perhaps you'd prefer to simply throw her out like spoilt milk?"

It was senseless to argue with his father. "No, of course not, Father. Your point is valid. She deserves consideration for all her years of faithful service."

Stepan set down his fork and leaned forward. "And where were you last evening? Another of your nocturnal excursions? The old woman fell down, and we could barely get her up. Gennady and I spent the better part of an hour getting her off the floor and into bed."

"Is that why she's walking so slowly today?" Elena asked.

"She walks slow every day, poor old thing." Stepan picked up his fork and jabbed the tines at Anton. "You didn't answer my question. Where were you last night? Out howling at the moon again?" He mumbled some animal metaphors about "tomcatting around" and "no better than a billy goat."

"I was visiting friends. As we agreed on my eighteenth birthday, I'm free to come and go as I see fit."

"We also agreed you would help out around here, but you're never around when I need you."

Anton sought a change of subject. His "nocturnal excursions" were becoming costly. His recent luck at cards was so abysmal, he'd been forced to write a promissory note. "Elena and I were talking in the stable this morning. She has a legitimate request. I think we should hear her out."

"And that is . . . ?" Stepan asked.

"Perhaps it's time she tried her hand at hunting."

"Please, Papa, I so want to."

Stepan's eyes shifted to his youngest daughter. "Oh, I suppose it won't hurt to give it a try. Anton and I will take you."

"Thank you, Papa!" Elena leapt from her chair and raced around the table to throw her arms around her father's neck.

Matriusha happened to be passing the doorway. "Elena, sit down like a lady and mind your manners." The old nanny turned to the butler. "Gennady, the cook needs you in the kitchen. And bring back some more kidney sauté and buttered toast."

Stepan directed his attention to Anton. "Have I told you about the possibilities of a six-year field rotation?"

Only a thousand times, Anton groaned inwardly.

"Gennady, get me a paper and pen. Gennady? Where's Gennady?"

"In the kitchen," his three children chorused.

Stepan rang the silver dinner bell and shouted for paper and pen. "And don't forget the ink."

Stepan retrieved his reading spectacles from his vest pocket and slipped the wire earpieces past the gray at his temples. "Look here, Anton, this is how it works." Stepan scribbled on the paper and shoved it toward his son. "See the beauty of it?"

Year 1	*fallow*
Year 2	*winter rye*
Year 3	*potatoes or lentils*
Year 4	*fallow*
Year 5	*winter rye*
Year 6	*spring oats, barley, or buckwheat*
Begin again Year 1	

Anton would prefer to bang his forehead against the table rather than endure yet another spiel about crop rotations. However, he was definitely eager to veer from the topic of his nightly activities, so he masked his face with rapt attentiveness. Allowing the old man to rattle on about agronomy was far safer than having him stumble onto his son's gambling debts.

CHAPTER 27

Maximov

1856

Sasha is standing up.
He begs, standing up.
My kulik is big,
and the hole is too small.
What is happening?
The key doesn't fit the lock.

ANTON CHEWED ON a piece of straw, hoping the peasant custom would put the girl at ease. He patted the pale gold straw beside him.

"Come here."

The girl, of course, could not refuse and shuffled a half step closer. She looked like a frightened, long-legged fawn, which appealed to Anton in a visceral way. He guessed her to be about thirteen. Her threadbare jumper was too small, its bodice cinched against her thin, budding figure.

She was a field serf who lived in the village. Anton had chatted with her a couple of times when she'd come to the estate house selling mushrooms or berries. The last time she was there, he showed off by juggling croquet balls. On that occasion, the wind caught her skirt and held it tight around her willowy thighs, and Anton knew he'd eventually have to sample what lay atop those legs. After all, sex was merely one more appetite to be sated.

"Come on. Don't be afraid. I thought we were friends. Aren't we friends?"

The girl stood her ground. Anton's eyes wandered down to her hands clutched in front of her narrow hips. He grew hard.

"Alvetina, please don't hurt my feelings. Sit here next to me for a minute or two, so we can talk. We so seldom get a chance to talk."

He removed the piece of straw from his mouth and tossed it aside. He stretched out his arm, seized her hand, and pulled her down beside him. The girl pinned her eyes on the far side of the stable.

He needed to hurry along. Natalya would skin him alive if he were late for her wedding.

"It's a little chilly, isn't it, Alvetina?"

Her gaze remained frozen.

He reached an arm behind her neck and clasped her shoulder. *God, she's bony,* he thought. *Don't these peasants eat?*

His free hand swiveled her chin toward him. "I simply want to be friends. Don't you?" His hand dropped from her chin to her chest. He massaged the juvenile knoll that would one day become a woman's breast.

She snuck a fleeting glance at his hand, then looked somewhere distant over his left ear.

Anton's hand slid down to pat her thigh. He felt the heat of her limbs. "You do believe that I mean you no harm, don't you? That's the beauty of friendship."

He slowly hitched up her skirt until her knees were exposed. Her nose inhaled a small gasp.

"Friends make each other feel good." His fingers continued to raise the homespun until the skirt's hem rested at midthigh. He placed his palm on her bare thigh and stroked it.

"Pretty, pretty Alvetina," he whispered, keeping a safe distance from the dark rings of grime in the creases of her neck. "Have any good friends done this to you before?"

The girl swallowed.

Anton's hand drifted upward. The inside of her thigh was sinewy, not soft and supple like the women he was accustomed to. His fingers spread her legs, then continued their ascent. The corners of his mouth twitched upward—like the other peasant women, she wasn't encumbered with undergarments.

Her legs snapped shut. He withdrew his hand and took hold of the skirt's hem. His gaze followed the faded cloth as it crept to her waist. She had only the slightest covering of soft down, the same pale color as the straw underneath her and as velvety as billiards felt. Anton watched as he inserted a finger.

"Does this feel good? Yes? I know something that feels even better."

HE ARRANGED THE orange blossom in the buttonhole of his dress coat and, with lazy indifference, glanced at the foyer's ponderous French Empire mirror. Natalya had teased him time and again about how unfairly handsome he was, but

Anton never saw it in the mirror. He gave no more heed to his imposing appearance than he did to his innate intelligence and charisma.

Natalya's wedding reception was at A.A. Gabrichevsky's mansion, which, quite unlike Petrovo's estate house, could comfortably accommodate three hundred guests. Gabrichevsky graciously assumed the exorbitant expenses.

Alongside Anton's image in the mirror appeared his father, cheeks puffed out. Stepan exhaled until his chest was deflated. "I'm going upstairs to talk some sense into your mother."

Following the church ceremony, Sophia had arrived at the Gabrichevsky mansion in a state of nervous collapse. She asked the hostess if she might briefly lie down on one of the beds. "At the precise moment Natalya and Ippolit were being joined in holy matrimony, the Weeping Virgin revealed herself to me. If I could please have a few moments to collect myself."

That was almost an hour ago.

Stepan put a foot on the bottom tread and lifted his gaze to the top of the staircase. "Of all days for her to commiserate with the Weeping Virgin." He took each step as if his boots were solid lead.

Anton tugged at each shirt cuff in turn. Why didn't the old man just divorce her? No one would blame him. Everyone knew she was as unhinged as the rusty fence gate at Petrovo's church.

But then again, the Orthodox Church made divorce virtually impossible, limiting the grounds to little beyond adultery, willful abandonment of at least five years' duration, or physical incapability to have conjugal relations. Although the wealthy could buy divorces, Anton knew his father's well-intentioned but misplaced principles could never abide such an unscrupulous action.

Anton smelled the bride's arrival beside him, marinated as she was in rosewater. He toasted her with his glass. "How fortunate that Gabrichevsky was able to secure the finest French champagne, despite the embargo."

Natalya exhaled her vexation. "Ugh." Even as a young girl, Natalya's sights were set on a honeymoon in Paris, and Stepan long ago promised her the trip as a wedding gift. But Russia and France were on ill terms, having just bloodied each other in a war. Her long-awaited honeymoon foiled, Natalya didn't hesitate to let everyone know of her profound disapproval of the Tsar's foul timing.

Rather than embark on their honeymoon, Natalya and Ippolit would travel straight to their new home in St. Petersburg. Ippolit stood to eventually inherit his father's lucrative textile mills there, and the young man appeared to have an aptitude for business. Natalya's materialistic longings would be fulfilled to the hilt.

The bridegroom entered the foyer, his eyes entrapped by the beauty of his new wife. Natalya was truly dazzling in her white silk wedding dress trimmed with orange blossoms. Her lace veil flowed from the crown of her head to the floor.

Anton extended a hand to shake in Western style. "I congratulate you, Ippolit Filippovich. You and my sister make a sterling match."

"Thank you, Anton Stepanovich. I am indeed a fortunate man."

Anton's engaging smile widened as he kept his response to himself. *Wait until your mother-in-law visits you in St. Petersburg for a month. See how fortunate you feel then.*

Anton followed Natalya's gaze toward the top of the staircase. Stepan was descending, his shoulders bowed as if carrying the weight of the world.

"Mother won't come down?" Natalya whispered when her father reached her side.

Stepan shook his head.

"The Weeping Virgin?" Anton asked.

"Yes. And she's in a fit of despair that Sergei is returning to St. Petersburg in two days."

Ippolit noted, "But at least the War is over. No more worries that he might be sent to the front."

"From the sound of it, Sergei has no more worries whatsoever." Anton winked.

During the week Sergei had been at Petrovo, he prattled incessantly about a girl named Matriona Mikhailovna Bakhrushina. According to Sergei, not only was she beautiful, but her father was a shipbuilder who was making money hand over fist due to his long-standing connections to the Navy. Since the start of the Crimean War, orders—and rubles—had been spilling into Bakhrushin's lap faster than his shipyard could keep pace.

Anton wasn't one to begrudge other people's success, but he was dumbfounded that his boring, bigoted, squirrel-headed brother had blundered onto such an inconceivable run of good luck. First, he'd been accepted into the Guards, the most illustrious branch of the military, where he was already up for promotion. Second, he had managed to stay in the comfort of St. Petersburg while poor suckers like Cousin Rodya Shelgunov were shipped to the Crimean front as fast as the schools could graduate them. Then a beautiful girl of untold wealth had fallen in love with him. What next? Appointment as Official Dolt of the Tsar's Court?

Natalya's dismayed whisper broke into his thoughts. "Nobody turn around.

Victor Rusakov just walked in, and I don't want him to come over here. I wish I didn't have to invite him to the wedding."

"Natalya, such harsh words." Scowling eyebrows and thinly pressed lips added unflattering years to Stepan's already haggard appearance.

The bride defended herself. "Even his own parents don't like him. He constantly embarrasses them."

Vladimir and Yustina's model son had recently become an enigma to them. Victor had paid an extended visit to St. Petersburg last summer, and he'd returned home with, in Victor's words, "an awakened social conscience."

His parents said he had developed a new circle of radical friends in the capital city. After Victor fell victim to the agitators, he effectively separated himself from conventional society, by both his appearance and his attitude. He moved back into his father's house sporting long hair, frayed laborer's clothing, and blue-tinted glasses. He argued incessantly with Vladimir about the evilness of serfdom, spewing out trendy phrases like "serfdom—a barbarous relic of an unenlightened past" and "Russia—home of semi-savages who have been glazed over with a veneer of polish."

Anton didn't care for his sister's demeanor, but truth be told, he likewise found the newly awakened version of Victor hard to endure. "I believe I'll get a bite to eat."

"Do try the pastries, Antoshka!" Natalya exclaimed. "They're light as air. The Gabrichevskys' confectioner made them. He was a pupil of Tremblé."

"A pupil of Tremblé!" Anton's ardor was equal to Natalya's. *Whoever the hell Tremblé is.*

Ippolit told Anton, "Join us at your leisure in the library for conversation and cigars."

Anton greeted several of the guests as he waded through the smaller of the two ballrooms toward the lavish repast. He helped himself to pâté with truffles along with cold sturgeon in aspic. And another glass of champagne.

He looked up to see a pair of breasts the size of hefty melons bursting from the dangerously low neckline of a silk gown of the palest peach. He obliged his eyes to move up and look at the face that belonged to the lush sweep of breast.

"Feona Ivanovna! Always a pleasure to see you." He bent to kiss her proffered hand, his eyes lingering on the diamond pendant nestled in her cleavage where his own head had burrowed several times.

Her lips stretched into a tight smile. Her eyes cast about for eavesdroppers. "Anton Stepanovich," her voice was hushed, "I need to talk to you this afternoon."

"Of course. Anytime."

"Meet me in the orangery immediately after your sister and Ippolit Filippovich depart."

As she walked away, he watched the little peach bows that covered the clasps of her gown, molding it against the curve of her spine. He pondered the cause of her urgency. Feona Ivanovna was eight years his senior, and her husband was fifteen years older than her. Perhaps her needs hadn't been satisfied in a while.

As Anton topped a cracker with red caviar, he surveyed the swell of people in the ballroom one last time. Despite the silks, satins, and brocades and the feathers, jade, and diamonds, no one captured his interest.

Anton took note of Yustina Rusakova reclining against a fluted pillar, her upturned face mawkishly sweet as she chatted with Stepan. The old man gazed at her with naked longing.

It was the identical pose Anton had stumbled upon during that silly Maximov Ball when he had gone outside to relieve his bladder and take a nip from his flask. The close posturing of his father and his mother's sole friend had caught the fourteen-year-old off guard, so he dallied to watch what else might happen. He hadn't been disappointed—the touching, the embrace, the kiss.

Anton gave a wry smile as he popped the caviar-laden cracker into his mouth and pictured his father humping his best pal's wife.

He left the tinkle of china and followed the drift of expensive tobacco leaf down a long corridor of thick Persian carpet. Past the alcoves filled with Petrine antiques and nude statues of Venus and Hercules, he found the double doors of the oak-paneled library.

The room stirred a nostalgia in Anton. Tiers of leather-bound books climbed from floor to ceiling, all tucked behind leaded glass cabinet doors with Wedgwood medallions. The air was steeped with the scent of cigars, brandy, wax, and leather, a combination Anton found second in appeal only to the scent of a woman. He had always been attracted to the life of the intellectual and had a long-standing image of himself sunk in a supple armchair in a nicely appointed sanctuary, debating politics with the best minds in Moscow.

Someday, he again pledged, he'd say good-bye to the flatness of country life and partake of the ambrosia the city had to offer. Someday.

While Rusakov's wife cooed at Stepan in the parlor, Vladimir, along with his radical son, had joined a group of a dozen men installed on the library's wing chairs and plump sofas. Victor was slouched in a cushioned chair, a miasma of cigarette smoke circling his head.

"So tell us, Sergei Stepanovich," the bridegroom was saying to his new brother-in-law, "as an up-and-coming member of the Guards, what are your thoughts on why the War went so badly for us?"

Anton sipped a glass of Benedictine, allowing the pungent spice-and-herb flavor to calm his irritation at an answer that was certain to be nothing but rubbish.

"I can tell you this much." Sergei swirled a snifter of brandy. "The shortcoming lies not with the Russian soldier. He never falters, no matter in what part of the world he is put to the test and no matter against whom."

A.A. Gabrichevsky leaned forward over his paunch, one hand atop his elmwood cane and the other holding an ear horn ready at a moment's notice. "Things would have gone differently if the English and the French hadn't interfered with this War." Over the years, Gabrichevsky had become even more enamored with the sound of his own voice, which boomed now that he was hard of hearing.

Sergei offered his insights into military strategy. "The English and the French betrayed us through their alliance with Satan." He gave an energetic nod, as if in firm agreement with himself.

Oh, good God. Anton ran a finger along the inside of the stiff collar that stood at attention above his blue satin cravat. Sergei possessed the intellectual capacity of a stump. Like Russia's fabled Army, the coxcomb was all veneer and no substance.

An assured voice stated, "Russia's casualties extend far beyond the battlefields. Her ultimate wound is the loss of standing among other nations." The speaker was Natalya's new father-in-law, Filip Ilyich Gabrichevsky. "The whole of Russia had its roof torn off and was exposed for what it is."

Several voices asked what he meant.

"For one thing, our bitter defeat revealed the weakness of having an Army composed largely of peasants." Filip twisted a curled end of his moustache. "There are those who say to move east from Europe into Russia is to go backward in time."

Victor Rusakov sprang to life. "And behind it will stay . . . unless our new Tsar has the fortitude to make the changes his father didn't."

"May the memory of Nicholas be forever blessed." Old Man Gabrichevsky crossed himself with the hand holding the ear horn.

Victor's chin rose in belligerence. "When Nicholas died, a sore was taken out of the eye of humanity."

The men inhaled collectively. Like a dozen brooms, their eyes swept over one another. Vladimir sank into his armchair and hid his mortified face behind his hand.

The groom's father, however, remained unruffled. "Perhaps our bitter loss in the Crimea has handed the new Imperial Majesty the opportunity to make changes. Some believe once he gets his feet under him, he'll pursue a domestic policy diametrically opposed to that of his father."

"He's already started," Anton said. "Certainly you've read the recent statement he made at an assembly of the Moscow nobility." He was referring to Alexander II's worrisome declaration, *It is better to abolish serfdom from above than to wait for it to abolish itself from below.*

Natalya's new husband almost spewed out his Benedictine. "You don't think he'll actually emancipate the serfs?"

"A Western wind is blowing into Russia." Victor's tone was low and defiant. "If Alexander Nikolaevich has the intelligence of even a peahen, he will understand it's blowing in great gusts against the relic of bondage." He took a long draw on his cigarette and arched his neck to exhale like a smokestack toward the coffered ceiling.

"Bah!" Old Man Gabrichevsky thumped the malachite tip of his cane into the Persian carpet. "There's been talk about freeing the serfs my entire life. It'll never happen."

Victor's composure splintered. He planted both feet on the floor and pitched his torso forward. Blistering malice infused his voice. "Human rights should not be conferred by society or state. They are inalienable by virtue of being born." He swiped aside the grimy hair that fell over his eyes. "As it stands now, the serfs are as trapped as animals in a pen."

"Please, Victor, don't get up a scene." Vladimir appeared ready to crawl under his chair.

The room fell silent. Anton watched Sergei open his mouth as if to speak, flop his tongue about, then—thank Heaven—clap his lips closed.

Filip Gabrichevsky, ever the mediator, took control. "We gentry don't like hearing what the young man says, but he has a point. The informed mind will have to accept that unfree labor will never work well or honestly. Russia's economy is being mortally wounded by the institution of serfdom."

"But what would we do without serfs?" Glasses slammed onto end tables. Fists pounded knees. Men itched to leap from their seats.

Filip removed a leather tobacco pouch from his coat pocket. "We may not like it, but I'm afraid reform is inevitable. And reform is always risky business."

AFTER THE TUNISIAN doves were released in the ballroom, the bride went upstairs to change into her traveling outfit, which included a monstrously large crinoline with rigid birdcage hoops.

Despite hours of practice, Natalya had a devil of a time fitting her enormous hoops though the door of the carriage. After two failed attempts to back in, she attacked the door headfirst, giving the appearance of a peacock contending with the wind. Once inside the carriage, the understructure puffed out like a vast cloud and took up one whole seat, leaving Ippolit to sit opposite his bride.

Anton found the crinoline fashion to be intensely seductive when it revealed tantalizing glimpses of legs as it swung in walking or was lifted for stairs. To achieve the desirable hourglass figure, tight corsets hindered breathing such that the bosom panted upon the slightest exertion. Anton regarded the movement as not in the least disagreeable.

Which reminded him of his engagement in the orangery. He set off in search of Feona Ivanovna's breasts.

CHAPTER 28

Elizaveta

1856

Who fleeces the living and
the dead alike?

A priest.

ELIZAVETA POURED THE scalding water into the washtub and added an armful of raw wool. Steam billowed from the tub and, in the cool May air of the izba's workyard, condensed in little droplets on her face. She was pleased. The hotter the water, the better the grease would be removed. The wool would soak overnight. Then, in the morning, she'd spread it out in the shade for drying. As she walked toward the izba, she pressed her hands against the constant ache in the small of her back.

The bread needed more time in the oven, so she sank into the rocking chair and massaged her muscles against its back. Except for the occasional pop of an ember in the stove, there was only silence. She swathed herself in the blissful luxury of being alone in her own home.

The last traces of snow had melted, and outdoor chores scattered the Vorontsovs in different directions. Ermak and Grigorii were hauling manure to fields. Uncle Stanislav was hollowing out a split log to serve as a new laundry trough. Stanislav's wife was collecting birch leaves to use for dyeing linen. Their son Onufrii was gathering strips of linden tree bark to weave into bast shoes.

Meanwhile, Elizaveta had the serenity of solitude. Serenity and a half-filled feeling of contentment was the best she could hope for. Especially now that Feodor was married.

He finally had taken a bride after years of being goaded with sayings such as *"A bachelor is a goose without water"* and *"A man without a wife is a man out in January without a fur cap."*

Three years ago, he married a pretty, hardworking girl with an impeccable reputation. Although she was a bit young for someone of Feodor's age, any man would have welcomed her as his bride.

Despite being sick at heart at the wedding reception, Elizaveta had put forth a smile, albeit a stiff one. She'd kissed the radiant bride on both cheeks, then recited the bright and bouncy words she had rehearsed.

"I've known Feodor since we were toddlers. If you need advice on how to keep that rascal in line, just ask me!" She gave the girl a conspiratorial, woman-to-woman wink, but was unable to meet Feodor's eyes. She backed away from the newlyweds and, wholly out of character, proceeded to toss back vodka until she hiccupped her way home.

Nikifor Zhemchuzhnikov didn't live long enough to see his eldest son married. At the time of the engagement, the cold, rainy spring had already settled in his lungs, and he coughed his way through the labors of summer. He continued to weaken until his soul quit his body at the first sharp bite of autumn air. Although the entire village felt the loss of the man who consistently demonstrated both wisdom and fairness, they whispered among themselves that the Zhemchuzhnikovs should have never planted those potatoes in their kitchen garden. God had sought His retribution.

For weeks after Nikifor's death, Elizaveta's father had pulled at his beard as he wept beside the grave of his lifelong friend. The following year, Erafei bore another heartbreak when his youngest son vanished into thin air in the Crimea. Putting his faith in the rumor that the Tsar would free any serf who volunteered for the War, the boy marched out of Petrovo. Alongside him was the younger of Uncle Stanislav's two sons. During the two years they'd been gone, not a word was heard from or about them. Both families mourned their loss, presuming the boys were departed souls.

Elizaveta's eyes closed as her head dropped against the back of the chair. All in all, the past year had been much better than the previous three. Grain was still piled high from last summer's plentiful harvest. Months had passed since Ermak had felt the need to discipline her. Enough time had gone by since her string of pregnancies that she was feeling motherly tenderness toward the child growing in her womb. So certain was she that the baby was a boy, she had already named him.

Elizaveta expected Zinovy to be born around the same time her little sister Yulia would have her second child. Six years ago, the red-headed widower Demian Osokin had taken Yulia as his bride, and he still couldn't keep his eyes off her. The scorn he had experienced as a youngster engendered the slender-framed, ginger-haired man with compassion and humility. He cherished Yulia, who returned his love unequivocally.

Last autumn, Uncle Stanislav's Onufrii married a girl who proved to be a diligent worker, was as quiet as a mouse, and appeared content to acquiesce to the Vorontsovs' high-handedness.

Later that same month, another wedding ensued that whipped the villagers' tongues into a frenzied clacking. Out of the blue, Evdokim Seleznyov announced that his only child, the widowed Zhanna, would marry Illarion Loktev. Petrovo's stunned peasants accused Seleznyov of casting pearls before swine. Why take an incurable liar for a son-in-law, particularly when his man parts were rumored to be out of whack ever since he smeared lye on his sac to avoid military conscription?

Speculation coursed through the izbas. How long had Zhanna been married before her husband died of cholera? Eight years? Why no children? Was she barren? Maybe Seleznyov's true motive had nothing to do with propagating offspring. Everyone knew Seleznyov was tired of the tavern's late nights and drunken brawls. Perhaps Illarion was a good business match. His penchant for gossip would draw business into the tavern and allow aging Selezynov more time to soak up the warmth of the stove.

While one palm caressed her swollen belly, Elizaveta's other hand stroked the smooth wooden arm of the chair. At an evening meal in February, her father-in-law had declared that he, Ermak, Grigorii, and Onufrii would build a chair like the one he had sat on while in a pawn shop during his previous trip to Sukhanovo. The announcement caught everyone off guard, none more so than his three helpers.

Sidor described how the chair pitched forward and backward on wooden legs the shape of crescent moons. The store clerk had told him that the motion was quite wholesome for unborn children. Elizaveta's baby was due at the end of summer, and Onufrii's wife surely would provide him with a son within a year or two. And the Vorontsovs always held on to a glimmer of hope that Avdotya might perform her womanly duty.

"It's called a rocking chair," Sidor explained. "And it will be the envy of the entire village! I doubt even the Maximovs have such a chair!"

At the Easter meal, the rocking chair was presented to the family with a prodigious flourish. It was devoid of embellishments, had rockers that were a bit choppy when set into motion, and possessed a tendency to flip backwards if propelled too enthusiastically in that direction. Nevertheless, it was the first true chair to enter the Vorontsov izba. Rarely was it empty, leaving Elizaveta and her expanding belly to sit on a bench.

Today's heat from the stove caressed Elizaveta's face while the chair responded to the languid rhythm of her bare feet as they rose and fell against the plank floor. For the moment, she was as cozy as if she were on Christ's bosom.

Elizaveta's peace of mind chilled. Was that a spider crawling down the wall? A spider crawling up the wall foretold of good fortune, but one crawling down the wall . . . Elizaveta shooed away the omen. It was too nice a day for bad news to come knocking.

She gripped the arms of the chair and pushed herself up. She had dallied as long as she could in the izba's luscious quiet. The bread was finished baking. And she needed to help her mother-in-law and Avdotya at the river, where they were bleaching newly woven hemp cloth and keeping an eye on Elizaveta's children.

Elizaveta frowned as she slid the long-handled, wooden bread shovel into the oven. The loaves' crusts were tilted toward the rear of the stove, a sign that misfortune was on its way. First the spider. Now the misshapen loaves. Elizaveta vowed to watch her step the rest of the day.

She followed the trail of laughter to a small cove where the water spread out and formed languid eddies. Dozens of youngsters were loosely supervised by women who were washing clothes or bathing small children in hollowed-out logs. She spotted the sun-streaked hair of Ilya and Gerasim as they stood at the water's edge with their pals, their trousers rolled up and fishing lines cast into the river. Serafima was sitting with her girlfriends, their toes wiggling in the spring-cool water and their heads bent in serious discussion. Anna was engaged in a carefree frenzy of blind man's bluff with a covey of five- and six-year-olds.

Elizaveta joined Avdotya beneath a misshapen willow tree that bowed toward the water courtesy of an unrelenting wind. She couldn't help but feel a poignant reverence toward the old tree. Its long, drooping branches had provided a shaded canopy where she, Katya, and Feodor had whiled away hours upon hours of their childhood.

"Where's Vera?" Elizaveta asked Avdotya.

Avdotya's eyes and mouth tightened with exasperation, an expression she never allowed any of the Vorontsovs except Elizaveta to witness. "She went to her sister's izba to help her. She said she'd come right back. But she didn't."

Bleaching required more than one woman. Thirty or forty pieces of material were placed in a cauldron and covered with a piece of old material. Wood ashes were spread on top, followed by the addition of twenty pails of boiling water, which had been heated in another large pot. When the water in the cauldron grew cold, the plug was pulled and the ash water was collected in a wooden bucket for reheating. After two dozen or so repetitions, weary arms rinsed, beat, and spread the linen out to dry. The process took as many hours as there was daylight, and the women's backs and shoulders ached for days afterward.

Elizaveta was filling the cauldron when her daughter stepped up. Anna's arms were extended straight forward, one hand cupped over the other.

"Look, Mamasha. I saved her." The hands opened ever so slightly to reveal a dragonfly. Its iridescent wings fluttered, and the hands snapped closed.

"You did what?" Elizaveta scowled. What was her youngest child gibbering about?

"She was drowning, and I saved her."

Elizaveta heaved a weary sigh. Anna taxed her mother's patience to the limit. The girl gushed with tenderness and didn't possess a spoon's worth of practical sense.

Anna continued her babbling. "I know she's a girl, because she's so beautiful."

"What do you plan to do with her?" Elizaveta hated the irritation she heard in her own voice.

Anna nibbled her lower lip as she scoured the options first to her right and then to her left. She had performed the charitable act without thought of a subsequent next step. "Ummm, I'll put her on those reeds over there. Would that be good?"

"Yes, that would be good."

Her mother's sanction of the plan unfurled Anna's bow-shaped mouth into a smile, which immediately withered when Elizaveta added, "Don't rescue any more."

Elizaveta watched her daughter walk to the reeds as warily as if she were carrying a filled-to-the-brim mug of kvass. She feared a child with such a gentle spirit would be too fragile for life's harshness. Anna would have to toughen up if she were to survive.

When she had been a toddler, Anna's older brothers found her sitting on a hen's nest. They ridiculed her mercilessly. Anna sniveled that she didn't want the unhatched babies to freeze while the hen was off the nest. And just the other day, she cried a river when told to collect the eggs from the chicken house. She said it wasn't fair to steal from the mother hen. Elizaveta had once again reminded her, "No one said life was fair."

Today Elizaveta studied her peculiar youngest child as the dragonfly was tenderly released on the tallest of the reeds. Not only was Anna one of the few blue-eyed blondes in a village of dark-eyed brunettes, but the teardrop birthmark also set her apart from all the other villagers. When neighbor children mocked her birthmark, tears of hurt would stream down her face, and Elizaveta would yet again issue her customary admonishment about life's unfairness.

"There's Varlaam Gorbunov." Avdotya's voice was hushed as she bent next to Elizaveta and set down a basket of wet linen.

"Who?"

"Varlaam Gorbunov, the holy beggar."

Elizaveta lifted a hand to shield her eyes from the glaring sunlight. Walking toward them was a tall, gaunt man wearing trousers floured with dust and faded with age. His linen shirt was cinched at the waist with a sash. He carried his head high and purposefully.

During the past two days, word had raced through the village about the arrival of a holy beggar. He was a self-proclaimed man of God who was continuously on the move, traveling on foot from one end of Russia to the other, accompanied only by his knapsack and a walking stick. The women at the well had already labeled him pious to the point of mysticism, and they speculated he could predict the future.

"Varlaam Gorbunov," Avdotya called, "good day to you!"

"Good day to you, Avdotya. And the Lord be with you." The slender man reached for Avdotya's hand with both of his and brought it to his lips.

"Varlaam Gorbunov, this is my sister-in-law, Elizaveta Vorontsova."

His penetrating scrutiny pierced Elizaveta like a knife thrust through the soft belly of a fish. "And the Lord be with you, Elizaveta Vorontsova." As he had done with Avdotya, Gorbunov raised Elizaveta's hand. For the first time in her life, a man's lips brushed her knuckles.

Taken aback, Elizaveta stammered, "I understand you're staying in Avdotya's parents' barn."

The man stroked his tatty beard as he turned his gaze onto Avdotya. "Yes, Avdotya's virtuous family has kindly taken me in and treated me with the same generosity they would grant to a saint."

"There are some who say you are a saint in disguise." Avdotya's cheeks flushed with color.

"I am nothing but a holy pilgrim who wanders from pillar to post across the expanse of Mother Russia, befriending all I can along the way."

Sharing Petrovo's communal suspicion of strangers, Elizaveta wasted no time taking stock of the reedy man, whom she judged to be a couple of years older than her own age of thirty. Other than being as dark as a gypsy, Gorbunov's most predominant feature was his eyes, which were set on a ledge of high cheekbones over sucked-in cheeks. One eye was covered with a milky film. The other was dark, its iris the color of midnight. His sighted eye rarely blinked and never wandered from its item of interest.

A forked beard rippled down to the middle of his chest, the slit in the middle revealing a silver cross hanging by a chain around his neck. His brown hair was parted down the center and hung loose below his shoulders like a priest's. The scraggly locks were tucked behind his ears, which themselves were most unusual. They lay flat against the sides of his head, like those of a dog readying itself for a fight. Also as with a dog's ears, their tops were not rounded peaks or tapered arches, but pointed like the tip of a spear.

Avdotya told Elizaveta, "Tomorrow, I plan to take Father Varlaam to meet the nuns and minister to the orphans."

"*Father* Varlaam? You're a priest?" Elizaveta asked.

Gorbunov shook his head from side to side, but his good eye remained fixed on Elizaveta. "No. I am only a holy fool wandering about the face of Russia. But some people refer to me as 'Father' because I have dedicated my life to God's will."

Elizaveta felt an innate distrust of the man. "So you've never been to a monastery?"

"Only to visit. And to learn."

"To learn what?"

"To learn how to best be a disciple of Christ. To learn about virtue." His voice was both subdued and strongly compelling at the same time. "You see, I'm already familiar with all there is to know about sin."

Unsettled by his disconcerting statement and the smoldering embers lurking behind his good eye, Elizaveta knelt to stoke the fire under the ash water.

"And what about you? Are you already a mother?" His unblinking eye swept to her enlarged belly.

"I have four children. This will be the seventh I've borne."

"Then you've already given two up to the Lord."

Elizaveta rose from the fire. "My first died shortly after birth. And my son when he was but a half year."

"I should like to visit their graves. Is there space beside them for the others in the family?" Receiving Elizaveta's nod of stunned silence, he continued, "We shall all visit their graves before long."

"We'll go to the cemetery tomorrow on the way to the orphanage," Avdotya said, as if Gorbunov's comment wasn't at all odd.

He diverted his attention from Elizaveta back to Avdotya. "I look forward to it." He bent and kissed Avdotya's hand farewell—first its back, then the palm. He gave Elizaveta a shallow bow and, upon straightening, stared long and hard into her eyes. She again felt the sensation of being pierced by something sharp and deadly. He poked his stringy long hair behind his wolflike ears.

Once he was out of earshot, Elizaveta said, "Why did he ask if there was room beside them for the rest of the family? And what did he mean by 'We shall all visit their graves'?"

Avdotya's stick began swirling the linen in the cauldron. "I'm sure he was referring to the inevitable, that we'll all end up in the grave sooner or later."

"No, he said we'd all visit their graves 'before long.'"

"Don't take it so personally. After all, I'm part of your family, and I'm not the least worried."

Elizaveta closed her eyes to get a clear image of the self-ordained holy man, but all she could picture was his unabashed, enigmatic, one-eyed stare. Her lids snapped open.

"He's scary. Why did your parents ever agree to let him stay with them?"

"Because my parents see him as a man of God who should be treated accordingly." Avdotya's voice was tinted with uncharacteristic impatience, and her normally hooded eyes were bright with passion.

When the two women had accomplished as much as their strength and the sun's fading light would allow, Elizaveta sent Avdotya home. "I'll wait while this final batch dries. Send one of the men down with the cart to haul the cauldron home."

The night insects began to croon, and the bank emptied of everyone except Elizaveta and a few frogs plopping into the river. Yet none of the Vorontsovs fetched the cauldron. Elizaveta faced a dilemma. She couldn't leave the pot for someone to steal, yet it was too heavy for her to lug. Eventually, she walked home without it.

When Elizaveta opened the door to the izba, her basket of linen fell to the floor. Avdotya was bent over the table, her skirt bunched over her shoulders. The side of her face was crammed into the table's boards by a hairy paw. Stanislav's trousers were around his ankles.

"Bastard!"

Elizaveta seized the stirrer stick she had used to mix the bread dough and attacked Stanislav about the head as he tugged at his trousers. Elizaveta got one good blow to Stanislav's face before he deflected her thrashing. Whacking his arm, the stirrer's wooden cross snapped off and clattered to the floor. Elizaveta drove the broken end toward his eyes. It grazed his eyebrow, making a thin pink line. She stabbed the jagged stick again. And again. She'd spear out his eye. Both eyes! She'd blind the vile piece of shit!

A hand came from behind her and seized her wrist. In the blink of an eye, her arm was wrenched behind her back. Pain seared from her wrist up to her shoulder. She twisted her neck around and saw Ermak's face, hideous with rage.

Stanislav's open palm struck her exposed cheek, propelling her head around further. The bones in her neck cracked. Ermak yanked off her kerchief and grabbed her hair. While she thrashed, he marched her, arm still contorted behind her back, to the izba's wall. He slammed her forehead against the boards. A bonfire of sparks filled her head.

He pulled her head back and crashed it a second time against the wall.

CHAPTER 29

Elizaveta

1856

Who wasn't born,
yet died?

Adam and Eve.

WHEN ELIZAVETA PRIED her eyes open, the room was dark except for a burning splinter. Its dull light sent swells of nausea over her. A hand gripped hers. A small hand. A woman's hand.

"Avdotya?"

"Yes, darling, it's me." As Avdotya leaned forward, the rocking chair creaked, shooting thunderbolts of pain through Elizaveta's head.

Why did she feel worse than she'd ever felt in her life? Images came to her in bits and pieces. Avdotya slammed against the table. Vile Stanislav. Ermak's brutality.

She pinched her eyelids shut. Avdotya took something from her forehead. Elizaveta heard the dribble of water, then the rag was replaced across her brow. Its wet coolness offered solace.

"Go to sleep," Avdotya murmured.

Yes, numbing sleep.

When next she woke, Avdotya was still in the rocking chair. Her head tilted to one side, and rhythmic breaths fluttered from her slack mouth.

Even the moonlight coming through the window, dim as it was, made the blood pound in Elizaveta's head. She laid a hand on her pulsating forehead.

How could she continue to live in this madhouse?

Grief battered her head, making the room spin crazily. She sucked in a deep breath, giving rise to a pain that sliced through her belly like the blade of an ax. She slid her hand under the sheepskin blanket, onto her stomach.

"My baby!"

Elizaveta's cry woke Avdotya. She moved from the rocking chair to the edge of the sleeping bench. "Shush. You'll wake the family."

"Where?" Elizaveta pleaded.

Avdotya slipped a hand under the blanket. Her fingers intertwined Elizaveta's. "Your baby's gone."

"No!" The single word was like a wolf's howl into the night.

"Shush."

"Tell me."

With halting words, Avdotya recounted how Elizaveta's contractions came after she passed out. Fortunately, Vera returned to the izba and ordered Stanislav and Ermak to carry Elizaveta to the bathhouse while Avdotya fetched Father Diakonov.

Little Zinovy was dead! The baby Ermak created, then killed!

Elizaveta turned her face toward the wall. She saw the piercing black eye of the holy beggar. *Is there space beside them for the others in the family? We shall all visit their graves before long.* Had he truly known this would happen? *Others.* Were more to die? Oh, Holy Savior, who next?

Elizaveta swiveled her head back toward the timorous woman. "Thank you, Avdotya."

Avdotya's thin-boned hand tightened around Elizaveta's. "I'm the one who owes you. For trying to save me from . . . from . . ."

"If only I had gotten home sooner . . ."

Avdotya pulled both lips inward and pressed them against her teeth. Elizaveta felt there was more that wasn't being said.

"What is it? Avdotya, what?"

"You rest. We'll talk later."

Elizaveta took a mental inventory of her body. She wiggled her toes, moved her legs, ran her tongue over her teeth. "The children? Did that son of Satan hurt my children?"

"No, no." Avdotya put a finger to her lips. "Shhhh."

With what little strength she had, Elizaveta squeezed Avdotya's hand. "If you love me like a true sister, you'll tell me."

Avdotya's eyes were pools of misery as she told the story.

Upon hearing what happened to his daughter, Erafei Anafrev had flown into a frenzy and threatened to kill Ermak. When his wife and Uncle Artamon and Aunt Marina tried to keep him from leaving the izba, he turned red in the face and fell over.

"Fell over?"

Avdotya hung her head and stared at the skirt she was twisting into tight knots.

"You mean . . . you mean . . ." Elizaveta clutched Avdotya's arm. "Dead?"

Avdotya's thin shoulders trembled.

"Ahhhhh," Elizaveta wailed, not caring if she woke up the whole village. "Oh, God, not Papa!" She felt the cool hands of Avdotya trying to soothe her, but she wasn't interested in being soothed. She wanted to release her agony over the miserable life to which she'd been condemned. She needed to announce to the world how unfair it all was.

Poor Papasha! He should have had the opportunity to reap the benefits of having conquered the hardships of life. Deprivation, disease, endless toil—he had withstood them all. His final years should have been spent with less time laboring in the fields and more time soaking his bones with the heat from the stove. He should have seen every last one of his grandchildren be brought into this world.

As she wailed into the night, only one Vorontsov rose to offer comfort. Her mother-in-law cradled Elizaveta's head in her arm and tilted a cup to her lips. "Sip this."

Elizaveta flung her arm against Vera's. The wooden cup sailed across the room and bounced on the floor.

"I want Ermak Vorontsov dead! He killed my child! He killed my father!" She didn't care that Ermak was Vera's son. She wanted his life just as he had taken the lives of those she loved.

Vera recoiled from Elizaveta and climbed onto her sleeping bench above the stove. At some point, Avdotya had disappeared into the darkness. Elizaveta mourned alone.

CHAPTER 30

Elizaveta

1856

From the front I am a man,
but from behind I am a woman.
What am I?

A priest.

HER BATTERED BODY craved sleep, but ghoulish nightmares drained her further. Babies were tossed into graves while the cryptic eye of the holy beggar silently screamed, "I warned you!"

Jagged spears of lightning lit up the gray sky the afternoon of her father's interment. Elizaveta was alone in the Vorontsov izba, incapable of attending either the burial or the funeral repast at the Anafrevs'. The storm-darkened room flickered with two candles saved from the Church services the previous Epiphany. Vera lit them before leaving for the funeral as a divine safeguard to protect the wood-and-thatch izba from lightning.

Elizaveta's fists pounded her sleeping bench. How unfair that she was trapped here, unable to see her own flesh and blood being handed over to the next world. Meanwhile, Ermak, who, in Elizaveta's mind, had killed his father-in-law the same as if he had stabbed him with a knife, sanctimoniously watched the coffin being placed into the earth before gorging himself at the memorial supper.

Fourteen years ago she had been transferred from a loving family into a house of horrors with no escape. How many more savage assaults could she withstand? What if someday he killed her? Oh, yes, the village assembly would find him guilty of excessive discipline, but what good would that do? If she were to die, who would protect her children?

She wiped away her tears with the back of her hand and looked into the dimness of the rafters. She felt the roof descending like the lid of her own coffin. Voices of the dead called to her. Her father. Mother. Grandparents. Youngest brother. Newborn daughter. Little Mitya. Unborn Zinovy.

Ermak is the one who should be wrapped in a burial shroud, she seethed. *Along with his evil uncle. And may both their black souls rot in Hell!*

A fist pounded on the door. *Go away,* she mouthed silently as she rolled onto her side and faced the wall.

The hinges creaked. "Elizaveta, my poor child."

Her stomach churned at the low resonance of the holy beggar. "I'm sleeping. I'm sick."

The soles of his leather boots clumped across the wood floor. Pain shot up Elizaveta's neck as she turned toward Gorbunov. With each step, the boots' wet toes poked from beneath the heavy folds of his priestly habit. She raised her gaze to the imposing silver cross that beamed on his chest, its bottom reaching almost to his belted waist. Two eyes, one milky, one penetrating, stared down at her.

"My sad, sad woman. I read people's hearts, and I know yours is weeping. Permit me to help you sit up."

Gorbunov put a hand under each of her arms. As he hoisted her to a sitting position, the hay jabbed and scratched the backs of her thighs and calves. Her back rested against the plank wall while her legs stretched out beneath the sheepskin blanket.

Gorbunov pulled a stool beside the bench, sat down, and tucked his long locks of dripping hair behind his peculiar wolf-ears. His eye drilled into her until she had to glance away.

"May I pray for you and the souls of your departed loved ones?" He spoke with velvety persuasion.

"I have no money in exchange for your prayers."

He raised a hand to silence her. "I come not for money. I wouldn't accept any from you, and what I get from others, I give away. You see, I've stripped myself of all earthly possessions and pretenses."

Despite his righteous words, an evil scent lingered about him. "Why are you here?" she asked.

"I came to offer what comfort I could. God told me of the burden he was going to place on you. All strength and all mercy come from Him." His eye, unblinking and unyielding, was trying to pierce her soul.

Thunder crashed overhead. Elizaveta shuddered. "You say you talk to God? Ask Him why He cursed me. Why He put this grief on me."

"Suffering is good in God's sight. It restores our reliance on Him. There is no one to depend on but the Lord God."

Elizaveta shook her hands, splayed like cat claws, beside her head. "If God is so merciful, why won't He leave my soul in peace!" The exertion nauseated her. She slid her hands back under the blanket and crossed her arms over her waist.

"God always provides the strength to bear our crosses. You need only ask Him. Tell me, Elizaveta Vorontsova, do you believe?"

"Of course I believe." Her lower lip stuck out in defiance.

"Then you must have faith in His mercy, for in Him alone can we find truth and peace." He stared at her, his eye a beacon of passion. "I see God's face. He is here." He brought up an arm to cover his heart. "And here, in this izba." He lifted his palms and his eyes toward the dusty roof beams.

"Why are you allowed to see God and the rest of us aren't?"

"Why was I chosen? I do not know." He bent so close to her, she felt his breath on her face. "But the Holy Virgin reached out Her hand one day and touched me, and revealed much that remains hidden to others." Like the Virgin's, his arm reached out until his hand rested on Elizaveta's shoulder. "I have never been the same."

The izba behind him was dark and obscure. His robe, his cross, his long hair, his pointed ears were merged together in a steamy haze. Only his glaring, hypnotic eye was distinct.

"I wish you wouldn't fight me. I wish you wouldn't fight God." He squeezed her shoulder before releasing it, then reached under the blanket and thrust his fingers into the clenched hollow of her palm. "In the end, His will always triumphs."

He leaned forward, closing in on her. Silver lightning flashed through the window, blanching half his face.

Elizaveta averted her eyes. "I'm tired. Please leave me alone."

"I want to get to know you very well, Elizaveta, before I go forth from this village. Will you allow me that?" When she didn't answer, he released her hand. "Sleep well, my child." His robes rustled as he rose from the stool.

When the izba was free of him, Elizaveta rubbed the palm of her hand against her sleeping shirt. That he'd touch her with such familiarity! The man was a fake. The filthy old fool was nothing more than an itinerant peddler whose wares included only himself.

Moments later, a knock again came at the door. Elizaveta set her jaw. She couldn't and wouldn't put up with any more of that phony holy man.

A voice emerged from the blackness like a dream. "Liza?"

Her blood, her strength, her thoughts all drained from her. "Feodor?" Did she dare allow herself to believe he was walking across the murky darkness?

CHAPTER 31

Elizaveta
1856

Two brothers:
one everyone sees but doesn't hear,
the other everyone hears but doesn't see.
Who are they?
Lightning and thunder.

"FEODOR?" SHE REPEATED, and winced at how ridiculous she sounded, like a crow cawing over and over. But his name was the only sound her tongue would make.

It had been an eternity since they had exchanged anything beyond the most fleeting of words. Now here he was, walking toward her as he wiped the rainwater from his face. Without thought, she reached an arm straight toward him, bidding him to come closer. It felt like a completely natural thing to do.

He took her outstretched hand in both of his, kicked aside Gorbunov's stool, and sat on the straw of her sleeping bench. "Liza, all of my sympathy goes to you."

He brought her hand to his mouth. It was kissed for the second time in less than a week. His gaze locked on hers, he bent forward the slightest amount, paused, then continued. She closed her eyelids and felt his lips on her forehead.

Oh, Feodor, she cried inside. *Take me in your arms and hold me. Take me into your world and away from mine.*

All too soon, she felt his body pull away. But he kept her hand secure in his. She opened her eyes and feasted on his face. His features, once baby-soft, were now angled, carved with life's hard lines. Although he was still lean, he bore no more semblance to a gangly scarecrow than a young turkey poult bore to a strutting tom.

She longed to trace her fingers across the etchings in his forehead and down the sinews of his neck. She wanted to feel the strength of his shoulders under her hands. She yearned to memorize the most insignificant details, so later she could rebuild the image in her heart.

"I hoped you'd be alone." His voice no longer cracked like a teenager's, but resonated with the surety of a man.

"You came at the right time. The holy beggar, Gorbunov, just left. He's nothing but a cunning imposter."

The twinkle in his eyes was amused and tender. "You were never one to hide your feelings."

"He's hustling handouts, that's all."

"Hustling handouts," Feodor repeated. "Oh, Liza, I've always loved how you never take things at face value, like the rest of the village does." His teeth tugged at his lower lip. "I know you're not well or else you'd have gone to the funeral. But are you feeling better?"

"Yes, a little. But in a way, I'm glad not to go to the funeral." The words blurted out without her knowing where they had come from.

Feodor's brow wrinkled in confusion. "What do you mean?"

She looked down at his hand, rough and calloused from work, and shook her head. "I don't know what I mean." When she looked up, the perfect sincerity of his eyes laid bare her very soul. Years and years ago when they were children, they had sworn never to lie to each other. Each had swallowed a small handful of dirt to seal their unbreakable promise. "I guess I mean I can't stand to be around the Vorontsovs."

"It's being said that . . ." His voice was hesitant and compassionate. "That your injuries are from Ermak." The tip of his finger gently glided the length of her twisted little finger. "He did this, too?"

She gave a single nod.

Sorrow overspread Feodor's face. "Liza." His hand moved to cover the misshapen finger from sight. "You can't live like this."

"What choice do I have." Rather than a question, it was a declaration of complete hopelessness.

His only response was the tightened corners of his jaw.

Elizaveta slipped her other hand over the back of his. "How I wish we were fifteen again." The hungry words echoed off the plank walls and the table and the whitewashed stove and everything Vorontsov.

His head fell forward, dropping his beard onto his chest and his gaze onto their overlapping hands. "I can't tell you how many nights I've thrashed about, searching for a way for us." His words became strangled. "I thought about it while working in the Count's distillery. While in the fields. Watching you from across the church. There simply isn't an answer. We're powerless to control our own lives."

He lifted his head and slid his free hand to cup the back of her neck. His thumb caressed her cheek as his eyes traveled over her face. "I need for you to understand, I had no choice but to marry. Mama, Papa, the Count, they were all pressuring me."

"I understand." All too well, she understood choicelessness and oppression and subservience.

"Not a day goes by that I don't wish you were the woman beside me."

Elizaveta was too much of a realist to think that today's words would change anything. But for the moment, it was enough to know that he had never stopped loving her.

Her head darted to one side. There was a movement outside the window. Elizaveta froze as she saw the face of the holy beggar peeking inside her window. Varlaam Gorbunov gave a jaunty wave and pointed to the door.

"It's that damn holy man," she whispered.

Feodor removed his hand from behind her neck and squeezed her fingers before releasing her hand from his.

Gorbunov stepped into the izba, rainwater running off him. "I tried knocking, but you couldn't hear me over the storm."

Elizaveta doubted the truth of that statement.

"I was halfway across the village when the rain came again, and I remembered I left my cloak here. I must have been too busy thinking about you, Elizaveta, and not thinking about myself." He squeezed the water out of his beard as he gazed at Feodor. "I'm Varlaam Gorbunov."

Feodor stood. "Feodor Nikiforovich Zhemchuzhnikov."

"I was here earlier to pray for our dear Elizaveta during this dark hour." His shrewd eye radiated barbed mirth. "Is that likewise why you are here?"

"I came to extend my sympathy. Elizaveta and I have been friends since childhood."

"Yes," she said with pluck. "Feodor's family and my birth family are very close. And Feodor is one of my dearest friends, one I seldom get to see."

Gorbunov stroked his beard. "A most interesting little village, I must say. I shall regret leaving it."

Leaving? Elizaveta liked the sound of that word. "When do you intend to go?"

"I don't know. Next week perhaps. Or next year. Nor do I know where I will go. Perhaps to the Crimea. There are rumors that peasants are needed to resettle the war-torn area and will be given their freedom if they do. They will require God's ministry. I need only listen, and God will tell me when to leave and which direction to go."

There was a clatter at the door as Avdotya entered with Elizaveta's daughters. The two girls shook themselves like ducks, flinging rainwater everywhere. Serafima averted her gaze from the holy man and busied herself at the stove while Anna walked over and stood patiently at the far end of Elizaveta's sleeping bench.

"Good afternoon, Father Varlaam," Avdotya said as she hung her jacket on a peg. "I didn't realize you were here."

"Feodor and I stopped by to give Elizaveta what comfort we could."

Elizaveta used Anna to get rid of the man. "Please excuse me. My daughter is waiting to tell me something."

Gorbunov bent forward to place his lips on her forehead. Elizaveta was certain he was mimicking what he had seen through the window. In a silky tone, he said, "Remember what I said, Elizaveta. In the end, God's will always triumphs." His breath lingered on her forehead.

He straightened and made the sign of the Cross over her. Avdotya was immediately by his side, taking his arm to lead him to his black cloak hanging beside the door.

Elizaveta told Anna, "Sit at the table 'til I'm done talking."

As the girl moved away, Feodor reseated himself on her sleeping bench and took one of Elizaveta's hands in each of his. He bent close, his low voice husky with emotion. "The holy beggar speaks at least some truth. In the end, God's will always triumphs. And I've always known"—he clamped down on her hands, tighter, and then yet tighter—"I've always known, in the very deepest part of me, His will is for us to be together." He pulled back. "I'm going now, so you can talk to your beautiful daughter."

Beautiful daughter? The words jolted her back to the reality of her world. "Beautiful?" she mouthed, her face scrunched in disbelief.

Feodor's eyes widened a sliver as his head cocked ever so slightly. His voice was a whisper. "Oh, Liza, certainly you don't listen to the malicious meddling of others? She's not marked by the Devil."

"Whether it's the mark of the Devil or not, everyone thinks it is."

Feodor reflected a moment. "I have two things to say to you. First, she's a fine girl, every bit as fine as Serafima and every bit as fine as your first daughter had she lived."

Elizaveta started to speak, but he silenced her with a raised hand.

"Second, of this whole village, my father and I are the only ones who've traveled beyond the district capital. I told you this before, many years ago. Remember? The world is very big, much bigger than any of us can imagine. And its people have many different beliefs. The prejudice and injustice your daughter faces are not the result of any shortcomings in her or in you. It's due to the small minds of the people in this small village—peasants who needlessly cling to their fears."

Even as a boy, Feodor had spoken from principle and not from cursory judgments. And he was still incapable of anything except untainted truth. And she still loved him for it.

"Thank you, Feodor. And as I told you many years ago, I'm forever grateful for your clear vision and for your kindness."

He squeezed her hands, then released them.

The moment Feodor left her side, the reed-thin girl was at her mother's elbow. Her blue eyes were ready to spill tears of empathy. "Mamasha, I'm so sorry for you."

Elizaveta reached for the hand of her kindhearted child. "Thank you, Anna."

"I'm sad for Grandpapa and for the baby."

"I'm very sad, too, but I'm glad I have you with me." Elizaveta wanted to hug her youngest child, but she was too exhausted and too sore. She pulled Anna forward and gave her a kiss on her cheek.

Anna straightened and chewed on her lower lip. "Is your baby dead like Martishka?"

"Who's Martishka?"

"Cousin Lukeria's cloth baby." Lukeria was the daughter of Elizaveta's sister Katya.

Elizaveta's mind was tired and so full of Feodor, she couldn't grasp what the girl was saying. "Martishka is Lukeria's cloth baby? And she's dead?"

"I think she's dead, like our baby. She got busted open and her straw fell out."

Elizaveta wasn't in the mood to discuss dead babies made of old rags. She wanted to go over and over in her mind everything Feodor had said while he was here, before any of it slipped away. He had been next to her, in that very divot of hay. She put her hand on the spot. It was still warm.

She dragged her attention back to her daughter. "Cloth babies don't die, honey. They get ripped or torn or broken. Things that have never been alive can't die."

"Then I guess Martishka is broken, not dead."

"Did you try to help Lukeria fix Martishka?"

"No. But I helped Lukeria cry."

Visions of Feodor slipped away as Elizaveta looked at the fragile, compassionate girl. Tears stung her own eyes. Her arms opened wide to her daughter. Anna scrambled onto the bench. As the little girl pressed against her mother, Elizaveta's cheeks became wet with a million silent tears. What Anna supplied Lukeria was exactly what Elizaveta needed.

Someone to help her cry.

CHAPTER 32

Maximov

1856

In the city is a tsar.
The tsar has many warriors.
Each warrior has a spear.
What city is this?

A beehive.

ANTON STARTED THE day the same as he had every day for the past four months: He examined his penis. At Natalya's wedding, Feona Ivanovna hadn't been in pursuit of a little romp beneath the nectarine trees in Old Man Gabrichevsky's hothouse. Rather, she wanted to let him know that her husband was under the private care of a physician in St. Petersburg.

"Just a little problem with the French pox. I thought it best to let you know because of our . . . well . . . just in case . . . well . . . you understand. I trust my divulgence will go no further."

Anton's peace of mind remained intact—this morning his pecker looked as serviceable as ever. Although he was panting for a visit to St. Petersburg, receiving months of gruesome mercury injections wasn't what he had in mind. Besides being costly both financially and to one's reputation, the treatment wasn't always successful and its side effects were hideous.

Outside his bedroom door, Matriusha was telling his mother that she had just seen the cat washing its face and purring at the same time, a sure sign the expected visitors would arrive today. The Shelgunovs had written that they planned to stop in Petrovo for a few days in early September while on their return from Orenburg to Moscow.

Anton heard Sophia's slippers shuffle to her bedroom, presumably so she could change from her nightclothes into more suitable attire, though undoubtedly of a bygone fashion.

Much to the nanny's smug satisfaction, Stepan's cousin Valeryan, his wife, and their youngest daughter, Nadya, arrived as predicted, in time to share the Maximovs' midday meal. While the Shelgunovs were upstairs brushing the road dust from their clothes, their hosts gathered around the table. Anton amused himself by contemplating the rounded derrière of Dasha the housegirl, as she stretched over the table to place the trivets for the forthcoming dishes. He appreciated a robust set of hips on a woman. His carnal deliberation lingered on the past and future entertainment offered by those particular buttocks. When Dasha moved beside him to light the candelabra, his hand reached below the white tablecloth and stroked her calf.

The spread of roast goose and fresh perch with six side dishes was excessive for the few people seated around the half-empty table. Natalya and Sergei lived in St. Petersburg. The Shelgunovs' son Rodya had died of the bloody flux while serving in the War. Their oldest daughter Sonya remained in Moscow finalizing her wedding arrangements.

As they overburdened their stomachs with a dessert of ginger cake dribbled with thick cream, Stepan queried whether the visitors would like to do anything in particular while at Petrovo.

"I'd like to ride in the canoe, Cousin Stepan," Nadya said.

Anton gave a dip of his head. "A fine suggestion. And most assuredly one we'll carry out."

"Is that old thing still seaworthy?" Valeryan asked. "We whittled on that log, what, nine or ten years ago?"

"Papa saysh it was made the spring before I was born, so twelve years ago," Elena lisped. "And I use it all the time." Half her mouth was deadened by the toothache powder applied to an erupting back molar. Plus, yesterday's bee sting had provoked that section of her upper lip to blossom to the size of a maraschino cherry.

Anton couldn't help but notice that sixteen-year-old Cousin Nadya had also blossomed—like wildflowers after a rain. The bodice of her pink frock traced her developing figure, while the outer layers of her skirts were a delicate, misty film that begged his eyes to speculate what lay beneath.

"Perhaps you two young ladies would like to rest for an hour after eating?" Anton poured his most glorious smile over Nadya. "Then we'll embark upon a scenic voyage to the far reaches of the pond!"

Nadya's shimmering smile matched his.

TO COOL HIS heels, Anton retreated to the stable, specifically to a small, informal office Stepan had cobbled together from two horse stalls. The cubbyhole housed a few bottles and tins of equine medicines; a secondhand, mostly empty gun case; a small woodstove; and the wobbly, square table that had been in the kitchen when Anton was a child. It also contained an old wall cupboard in which Anton kept a stash of libations for those occasions when either he was too lazy to go to the house or he wanted to drink on the sly.

As Anton dropped onto a chair, something nudged his elbow. He extended his hand, palm up. The goat wrapped his lips around the chunk of carrot.

"Here. The cook also sent you this." Anton handed Vaska the stump of a loaf of stale bread.

Anton leaned back in his chair and planted both boot heels on the old tabletop. Never a single day went by that his father didn't infuriate him. During today's meal, Stepan had made a snide remark to Valeryan about Anton's inability to make a connection between work and income. Yesterday's badgering was that Anton had no more interest in earning a living than a peasant had in fixing a leaking roof.

Just wait, you contrary old fool, I'll show you, Anton silently vowed. *Sure, I've had a string of bad luck lately at the card tables, but that's about to change. I'll cast off this countryside and its stagnant eighteenth-century mores, and I'll live in Moscow and rub elbows with progressive, forward-looking men. And I'll travel, travel to places you've never even heard of. There's a huge world out there with an abundance of pleasures, and I intend to sample—*

"Your herdsman said I could find you in here." The unexpected caller was Veniamin Savelyevich Pichshenko, the chief inspector for the enterprise that purchased Petrovo's vodka.

Anton lowered one of his legs and kicked a chair away from the table. "Have a seat." He casually recrossed his ankles.

Pichshenko took the indicated chair. "By all means, please don't get up on my account."

"If you insist." As he did with most people, Anton had a cordial relationship with the short, middle-aged man. A cunningly ambitious fellow with a glib tongue, Pichshenko had muscled his way up from the role of a ward agent to a lofty position of authority in the 120-employee business. Anton regarded him as a crow dressed in peacock feathers.

"I was passing through and thought I'd stop to see how things are on the estate." Pichshenko eyed the creature nuzzling his fingers. "I must say, you and your father are certainly fond of that goat."

"He's a nuisance, to be sure. Show him your empty hands, and he'll go away."

Pichshenko gladly obliged. "Speaking of your father, how is he?"

Anton downed his brandy and poured another. "My father is the same as ever, thank you very much." He lifted his glass toward Pichshenko. "If you care to join me, the glasses are in the wall cupboard." Anton had no intention of playing the role of polite host to the employee of a common liquor tax farmer.

Contrary to the name, a tax farmer wasn't a farmer or even a person. It was a business that cultivated taxes.

Pichshenko's employer, Rodionov, owned several of the over two hundred tax farms in central European Russia. Many years ago at the government's tax farm auction, Rodionov had been the highest bidder for the local district, thereby obtaining the right to be a business that collects liquor taxes for that district. Whenever the four-year auctions had rolled around, he not only continued to outbid the other contenders for that specific locale, but he succeeded in garnering considerably more districts.

The tax farmer's purpose was to serve as the Empire's agent in collecting a mishmash of liquor excise taxes, licenses, and fees, and then forwarding those rubles to the Imperial government. However, the tax farmer owed only the amount he bid at the auction. Any rubles the tax farmer collected beyond that amount comprised the tax farmer's profit, which was usually outlandish.

In addition to collecting taxes, tax farmers bought the distilleries' vodka, rebottled it for retail, and sold it to every tavern, bottle shop, and temporary liquor stall in their district. Increased vodka consumption equated not only to more direct product sales, but also to more taxes, licenses, and fees over and above the amount the tax farmer owed the government.

Pichshenko poured himself a drink. "To your good health."

Anton held up his glass. "And to yours."

After tossing back the amber liquid, Pichshenko wiped the corners of his mouth with his thumb and forefinger. "Speaking of your father, the last time I saw him he mentioned he might need a cash advance this autumn. He said he'd come up with a '*champion strategy*' for expanding the distillery."

Anton lazily threaded his fingers behind his head. "He toys with the idea every year, but nothing ever comes of it. And this year, he's scared off by rumors that tax farming will be abolished altogether and vodka prices will fall."

"A bunch of drivel!" Pichshenko waved away the concerns as if they were smoke. "Alexander will eliminate serfdom before he eliminates tax farming! The tax on vodka is His Majesty's most important source of revenue. Courtesy of the tax farms, the Treasury, with very little effort on its part, receives regular, fixed payments, district by district, year after year. Without tax farmers, the government itself would have to license and collect taxes from each wholesaler and retailer. A nightmarish bureaucratic labyrinth, to be sure."

"You have a point." Anton unlaced his fingers from behind his head and lowered his feet to the floor pavers. His forefinger traced the chinks in the table etched by knives decades ago. "But the price of vodka keeps going up, and the peasants are continually griping the product has become so dilute, it does no one any good. The peasants will simply stop buying it."

"Impossible," Pichshenko said with a conviction that offered no room for second thoughts. "Think about it, Anton Stepanovich. How do the peasants cool themselves in summer? Vodka. How do they warm themselves in winter? Vodka. How do they console themselves in times of grief? And when times are good, how do they make things even better? Why, the idea of a wedding or a funeral without vodka, it's enough to make a chicken laugh."

"So you believe the peasants will pay whatever price for a product that is becoming increasingly inferior?" Anton poured himself another drink and slid the bottle across the table to the chief inspector.

Pichshenko declined the offering. "Vodka is everything to the peasants. It's their champagne, sherry, port, cognac, balls, concerts, whist, literature, all combined into one easy-to-pour bottle." He leaned across the table and lowered his voice. "I'll let you in on something. The next few years will be superb for liquor sales. The peasants are recovering from the War and are enjoying a good harvest and high grain prices. Distillers will garner some of the proceeds. But reaping the largest profits will be the government"—Pichshenko held up first an index finger, then a second finger—"and the tax farmers."

"Why are the distillers left behind?"

Pichshenko stroked his pointed goatee like a university professor. "You're far too astute not to realize most profits are made under-the-counter. Consider the process. Petrovo's vodka leaves here in concentrated form to save on cooperage and transportation costs. It's then diluted to standard strengths, bottled, and sold in taverns. The urge to add more water than necessary is irresistible to the tax farmer and his employees right down the line, including the cellar, the wholesaler, and the tavernkeeper. By the time the vodka crosses the peasants' lips, it's been diluted anywhere from ten to thirty percent from its official strength."

Anton's head jolted back. "Thirty percent?"

"Everyone in the vodka trade turns a tidy profit *except* the distiller." The right side of Pichshenko's mouth curled into a satiric grin. "You need to think about getting into the tax-farming end of the business."

While Pichshenko made his suggestion, Anton was thinking about how some extra income would help offset his gambling debts. But Pichshenko hit the nail squarely on its head with his next words. "I know you want more from life than Petrovo's monotonous fields. Tax farming has made many a man wealthy. And will continue to do so."

"An interesting proposition. But right now I have more pressing issues to tend to. I'm taking my sister and cousin for a canoe ride."

"While you're paddling, give it some serious thought."

THE WARM FOREST air lay undisturbed as they pushed from shore. Anton worked the rear paddle and Elena the front. Nadya sat in the middle, facing forward, her shawl folded beneath her for cushioning against the wooden bench. Anton wasn't pleased to have his view restricted to her parasol and the folds of blush-pink material that flowed over the wooden bench.

"Does your lip hurt?" Nadya asked Elena.

"No, not too much. But it thure feelth peculiar." Elena's strong arms dug the paddle into the water to break through a tangle of lily pads.

"What were you doing that a bee stung you?"

"Searching for honey."

"Why were you doing that?"

"Because we have tho much honey thith year, the hiveth need to be emptied more often."

Nadya fell silent for several strokes of the paddles. "But why were *you* doing it?"

Elena likewise paused, seemingly unsure of the intent of the inquiry. "Because the hives need to be emptied at leath once a week, thometimes even every other day. We had them blethed."

Another hesitation from Nadya. "You mean, you had the hives blessed?"

"And the beeth."

Nadya turned her head and raised her eyebrows at Anton.

Anton gave her a conspiratorial wink. "Elena, tell Nadya about the Honey Savior."

"You know about the Honey Thavior, don't you?"

"No, I'm afraid I don't."

Elena swiveled her head, her eyes narrowed as if she were trying to see if Nadya was jesting or was truly ignorant of bee blessings.

"Every August, Father Diakonov leadth a procession of all the boyth who tend the hiveth. They carry icons and go from the village to the wooth. That's where he sprinkleth the hives with holy water." Elena turned again to query Nadya. "Don't you have that in Mothcow?"

"No, we don't. Is that all there is to it, merely holy water and icons?"

"Well, it'th very solemn. And very important."

"Oh. And you believe it works?"

"Certainly it works. There'th more honey, and there'th more wax."

The sixteen-year-old threw her head back in a throaty laugh, which to Anton had the summons of a sensual ingénue. "Oh, Elena, I couldn't ask for a more interesting and delightful cousin!"

Heat swelling in Anton's groin, he asked, "Nadya, would you like to cap off the afternoon with a visit to the hives?"

She pivoted partway around, affording him a pleasing profile of her breasts. "A splendid idea, Cousin Anton! Will you be joining us, Elena?"

"Wisth that I could, but afternoon choreths are waiting for me in the barn." Elena answered exactly as Anton knew she would.

On the way back to shore, he eyed the charcoal clouds on the horizon and assessed the accelerating breeze. He gauged the pace their walk would have to assume in order to arrive at the hunting lodge concurrently with the rain.

The paddlers gave a final thrust that drove the canoe aground. Anton stepped on shore and offered his hand to Nadya. As she rose, the canoe pitched precariously. He steadied her with an arm around her slim waist.

"You and Elena make it look so easy," she tittered. Her free hand lifted her skirt as she stepped onto the mossy bank, exposing a generous portion of calf.

Anton gathered her shawl from the bench and handed it to her. As she wrapped it about her shoulders, a wind gust blew one end loose. It flapped against her back until he snared the errant end. He brought it around her shoulder, paused his hand at her breastbone, and dipped his dark eyes into her sapphire ones. She thanked him with a dimpled smile.

After helping Elena flip the canoe upside down on the bank, he turned toward

Nadya. She made an extraordinarily pretty picture, standing among the white trunks of the slender birches contrasted with the yellow and oranges of the autumn leaves.

When Elena headed toward the barns, Anton took Nadya's elbow to guide her into the forest. "Keep your eyes alert. The peasants tell me they've seen *leshii* in these woods."

"Leshii? What's that?"

"Wood sprites. Very evil and very dangerous."

She reached an arm from under her shawl and gave his shoulder a prankish jab. "Oh, Cousin Anton, I'm here to look at beehives, and you're trying to scare me with silly folklore."

"I'm merely sharing with you what the peasants shared with me." He raised a shifty eyebrow toward her. "Who's to say wood goblins don't actually exist? Of course, leshii aren't nearly as dangerous as the *vodyanoi*."

"The vodyanoi?"

"The hideous water devil. He lives at the bottom of pools of water and has only one purpose—to drown people."

Nadya's lips unfurled into the most mischievous grin. "As a gracious host, you have the obligation to protect me from these horrid creatures."

Lightning threw a lance over a nearby meadow. Anton sniffed the encroaching rain. It would blow in at about the same time they'd arrive at the lodge. Everything was progressing according to plan.

The corners of his mouth curved upward. This was going to be so easy. Even easier than it had been with her older sister.

CHAPTER 33

Elizaveta

1857

Five hold on
and five shove in;
two watch to see
whether they're shoving all right.
What is happening?

Threading a needle.

"I HAVE A thirst!" the head of the household bellowed as soon as Avdotya and her freshly born son were brought in from the bathhouse, the preferred location for giving birth. "Bring out the vodka!"

Despite the early morning hour, the Vorontsov men—baby Platon's father and grandfather, his uncles Ermak and Stanislav, plus Stanislav's son Onufrii—assembled at the table quicker than hummingbirds gather around nectar.

When Grigorii had announced his wife's pregnancy, everyone had been caught by surprise, none more than Elizaveta. During the ensuing spring, there were days when the family wondered if Avdotya would be able to fulfill her obligation to deliver a healthy baby. She suffered from headaches, dizziness, and nausea. Her hands and lower legs swelled like the udder of a cow on the eve of calving. The veins in her neck stood out like ropes.

As soon as the baby was swaddled and placed in a hanging cradle, exhausted Avdotya fell into a stupor on a sleeping bench beside the stove.

Sidor toasted, "Here's to the son we thought Grigorii would never have."

Stanislav seconded with "Sons. We raise them to bring us joy when they are little, to help us work when they are grown, and to remember us after we die." He let out an extended belch that originated in his toes. Two unglazed mugs, two wooden cups, and one glass clinked together.

His son's future was too elusive for Grigorii to grab on to, so he addressed a more immediate concern. "This is nothing but pure, blunt misery." He held up the bottle to examine its contents in the window's light. Despite the loathsomeness of the liquid, Grigorii drew a long pull from the container. "So foul, it would gag an offal hauler."

Sidor took the half-empty bottle from his son and swirled it beneath his nose. "What's in here, Stanislav? Honey? Molasses? Why'd you buy this expensive stuff?"

"It's all Seleznyov had."

"That's always how it is nowadays," Ermak said. "You pay more, and it rots your gut, tears your mouth, and still leaves you sober."

"It's more watery than water." Sidor went on to describe, for the umpteenth time, an assembly meeting the previous winter when several of the men forced Seleznyov to put a bottle of vodka out in the snow. Before the meeting was over, the liquid was frozen solid.

Grigorii proclaimed, "If only the Tsar knew what they were feeding us."

Onufrii opted for the next higher in the hierarchical line. "May God punish Evdokim Seleznyov for swindling us with donkey piss."

As soon as Sidor asserted, "God is too high, and the Tsar is too far away," the contemptible beverage was tossed to the back of his throat.

After the watery spirits made another round of the table, Stanislav waved the empty bottle.

"Let's drown some more worms!" Onufrii exclaimed as they headed for more donkey piss at the lout Seleznyov's tavern.

Elizaveta went over to the hanging cradle to look at the tiny bundle that had arrived earlier than expected. His eyeballs were tinged pale yellow, and his translucent skin was the color of the outer layer of an onion. Elizaveta put her smallest finger to the infant's lips and was rewarded by a distinct, if feeble, sucking. "You weigh less than an empty honeycomb."

She lingered at the cradle, and when she finally turned from it, she caught sight of her mother-in-law with a torn shirt of Sidor's in her lap. Vera held a needle out at arm's length. The sagging skin of her chin stretched as her head arched back. She moistened the end of the thread with her tongue, screwed up her eyes, and made a tremorous stab at threading the needle. Failing, she made a second attempt.

Only in their own izba, and then only on rare occasions, did Sidor's and Stanislav's wives neglect to cover their heads with a kerchief. Of course, it was natural for the hair of women in their early fifties to fade to the color of old age, but Elizaveta's mind still pictured the two women as they'd looked when their first grandbabies had been born—brunettes, firm of hand and eye.

While Elizaveta threaded Vera's needle, the men careened from the tavern with two bottles of vodka and settled in at the table, ready to drink themselves to blank-eyed abstraction in honor of Grigorii's long-awaited son.

Elizaveta knew it was simply a matter of time before one of the women brought the men an assortment of onions, cucumbers, fish, and beets—all of which were pickled—to soak up the vodka swishing in their bellies. The salt would increase the men's thirst, and so the cycle of eating and drinking would spiral. Later, as the sun dropped below the horizon on this longest day of the summer, the men would tuck their faces into the crooks of their arms and sleep like ducks with their heads under their wings.

Onufrii announced to the women that while they were at the tavern, they heard that Feodor Zhemchuzhnikov's new baby boy was weak and puny and wasn't expected to live. His wife had bled to death after going into premature labor with her firstborn.

A flutter of joy seized Elizaveta's heart, but she quickly crossed herself and whispered, "God forgive me."

Elizaveta believed, truly believed, that the death of someone that young and full of life was altogether a very sad thing. Yet she couldn't quell the contradictory and shameful emotion of relief. There were days when thinking of another woman with Feodor, talking to him, laughing with him, lying beside him, drove Elizaveta to near madness.

"Remember those rumors about Feodor when he was a teenager?" Vera asked.

Elizaveta's head jerked toward her mother-in-law.

"What rumors?" Stanislav's wife asked.

"*Those* rumors."

"Oh, *those* rumors."

"What rumors?" asked Onufrii's wife.

Vera motioned the women to the other side of the room, away from the men. "Those rumors about Feodor having solitary sex as a teenager."

Elizaveta flushed hot with anger. "What makes you say that?"

"Think how spindly he was back then," Vera said. "And how long he waited to take a wife. And now with his baby being born frail, it all makes sense."

It all made sense to everyone except Elizaveta. It was a known fact that solitary sex hindered growth in youths, hence Vera's explanation of Feodor's scrawniness as a youngster. It was also perceived that youths who masturbated had trouble getting an erection as married men. And if they were able to impregnate their wives, the children resulting from that diluted seed would be weak. Therefore, the logical conclusion in this illogical progression of cause-and-effect was that the baby might die because Feodor had abused himself as a teenager.

Elizaveta put her hands on her hips, disgusted with the women's opinionated, meddlesome minds. "I don't suppose the baby's weakness had anything to do with his being born early, just like Platon."

Just as she finished speaking, a cry came from the sleeping bench beside the stove. The four women rushed to the new mother's side. Avdotya's rigid neck held her head off the straw, and her lips pulled back, leaving a gaping hole for her mouth. Her wide eyes appeared terrifyingly close to popping out of their sockets.

Elizaveta reached under the sheepskin for her sister-in-law's hand. "Avdotya, darling, what is it?" Every muscle in Avdotya's body clenched into knots, and her neck veins pulsated wildly. Avdotya's hand bore down on Elizaveta's with bone-crushing pressure.

Vera ordered, "Get something in her mouth so she doesn't swallow her tongue."

Stanislav's wife twisted a rag until it was tight as a rope, then thrust it between Avdotya's teeth.

"Avdotya! Can you hear me?" Elizaveta screamed to the body that writhed as though possessed by demons.

"What the hell's wrong with my wife?" Grigorii shouted from the table.

The spasm released its grip on Avdotya, and her body collapsed like a wilted petal. No one spoke until Avdotya's breathing returned to normal.

"What the hell was that?" Grigorii rephrased his question.

"This isn't a good sign," Vera said.

"That's fucking obvious."

Sidor cuffed the back of his son's head. "Respect your mother."

When it became clear that Avdotya was slowly returning to her senses, Onufrii was sent to get her mother.

When Evfrosinya Sharovatova held Platon to her daughter's breast, his mouth grabbed at the nipple until his tummy pouched. But no sooner was the newborn tucked into his hanging cradle than a violent twitching occurred under the sheepskin. The women once again rushed to Avdotya's side while the men mutely watched from across the izba. The tremors intensified into another ruthless spasm, lifting Avdotya's rigid legs off the bench and savagely coiling her body.

The fits came steadily, just minutes apart. Avdotya's big, scared eyes rolled up into her head and her face was beetroot red. Her breath came in gasps through clenched jaws. Between spasms, her skin was ashen, and the vessels in her forehead protruded like tiny frozen snakes.

Avdotya slowly sank into oblivion. Her heaving chest slowed until her breath became sluggish. The veins disappeared from her neck and forehead, and her hands turned ice cold. Her eyes, fixed on some unseen object, chilled Elizaveta to the bone. Unable to stand the eerie, sightless gaze, she gingerly closed Avdotya's wide, timid eyes for the last time. Moments later, Avdotya died in her mother's arms.

The women fell to their knees, beating their breasts and wailing. Grigorii walked over to the bench for a final look at his shy, long-suffering wife before stomping out of the izba.

Elizaveta silently asked the eternal question: *How could a merciful God allow this to happen? How unfair that such a fine person marry a brute and live a fearful, childless life, only to die so young.* But, as she regularly reminded herself and everyone else, no one said life would be fair.

Elizaveta tiptoed to the cradle and bent over her new nephew. The infant's unfocused eyes drifted in her direction as she cooed at him.

"Hello, little fellow. I'm your Auntie Elizaveta. Your mama, she was a wonderful person, but she's with the angels now. Your papa, well, you can't count on him for much, but you can count on me for everything. And soon I'll be your godmother, just like your mama wanted."

Platon exhaled a sigh, heavy with the chaste scent of his mother's milk.

"I'll sing you to sleep with lullabies. And I'll make your first pair of trousers. And I'll spoil you and kiss you all over. How does that sound?" She rubbed the bend of her knuckle against a cheek that was as soft as a butterfly wing.

As she straightened to leave, she peered at the small bundle that had entered her life on the same day Avdotya was taken from it. Bald as a turnip, he lacked the irresistible cuteness that accompanied babies. But that charm would develop with time. Elizaveta tried to find Avdotya's likeness in him but found little resemblance in the shriveled head. He was too young to have distinguishing features, except for—

Elizaveta gasped and took a step backward. *Oh, Mother of God, let me be mistaken!*

But there was no mistaking the ears, pointed like a dog's and held flat against the tiny skull.

How long had the holy beggar been gone from Petrovo? A half year or so?

Avdotya's passing. The death of Feodor's wife. And now a bastard child. The pressure built in Elizaveta's head. She had to escape the cramped izba before she went mad.

She moved beside Avdotya's sobbing mother and placed a hand on her shoulder. "Evfrosinya, would you like me to go to your izba and tell the rest of your family?"

AFTER DELIVERING THE heartbreaking news to Avdotya's birth family, Elizaveta settled in among the exposed roots of the old bent willow near the river's cove. To calm her whirlwind of thoughts, she shut her eyes and listened to the murmur of the water.

She reasoned that Grigorii knew Platon wasn't his child. However, he would never embarrass himself by publicly admitting he was less than a man. So maybe Avdotya was fortunate she was in a better place than among the living. Eventually, Grigorii would have made his wife atone for her sins.

Elizaveta heard distant childish laughter coming from Darovoe, the village around the river's bend. The sound filled her mind with the echoes of youthful, carefree summers. Summers when molten sunshine dripped like honey between the leaves. Summers she and Katya and Feodor had taken for granted as they idled away dreamy hours under this very willow.

If memories were supposed to fade with time, why did hers grow more painful? A sadness so intense rolled over Elizaveta, it threatened to smother her. She grieved for things wished for and unfulfilled, things she had expected and not received. She had been full of fantasies about a future without blemishes. Yet the turbulent river of life was full of treacherous rapids and undertows. A lost love. A miserable marriage. A dead baby. Too little rain. A freak hailstorm. A late spring. A dead horse.

Three women from the Naryshkin family appeared with laundry baskets and a passel of small children. In no mood for conversation, Elizaveta rose and crossed the bridge. She veered from the Count's road and entered the woods. The fermented aroma of the rich, moist undergrowth hung still and heavy. The leaves of the silver birches quivered with the gentlest of breezes. Amid the soft summer sound of the wrens' airy bubbling, she found the solitude she sought.

Feodor's words echoed through her entire being. *I've always known His will is for us to be together.* Was there any more hope now than when he had been a bachelor? No. It was the same snarl of thorns that had blocked their paths years ago as teenagers.

Years ago. How could it have been years ago that they had whispered sweet intimacies while entwined around each other like tendrils? How could she be an adult woman with half-grown children and still mourn the loss of her childhood sweetheart?

Elizaveta stopped in midstride. What was that noise? Was it human? Or just an animal? Where was she? She'd been in such an emotional fog, she had wandered deep into the forest, much farther than she'd ever gone, for fear of wood goblins.

Her heart pounded as she realized dusk was settling. What if the noise were the leshii! She turned in a full circle, her eyes flicking to each tree and bush. Something caught her attention, something with straight lines that wasn't part of the forest. She squinted. It was a hut of some sort.

She moved a few steps closer, her bark sandals rustling dried leaves. The cottage looked like a woebegone orphan. The window was opaque with layers of rain-smeared dust. Vines draped the red bricks, then reached up and over the mildewed, wood-shingled roof. Saplings intruded on the once-razed clearing. No trodden path led to the mossy stones outside the door.

She heard the noise again. It came from inside.

Elizaveta dropped to the ground and plunged into a tangle of underbrush. The door flung open. Anton Stepanovich Maximov emerged.

She thanked the Blessed Virgin when he headed in the direction opposite from her. He walked with a sauntering amble, his black curls covering the back of his collar like lazy fleece.

Elizaveta stayed low, for fear he might return. What if he found her nosing around where she had no business? Best to be patient.

The door opened. Out stepped a woman.

Zhanna!

Yet the resemblance to Zhanna was only superficial. This woman moved like a snail carrying the weight of her house on her back. Her mouth, once red and plump, was now thin and drooped.

Something caught Zhanna's attention, and she looked straight at Elizaveta with eyes that were round and scared and tormented. Zhanna froze, exactly as she had in the Widow Shabanova's barn half a lifetime ago. Then she clutched her skirt and ran.

Unlike that afternoon in the Widow Shabanova's barn, there was no haughtiness in Zhanna today. The once-beautiful woman had the look of a blossom that had been trampled by a heavy footstep.

CHAPTER 34

Maximov

1858

I shall arise early, fair and rosy;
I shall wash in the dew;
I shall let down my golden tresses.
When I ascend the hills in a
    golden crown
and look with radiant eyes,
both man and beast will rejoice.
What am I?

Sunrise.

SOMEONE WAS TRYING to get in bed with him. It was his mother. He was
nine years old, and Sophia was sliding under the covers. She was sobbing.

"Oh, Antoshka!"

No, it wasn't his mother. He struggled to swim out of the abyss of sleep.

"Antoshka!" the voice repeated, followed by the gasps of someone trying not
to cry.

"Elena?" He could barely see past the fringe of his eyelashes. She wasn't in bed
with him. She was kneeling on the floor, her torso prone across the mattress, her
eyes level with his.

What time is it? What is she upset about? What is that smell? He peeled his alco-
hol-laden tongue from the roof of his mouth. "Pigeon?"

"It's so horrible." Her face was as pale as plaster. "And I can't find Papa."

Does she have to wail so loudly? "What's horrible?"

"I was taking care of my cows, and I . . . I . . ."

She'd been with her cows. That explained the pungent aroma.

She seemed incapable of telling the rest of the story, so Anton took a stab.
"Something wrong with Malinka?" *Malinka One? Malinka Two? Malinka Three?*

How many Malinkas existed now? "What happened while you were taking care of your cows?" He hoisted himself onto an elbow.

"I didn't see her at first." She slid off the bed and rested her weight on the back of her heels. "That peasant from the village. The tavern owner's daughter . . . She's dead."

"Dead?" The stupor was knocked out of him.

"In the barn."

"In *our* barn?"

"I found her." She crumpled forward and sank her head into the quilt.

Anton stroked her hair. "I'm so sorry, Pigeon. How awful for you. Tell me about it."

The quilt muffled her strangled sounds.

"Elena, honey, I can't understand you."

She lifted her tear-streaked face. "Hung herself."

Anton stopped breathing. Last summer, he'd ceased taking Zhanna to the hunting lodge in response to her thickening waist. He recently heard that she had given birth to a girl with a misshapen arm.

"Yegorka . . . Yegorka . . ." Elena fought to control her sobs. "He cut the rope. Took her down. She looked so terrible!" Her face plunged back into the quilt.

Anton stroked her hair and murmured consoling words while his mind raced. He needed to deal with this quickly and discreetly. And before his father, wherever he was, showed up.

After putting Elena under the care of Matriusha, Anton layered on his clothes and ran to the barn, the savage cold pricking his lungs. He found the woman lying face up on the dirt floor. Yegorka and two other servants hovered twenty paces away, their slack mouths releasing plumes of frost.

Anton turned away from Zhanna, loathe to look at her bloated face the color of pewter, her engorged tongue protruding between purple lips. He directed the three serfs to roll her in a blanket and take her to her parents' izba.

Anton headed for the little stable office to warm his body and comfort his soul. He poured a glass of vodka and relished the feel of the fiery silk as it glided down his throat. After starting up the woodstove, he dropped into a chair and put his elbows on the bruised boards of the old kitchen table. Both hands tunneled through his hair, and his cupped palms cradled his forehead. All things considered, he was fortunate he'd fathered only one bastard. Or, at least, only one that he knew of.

Why was it he needed women as much as he did? The peculiar thing was, despite his extensive amorous activity, he had never courted a woman. Sure, there had been some he laughed with, and some whose company he enjoyed beyond the bedroom, but he kept his relationships uncomplicated.

One woman in particular came to mind. Feisty, long-stemmed Tonia Seminovna. For a year, maybe more, he had dropped in on her whenever he was in Sukhanovo. During their final parting, she proclaimed that he was emotionally sterile and incapable of loving a family.

Anton poured a second drink. The first one had done an exemplary job of settling his nerves, just as he knew it would. He inhaled with deep satisfaction. Yes, the jitters were starting to dissipate.

He pondered the words Tonia Seminovna had flung at him. She obviously didn't know what she was talking about. He loved Elena beyond measure. He pampered her in ways their parents never had. Who taught her how to tread water and then swim when Stepan was too busy tending to his potatoes? And chasing his daydreams of renovating the distillery? And obsessing over his four- and five- and six-year crop rotations? Who took Elena canoeing on the river when Stepan didn't have room for his daughter in his harmoniously organized milieu of cultivated fields and mown hay meadows?

His father's grandiose dream of the quintessential estate was enough to drive anyone to drink. So Anton poured another glass.

And who took care of Sophia when her husband turned his back on her? A six-year-old kid, that's who. He's the one who had listened to her cry, watched her face contort with agony, held her hand when she collapsed with her hypochondriac affectations. That was asking a lot from a kid. When Stepan had turned away from his wife, who went to church with her to pray for dead Dmitry's soul? And because she couldn't endure a night alone, who'd slept in her bed while her husband frolicked about on his three-week airing in Nizhny Novgorod?

Anton's jaws ground back and forth. Who had put up with all the caressing and cuddling that Sophia had to bestow on someone when she couldn't give it to Dmitry? Young Anton had endured it, regardless of how awkward he felt when she kissed the top of his head, his cheek, his lips. Regardless of how she came to his room at night, wearing only her muslin nightgown and wafting the scent of votive candles. Regardless of how she slipped into bed with him and folded herself around his back so that he could feel every bit of her, from her breath on his neck to the silkiness of her bare calves. Regardless of how she made him put his head on her stomach.

"Yes, Antoshka, that's where mamas carry their babies before they're born. But your papa won't give your mama any more babies."

Then her arms would coax him to lay his head in the nook where her shoulder met her body, where he couldn't help but see her muslin-covered breast moving up and down. Eight years old, ten years old, twelve years old, far older than was natural for a boy to cuddle against his nearly disrobed mother. Long before he reached his teens, he knew what men did with women's breasts. What would have been her reaction if he had put his mouth over her nipple? He had the hideous feeling she would have let him.

As a youth, to escape to the Cadet's College and away from his mother's clinging need for intimacy was an answered prayer. Thank Heaven, by the time he returned to Petrovo, Sophia was so tormented, she sought her comfort from the spiritual realm.

Now he needed another escape—from the triviality of provincial life. The unvarying routine. The mournful boredom. The unbroken view of endless fields. His father's incessant carping.

He needed out!

Anton's original plan was that by age twenty-four—barely one month from now—his prowess at cards would have brought in enough rubles to pave his way to Moscow. But a string of bad luck had put those disillusioned hopes squarely in their place.

When and how in God's name would he be able to commence a fresh, unrepressed life in Moscow?

Anton reached for the bottle. He knew with precision that one drink gave his spirits a little lift while the second and third offered relief from anger, hurt, and disillusionment. Alcohol was more predictable than his mother and more comforting than his father.

Anton's head jerked around.

Snarling. Growling. Shrieks of pain.

He grabbed the rifle and ran out to the blistering cold. Vaska lay on his side in the corral. Two wild dogs were yapping and lunging at the goat while a third tore chunks out of his flank. The downed animal thrashed his head and bawled. His arthritic legs flailed at his torturers.

Anton fired into the air. The skinny curs tore from the corral.

A haunting silence ensued. Anton's heart hammered his breastbone as he approached the recumbent goat. Vaska threw his head back and released a long, pitiful bleat. Blood coursed from holes in the animal's neck, turning the snow red. Raw chunks of meat hung from his thigh. His caramel eyes stared up at Anton.

Christ! The servants needed to end the poor creature's suffering. Where were the worthless oafs?

The gun at the end of his arm felt heavier than a block of granite. God, could he do it? Could he put a bullet through the head of docile, irksome Vaska, his childhood companion?

Anton reloaded while Vaska's head thrashed about as the animal tried in vain to right himself. Blood crusted around the goat's lips and nostrils as the side of his face beat the packed snow. He gave a throaty, soul-wrenching wail.

Do it, Anton. Do it now.

He moved behind Vaska's head, to where he couldn't see the scared, guileless eyes. He took aim but couldn't stop the weapon's tremor. He blinked to clear his watery vision. His thumb clicked the cold, impassive steel of the hammer.

Do it, you spineless bastard. Reach inside and find the gumption.

Teeth clenched, throat constricted, Anton fired. Vaska lay still.

Even before the blast stopped ricocheting, Anton headed for the stable and another drink.

CHAPTER 35

Maximov

1859

Nice and round,
it skips from person to person;
it'll skip clear around the world.
It's good for nothing itself,
but everybody wants it.
What is it?

A coin.

ONE YEAR TO the date of Zhanna's suicide, on the Saturday prior to the commencement of Lent, Anton was stocking his new oak cellaret when his father and August Roeglin entered the tiny stable office. Roeglin removed his hat and knocked off its snow with his gloved hand.

Stepan warmed his hands at the woodstove. "So what is it you wanted to discuss?"

"Two things. First, I . . . Hilda and I . . ." He pulled off his gloves and started over. "Hilda and I . . ."

"Stop sputtering, Roeglin."

"What I need to tell you is that . . . well . . . we all realize it's time for us to move on. Elena will be sixteen on her next birthday. She's finished any education Hilda can offer her." He lowered his gaze to the snow melting from his worn-down boots. "I've located a position in Saratov. In addition to a steward, the family needs a tutor for their five children." Roeglin picked at a hangnail. "Anyway, we're going next week for an interview, and if they like us . . ."

Stepan's lips barely moved. "You'll be leaving us." The air left his chest, and he swallowed hard. For a moment, Anton thought the old man was going to topple over onto the brick pavers. Instead, Stepan lowered himself onto a chair. The only sounds were the crackle of the fire and the screech of the wind across the fields.

"Yes, yes, of course." Stepan's voice wavered as though he were trying to see the picture through blurry swamp water. "It's obvious Hilda's work here will soon be completed. All four children received a first-rate education. Equal to the best boarding school. Of course, it's time for you to move on. You and Hilda have things to do. We all have things to do." Stepan seemed to have lost the thread of his thoughts.

Anton curtailed the nostalgia by asking Roeglin the size of the estate, the ages of the children, and other passionless details. His father gave no sign of hearing the conversation.

"How long has it been, Roeglin?" Stepan interjected.

"Almost a quarter of a century."

"We were young then, weren't we?"

"Yes, sir, we were."

Stepan's jaws ground as he chewed on his thoughts. "Do you think we've done sufficiently well here?"

"Yes, sir, we've done a very fine job."

Stepan nodded absently. "We tried. Both of us. We tried."

Having had his fill of the two men's reserved sentimentality, Anton broached a new subject. "You said you had two things to discuss."

"It seems the peasants have taken an oath of sobriety."

"They've sworn off vodka? Completely?" Stepan's voice once again found its thunder.

"Except for weddings, baptisms, and each of the twelve main Church festivals."

"Well, that's plenty of exceptions." Stepan pushed out his caved-in chest and regained his composure as the pomeshchik of Petrovo.

Roeglin added, "And the sick are allowed vodka for medicinal purposes."

"But of course." No sooner did Roeglin lower his hefty frame into a chair than Stepan rose and paced about the cramped quarters. "And if they don't comply with this misnamed oath of sobriety?"

"The village is monitoring itself. Offenders will be fined two rubles. If the offender has no money, he can be flogged."

"So you're telling me that my peasants won't get drunk ever again, except on holidays?"

"No, Father," Anton said in a voice usually reserved for addressing six-year-olds. "What he's saying is that the village assembly, while they were duly drunk at their last meeting, swore to stop drinking. The fall wedding season is over, as is Yuletide. The Lenten fast starts in a few days. It's an opportune time of year to climb on the sobriety wagon."

"How did you hear about all of this?" Stepan asked Roeglin.

"Feodor Zhemchuzhnikov brought it up to me by way of conversation. Apparently it was the pathetic vodka at last fall's weddings that sealed their decision. According to Zhemchuzhnikov, in the old days, good weddings needed two buckets of vodka. Now they need six buckets of the watered-down stuff, the cost of which is sky-high."

Stepan picked up a copy of the *Landowners' Journal* and rolled it into a tight cylinder. "Well, I think it would be downright champion if my peasants stopped drinking for the remainder of their lives and their children's lives."

"Not a ghost of a chance," Anton snorted. "You'd have better odds trying to pick up water with a fork."

"There's more." Roeglin let Stepan's eyebrows vault over his nose before he continued. "There's some talk about possibly having a more visible demonstration than merely a boycott."

"Such as?"

"Perhaps a little roughhousing. Maybe smashing Seleznyov's glasses. Burning his tables."

"Why can't peasants see beyond their own noses? Don't they realize that Seleznyov can sell only what that crooked tax farmer delivers to him?" Still pacing, Stepan slapped the rolled *Journal* into the palm of his other hand. "Exactly who are the instigators of this juvenile display of discontent?" Stepan's empty hand flew forward, palm out. "Wait! Let me guess. Probably the usual rabble-rousers. A couple of Loktevs. And the Vorontsov brothers."

Roeglin nodded. "Plus some of the Novikov clan."

Stepan whacked the paper baton against the gun cabinet. "I ought to send every last one of those knotheads to Siberia."

THE MAXIMOVS WEREN'T the least surprised by the peasants' boycott. For months, the family had been following newspaper reports on how bad vodka was incurring the wrath of the lower classes across Russia. But the articles also had tackled a broader issue. Because the Empire's coffers depended on the taxes garnered from the sale of vodka, the press accused the government of relying on the thirst of the increasingly intoxicated peasantry to satisfy its own thirst for easy revenue. According to the newspapers' predications, if tax farming wasn't abolished, the soul of the Russian people would drown in liquor.

The peasants' abstinence fever was abetted by some of the more righteous of

Russia's upper classes. Everyone who consumed vodka contributed to the public purse. But the pockets of working-class drinkers were tapped the deepest, decried the sympathetic gentility. The excise taxes placed on vodka were so extreme that if they had been direct rather than covert taxes, the populace would have reacted with riots.

The resulting boycotts posed a devil of a quandary for the Imperial state. How could it disapprove of sobriety and morality? Yet if the populace stopped drinking, the government would go bankrupt. And beyond that, the peasantry's actions were an unnerving display of an independent political movement, sentiments particularly worrisome to a monarchy that was contemplating the emancipation of a third of the Empire's population.

A week following Roeglin's announcement, Anton was on his way from the house to the stable office when he saw a carriage parked near the barns. The well-appointed coach had leather upholstery and a crest emblazoned on the side. White mist billowed from the horse's nostrils. The coachman hunkered in the driver's seat beneath a pile of blankets.

When Anton reached the warmth of the barn's office, he found Veniamin Savelyevich Pichshenko, the tax farmer's employee, perched at the table on the straw-plaited seat of a stool. "I see you've expanded your inventory." He held his glass tumbler of amber liquid up to Anton. "Your choice of brandy is unsurpassed anywhere in the district."

"Glad you find it suitable." Anton doffed his coat and tossed another log into the woodstove. "I'm not the only one with refined tastes. New carriage. And a driver too, I see. Business must be going well." Anton retrieved a glass from the cellaret and joined Pichshenko at the table.

"The carriage and driver are out of necessity. I'm certain you realize the precariousness of my riding through the countryside alone in an open buggy at the present time. The coachman is an excellent marksman." Pichshenko was referring to how, with increasing frequency, the peasants' unobtrusive pledges of sobriety were turning violent against anyone associated with the vodka trade. "As for my visit, it's strictly personal."

Anton tented his eyebrows.

"Are you aware that your former serf hasn't completely divested himself of the vodka business? Rumor has it that even with his crossed eyes, he can find his way into the distillery. While your family is sleeping, Maximov vodka is routinely tapped and peddled to the villagers."

"How did you learn of this?"

"Trust me, my sources are reliable. Consider me as an asset, Anton Stepanovich. Which brings me to the second reason for my visit. We'd make a good partnership: my knowledge, experience, and contacts with your investment."

"So you've told me before."

"But I have an even more interesting proposition this time." Pichshenko ran his thumb and forefinger down the outer edges of his goatee, pausing at its pointed end. "My boss faces a cash flow problem and can't make his payments to the government and other creditors. In fact, Rodionov is teetering on bankruptcy. He'll let his tax farm go for seventy-five percent of what he contracted with the government."

Anton's snort was sardonic. "Why would I want to invest in something that has already brought one man to the edge of ruin?"

"Extravagant living was Rodionov's ruin. It had nothing to do with his business. The beauty of the situation is that you and I can purchase the lease for significantly less than its rightful price."

"The price of leasing a tax farm goes higher and higher every year. Tax farmers must resort to greater and greater reprehensible actions just to meet their obligations. It's a house of cards that has to crash at some point." Anton tapped his forehead, implying only an idiot would fail to understand that.

"The government will always take care of its tax farmers. It can't afford to do otherwise." Pichshenko finished his single drink, which was all he ever imbibed while visiting Anton's retreat. Meanwhile, Anton, true to form, was pouring his second.

"You told me yourself the Shatsk district has seen lease prices rise more than one thousand percent over those of the previous period. How can the tax farmer ever hope to make money while shouldering that much overhead? Especially considering the legal price of vodka has remained unchanged for fifteen years?"

Pichshenko conversed as if engaged in a game of chess, always anticipating the next move. "Visit any tavern in Shatsk and you'll find the cheapest vodka on the shelves is ten rubles. Of course, it's lavished with fruit and bottled in fancy containers and therefore can't be sold as ordinary vodka for the normal three rubles."

"Sounds as though the peasants have a right to be riled."

"Let's not muddy the pond with high-minded righteousness. The grim fact is that no one makes it in this life if he isn't willing to practice a little cunning. Take, for example, how the tax farmer docks the distiller for casks that aren't completely filled when they reach the warehouse. Of course, the casks were filled to the brim when they left the estate."

Anton's eyebrows bounded upward.

"Don't look so shocked. It happens all the time. Zhemchuzhnikov always puts up a fight when we tell him he shortchanged us. Sometimes we let him win, but more times than not, it's deducted from your father's compensation."

"You dishonest bastard."

Pichshenko gave a thin laugh. "It's the way of the world."

"And the government is aware of it?"

"The government knows that out of honest businesses, its citizens can't build stone mansions. Want another example? Someone brings in his own flagon, and the tavernkeeper pours the vodka in full view of the customer. But partway through the process, he slips a little ball from his palm into the funnel, then taps the funnel to lodge the ball in the neck. When he lifts the funnel from the flagon, the peasant sees no more liquid coming out." Pichshenko innocently lifted his upturned palms toward Heaven. "Apparently it's all been poured. Then the tavernkeeper puts the funnel, and the vodka it still contains, behind the counter."

Pichshenko went on to describe a witches' Sabbath of tricks used by tax farmers and their employees, but he could have saved his breath. Ever since Pichshenko had first proposed a partnership two and a half years earlier, Anton's nimble mind had been transforming the income from a tax farm into a cultured, colorful life in Moscow. The vision burned constantly in his thoughts—stepping into a coach and forever leaving the suffocating dreariness of provincial life.

One stumbling block to the new venture was the government's requirement for collateral from the lease-holding tax farmer. To overcome that snag, Anton had already contrived a scheme to collateralize the inherited Moscow mansion while keeping Sergei in the dark about the undertaking.

He reflected on the deceitful action he was planning and on the fraudulent career upon which he was about to embark. His fingertips ran along the old knife grooves that embellished the wobbly table. Hovering over him were the memories of his family gathered around the table on the Feast of the Honey Savior and the aroma of freshly baked poppy seed pie, poignant reminders with virtuous principles that were doing their damnedest to dissuade him.

Anton pushed aside the gilded recollections. He was no longer a child. He was a man, and he had to make adult decisions. He craved—no, he *required*—a more expansive life than Petrovo could offer. His very sanity was at risk.

But Anton had one more challenge to throw at Pichshenko. "Why shouldn't I simply purchase the lease and cut you out of the picture? Then all the profit would be mine."

Pichshenko's eyebrows rose eloquently as he leaned his forearms on the table. "Tell me, how many taverns can this lease legally operate? How many rooms can each establishment have? What types of furnishings are allowed? What types of food can be sold? The latest law on tax farms contains 517 articles. Next year, another twenty-five or fifty will undoubtedly be added. What are the legal ways tax farmers can purchase, transport, and sell vodka? And at what strengths and prices? How much honey can be added? How does one go about adding nicotine to give more kick to the watered-down slop?"

Pichshenko let the questions float about the air before concluding, "There you have it: you and me, an instinctual union of gentry capital and merchant expertise."

The chief inspector rose and stood beside the table, forcing Anton to look up at him. "I am fully aware that Evdokim Seleznyov runs an unlicensed clandestine tavern and that he obtains a portion of his vodka directly from you and your family. Running a tavern and selling vodka outside the tax farm system are both criminal offenses. If you want to keep the government in blinders regarding your family's role in that tavern—"

"Hold on! We don't sell to Seleznyov except when his vodka runs out and the roads between here and Sukhanovo are impassable mud pits. It never amounts to more than a cask or two a year."

"It's not the quantity. It's the deed." Pichshenko pulled on his heavy bearskin coat and tucked in the tails of his muffler. "Give my proposal some serious thought." He patted his fur turban into place. "But don't take too much time."

CHAPTER 36

Elizaveta

1859

A hole toward the sky,
a hole toward the ground;
in the middle is fire,
all around is water.
What am I?

A samovar.

"TASTES LIKE SNAKE piss!"

Grigorii Vorontsov was enjoying himself. He was playing to a new and enlarged audience. Elizaveta's Uncle Artamon and his wife had invited anyone who was even tenuously related to them to celebrate the christening of their first grandchild. On the last Sunday before Lent, Elizaveta's childhood home was full to bursting.

Following Erafei's death almost three years earlier, Artamon had become the bolshak of the Anafrev extended family—ten healthy adults and three children. The abundance of adults meant the family received a sizeable land allotment from Maximov. In addition, they had plenty of labor to work the fields from sunup until sundown, making the Anafrevs' strips of land among the most productive on the estate. The family was at an exceptionally affluent stage of its evolution.

A bountiful harvest in 1858 combined with good prices for his excess grain deposited actual cash into Artamon's pockets, a rare occurrence at best. Feeling his oats during this time of plenty, Artamon made sure today's tables overflowed with food and beverage. Instead of the usual three-ruble christening party, he spent five times that amount, not counting the samovar.

Flush with prosperity, Artamon had cast all fiscal caution to the wind and purchased a samovar for the occasion. It was the second such teapot in the village, the other one holding a place of honor in Seleznyov's tavern. Tea was a rare luxury, and today's guests weren't about to insult their host by not partaking of his openhanded generosity.

It was at this holy celebration honoring the entrance of Artamon's first grandchild into the sacred world of Orthodoxy that Grigorii made his comparison between vodka and snake piss.

As a former member of the household, Elizaveta worked beside the Anafreva women to keep bowls stocked, cups filled, and children out from underfoot. As Elizaveta maneuvered between the tightly packed borrowed tables, talk centered on the vague but ever-hopeful topic of "when the Tsar frees us serfs from Maximov's clutches" and "when the land rightfully becomes ours." According to rumors, Alexander II had already freed the serfs, but the government officials and the pomeshchiks wouldn't allow the news to reach the peasants.

Elizaveta was searching for a ladle among the utensils hanging on the wall pegs when every muscle in her body tensed.

Feodor's handheld mirror from Nizhny Novgorod.

Its handle was blackened from years of clasping, and a diagonal crack scarred the glass. Despite its blemishes, it carried her back to a bygone summer day brimming with youthful dreams.

What had happened to that young girl? Who was the sour old woman staring back at her today with small, hard eyes and tight, unyielding lips?

In the mirror, Feodor's reflection appeared above her shoulder. But it wasn't her overwrought imagination. It was a fluke of timing.

His presence didn't surprise her. The two of them typically made courteous appearances at their respective families' gatherings. They'd exchange hasty pleasantries, then fall back into the gaggle of family before making a premature departure.

But this afternoon, Elizaveta received the shock of her life when Feodor took a seat at her in-laws' table. Why in Heaven's name would he sit there?

She centered her chores near their table so she could keep an ear on the men's talk.

Stanislav elaborated on Grigorii's snake-piss complaint. "A peasant can give the tavernkeeper his coat, hat, ax, and cart and still get bad vodka!"

"Maybe we should see to it that Seleznyov gets his just deserts." Despite his age, Grigorii maintained his adolescent bravado.

"We already have," said Stanislav's son, Onufrii. "The whole village has sworn off drinking, starting in three days."

"Maybe speed things up a little?" The men turned glassy eyes toward Grigorii. "As I've said for some time, our point would be better made with some broken mugs. Some overturned tables."

"A smashed window." The suggestion came from Ermak, for whom violence was a way of life.

"You might think twice about that," advised Feodor.

Grigorii wiped the corner of his mouth with the back of his hand. "Huh?"

"The Count is often at the distillery, and I've come to know him pretty well. I know he won't tolerate violence. If you seek revenge on Seleznyov, you'd be looking at flogging at best, Siberia at worst."

"I'm not talking about a serious ruckus. Just a little arm-twisting." Grigorii popped a chunk of garlic in his mouth. His jaws ground from side to side like a cow angry at her cud.

Feodor rephrased his cautionary words. "Whether you fellows want to create so much damage as to place sin on your souls is your concern. I'm merely telling you what lies ahead if you annoy the Count."

The discussion ended as Artamon slid onto the bench beside Elizaveta's father-in-law. Sidor hoisted his empty glass. "To your new grandson, who will spend his life as a free man!"

"May your grandson never know the humiliation of ploughing another man's land!" Stanislav tilted the bottle toward Artamon's glass.

"Only half a glass." Artamon blinked as he strained to focus on Stanislav's face. "You already have two noses."

"I may have two noses, but you only have one first grandson. Drink up!" Stanislav had little respect for anyone who didn't regularly consume his weight in liquor. He filled Artamon's glass to the brim, then waved the empty bottle in front of the host's face.

"Liza, darling," Artamon called over his shoulder, "bring another bottle." He leaned toward Sidor and gave a tipsy hiccup. "I need to ask a favor of you."

"Of course, Artamon, whatever I can do."

"I'd like you"—Artamon jabbed his forefinger into Sidor's chest, then punched his own chest with his thumb—"to show me how to build one of those roll-about chairs for my daughters-in-law and their babies."

"You mean my rocking chair?" Sidor's chest visibly swelled. "I'd be happy to!"

"Good!" Artamon's calloused hand whacked Sidor on the back. "I want it made out of good, straight boards from a mill. Buy the lumber you need in Sukhanovo. I have rubles for you to spend."

"Tomorrow I'm hauling a load of the Count's milk to Sukhanovo," Feodor said. "You're welcome to ride along."

Stanislav leapt into the conversation. "Sidor, you and I vowed to mend that old plough tomorrow. Why not send Grigorii to Sukhanovo with Feodor?" While Stanislav twirled the end of his beard, his eyes bored into Grigorii's. "You helped build that chair. You know what wood is needed." He paused to let his next words sink into his nephew's soused brain. "You can pick up a few other things while you are in town."

As Elizaveta set the new bottle of vodka on the table, she fully understood the true intent of Stanislav's words. Peasants didn't "pick up a few things" in their district capital. Their purchases were infrequent and painstakingly deliberated. The underlying truth was that Stanislav was no more capable of honoring the sobriety pledge than the autumn was capable of staving off the winter. He wanted Grigorii to load up on vodka in Sukhanovo, away from the prying eyes of Seleznyov and the entire village.

Grigorii gave a sloppy, boozy grin. "Sure. I'll go."

"Pick you up at sunrise," Feodor told Grigorii before turning to address Artamon. "I think I'll have some of your tea." He rose and, moving toward the samovar, caught and held Elizaveta's eye. His head inclined with a barely perceptible beckoning.

She scrambled beside him, her legs as flaccid as caterpillars.

He swiveled the valve handle on the gurgling samovar. "Meet me, Liza." His lips barely moved.

The world inside her went still.

"I must talk to you." His voice was raspy, like a mouse scratching to get into some dark hiding place.

"When?"

His eyes remained fixed on the steamy liquid flowing from the spout. "When Grigorii and I get back tomorrow. In the woods on the other side of the bridge."

"Yes."

He closed the tap and returned to the table with his glass of tea.

CHAPTER 37

Maximov

1859

What is sharper than a sword?
A piercing look.

"ST. PETERSBURG OR Siberia. Take your pick."

While the Anafrevs were rejoicing the baptism of the family's newest member, Anton leaned against the side of the sledge, ankles and arms crossed, and gave Cockeyes the ultimatum.

Pichshenko's exposé the previous day about Cockeyes pilfering vodka certainly wasn't news to Anton. Not only had Anton masterminded the plan to split the profits with the serf, he had also given Cockeyes a key to the distillery's padlock. Anton regretted having to terminate the arrangement, even though the fiscal rewards had been slender. He had kept the amount of filched vodka at a minimum to prevent his father from discovering the discrepancy. However, the black-market sales put enough rubles in Anton's wallet to ante into a few card games.

On the other hand, the partnership's dissolution markedly altered Cockeyes's existence. As a serf without a home, he lived hand to mouth. His vodka sales augmented his begging, allowing him to at least keep flesh on his bones.

Pichshenko's tip-off had thrown Anton into a moral dilemma, territory that was foreign to him. If Pichshenko knew about the illegal sales, then other people also knew. It was simply a matter of time before the scuttlebutt reached Stepan. Anton didn't want to see his childhood friend sent in leg irons to the Siberian tundra. Anton owed the serf. Ol' Cockeyes had covered for him countless times when his father came within a hair's breadth of catching him tipping the bottle as a teenager.

"Stop wringing your hands and take this." Anton thrust a sealed envelope at Cockeyes. "Inside is the address in St. Petersburg. Anyone can direct you to the house. Insist that you personally hand the envelope to Maksim Semenovich

Zinoviev. The letter explains that you, as a serf, are payment in full for my debts to Monsieur Zinoviev. Repeat the name to me. Maksim Semenovich Zinoviev."

Anton's debts to Zinoviev were promissory notes for gambling losses that had accrued over the years when he visited his siblings in St. Petersburg. Zinoviev's letters were becoming tetchy about Anton's arrears and insinuated possible legal action. Transferring Cockeyes to Zinoviev would cover his obligations. And Cockeyes—an outcast who lived on the fringes of village society—wouldn't be missed by Stepan or anyone else.

Cockeyes hung his head as he repeated his new master's name. "No choice?"

"None."

The serf lifted his unruly eyes and focused one on Anton and one on some ill-defined place across the shed. He rubbed his forehead as if attempting to generate some logical thought. "Who's the snitch?"

Anton started to say that Pichshenko had somehow found out. But perhaps it would be best to keep his conversations with the tax farm employee discreet. Instead he said the first name that came to him. "Zhemchuzhnikov."

Cockeyes's lip curled back. "Zhemchuzhnikov? How did he find out?"

"How the hell do I know?" Anton pulled himself upright from the sledge's sideboards. "I'm driving you to Sukhanovo this afternoon. I'll secure your passage to St. Petersburg, and you'll be on your way in a day or two."

The man's wayward eyes became hot embers, focused on nothing except his anger. His voice resonated with brutish rancor. "Take me to Sukhanovo tomorrow. Today, I have to repay Feodor Zhemchuzhnikov."

"No. I want you off Petrovo today. There'll be no settling any score with Zhemchuzhnikov."

One of his eyes came back to Anton as Cockeyes raised a clenched fist. "I owe him."

"Too bad. He's leaving tomorrow at first light to haul milk to Sukhanovo. I want you gone from Petrovo by then. You can be a cunning old bastard, and I won't have you seeking revenge."

"Zhemchuzhnikov will get what he deserves."

"Not from you, he won't."

"We'll see about that." He spat onto the dirt floor of the shed.

"Forget about Zhemchuzhnikov. Go gather your things."

"What things?"

Anton eyed the shriveled man and the rags he was wearing in air that was brittle with frost. How old was he? Early forties?

Amazing, Anton thought. Cockeyes had been homeless for seven years, yet managed to stay alive in the village by sleeping in barns and begging for food. Did the bonehead have the wherewithal to make it to St. Petersburg? Even if he did, the uncultured country serf had never even seen the inside of the Maximov manor house. How would he ever fit in with his fellow servants or meet the demands of his urbane master?

Anton shrugged. Those were Cockeyes's problems, not his.

"Walk your ass toward the orphanage. I'll pick you up along the road."

Anton left the shed and headed back to the manor house to get the serf's legal documents and a passport from the safe. He knew from experience that he could pen his father's signature. While he was in the house, he'd grab some warm clothes for Cockeyes.

He opened his pocket watch. The villagers would still be kicking up their heels at the Anafrevs' christening party. No one would see him picking up the beggar along the roadside.

CHAPTER 38

Elizaveta

1859

The walls are sturdy,
but few are keen on the place.
What am I?

Jail.

VERA SHOOK GRIGORII'S shoulder. "Up. No one should sleep beyond the dark."

Grigorii grunted and rolled over in his straw, giving his mother only his back to fuss at.

"Zhemchuzhnikov will want to get back before nightfall." She gave a jab between the unresponsive shoulder blades and walked away muttering, "Sleep himself to death."

Platon sat on Elizaveta's lap, allowing kasha to be spooned into his mouth. "Yes, little Platoshka, Feodor will be here soon," she whispered in his pointed ear as her heart galloped in her chest.

She had spent the night turning over Feodor's hushed, clipped words, examining them from all angles. Why now? What did he have in mind?

"Here's what I have in mind for you, little fellow. Enough pampering. It's time your chubby little hand learned to hold its own spoon."

Platon's deep-set eyes twinkled up at his godmother in anticipation of life's newest adventure. Since the day of his birth, the sweet-souled boy had surveyed the world with exuberance, continually seeking out wondrous objects that could be placed in his mouth or ears. Elizaveta had long ago brushed aside the identity of the child's father. The holy beggar had not been seen or heard from since he left Petrovo. The child was ignored by Grigorii, who possessed the fatherly instinct of a snapping turtle. Elizaveta considered Platon her own. And she shared her maternal pleasures with, of all people, her daughter.

Platon had lived his entire first year in his Cousin Anna's arms. Unlike the other village children who spent their infancy motionless in a cradle, bound like a mummy in swaddling, Platon had explored the world with his eight-year-old cousin. She introduced him to the hens and charmed him into rubbing noses with the mare. He squeezed the moist garden soil, thrilled when it oozed between his fingers.

Elizaveta didn't often admit it to herself, but Platon was marching through the phases of childhood faster than any of her children. She couldn't bear the possibility that the boy's smarts and skills had come from that dreadful Varlaam Gorbunov. So now, as always, she centered her thoughts on her love for the child.

Grigorii tumbled from his straw and staggered to the barrel of pickles. Using his cupped hand, he took several gulps of pickle juice to dampen his hangover. As he wiped the dribbles from his beard onto his shirtsleeve, from outside came the sound of snow crunching beneath the hooves of Feodor's horses. Vera thrust Grigorii into an overcoat, hat, scarf, and gloves. She wrapped his fingers around a sack that contained a chunk of bread for breakfast plus additional bread and dried pork for a midday meal.

Elizaveta listened to the retreating tinkle of the bell hanging from the arching bow-shaft of the horse collar. *Only half a day from now, Feodor. Only half a day.*

Following the morning's chores, she couldn't bear the cheerless izba another moment. She bundled the children against Grandfather Frost and took them to the cemetery to offer the traditional fried eggs to the dead of the family.

Few places underscore the passage of time as does a graveyard. Elizaveta looked back on year after year of pining for Feodor, dwelling on her loss, allowing it to consume her. Were her feelings the remnants of mere childish infatuation? Was she carrying around dreams that should have been laid to rest years ago? Their love had been so intense. On the other hand, they had been so young. Was she more in love with the memories than she was with the person?

The church bell clanged two times, too early to expect the men's return from Sukhanovo. But she couldn't run the risk of missing Feodor, so she shepherded the children to the izba to await Grigorii's return. Her back was knotted with tension, and she quaked with impatience. Perhaps the arduous, repetitious work of weaving would calm her.

She sat at the massive loom, her leg moving the heddle up and down, up and down, over and over, hoping her mind would sink into a stupor. Her muscles loosened, and her face grew moist with sweat. But her insides continued to churn with anxiety.

Meet me, Liza. I must talk to you.

What did he mean? What did he want? Why now?

Elizaveta gave herself a good tongue-lashing. How foolish to spin all sorts of fantasies and futures around those simple words! Not only foolish, but dangerous.

Four bells.

Soon. They must arrive soon, otherwise it would be too dark for her to cross the bridge. Her arms were weary. Her face was grimy with a paste of hemp dust and sweat. She was too fatigued to continue weaving.

Feeling she couldn't get enough breath into her chest, she went outside, the air keen with frost. She wrapped her arms around herself and, for no good reason, stared down the dirt road, as if the sledge would appear at any moment. Clouds had rolled in, and the wind was picking up. The air was heavy with the feel of approaching snow.

At the family's evening meal, talk touched upon Grigorii's delinquent return, but it was of minor concern. Any number of things could have delayed them.

A second night stretched on for an eternity as Elizaveta lay awake listening to the Vorontsovs' night-breathing and the scurrying of mice searching for fallen breadcrumbs.

At first light, she slogged through the new snow and broke up the ice atop the livestock's water. Oh, dear God! What if they were snowbound in the backcountry, freezing to death?

As it was Shrove Tuesday, Vera served the traditional butter-rich buckwheat pancakes at the noon meal, but they provided little joy. By now, the rest of the family was tense about Grigorii's safety.

After the meal, Elizaveta fled the house, taking the youngsters to see the procession of sleighs and horses with ribbons and bells parading up and down the frozen river. Afterward, she and the children huddled beside bonfires with other families, singing songs that urged winter to depart. She spotted Feodor's younger brother among the crowd.

"Have you heard from Feodor?" she asked. "We expected Grigorii back yesterday, and we're sick with worry."

No, the Zhemchuzhnikovs had heard nothing. They, too, were fretful.

That night, Elizaveta's exhausted mind and body demanded rest. Yet her sleep was so fitful, the next morning she felt as though she had been up all night with a colicky baby.

Her chest was tight, as though it were about to collapse with anguish. She'd give her very soul to be at the Zhemchuzhnikovs' izba, surrounded by Feodor's family as they waited for his return. Instead she was trapped in this stale, loveless izba, where people agonized over a man so despicable, he deserved the fires of Hell.

Feodor, where are you? All morning and into the afternoon, every possibility looped round and round in her head. Her mind's turmoil was halted only by a knock on the door.

Feodor's brother! The family yanked him inside and clustered around him while he told the story.

Maximov's serf Yegorka had come to the Zhemchuzhnikov izba with news that the Count had received a letter. Feodor wrote that when he and Grigorii had reached the outskirts of the district capital, they were stopped by a temporary cordon set up on the road as a safeguard against peasant unrest over the vodka situation. Upon inspecting the bed of Feodor's sledge, one of the cordon guards had found vodka hidden in a bag of oats. The two large flasks lacked a State seal and were therefore considered smuggled contraband. The guards had carted Feodor and Grigorii to Sukhanovo's jail.

Zhemchuzhnikov finished the story with "Count Maximov will leave for Sukhanovo at sunup to get to the bottom of this."

Vera pressed her hands against her cheeks. "Oh, Lord, help us! In jail!"

During the evening meal, the Vorontsovs brooded over how the short trip to Sukhanovo could have taken such an appalling twist. The charges against Feodor didn't make any sense. Besides being law-abiding citizens, the Zhemchuzhnikovs were a family of sobriety, consuming less vodka than any other household in Petrovo. Although Grigorii didn't have the same high standards, the Vorontsovs knew for certain he wasn't carrying a bag of oats and flasks of vodka when he left the izba. After all, Vera had dressed him.

The following day, Elizaveta was ready to fly apart with nervousness. Finally, as winter's brief daylight was drawing to a close, the long-awaited jangle of the harness bell was heard. The Vorontsovs rushed outside to find Feodor alone in the sledge. A dozen questions were shouted in short, white squalls.

"Quiet! Let the man talk!" Sidor bellowed as he shoved Feodor into the izba and toward the table.

Feodor's Adam's apple rose and fell. "I'm afraid Grigorii won't be coming home."

"What are you saying?"

"What happened?"

"Let him talk!" Sidor roared again.

Feodor stammered, "He . . . he was sent to Siberia."

Wordless gasps encircled the table.

Feodor's fingers traced the wrinkles on his forehead. "If only he hadn't kicked that guard . . ."

"Start from the beginning," Stanislav demanded.

The cordon guard had inspected Feodor's load and found the illegal vodka hidden in a sack of oats. Both Feodor and Grigorii were bound, thrown in the back of the sledge, and carted to the jail.

Grigorii flew into a temper. He fought the guards, the ropes that shackled his hands, and everything else that constrained him. When he kicked a guard, they knocked him to his knees and tied his feet together. When he spat on the guard, they put a gag in his mouth.

"I think Count Maximov had to pay a lot of rubles for me to be freed. Plus an awful amount to get the horse and sledge out of the livery."

"What about my son?" Vera wailed.

"They wanted extra rubles for Grigorii, because he kicked the guard. The Count said he'd known me since I was a youngster but the same wasn't true with Grigorii, and, well . . ." Feodor was imprecise about exactly what Maximov had said. "I'm sorry. I truly am." Feodor's eyes pleaded with Grigorii's parents. "I swear on the Cross, I tried to convince the Count to bail out Grigorii, but he had deaf ears. Grigorii dictated a letter for me to write down for you." He glanced around the table, stopping for an extra beat on Elizaveta. "I forgot it in the sledge."

She jumped to her feet. "I'll go with you to get it, then you can hurry back to your family."

When they reached the far side of the sledge, Feodor said, "I did what I could for Grigorii."

"One reaps what one sows. It was you I was worried about." She gazed into brown eyes that were picking up the gold of the setting sun. "But why was the vodka in your sledge?"

"I don't know. The vodka or the sack of oats, neither were there Sunday morning when I loaded the milk. Then I padlocked the sledge inside the shed until I left Monday morning."

"Did the guards plant the bottle, so they could collect bribes?"

"They didn't try to bribe us." He shook his head in confusion. "They seemed to be expecting us, as if they knew the vodka was in the sledge. And it was odd how they went straight to the sack of oats. Everything was just too coincidental."

"Someone set you up on purpose? Who?"

He lifted his shoulders. "I don't know of anyone who hates me that much. It would have to be someone with a key to the shed's padlock. And who could have alerted Sukhanovo's guards?"

"At least you're safe, and I can stop worrying."

His fingers reached into the fleecy lining of her sheepskin's pocket. "Tomorrow?"

Her fingers threaded through his. "When?"

"One bell."

Elizaveta was at peace as she entered the izba. She watched Anna curl the sleepy-eyed Platon in her arms while one by one, the rest of the family members headed for their sleeping benches along with their silent memories of the unruly youngest son of Sidor and Vera Vorontsov.

Anna's toes set the rocking chair in motion and the girl began to sing softly.

> Sleep by night,
> and grow by the hour.
> Sleep well,
> arise happy.

Arise happy. Yes. Elizaveta thought she'd do exactly that.

CHAPTER 39

Elizaveta

1859

What has four legs
but isn't a beast;
feathers,
but isn't a bird?

A bed.

ELIZAVETA CROSSED OVER the ice-lacquered bridge, her white breath coming in short, timorous flutters. Over half a lifetime ago, her godbrother first placed his lips on hers in that extraordinary way that was decidedly not fraternal. During the countless kisses that followed, the two of them had been little more than children.

When she and Feodor came together this afternoon, it would be as adults. They were two mature people, making their choices with a full understanding of the consequences.

Over the years, she had indulged in heated fantasies of Feodor's mouth on hers. In those daydreams, his hands caressed a waist that was slim and supple and breasts that were high and firm. What would he think of her thickened middle and breasts that drooped like the teats of a nanny goat?

There he was, deep within the trees. Her breath raced to keep pace with the pounding of her heart.

His arms opened wide to her.

She glanced about. No one in sight. She darted across the frozen ground. As she sank into his embrace, all doubts, all insecurities, all unease vanished.

Finally! Finally! Please, Heaven above, don't let this be a dream.

But it couldn't be a dream. If it were, her cheek would be buffing against adolescent peach fuzz rather than nestling into the bristle of a beard. And his shoulders would be boney and hunched instead of feeling like a broad shield of protection.

"Liza, I can't begin to tell you." He placed a hand on the back of her head and pressed her closer until she felt part of his very being.

They clung together, inseverable. There was no rush to kiss, like in the old days. There was only the need to hold tight. When they tore from one another's arms, she saw a yearning in his unveiled eyes that matched hers.

He began walking. She fell into place beside him, matching him stride for stride through a forest silenced by a mantle of snow. They reached what Elizaveta had come to think of as Zhanna's hut. "What is this place?"

"It's the Maximovs' hunting lodge."

"Their what?"

"When the Count's sons were young, they'd go hunting and sleep here."

That made no sense to her. Why sleep here when it was only a brief walk to their big house? He went up to the door, but she hung back. "Can we go in there?"

"It's all right. It's my responsibility to clean it up, chase out the mice, and make repairs."

He pushed open the door. The rasp of its rusty hinges hurled her back in time to the Widow Shabanova's barn. How unbelievable that as adults in their middle years, they were still seizing stolen moments away from village eyes.

Inside, Elizaveta stomped the snow off her felt boots and onto a floor of flat, smooth stones. An entire floor of stone! Her eyes probed the cabinets, table, and chairs—not stools, but chairs with backs, like her rocking chair had!

And what was this? Beds! Two of them! A few years ago she had seen one when she had to fetch the priest from his izba.

She edged toward one of the mattresses and eyeballed the pillows and the soft woolen blanket. Feodor moved beside her and turned down what she'd thought was a single blanket. But there were three!

"Sit on it. You'll like it." Merry little creases radiated from the corners of his eyes.

She removed her gloves and gingerly pressed her fingertips into the contraption.

He chuckled. "It won't swallow you up, I promise."

She tucked her coat under her and sheepishly sat down. Summoning courage, she bounced. She buoyed like a fallen leaf on top of waves. He laughed again, and she giggled with him, simply because it felt so good to do so.

He reached down and slid the wool scarf from her head and shoulders, then draped it over the iron rail of the headboard. His fingers loosened the sash of her coat. "Warm up under the blankets. I'll start a fire."

Feodor walked to a black metal object that was slightly larger than a pickle barrel. He opened a small door and tossed in twigs and logs.

Elizaveta's eyes darted about, searching for the familiar huge, whitewashed clay stove. But there wasn't one! Certainly that little, silly-looking black thing wasn't for both heating and cooking? It wasn't large enough to accomplish either!

She hung her coat on a wall peg and removed her boots. As she returned to the bed, she gave it a long, hard stare, as if it were a snake that could strike at any moment. She thought it too brazen to lie down while waiting for Feodor. But she wasn't sure what else to do, since lying down was exactly what beds were for.

She ran the back of her hand over the smooth, white pillow. Her eyes closed while her fingertips traced a return path across the doughy softness. She moved the pillow aside, placing it atop the other one.

Icy shivers racing every direction, she tucked her legs under the blanket and propped her back against the curlicue metal headboard.

She pulled the blankets—all three—as high as she could. The wool didn't make her sneeze with dust the way her sheepskin blanket did. And quite unlike her pallet at home, the bed didn't poke her with the ends of stiff straw.

When the fire took hold, Feodor removed his coat and tossed it over a chair. He slid under the blankets and positioned the two pillows behind his back. He opened an arm. She cuddled into it and nuzzled her cheek against his shoulder, just like in Shabanova's barn. Except now, hairs poked above the neck of his shirt.

"Time and again I argued with myself about whether I should ask you to come here. Even though good sense told me not to," his voice wavered, "I simply can't face the rest of my life without you."

Elizaveta reached her arm across Feodor's chest, snuggled in tight, and sent a prayer of gratitude to the Holy Mother of God for this singular moment in her life.

His Adam's apple bobbed. "If we go on, who knows what pain and heartache we may bring upon ourselves."

She didn't know if "going on" referred to today's lovemaking or to their continued meetings. But it didn't matter. "We have to go on," she whispered, "now that I know you haven't forgotten about me."

"Forgotten about you? I constantly imagine you beside me. Every. Single. Day."

She squeezed back tears. She couldn't cry. The two of them needed to talk the language of adults. They had but a short time together. She wouldn't ruin it with hysterics.

"If we keep meeting like this, can you live with yourself?" he asked. "Can you bear the guilt? The risk?"

Elizaveta had already worked through those worries during her sleepless nights. What they were about to do was altogether wrong. But her conscience was clear even though her actions were sinful. She hated lies and couldn't tolerate deception, but her love for Feodor knew no remorse.

"I have no guilt. And you?"

His beard moved side to side. "But if we're caught, you're the one who will pay the price."

"I already thought about that."

"Of course you did. You've never been a person who stumbles blindly through life." His lips lingered in a kiss atop her head. "I'll protect you at any cost. You have my word."

"I can be happy as long as I have you for a few stolen minutes."

He surprised her with a stern admonishment. "Consider what you're saying. We mustn't fool ourselves that what we want today will be enough tomorrow."

She pulled herself away and dipped her eyes into his. They were still the color of weathered acorns. "But I can't see past today."

He cradled the point of her chin between his thumb and forefinger and drew her mouth to his.

His lips, at first as soft as moss, grew hungry. He slipped a hand around the small of her back and slid her full-length onto the mattress. As her arms went around his neck, the whole of his body pressed upon hers. His mouth moved from her lips to her chin, then below her ear.

He buried his face against her shoulder. "Oh, my soul, Liza." His voice was like thick porridge, heavy with cream. "I have never stopped loving you."

"And I, you," she whispered.

His breath wove through her shirt, making her body feel like warm honey. Flowing. Formless. Yielding.

Her hands pressed his head against her chest as she stirred with responses she didn't recognize. For so long, her frozen heart had been buried beneath a blanket of snow. But now a smoldering ecstasy was melting all that away.

Unbidden, his words returned to her. *We mustn't fool ourselves into thinking what we want today will be enough tomorrow.*

Tomorrow's wants would have to wait. Right now, there was the obliterating sensation of two people with a bottomless longing.

CHAPTER 40

Elizaveta

1861

Who among us is good-natured?

The dog.

ILYA AND GERASIM held Platon upside down out the window, swaying him back and forth like a canister of incense, while a yapping puppy licked the terrorized youngster's face.

"That's enough!" Elizaveta's voice was stretched with weary exasperation. "And shut that dog up."

Elizaveta's two teenagers hoisted Platon by the seat of his trousers into the izba. He hurdled himself across the room and into Anna's arms, biting his lip to keep from crying.

"My poor little lamb. Ilya and Gerasim were just teasing you," Anna assured him. "They would never harm so much as a hair on your head."

"By accident. They could have dropped me by accident." Platon's moist eyes told of the imminent danger he had been in.

"But Ilya and Gerasim are strong. They wouldn't drop our little darling Platoshka."

"That's right," Elizaveta quipped as she opened the door to leave. "Ilya and Gerasim are strong young men. You'd think rather than tormenting their young cousin, they'd be interested in learning about their new lives as free men." She looked pointedly at her sons, who had recently passed their sixteenth and fifteenth birthdays. "Get to the meeting, before I wallop you both with a broom handle."

As she stepped outside, she stumbled over the pup that was waiting for another rough-and-tumble game. In a never-ending quest for fun, the pooch cocked his head to one side while his tail wagged his body.

The brown-and-black pup had shown up two weeks ago with an empty belly and a long gash on his back leg. Sidor allowed the dog to stay because Anna and Platon were merciless with their entreaties. The dog's injury tore at Anna's heart, and Platon was enchanted with the pup's mirthful eyes—one was dog-brown in color while the other was gray blue.

With the happy incoordination common to all canine youngsters, the dog planted two oversized paws on Elizaveta's skirt. She kicked at the pup. "Platon, get your dog away from me!"

Platon ran, arms extended, toward his furry friend. "Sharik. I named him Sharik." The boy's cheeks grew fat with his smile.

The pup bounded into the open arms of the almost-four-year-old and the increasingly familiar sound of "Sharik."

As Elizaveta hurried toward the village square, her annoyance with her children shrouded her with remorse. When had she become so crabby, so short-tempered? Had living with the Vorontsovs hardened her into a snappish old woman?

And why did she feel a special place in her heart for Platon? Was she partial to him because of his secret? Or because he wasn't from Vorontsov loins? Or was it in remembrance of Avdotya?

The unanswered questions were set aside as she joined the crowd gathered about the well. Almost every adult in Petrovo was present, anxious to hear the new peace mediator explain the particulars of the serfs' emancipation.

Elizaveta snaked her way through the villagers until she reached Feodor. She turned her eyes toward the overcast sky. "Do you think it will rain on Friday?"

He nodded. "Oh, yes, I definitely hope it will rain Friday."

Elizaveta walked away, doing a poor job of concealing her smile or the spring in her step. Friday! The Maximovs' lodge! She and Feodor didn't dare risk meeting more than once a month.

She strode past the Vorontsovs in order to stand beside her sister Katya.

"This is Victor Vladimirovich Rusakov," Father Diakonov shouted, his hands cupped around his mouth and his old age bending him like a scythe. "He is the peace mediator our Tsar sent to explain our freedom. He will answer your questions truthfully."

The *Regulations Concerning Peasants Leaving Serf Dependence* infuriated both the nobility and the peasants across Russia, each believing themselves despoiled. Social order was but a few slight nudges away from collapse. Worried the situation was sufficiently charged to light a conflagration that could consume the entire Empire, the Tsar had sent forth an armada of newly hired peace mediators to diffuse animosity.

Rusakov, dressed in a starched civil service uniform and creaky leather boots, stood on a plank spanning two barrels. With theatrical aplomb, he raised a thick document above his head. "This law, signed by our Emperor, Alexander

Nicholaevich Romanov, grants the serfs of Russia full rights as free citizens. No longer will you have to answer to other men's demands."

"Praise God!"

"Glory to our Blessed Redeemer!"

"I'm free!"

When the worshipful murmuring subsided, Rusakov continued. "No longer will you be serfs. You will be called 'free rural inhabitants.' As such, Count Maximov cannot tell you how to run your lives or farm your fields. Members of your village assembly will elect from among themselves an official court, at which you can appeal petty civil disputes. Count Maximov cannot overturn the court's decisions."

"Petty civil disputes?" a voice called. "What's that?"

"Disagreements amongst yourselves. Violation of promises. Separation of husbands and wives. Reneging on agreements. Those types of things."

The crowd broke out in the hymn "God Save the Tsar," but Elizaveta didn't join the singing. She was clutching at the words *separation of husbands and wives.* Did that include divorce?

When the singing stopped, Rusakov got down to the nitty-gritty of how the land would be divided. The peasants' transition from tilling their pomeshchik's land to owning their own land would be gradual, ranging anywhere from two years to twenty years.

Two years to twenty years? The villagers' euphoria evaporated.

The peasants, although free, would work for Count Maximov in exchange for the right to grow grain on the land the Count allotted them. The village was to work as a single unit, precisely as it did now. All were required to uphold their end of the bargain.

A momentary silence gripped the crowd before it erupted. "What! Continue to work for Maximov?"

Seeking to restore peace, Rusakov faced the crowd with open palms and unfurled fingers. "Only for two years. During those two years"—his palms closed, leaving two fingers extended on each hand—"your village assembly will negotiate with the Count to determine how much land you will own. As the peace mediator, I will work with you and the Count to ensure a fair agreement is reached. That agreement will be put in writing in a document known as a land charter."

"We don't care a fig about a charter," Gavriil Naryshkin exclaimed. "Tell us about the land we're receiving."

"We—meaning your village assembly, Count Maximov, and myself—will jointly determine what price you will pay for your land."

"Pay for land? That land is ours because we plough it!"

"What next? Pay for the river? And then pay for its fish?"

"Will we have to buy our sunshine, too?"

Curses showered the air like wind-driven sparks from a burning thatch roof. Father Diakonov's hands flapped up and down to quiet the angry ruckus.

Rusakov continued, "After we settle on a price for the land, we will set a date when you will start *redeeming* your land. *Redeeming* means you start paying for your land. On that exact date, the land becomes yours. As I said, that date can be as soon as two years from now, if you choose to act quickly." He flashed the crowd a constricted smile. "However, if you drag your feet, you will have to compensate Count Maximov with either rent money or labor in exchange for grazing his meadows and growing your crops in his fields."

A murderous growl rose from the peasants.

"That makes no sense."

"There's been a mistake."

"In a pig's ear!"

"Don't fret," Rusakov urged. "I am here to help divide the land between you and Count Maximov, plus set its price according to what your Tsar has determined to be fair."

"I want to make sure I understand this," Feodor called out. "We no longer answer to Count Maximov. However, we'll work for him for two years or until the assembly and the Count agree on how much land will be ours to till?"

"Exactly!" Rusakov punched his fist across the air in front of his chest, relieved someone grasped his message. "And in the same way, you will negotiate at what price you will redeem that land."

Elizaveta's Uncle Artamon hollered, "*Redeem*? I don't understand that word."

Rusakov explained that the peasants would pay rubles to the government over a period of forty-nine years.

"Forty-nine years!" Anger was hurled at Rusakov with the ferocity of bees attacking a honey-pilfering bear.

"Why are we paying money to the government?" Evdokim Seleznyov's face was blotched with anger. "The land doesn't belong to the government."

"You and Count Maximov, with my help, will settle on the redemption price—that is, how many rubles the land is worth. Then the government will pay the Count that exact amount for the land, and the land is transferred to you. Therefore, you will owe the government rather than Count Maximov."

"But the land is ours."

"God made the land for the people."

"Why should we pay for it?"

"The land belongs to the Count," Rusakov explained. "His great-grandfather had to earn the right to own the land. Is it not fair that the Count be compensated? The Tsar isn't asking any more of you than the Tsar's forebears asked of Count Maximov's forebears."

"We've tilled that land since we were knee-high!" Sidor Vorontsov shouted.

Avdotya's brother Timofei Sharovatov yelled, "For generations, our families have sweated over this land, labored over it, tended it with loving care!"

Gavriil Naryshkin raised both fists in the air. "We have more right to the land than does Maximov!"

"What if we don't want any of this?" Ermak cracked his knuckles in a torrent of outrage. "Can we leave? Go to the city and earn a living?"

"What do you mean? Not redeem the land?" Vasya Karpov retorted. "We can't leave the land. Farming is a duty imposed by God."

"Shut up, so the man can answer my question!"

Rusakov pulled at his starched collar. "At some point, the village as a whole will have to accept a piece of earth and accept responsibility for making redemption payments for that piece of earth. If you want to leave Petrovo, you won't have to ask Count Maximov for a passport. Instead, the village assembly will issue your passport, and you will be free to leave. But your family is still responsible for its portion of the redemption payments."

Go to the city and earn a living. The assembly will issue your passport, and you will be free to leave. If she could divorce Ermak, perhaps the assembly would grant her and Feodor passports, and they could forever leave this dismal village and its gossip. Even without a divorce, maybe she could get a passport. When did all this take effect? Like everyone else, she had only the mistiest notion of what would occur and when.

Red-headed Demian Osokin said, "Feodor, take a look at that document. Tell us what it says."

Rusakov relinquished the proclamation to Feodor, who examined the richly inked first page, turned a page and then another, and went back to the first page. He opened his mouth to speak, then closed it. His brow wrinkled. He turned his head to one side and peered at the page like a chicken eyeing a grasshopper.

"The words are too big, the sentences too long. I'm not sure what it means." In defeat, he handed the manuscript back to Rusakov.

Suddenly Illarion Loktev bounded onto a short bench by the well. He pointed at Rusakov. "We know what you're telling us is not what our Tsar has proclaimed."

"We will die for God and the Tsar," Timofei Sharovatov declared.

Imitating the peace mediator, Illarion held a small bundle of papers above his head. "I have here—the Golden Charters."

Ahhh. A communal sigh of relief settled over the crowd like a rain shower after a drought. The long-rumored Golden Charters had finally surfaced. To the villagers, there wasn't a shadow of a doubt that the pages waved about by that asinine peace mediator were false.

Illarion motioned Feodor to again step forward. "Read these words to your neighbors. They are our Tsar's true wishes for his people."

Elizaveta rolled her eyes. The nerve of that wicked liar to even speak the word *true.*

Feodor gave the document a shake, cleared his throat, and began to read.

> *Article 1: His Imperial Majesty explains: My beloved children, I send you happiness and abundance. Do not listen either to the pomeshchik or to the priests for they will deceive you, but find yourselves a man of good will. He will read to you my favor correctly, and you pay him a silver kopek each. Listen to what he will read, and do as it says.*

> *Article 2: All the pomeshchik's land is given to the peasants, and for the pomeshchik there remain marsh grasses and the swamps, in order that they may have a place to nest, like the devils.*

> *Article 3: At harvest time do not go to work for the pomeshchik, but let him gather grain with his family; what he gathers, this is his, but if there remains unharvested grain, then it shall be gathered by the village and divided by the village.*

> *Article 4: Pay no kind of taxes or obligations for five years. The Sovereign pardons them.*

The document went on in like vein for four additional articles.

As soon as her beloved finished speaking, Elizaveta trudged home, pondering the connection between freedom and passports, between elected courts and separation of husbands and wives.

CHAPTER 41

Elizaveta

1861

What was born into the world twice?
A hen.

WHEN THE VORONTSOVS arrived home for the midday meal, Stanislav declared the peace mediator was as empty-headed as a potato. "There's talk of the men banding together to put Maximov in his place. We'll show him whose side God is on!"

"Our Tsar would never expect us to work for Maximov two more years." Vera's head swung side to side.

"Worse than that, we have to buy our land!" Ermak's knuckle-cracking anger was at a fevered pitch.

"That can't be true," Elizaveta said. "We've always said we may belong to the Count, but the land is ours."

Vera's shoulders drooped like wilted carrot tops. "Father Diakonov said the peace mediator would tell us the truth."

Stanislav snorted. "Diakonov. Humph! I bet that pious bastard—"

"Stanislav, please," his wife injected. "Show some respect."

"Respect? For a long-haired imbecile who has an unholy alliance with the peace mediator and with Maximov?"

"What are you saying, Papa?" Onufrii asked as he scooped another potato from the pot.

Ermak stopped cracking his joints and heatedly bounced his wooden spoon against the tabletop. "He's saying that a few pretty silver rubles have been slipped to that clerical dirt, so he'll agree with whatever lies come from the lout Maximov and the featherheaded peace mediator."

"Exactly what I'm saying." Stanislav took a long draught of kvass and gave a powerful belch before turning toward Platon. "And I have something to say to you, little boy. Get rid of that dog."

Platon's eyes went wide. Anna spewed out her half-chewed beets. Everyone at the table peered at Stanislav, stunned by his abrupt change of topic.

"There's a dead hen in the workyard. The dog has to go."

Tears jumped to Platon's eyes. "Noooo . . ."

Stanislav held up his hand. "Can't have a chicken-killer. Next thing you know, the pup'll be a full-grown dog slitting open the necks of our sheep."

"Uncle Stanislav, please, no!" Anna cried.

Stanislav ignored the pleadings of the children and addressed his wife. "Sun's warm today. You'll want to pluck and gut that chicken before it starts to stink."

Platon's tears came full-force. "Please, Uncle Stanislav."

"Get rid of the dog."

Anna pleaded, "But Uncle Sta—"

"Not another word!" Stanislav, his blood already in full boil over the peace mediator's words, wasn't about to put up with whiny children.

Stanislav's wife grimaced. "Isn't it expecting too much of a four-year-old to dispose of a dog?"

"Then you do it."

Platon flung himself facedown on the bench and flailed his legs and arms.

Ermak's scowl was dark as thunder. "Elizaveta, get that sniveling little idiot under control."

Elizaveta pitied the pup. He was a nuisance, but youngsters of all species were more bother than they were worth. She strove for a condescending tone. "Uncle Stanislav, the dog is just a pup. We can teach him not to—"

Stanislav cut her off. "What kind of senseless woman did you bring into this family, Ermak? She'll sacrifice the chickens and their meat and eggs that feed this family just to appease that bellyaching kid of Avdotya's."

Sidor, as the bolshak, had the final say. "Once a dog tastes a chicken, nothing's going to stop him. The dog has to go today."

Anna burst into tears, ran from the table, and burrowed beneath a sheepskin on her sleeping bench. Platon trailed after and joined her under the blanket. They bellowed like a couple of calves.

Knuckles cracked beneath the table. Ermak's lips went as thin and white as eggshells.

Elizaveta tensed, ready to spring from the bench. She vividly remembered a time when she hadn't acted quickly enough, and Ermak had shoved seven-year-old Gerasim's hand into a pot of boiling soup as punishment for snitching an extra fritter. Today, eight years later, she glanced at her son's hand that still bore the scars.

"I've heard all I can take!" Ermak slung his spoon across the room toward the two children. *Thunk*, against the wall planks. His stool screeched on the floorboards as he pushed back from the table.

Elizaveta sprang up and grabbed a knife.

She raced Ermak to the sleeping bench and slid between her husband and the two children. Nostrils flared, she poised the knife straight out from her breastbone. Her tight-lipped voice was for his ears only.

"If you lay a finger on them, I swear on the tears of Christ, I'll drive this knife through your liver."

She and Ermak glared at each other, mutual hatred in their eyes. When moments went by and he didn't move, she knew this small victory was hers. But he'd eventually have his day of reckoning.

Eyes fixed on her husband and arm ready to plunge the knife, she extended her other hand behind her and gestured to the youngsters. "Come along. Out to the barn. We'll talk about this."

CHAPTER 42

Elizaveta

1861

Twice are they born,
not once are they baptized.
What are they?

Teeth.

"SERAFIMA!" ELIZAVETA HISSED. "What are you doing?"

Her daughter, squatting in the garden, looked up. "Planting cucumbers."

Elizaveta glanced about the workyard to ensure no others were witnessing this unfortunate event. "Out of there right now!"

Serafima rose as she contemplated the maniacal woman before her.

"Out!"

Serafima's face scrunched in confusion. She was being chastised for being a diligent worker?

Elizaveta grabbed her daughter's slender arm and yanked her clear of the tilled soil. "You know better than to be in the garden when you're under the curse of Eve."

"But Grandma told me to do it."

"She didn't realize your condition. You've been taught right from wrong."

Elizaveta gave the sigh of the weary. Hadn't she explained the many rules to Serafima? A woman under the curse must never look upon another person's naked body or the latter would immediately be covered with a rash. If a woman having her cycle climbed a pear or apple tree, it would wither. A bleeding woman was not allowed to light the icon candle in her own home. And so on.

"What if we have a poor garden this summer? Who do you think they'll blame?"

But Serafima acted as if her mother hadn't spoken. Her eyes were fixed on the rear of the workyard. Elizaveta swiveled about. Peering around the corner of the barn was a scruffy black-and-tan face with one brown eye and one gray eye.

"Where'd that dog come from?" Elizaveta put her hands on her hips. Stanislav's wife said she had taken the pup so far into the woods, it could never find its way back. Now, weeks later, here it was. Thank goodness, Anna and Platon were playing down at the river.

Elizaveta's eyes narrowed as the pup rounded the corner of the barn. It crouched low, its tail hanging straight between its legs, its nose pointed down at the ground. Its eyes were rolled up in their sockets, showing the white rims of its mismatched eyeballs. It slunk two paces forward, stopped, and fixed its eerie glare on Elizaveta.

Could this deranged dog really be the same one whose happy pink tongue had smothered Platon with kisses? The hair rose on the back of the animal's neck, and Elizaveta's heart quickened.

She stood as still as a corpse as she whispered, "Go inside and find Papa or Cousin Onufrii or someone. Move slow, but go fast." There wasn't time for logic.

The dog took a step closer.

With excruciating deliberation, Elizaveta bent over and picked up the pitchfork. The mongrel's lip curled. White teeth gleamed in the sunlight.

Elizaveta's breaths were quick, shallow pants. With protracted movements, she gripped the wooden handle with both hands and leveled its prongs toward the animal. Bolts of rage shot from the dog's demented eyes as it hunkered lower.

Elizaveta licked her lips. The dog's body was taut, ready to make the six or eight leaps to reach her. She wouldn't be able to fight it off. Although far from full-grown, it was a muscular animal. If she moved slowly, could she back into the izba without rousing the dog?

She took a cautious step back.

The dog pulled its lips tighter. The skin along its back twitched as though struck by lightning. The animal was about to pounce.

"Help!" she shrieked.

The barn door opened. The beast jerked its head around to look at Stanislav.

"What's that damn dog doing here?" He stepped back into the barn and reappeared with a shovel, its iron scoop tapering to a pointed end.

Fast, powerful legs streaked toward Stanislav. He raised the tool and hurled it like a spear. The weapon glanced off the animal's shoulder.

Propelled by fury, it lunged at Stanislav's legs, lather flinging from its mouth. Stanislav sidestepped the attack, hurling his back against the side of the barn.

The dog clenched on to Stanislav's trouser and whipped the pant leg back and forth.

Someone grabbed the pitchfork from Elizaveta. Relief flooded her as she saw Gerasim and, behind him, Ilya. Gratitude for her own respite was instantly replaced by fear for her sons' safety.

"Ahhhhh!" Ilya ran toward the animal, the stove's iron poker projected forward like a bayonet.

Stanislav's trouser gave way, exposing his calf. Shreds of cloth hung from the dog's foaming mouth as it lunged at Stanislav's bare leg.

Ilya stabbed the poker into the dog's side. The crazed animal continued to tear its fangs into Stanislav's flesh. Gerasim thrust the wooden pitchfork at the animal's head. *Crack.* One of the tines broke off.

Enraged, the dog hoisted itself onto its back legs. Its foamy mouth went for Stanislav's throat and head.

Stanislav lost his balance and fell to the ground. He curled into a ball, his back against the planks of the barn, his head covered with the thick sleeves of his quilted jacket.

Elizaveta was paralyzed with horror, yet she knew she had to help her sons.

The hatchet in the barn.

Hoisting her skirt, she charged past the terrible fight. Blood spattered her. Stumbling blindly inside the dim barn, she groped nothing but cobwebs.

Where's the hatchet? Where is it!

Her fingers brushed against it at last. She grabbed it and darted outside, blinded this time by the glare of the sunshine.

Gerasim had the dog trapped on its side on the ground, its neck pinned by the tines of the pitchfork. Ilya leaned on the handle of the poker, its point in the writhing animal's flank. Saliva flew as its head beat against the dirt in its struggle to rise. Stanislav slid from the dog's reach.

Ilya saw the hatchet in his mother's hands. "In the belly!"

How she wished she could hand the tool to one of the boys! She looked down at the thrashing animal. With both hands, she raised the hatchet above her head.

The dog's body contorted as it battled to free itself from the pitchfork. Its teeth snapped the air. Its gray eye stared, wild and violent, at its captors.

Elizaveta clutched the hatchet with all her strength and drove her arms down in the same arc she'd used boundless times to thresh grain. Her eyes snapped shut. She heard a howl as the sharp wedge sliced through spongy flesh, then met unyielding ground. She opened her eyes.

Blood rushed from the wound, yet still the dog thrashed. She raised the hatchet and again brought it down on the animal's soft belly. Her arms quivered. Her strength was leaving her.

But it didn't matter. The animal could no longer struggle. Gerasim removed the pitchfork from around the hairy neck. He repeatedly and unmercifully thrust it into the dog's intestines. The dog snapped at the source of its pain, then laid its head on the ground and died.

Gasping for breath, Elizaveta, Ilya, and Gerasim looked down at the battered body of the once playful pup. Such a fearless, unfounded attack—it must have been mad with rabies.

Elizaveta looked at her two sons, both of whose height had overtaken hers with the years. "You hurt?"

"No," they gulped as the terror-induced valor left their bodies.

Stanislav sat with his back against the barn. Blood puddled on the ground. The gash in his calf was deep. The wounds on his face were mingled with spatters of blood from the thrashing dog.

"I need help," he demanded of Elizaveta.

Memories speared her. The lust in his eyes as he stood too close to her. The atrocities he had committed with Avdotya. The family's precious rubles he'd squandered on vodka, not caring if stomachs were twisted in hunger.

Hatred seethed within her billowing chest. She turned on her heel and flung her words over her shoulder. "Warm sun today." Her tone mimicked Stanislav's when he had told his wife to dress the mangled hen. "You'll want to get rid of that dog's carcass before it starts to stink."

CHAPTER 43

Maximov

1861

I am my father's son,
but not my brother.
Who am I?

I myself.

ANTON WAS SQUINTING down the length of a billiards cue when Gennady the butler announced Count Maximov wanted to see his son immediately in the stable office.

"I thought he was at Gabrichevsky's estate, looking over the new brood mare."

"He returned a few moments ago."

Anton took a sip from a tumbler of cold vodka, bent over the table, and leisurely aligned the five ball with the side pocket. He saw no reason not to finish the game. His father probably wanted to talk about a six-year crop rotation versus an eight-year rotation versus . . . Hell, what was the upper limit? A twelve-year rotation? A lifetime rotation?

Anton realized agriculture wasn't the topic, however, as he neared the tiny stable office and alcohol seared his nostrils. He stood in the doorway, mouth agape, eyes skimming over the shattered bottles strewn atop the wet pavers.

Stepan sat at the table, his hands piously clasped, his arms triangulated on the table over an open copy of *The Moscow News*. "I ask that you ignore the mess I've made." Despite Stepan's casual posture, his voice was tight.

"I assume you're displeased about something?" When Stepan's mouth remained a grim slash, Anton continued. "You visited Gabrichevsky?" He received a nod. "Did the new mare arrive safely?"

"Yes. A spirited beauty from the Don." Stepan's face maintained the solemn rigidity of the dead.

What the fuck is the old man's problem? Anton threw back his shoulders, walked the three steps from the doorway to the table, and slid onto a chair. *Had the old goat gone berserk?* "I'd pour a toast to Gabrichevsky's new femme fatale, but it seems there's nothing left to toast with."

"My misguided attempt to straighten out your fouled-up life. Temporary insanity on my part." Stepan pushed aside *The Moscow News*, so his fingers could rhythmically drum the table.

Anton crossed his foot over the other knee and grabbed the ankle of his boot. Not only did the posture evoke a look of imperturbable calm, but it also gave his hand something to do, since clutching a drink wasn't an option.

"And whatever is upsetting you came up in conversation with Gabrichevsky?"

"He had quite a bit to say about you." Stepan's eyes were piercing icicles.

August's moist heat gathered in the closed room. Anton forced a spurious chuckle. "I hope he did me justice."

"Do you deserve justice?"

Anton resolved to remain unflappable.

"It appears our tax farmer, Pichshenko, has a silent partner."

A pulsating constriction gripped Anton's throat. "I was going to tell you."

"When?" Stepan's neck sinews twitched.

"When I felt the time was appropriate. You've been so preoccupied with the emancipation of the serfs, I didn't want to cause you further consternation."

"Further consternation? How very considerate of you. Like I'm a doddering old buffoon who needs his rash, reckless son to protect him from life's trials." His breath quickened and his cheeks flushed. "So it's true. You've degraded the name of Maximov by sinking into the decadent position of tax farmer." His fist struck the table, and it tottered back and forth on its ancient, uneven legs. "What in God's name were you thinking?"

Anton took his time to respond, vowing to preserve an unruffled composure. "You're the one who's hounded me to find a source of income. Go ahead and snub your high-and-mighty nose at people who strive to make an honest living, but there are plenty of tax farmers who can buy and sell you hundreds of times over."

Stepan gave a throaty snicker. "Honest living. That's funny, Anton. Cheating the peasants and the distillers doesn't have a thread of honesty in it. If you want to know what honest work is, take a good, hard look at these two hands." Stepan raised his palms toward Anton.

Anton fixed his eyes on Stepan's face, refusing to so much as glance at the man's sanctimonious display of his years of toil. He clamped his teeth to keep from rejoining that Petrovo was little more than an indigent farm and that nothing Stepan had done in the past thirty years had made a spit's worth of difference in either its prosperity or its net worth. Not only were such statements irrelevant to the conversation, they also would lengthen its duration, which was entirely contradictory to Anton's immediate objective of getting the hell out of that office.

"I entered a legal business venture."

"Another hilarious notion. You running a business. One might as well endeavor to teach a dog to catch a mouse."

Anton labored to steady his voice. "I intend to make a living for myself with the one thing I understand: vodka."

"You'll never make a living for yourself. You've always lived irresponsibly, and you always will. Here I am, entering the later years of my life, our world turned upside down by Alexander's absurd proclamation, wishing I had a responsible son who could help me make decisions and maneuver through God-only-knows what lies ahead . . ." Stepan's voice trailed off as if he were gathering his stray thoughts. "Never has anyone in the Maximov family stooped anywhere near so low as to be a tax farmer, the same parasite that has ruined and corrupted the peasants and stolen untold thousands of rubles from honest distillers like your own family."

Anton's prolonged sigh was nothing but pure exasperation. "Face facts. The old days are gone. After the humiliating loss in the Crimea and the emancipation of the serfs, the Russia we knew is dead."

"Morality never changes." Stepan propped his elbows on the table, threaded his fingers together, and rested his chin on his knuckles. "I suppose Pichshenko partnered with you to obtain money?"

The stable office, paltry in size to begin with, began to feel claustrophobic and airless. "I supplied the needed capital."

"And exactly where did you come up with that capital?"

"It's none of your concern. I'm an adult. I have a right to make decisions."

"Then as an adult, why don't you move out and live on your own, as young men your age tend to do?" Stepan smirked as if he had a hidden trump card. "Why don't you simply pack your bags and never take a backward glance at your childhood home, the home that has provided you with the luxuries you squander on card games?"

"Honestly, I don't have a good answer for you. I should have left years ago."

"Why not leave today?" Full-blown sarcasm entered Stepan's voice. "Why not evict the tenants in your inherited Moscow house and move there?"

The question hit its target like a rock from a slingshot. Anton's head jerked back.

"Why not? Because the Moscow house isn't yours to do with as you please? Does the government have a lien against it?"

"It isn't a lien."

"What is it then?"

"The government holds the property as surety."

"That sounds like a lien to me."

"It's different."

"The government is so stupid as to take half a house as surety? Or were you clever enough to get your brother to sign over his portion also?"

"Leave Sergei out of this. He's not involved."

"How can he not be involved? The house is half his." Stepan inhaled sharply through his nostrils. "Did you forge the papers? Did you somehow pass off the house as belonging solely to you?"

"No!" Anton moistened his lips. "I supplied the government with papers showing I am an owner of the house. Which I am."

Stepan's chin quivered. "You cheated your own brother. It's not enough that you waste your life staring at the bottom of a bottle. To be an incorrigible good-for-naught is one thing, but to dupe your own family is unconscionable!"

Anton's heart beat erratically. His safest course of action was to remain silent.

Stepan pressed his closed fist tightly against his mouth, collecting his thoughts and his breath. "So this is what it's come to." His hand dropped to the table, and his forefinger thumped its marred top. "You know, when you were young and we used to sit at this very table in the kitchen, I repeatedly defended you to your mother when she bemoaned your misspent youth. I told her that you were like a young horse, raring to go. And that after you exhausted yourself early in the ride, you'd learn to pace yourself. I assured her that eventually you'd realize honorable living has its own rewards."

The ranting tenor in Stepan's voice was replaced by one of sympathy. "The sad thing is, Anton, over the years, you've convinced me you will never have the fortitude to look life square in the face."

The conversation was going in circles, and Anton had had enough berating. His unwavering eyes latched on to his father's. His tone was composed, his sarcasm subtle but unmistakable. "I'm fully aware that I have been a wearisome disappointment to you the entirety of my life. Even as far back as our gatherings around this very table." He tapped the boards in mimicry of his father. "I apologize for all my shortcomings. If you'll excuse me, I'll fetch a servant to clean up this mess."

"I'm not finished. You see, I was going to have a little discussion with you today, even before I found out about your business venture."

Anton tilted his head at a bored get-on-with-it angle.

"I received a letter yesterday from Cousin Valeryan. Nadya's new husband is considering having the marriage annulled. It seems he is the old-fashioned type and takes a dim view of brides who aren't virgins on their wedding night."

Anton's skin twitched as if a league of spiders were crawling up his back.

"Sickened as I was by Valeryan's implication, I fully intended to rake you over the coals today. But I've already exhausted my waning energy. So I'll simply conclude by saying this." He inhaled deeply. "For years I prayed that you'd stop drifting about aimlessly, that you'd put your oars in the water and give direction to your life. But you've turned out to be nothing more than a panting example of dissolute leprosy."

Anton's anger at his father, at A.A. Gabrichevsky, at Nadya, at Valeryan, at himself, burst forth in a way that surprised even him. "We all have an ample number of faults, don't we?"

"What do you mean by that?"

"Never mind. It's apropos of nothing."

"Say it."

Anton leveled his gaze at his father. "Let's just say that Vladimir might be interested in knowing about his wife and his best friend."

Stepan sat stone-still. His lips barely moved. "What the hell are you talking about?"

"I'm talking about you and Yustina."

"There's nothing to say about Yustina and me except that we are old friends." Stepan's voice was deep with quiet anger. "Where did you come up with such a degenerate notion?"

Stepan sounded so sincere, so outraged, Anton wondered if he might be telling the truth. But something about the way the old man had blanched and his voice tightened allowed Anton's suspicions to linger. "You can drop your virtuous rhetoric. I'm not buying a word of it."

"I guess dissolute living has so distorted your thinking . . ." Sweat glistened on Stepan's brow as the back of his hand grazed the stubble on his chin. "I'm putting an end to it right now." His words carried a tone of irrevocability.

Even as the walls continued to close in on him, Anton maintained an unperturbed cock to his head. "Meaning what?"

"Meaning you'll rue the day you ever thought about joining forces with Pichshenko. And the day you treated your cousin like a common harlot. I swear by all that is holy"—Stepan paused, allowing the silence to stretch on—"you'll never get so much as a handful of Petrovo's soil. I'm putting together a will. All of my money plus Petrovo will pass to Elena. Every last kopek."

Stripped of his inheritance! Panicked moisture streamed through Anton's palms, around his neck, under his arms. Protesting his father's decision would appear insufferably self-seeking, so he adjusted his argument accordingly. "What's so precious about Elena? Perhaps you feel I'm undeserving, but you have two other children you're likewise severing from their birthright."

"Sergei is set with his career and his well-heeled in-laws. And as for Natalya, Ippolit dotes on her and the children and will see to it she wants for nothing."

Stepan rose and strode, head high and back straight, to the door, each step pulverizing shards of glass. Halfway across the threshold he turned and nodded at the newspaper on the table. With a note of triumph in his voice, he said, "Oh, by the way, there's an article in the *News* that may be of interest to you." With cool composure, Stepan closed the door behind him.

As Anton glared at the door, a multitude of obscenities flew through his head. He swore in the deepest part of his soul, he'd find a way to get even with his father. Someday he'd thumb his nose at the old bastard and his puny little inheritance. By God, he'd come out on top. And in the meantime, he was leaving Petrovo. No longer could he endure living under the same roof with that man.

Anton wiped the perspiration from his upper lip as he craved the magical lull of alcohol. Then the opposite yearning came to him. How gratifying it would be to live a life independent of the bottle, to not long for its soothing respite. Someday. But not today. He'd wait a few minutes to make certain Stepan was gone, then he'd go to the hunting lodge to gather up the few dusty bottles of vodka and brandy stored there.

He glanced down at the newspaper. In the bottom corner was an article of international note about the rising conflict across the ocean. In the United States of America, opposing military forces clashed beside a small creek known as Bull Run.

Interesting article, but it couldn't be what his father was referencing.

He scanned a commentary on the new peasant-sponsored schools that were springing up in the provinces and then an article on the name-day celebration for one of Alexander II's children.

Finally he found it.

A newly enacted statute abolished tax farming. Effective in 1864, the right to manufacture and sell alcoholic beverages would be flung open to the populace. The only requirement was payment of an alcohol excise tax directly to the government.

Anton dropped his forehead into the upturned cup of his palm. *Insolvent.* A word he never thought would apply to him.

CHAPTER 44

Maximov

1861

In the morning I am on four legs;
at noon I am on two;
in the evening I am on three.
What am I?

A human.

ANTON'S PLANS TO move from his father's house met with disaster. During a sultry summer evening's card game in Sukhanovo, he approached an old chum about taking temporary lodging with him. Kazhekin, drunker than usual, replied that he had carried Anton's losses for too long. Not only was Anton not welcome to stay at Kazhekin's home, but until Anton paid off his debts, he wasn't welcome at his card table.

Words became heated. Anton told Kazhekin to be damned. Kazhekin shot back that Anton's shiftless lifestyle was best suited for living off his father's generosity. "That way, you can spend your days lollygagging with your tomboy sister, who acts more like a man than you do."

Thick, black rage flared unlike any Anton had ever known. He lowered his head, hunkered his shoulders, and ran full force into Kazhekin's chest, slamming him against the hearth. The other men tossed Anton onto the street.

Word of the encounter sped through Sukhanovo's scant upper class. The youth who could charm birds from the trees now found his friends scattered like a covey of quail.

Fate rubbed salt into Anton's wound as his business venture sank into a debacle. Tax farms would soon disappear forever. Yet he and Pichshenko had paid but a pittance of their obligations to the government. The two men had pocketed some of the proceeds, true, but most had been used to cover operating costs.

The next blow came as November's winds whipped snow across the fields, when Anton discovered Pichshenko was the fox who had kissed the hen—right down to her tail feathers. The goateed shyster had abandoned Anton to the government's exactions to secure repayment. Because Anton was the one who'd put up sureties for the tax farm, he was the one the government held liable for the payment of the outstanding debt. Shrewd Pichshenko got off scot-free while the bureaucrats relentlessly hounded Anton.

He used to think that his life had merely stalled. But now he found himself laid low by the unprecedented weight of anguished hopelessness. He was bereft of friends. He was up to his eyeballs in debt. His dreams of an invigorating life in Moscow had been snuffed out. He was wrung dry. Like a greedy child, Anton had devoured a life that could have supplied infinite sweetness.

All the cards were stacked against him. Except one. He'd never be homeless. Stepan wouldn't kick him off Petrovo; it would destroy Sophia. When Anton turned an eye toward the future, all he saw were squandered days of staring at bleak frozen fields and holding mind-numbing conversations with local gentry whose intellectual acumen only slightly exceeded that of the peasants. But at least he had a roof over his head, albeit not without his father's unremitting told-you-so smirks.

Christmas was a somber affair at the estate house. Stepan and Anton maintained feigned civility toward one another. Sophia was deep in her morbid winter depression. Even Elena's perpetual good spirits had plummeted into despondency. Two days previously, her favorite borzoi had disappeared during a hunt.

Also missing was the familiar creak of the floors beneath Matriusha's shambling feet, imparting a melancholic void in the estate house. After a lifetime of serving two generations of Maximovs, the stalwart nanny had been laid to rest beneath a cast-iron tombstone in the servants' cemetery.

Despite a general feeling of lassitude, Vladimir and Yustina Rusakov and the four Maximovs stayed true to their Christmas custom of attending the Divine Liturgy together, followed by an overindulgent breakfast.

At the table, Vladimir ran a liver-spotted hand through his thin hair. "As much as I hate to think it, I wonder if our Christmases together might be drawing to a close. Perhaps the time has come for Yustina and I to quit the provincial life and seek the comfort of St. Petersburg."

Sophia almost choked on her broiled squab.

"I'm sorry to hear that, Vladimir." Stepan sounded sincere. But when compared with his woebegone response when August Roeglin had announced his departure two years earlier, Anton found today's reaction somewhat lacking. This probably wasn't the first time his father had heard of the Rusakovs' plans.

Anton's gaze followed Stepan's as it gravitated toward Yustina. Her eyes were steady as they lingered on Stepan's for several seconds before she put down her fork, folded her hands on the edge of the table, and studied her plate.

Anton noted Yustina's graying hair was arranged in a smooth chignon, altogether the opposite of his mother's frizzy disarray. Yustina's chin was still firm and her back erect, quite unlike his father's sagging defeatism. Likewise, her bearing was the antithesis of her husband's, his shoulders hunched, a fork in one hand and a knife in the other, both motionless. The past couple of years had chiseled deep furrows in his face.

Vladimir's lengthy exhale was half sigh and half moan. "Our decision isn't merely because of the shambles Alexander has made of the serf situation. Even beyond that fiasco, the winters seem interminable. The cold leaks clear through to these squeaky old bones." His head rolled back as he stared at the chandelier. "Ahhh, the bliss of a warm apartment."

Sophia's fingertips massaged her forehead. "Have you prayed deeply about this? Asked for guidance?"

Vladimir gave a dismissive wave of his hand. "Dearest friends, Yustina and I are too old and too weary to continue rumbling around that drafty house, emancipation crashing our world down upon us."

"We'll come see you in St. Petersburg when we visit Natalya and Sergei." Elena never failed to find the silver lining.

A barb of self-pity stabbed Anton. He didn't begrudge the Rusakovs the financial wherewithal to move to the city and forever leave behind the rural humdrums. But why the devil couldn't his own prospects be so rosy?

The conversation was halted by a faint tapping at the mahogany door under the porte-cochere. All ears followed Gennady's footsteps to the foyer.

Stepan said, "It's probably the peasants wishing us a happy Christmas."

"I don't think the peasants feel compelled to do that anymore, Father." Anton's voice carried more than a pinch of sarcasm.

"Why not?"

Anton peered at Stepan, wondering if his query was sincere. Apparently it was, based on the bewildered rise of his eyebrows.

"Because the peasants are no longer yours."

"Ah, yes. Right."

The explanation seemed to satisfy Stepan, leaving Anton the one who was bewildered. Such a strange question to something so obvious. And how quick the old man was to accept the answer, as if his mind had become temporarily disengaged and simply needed realigning. Not to mention, hadn't Stepan heard the mockery, as thick as mud, in Anton's voice? The old man must be thoroughly distracted by the prospect of the Rusakovs—or more specifically, Yustina—moving to St. Petersburg.

Gennady entered the dining room. "A peasant girl is at the front entrance to see Mademoiselle Elena."

Elena rose from the table. Sophia hobbled with her cane after the girl—a mother can't stop being a mother simply because her daughter is eighteen years old. Stepan followed the two women. Yustina and Vladimir traipsed outside to the portico as though they were part of the family. Anton pulled some vodka from the liquor cabinet and spiked his apple juice before joining the others.

"Venerka!" White vapors burst from between Elena's lips. "I'd given up on you!" She threw her arms around the dog's neck as the borzoi twisted and turned and bounced. His pink tongue washed Elena's face while his tail battered the door frame. Venerka's exuberance was not the least impeded by an inflexible wrap of stiff linen around one of his back legs.

"Who is that?" Sophia's cane pointed toward the far side of the patio. All eyes focused on a peasant girl, slender as a sapling beneath a ponderous sheepskin coat.

"She's from the village, Mother. And you're shivering. Let's all go inside." Elena beckoned the peasant girl. "You, too."

Last to enter the foyer, the girl stepped as gingerly across the threshold as if she were passing through the pearly gates. While the adults reassembled in a semicircle, her huge blue eyes roved up the stairway, one step at a time.

Elena crouched beside the dog. "I guess you found him?" she asked the teenager.

The girl pivoted toward Elena, giving a start when she chanced upon her own reflection in the gilded wall mirror. At her flinch, the wool shawl slipped off her head, exposing her flaxen braid.

"Where did you find him?" Elena rephrased her question.

The girl licked her chapped lips. "Papa found him." The bevy of onlookers leaned forward to hear her soft words. "In the woods."

Anton didn't have to ask why Papa was slinking around the estate's forest in the dead of winter. He was filching either wood for the stove or small game to toss into the Christmas pot.

"And your papa put the splint on his leg?" Elena hugged the dog's neck. Venerka resumed thrashing his whip of a tail.

"I did." She sucked her lips inward between her teeth.

The semicircle cocked their heads. "You did?" Elena asked.

She gave a slight nod, trembling with cold, or perhaps with fear. Her arms hugged her sides and her hands seemed stitched to the inside of her sheepskin pockets.

Elena bestowed the warmest of smiles on the girl. "You did a very fine job. What is your name?"

"Anna."

"Anna what?"

"Vorontsova."

"Anna Vorontsova, it was most kind of you to return my Venerka to me. Such a special Christmas Day!"

"Vorontsova?" Anton asked. "You were related to Stanislav Vorontsov?"

"Uncle."

Anton gave a gracious bow of his head. "Our condolences. Rabies causes such a dreadful death."

The girl's miniscule nod about her uncle's grisly demise was as stoic as if a hen had gone missing from the workyard.

Elena told Gennady to get the girl a ruble for her troubles. "Wait." She held up a hand. "After all, it is Yuletide. Also bring Mademoiselle Vorontsova some soused apples and a tin of pistachio nougat. Plus a cake of that rose-scented soap Natalya sent us from St. Petersburg." Elena's eyes traveled the length of the girl, starting with her strawberry birthmark and ending at her felt boots. "And put it all in a nice basket."

Anna's eyes grew to the size of saucers.

"Take it to your family to celebrate the birth of Christ," Elena told the girl. "And no need to return the basket."

"Thank you," Anna whispered.

"Tell your parents if there is anything we can ever do for your family as repayment for Venerka's life, you must let us know."

At the sound of his name, the borzoi nuzzled his gray-flecked nose against his master's hand.

Stepan restated his daughter's intentions. "Most assuredly, we would welcome the opportunity to repay your kindness to the dog."

"A blessed Christmas to you, Anna Vorontsova," Elena said.

The girl silently mouthed, *Blessed Christmas.*

CHAPTER 45

Maximov

1861

They beat me, they drub me,
they turn me, they cut me;
I endure it all
and return good to all.
What am I?

The earth.

VICTOR RUSAKOV AND his family were on their way to his in-laws' for their Christmas repast when they paid a brief call on his parents and the Maximovs. Once the glasses of port were drained, the men retired to the study, so Stepan and Vladimir could, yet again, pick Victor's brain on how to best handle the devastation of their human resources.

Vladimir had poured his best efforts into dissuading his son from seeking the job of emancipation peace mediator. He warned that Victor would be in the middle of two warring factions—peasants insistent on receiving land without rendering compensation and the gentry dead set on preserving the status quo. Vladimir also predicted that, due to the size of the district, Victor would spend considerable time away from the family he adored. The strenuous job required personal sacrifice and considerable discomfort. And the paltry salary wasn't likely to increase. But Vladimir's warnings had gone through his son's ears as unchecked as the wind across the steppe.

With bottomless fortitude, Victor once again explained the stipulations of the Emancipation Statutes to the two men. The topic had been discussed so many times and at such grueling length, by all rights Stepan and Vladimir should have exhausted it. But like most landowners, they responded with stubborn incredulity. How could it be that suddenly they no longer controlled the people who worked their estate land and cleaned their houses and distilled their vodka? And how could the government require them to part with some of their estate land?

And how would the former serfs, none of whom had more than a handful of rubles, pay for that land?

Stepan waved about a letter he had received a few days previously. "According to Sergei—who was told in the strictest confidence—the Tsar is considering repealing the whole misguided Statute."

To keep from guffawing, Anton crossed his arms across his chest, his clenched hands almost strangling his biceps.

Victor gave a definitive back-and-forth wag of his head. "The capital abounds with rumors. I assure you, Alexander will stay his course."

"My improvements to Petrovo, all my effort, the commitment I made to this land . . . It's all come to naught." The sag under Stepan's chin fluttered like a turkey's wattle. "I might as well have let the fields languish."

Anton choked back an acerbic snigger. Hell, he could have told the old man that a decade ago. But his words were held in check by the piteous droop of his father's face.

"How am I going to farm my land?" Stepan seemed to shrivel into a miniature of himself, sinking into the imposing wingback chair. "I don't have the working capital to pay wages or purchase equipment."

Vladimir's faded eyes rested on his old friend. "Exactly my thoughts. Far more sensible to sell the estate outright, move to St. Petersburg, and invest in railroad shares or real estate." He pulled off his spectacles and gnawed on an earpiece.

"But the market is glutted with estates for sale." Stepan's index finger heatedly tapped the arm of his chair. "What it boils down to is state robbery. How am I supposed to survive when tens of thousands of rubles have dropped off my asset sheet due to the loss of my serfs? Not to mention, I'm forced to sell one-third of my land to the serfs with nothing to show for it but government bonds, which we all know may end up being completely worthless!"

As the discussion sank into the same old swirling mire of rage and confusion, Victor consulted his pocket watch and said that he needed to be on his way to his in-laws'. "But we can talk again, Stepan Stepanovich, if you'd like. I'll be back in Petrovo soon, to quell some of the peasants' fears."

"What do the peasants have to fear?" Anton asked Victor. "You'd think they'd be on their knees thanking God for their freedom. Isn't that what they wanted?"

"The reality is far more complex. For centuries, the land has held tremendous power over the peasant heart and soul. The peasants have consecrated their lives to the land, making the family, the village, and the land synonymous. And now they're being told that it will be years before they own what they already considered to be *their* land."

"But Alexander had no choice. Freeing the serfs and simultaneously giving them their pomeshchiks' land would have resulted in a conflagration that would have ravaged all of Russia."

Victor held up his hands, palms forward, in a gesture of concurrence. "Try telling that to the peasants. All they see is betrayal."

"But eventually they'll have legal title to the land."

"True. But when? Even without math skills, they understand that their children and their children's children will be in debt until early in the twentieth century."

"So the peasants point the finger of blame at the nobility. The nobility place the blame on the Tsar. And the Tsar blames . . . ?"

"Probably Western Europe, for making serfdom obsolete." Victor chortled as his knuckles stroked a sideburn. "It's the classic Russian question, isn't it? *Who is to blame?*"

Anton contemplated the man sitting across from him and compared him with the renegade at Natalya's wedding five years earlier—unkempt hair about his shoulders, clothes ill-fitting and seedy, a cocoon of detachment and indolence. Victor deserved credit. His job required that he attain the ability to speak out of both sides of his mouth. And he'd learned his lesson very well. No one-sided opinions. No biased statements. The insipid boy he and Sergei had called "namby-pamby" had transmuted into a dissident youth, who had then ripened into an arbitrator who kept peace in the Russian countryside.

Vladimir proceeded to the parlor to bid good-bye to his grandchild while Stepan went to order Victor's horse and carriage be brought around to the portico. The two younger men walked to the foyer.

"Our fathers can really get on a rampage," Victor said as he layered on his outer clothes.

"Can't they, though."

Victor chuckled, then turned serious. "Neither of them is coping well with change at this point in their lives. They've both been set adrift with no idea which course to chart. Or how to even chart a course."

Anton silently questioned Victor's phrase, *at this point in their lives.* "Yes, our fathers are getting older, but it's not as though they're infirm."

"But look at it from your father's perspective. His whole existence, and the existence of his forefathers, is in a state of upheaval. The life of privilege and gay carelessness—it's taken its final bow."

"Tradition dies a hard death." Anton took the simplest tactic, neither agreeing nor disputing.

"Your father has endured enough in his life." Victor tucked the tails of his muffler into his overcoat.

"My father? I don't understand."

"Why, your mother," Victor said, as if his meaning should have been intuitive.

"Oh, yes. Mother. She'll wear on anyone's nerves."

"Not just her, shall we say, 'eccentricities.' I was referring to how abandoned your father must feel."

Stepan, abandoned? Anton thought Victor must be making a wisecrack. But he didn't sound as though he were joking.

"Your father has no one to talk to, to lean on." Victor's voice quickened as he recognized his faux pas. "Not that you and Elena are *no one*. I meant a spouse. Someone his own age who shares the same past and the same outlook."

"Oh, that. I suppose you're right." It was decidedly easier to agree than to quibble with Victor, even though Anton thought Stepan "shared" a hell of a lot with Victor's own mother.

"Of course, you and I were too young at the time to pay attention to our parents' lives, but Mother has often said how Stepan was almost destroyed when your mother, well, when she . . ." For all his newfound diplomacy, Victor couldn't seem to locate the proper word.

"When she took leave of her senses?"

"To hear Mother tell it, Stepan was like a lost lamb for a number of years."

Stepan, a lost lamb? What fairy tale had Victor attached himself to?

After Victor and his family said their adieus, Anton retrieved a bottle of rowanberry vodka from the liquor cabinet. As he headed for the privacy of his bedroom, Victor's words ricocheted. *How abandoned your father must feel. Endured enough in his life.*

Anton took a hearty swallow from the bottle.

Stepan was almost destroyed.

Had his father, at one time, actually loved his mother? Before she pushed him to his limits with her melodramatic theatrics and her possessive dependency? Had Stepan felt as victimized by Sophia as Anton himself had felt?

Anton suspected that he had let Victor put quixotic notions in his head. But possibly Victor's words held some truth. His father did have an inherent intolerance of the irrational. When Grandfather Maximov's mind had slipped away, Stepan could withstand only the most cursory visits with the old crackpot. Perhaps Stepan simply didn't have the mettle to cope with Sophia's type of illness.

And had he himself, at a tender age, been so influenced by Sophia's perpetual grievances against Stepan that he never gave his father a chance to prove he wasn't the Devil incarnate? In a rare brush with self-doubt, Anton wondered if the resentments he harbored toward his father were actually warranted.

What justification was there for allowing his animosity toward Stepan to live in perpetuity? Should he try to patch things up with his father? Could they find a way to live in familial amicability? Or were father and son so alienated that even a halfhearted reconciliation was beyond reach?

Anton took another pull on the bottle. It tasted rotten, even though it was perfectly good vodka. Damn, he was tired of drinking! Tired of hiding liquor in every nook and cranny. Tired of "*accidentally*" pouring wine into his glass at breakfast, always ready with the pathetic excuse that he had mistaken it for cranberry juice.

It was an easy pattern to discern. He drank when he was bored. He drank when problems erupted with Stepan or Sophia. He drank when he was unfavorably compared with esteemed Victor or dumb-as-a-peg Sergei. He drank when he thought about the tax farm or the Moscow house. He drank whenever he felt his life wasn't under his control.

Introspection was an unfamiliar and uncomfortable visitor to Anton. To escape his soul-searching, he fell back upon his training at the Cadet's College. He plotted an intricate series of strategies and mapped a string of contingencies—all designed to minimize his need for the loathsome bottle.

An index finger went into the air. First, he'd switch completely from hard liquor to wine. A second finger joined the first. No longer would he take pleasure in the company of a carafe during the afternoon. He'd drink only at dinner. And after dinner. A third finger followed. Drinking outside those hours would be limited to weddings and other social occasions.

CHAPTER 46

Maximov

1865

You want me,
but you can't buy me.
You don't need me,
but you can't sell me.
What am I?

Youth and old age.

LEGS LANGUIDLY STRETCHED on the ottoman in the study, Anton perused *The Moscow News*'s latest critiques of Alexander II's liberal overhaul of the judicial system. Drawing upon the fundamental principles of Western jurisprudence, the restructured judiciary included not only equality of all citizens before the court but also trial by jury.

Anton was feeling very tolerant of Alexander and his ambitious Great Reforms. For over a year, Anton had been trying to keep the wolf from his door as he sought an extension on his past-due accounts for his defunct tax farm. Notice had arrived today that the government was content to lease out the Moscow mansion as it saw fit, crediting the income toward Anton's arrears.

Anton hoisted his glass in honor of the annoying pebble having finally been removed from his boot.

Plus, the pot had been sweetened further. If the obligation were cleared in less than ten years, the government offered him a substantial discount. Anton made a pact with himself to somehow pay off the debt in half that time. Five years from now, by God, he'd be in the city, immersed in its many pleasures.

Sophia teetered into the study wearing a decades-old black dress and house slippers that were only slightly newer. Leaning on a cane, she blew an aerial kiss toward the corner icon draped in embroidered scarves. After easing into a padded rocker, she tucked a flyaway wisp of gray hair under her omnipresent black knit cap. Her knobby fingers spread a crocheted afghan across her lap, and she picked up an embroidery hoop.

Except for the crackle of the hearth's logs and the ticking of the clock's pendulum, the house was as quiet as a tomb—and not just this evening. Stepan used every excuse he could to escape its walls. Elena sought the comfortable intimacy of the barns or the solitude of horseback. Guests were nonexistent other than Vladimir and Yustina, and they were spending extensive time in St. Petersburg, preparing for their move.

Following emancipation, most of the household serfs had drifted off to urban slums and factories. The only remaining servants were Yegorka, a couple of herdsmen, the cook, Gennady the butler, and the housegirl Dasha, who had long ceased being a girl and had grown wide of hip. Prior to their emancipation, Stepan had supplied the servants with food and shelter. Now he was obliged to also pay wages, which galled him no end.

"Are you reading something important?" Sophia asked Anton.

"No. Merely how the country's entire judicial system has been turned upside down and is no longer recognizable to us."

"Good, because I want to talk to you about an idea I have."

Anton exhaled slowly before lowering the newspaper and reaching for the cut-glass decanter handily placed on the end table.

"Do you realize how many of our peasants do not know their prayers or the Commandments? I could insist they pass my examination before being allowed to marry. It would force them to learn, would it not?"

Pity squeezed at Anton's heart. The timeworn woman was unable to fathom that the peasants were no longer hers. Either that, or she was getting as forgetful as her husband. Stepan had recently made some reckless and sometimes contradictory decisions and purchases. More than once he'd gone to Sukhanovo to buy an agricultural contrivance, only to return to Petrovo to find he had purchased the same item a month earlier.

Stepan entered the study with a newspaper under his arm and headed for his ragged India-red armchair. He looked about the room as if counting the number of people present. Both of them. "Where's your sister? It's almost dark."

Sophia posed her daily question. "When will you replace that ratty old chair?"

Stepan peered over his wire-rimmed spectacles. "I told you. It's comfortable."

"It's so old, it's practically an antique."

"All the more reason to keep it." Stepan snapped out the creases of *The Russian*

Gazette, pushed his spectacles higher on his nose, and submerged his grizzled head in the newspaper.

The lassitude of the study was shattered by a commotion in the foyer. Dasha appeared in the doorway of the study, her voice lurching with breathless fear. "Elena! Hurt! Bad!"

The three family members flew to the foyer to find Gennady struggling up the stairs with Elena in his arms. While Sophia pressured him to move faster and Stepan shouted questions, Anton took Elena from the aging butler and carried her to her bedroom.

As he eased her onto the bed, Elena screamed in raw pain. Her riding breeches angled unnaturally at her shins. In short phrases, Elena described that she had been riding in the forest when she was thrown from her horse. With both legs broken, all she could do was yell for help. Eventually, some peasants had found her.

"Go get that doctor from what's-his-name," Stepan ordered no one in particular.

"You mean from Gabrichevsky?" Anton asked.

"Yegorka just left to fetch him," Gennady said.

Sophia bent over Elena. "Lay still, little Pigeon. The doctor will mend you right up." She kissed her daughter's forehead. After securing her husband's promise to have the priest visit the estate house daily to pray over Elena's fractured tibias, Sophia crossed the room to light the votive candles under the icon.

Stepan's foot tapped. "When is the doctor going to get here?"

"Christ!" Anton shot back. "Yegorka just left to fetch him!"

"The doctor will be here shortly." Dasha soothed Stepan's anxiety while her fingertips gently brushed wayward strands of hair from Elena's face.

A.A. Gabrichevsky's physician arrived three hours later, utterly vexed that April's snow melt had turned the "deplorable roads into a mélange of potholes held together by slurries of mud!" He spent two hours administering laudanum and splinting both legs. He instructed Elena not walk for two months and suggested purchasing a wheelchair.

Rather than risking the return drive in the pitch-black night, the physician stayed until the following morning. Before departing, he handed over some fish-liver pills to help build Elena's strength plus a week's supply of laudanum.

Stepan demanded the doctor leave at least a two-week supply. "My God, man, can't you see the horrible pain she's in?"

Three days later, Yustina came to Petrovo to see how Elena was faring as well as to ensure that Sophia was coping with the trauma.

In the foyer, she peeled off her gloves and pushed back the hood of her cape while Anton explained that his parents were on an overnight trip to the provincial capital in search of a wheelchair. "And probably purchase a couple of trunkloads of votive candles." He turned to escort Yustina up the staircase to Elena's bedroom and mumbled, "And undoubtedly some milk pails or a new wagon seat or something else we don't need."

He felt a light hand on his arm. "Anton, before we go upstairs, allow me to ask you this. How do you think your father is doing? I mean, in general."

He tilted his head. "I don't understand your question."

"These needless purchases you just mentioned . . ." Her sigh indicated she might as well come out with it. "Does he seem distracted? His mind, perhaps, a little disordered?"

Anton didn't feel like having a heart-to-heart conversation with his father's lover. He shrugged his shoulders. "I think he's just unnerved by the serfs' emancipation. So many decisions to make."

"Practicalities aren't the only things that are setting him adrift. The old order of things has disappeared. And along with it, security and predictability. He sees the end of the Petrovo that generations of Maximovs have known. He'll require your help, Anton, to contend with the changes that are coming."

His head snapped back. "My help?"

"Yes. Your father needs someone to pay attention to his ideas."

"I thought you paid attention to him."

Yustina's withering look stated she fully understood his inference. She shifted her weight, not self-consciously, but as a declaration that she wasn't interested in putting up with his crass insinuations. "I try to be the best friend I can be. And so does Vladimir. But there's only so much we can do. What he really needs is your mother. And you, his son."

"Mother?"

"When your mother drifted away, he became like a boat torn loose of its moorings."

Anton knew he should yield to his better judgment and let the conversation drop. Instead, he challenged Yustina with "If he loved her so much, why didn't he help her?"

"You mean when Dmitry died? He did what he thought was best by trying to get her to put aside the baby's death. But that wasn't what your mother needed, and that's partly why she became . . . the way she is."

Yustina's gaze traveled over his face. "Trust me, I've seen it happen to others. A person has to be allowed to grieve. Fully grieve, for however long it takes. If that flood of emotion is denied, it becomes exiled to the darkest place in our soul. It evolves into something monstrous that wants to destroy us."

"And you believe that's what happened to Mother?"

"Definitely. To this day, your father doesn't know what he should have done differently. But in some intangible way, he feels he should have done something." She gave a melancholic smile. "I'm exercising an old woman's privilege to dole out advice. Give him another chance, will you? He's in his sundown years, and he's tired." She gripped Anton's hand and squeezed it. "No need to escort me to Elena's room. I certainly know the way." Yustina gathered her skirts and ascended the stairs, leaving behind the calm, clean scent of lilac.

Two voices spoke. One said, *Have a drink. You deserve it.* The other voice said, *No! Not until the evening meal.* Point. Counterpoint. It was an endless harangue that had beaten Anton about the head for more than three years, with temperance knuckling under more often than not.

He ached for the smooth, silky liquid. He ached so much his body quivered. *Find the strength*, he demanded of himself. *Dig deep and find the gumption.*

Anton grabbed an overcoat and sat on the terrace where he could think without a bottle within easy reach.

Tiny, sparrow-boned Yustina had surprised him. He had known her his entire life, but he'd completely overlooked her quiet stamina and perception. She had stood by Sophia and Stepan through thick and thin. Whether or not she was bedding Stepan seemed irrelevant at this juncture.

Anton had always been so certain he knew everything about his parents. But perhaps he didn't. All he knew were their crimes, both real and perceived, after fate had buffeted the two of them around. He had seen the hurt his father inflicted on Sophia. Now he was seeing the reverse—Stepan's hopelessness as Sophia licked her wounds, not to help them heal, but to make them raw.

Sophia's problems became Stepan's problems. And then, did those problems become his, Anton's, problems? Did all three harbor personal echoes of betrayal? Is that why he never married—aside from the fact that for the past year, his penis had been as limp as a wilted sunflower?

Something monstrous that wants to destroy us. It galled him that the bottle was summoning him back into the house. He loathed that bottle. And yet, he wanted to grab its neck and chug down the amber magic.

His thoughts were preempted by a herdsman coming from the barn. "My apologies for the interruption, sir, but the veterinary surgeon has arrived to castrate a colt. Your father likes to be here for those types of things. I guess he forgot, what with Mademoiselle Elena needing that wheelchair."

"Don't wait to cut the colt. Father won't be back for hours."

"Yes, sir, we took care of the colt, but there were some other things the Count wanted the veterinary to do. I don't know what they were. Do you?"

Both Anton and the herdsman knew the question was a long shot.

"No, but probably Elena does. I'll go upstairs and ask her."

Of course Elena knew. Her father wanted some colic medicine to keep on hand as well as cautery powder. And she wanted a hard quarter in Malinka Five's udder examined.

Creases formed between Elena's eyes. "How unlike Father to forget the veterinarian. I even reminded him yesterday."

THE WHEELCHAIR COULDN'T navigate the stairs, so her parents suggested moving Elena's bed downstairs to the parlor. Elena declined and, quite against her mother's wishes, moved into the windowless, low-ceilinged cubbyhole behind the kitchen that had been Matriusha's room.

Elena's strong arms had no trouble maneuvering the bulky wooden wheelchair around the house, but she couldn't reach high shelves nor retrieve items from the floor. Going to the privy was also a challenge. Simply wheeling the chair over the rough outside ground required the assistance of another person. And Elena, unable to visit the barns, floundered like a fish out of water.

"I've decided I need a helper, someone who can spend all day with me," Elena announced at the dinner table. "Perhaps we could bring up one of the peasants from the village."

Sophia stopped in midchew. "A peasant?" She scrunched her nose. "Out of the question. We will assign Dasha to tend to you for more hours during the day."

"But, Mother, Dasha *is* a peasant."

"Of course she is, dear. But she grew up in our household. She's been taught manners. And cleanliness."

Elena turned her eyes on her father. Realizing he was supposed to speak, Stepan admitted he hadn't been listening. After Elena restated her appeal, he said, "I'll check in the village tomorrow for someone suitable."

"I'd like Anna."

"Anna?" Sophia, Stepan, and Anton chorused.

"Anna Vorontsova."

"That slip of a girl who returned Venerka?" Anton asked. "With the port-wine mark on her face?"

"She obviously has healing skills, considering how splendidly she splinted Venerka's leg." Elena gave her father an irresistible smile. "Will you fetch her tomorrow?"

CHAPTER 47

Elizaveta

1865

Which animal is the most vicious?
An angry wife.

WITH THE HELP of a walking stick, Elizaveta dragged her crippled leg across the tavern's wooden floor, sticky with dried spit. Her face was mottled with fading yellow and mulberry blotches.

She was one of four peasants who had petitioned hearings from the new court. At one side of Seleznyov's tavern, three square tables had been pushed together edge to edge, behind which sat the official court, five men whom Elizaveta had known her whole life. Three dozen curious spectators sat on various benches and stools that were crammed into the small room. She didn't have to search the room to know that Ermak was present. She could hear the cracking of his knuckles over the chatter.

She sat next to her sister Katya, who was fanning her face in the June heat. Elizaveta folded her arms across her belly. Her insides felt as unsettled as an armful of feathers thrown into the air. The whole of her past and her future met at this precise moment in time.

Katya nudged her sister and flicked her head in the direction of the door. Arriving was the consummate liar Illarion Loktev, who had no reason to be at the hearings except to snoop into other people's business. Illarion stepped behind the judges and bent forward between Constantin Sipko and Mikhalek Karpov. Illarion put a hand on each of their shoulders, and they inclined their heads toward him as he whispered in their ears.

Is that maggot up to his old tricks of spreading lies? Elizaveta's dread grew heavier.

Hers was the first hearing that morning. In fact, it was the first to ever take place in Petrovo. Leaning on her stick before the stone-faced judges, she took an oath by swearing on the Cross.

Her dry tongue stumbled as she chronicled events that had occurred two weeks ago. Her quivering throat clamped down, and her story squeezed past in squeaks.

Ermak had been irritable at the thought of starting the monthlong fast of Saints Peter and Paul. He got mad during the noon meal when he wanted potatoes, and she told him there weren't any. Later that afternoon, when she had tripped coming up from the root cellar and spilled a crockery jar of milk, the beast in him broke loose. He pounded her face with her shoe and smashed her left knee with an iron skillet.

She modestly lifted her skirt and showed the judges her purple, melon-sized knee. The men's stoic faces revealed none of their thoughts.

Next was her lynchpin. She willed her voice to be steady but submissive.

"After hitting me with the skillet and causing me to almost faint, my husband climbed into my wedding trunk and defecated on my possessions—my most cherished and personal possessions. Then he demanded that I clean up his foulness."

Elizaveta knew this crucial point would make or break her case. Invading and befouling a woman's private trunk was an act of debasement just short of rape.

"I humbly ask permission to divorce my brutish husband, so I can live a life free of torture." Elizaveta delivered the conclusion with eloquence and persuasion, exactly as she had practiced it with Feodor.

She was directed to step aside, so Ermak could come forward and tell his side of the story. With cap in hand, he said he had disciplined her for two reasons. First, she had been careless with food her whole life, wasting it and spilling it. Second, she had refused him the night before.

"Why do you think we have so few children?" he asked both the judges and the spectators. "The woman won't offer me the comfort a wife owes a man."

Ermak was told to return to his seat. Elizaveta remained standing, sweat trickling down the small of her back.

Red-headed Demian Osokin was the first judge to speak. "Although some discipline may have been justified, it sounds like he is guilty of 'inhuman fighting with his wife.'"

Mikhalek Karpov responded, "I don't think Ermak's punishment was unreasonable for refusing to meet a husband's needs."

"If indeed she did refuse him," said Demian.

Constantin Sipko asked, "Did you refuse your husband?"

Elizaveta had refused Ermak so many times, she couldn't say with any certainty whether she had rebuffed him that particular night. "Can't remember," she muttered, fidgeting with her blouse's neckline.

Karpov leaned forward, so he could look down from the far end of the table at the man he used to call Little Red. "Then we have to accept the husband's story as truth."

Demian refused to drop his point. "But the woman can barely walk. I question whether she will ever again be of help in the fields. That is 'inhuman fighting.' We all know that fighting in the home can spill over into unruliness within our village."

Karpov tapped the table with his forefinger. "I remind you, a husband is the law for his wife."

The overstuffed room began to tighten around Elizaveta. Her blouse clung, itchy, to her moist skin.

Avdotya's brother, Timofei Sharovatov, cut to the chase. "Elizaveta Vorontsova is seeking a divorce. A few days ago, I questioned the peace mediator. He said only the Church can grant divorces. As township judges, we don't have that authority."

Elizaveta's mouth fell open. *Don't have that authority?* But all of her hopes had been based on the judges having that authority!

"Even if it were within this court's authority to grant a divorce," Karpov said, "her accusations aren't sufficient to justify shattering a holy union."

A holy union? At no point could her marriage have been termed "a holy union." Elizaveta's mind churned like a boiling pot as she strained to think of a response. "Are you sure you can't grant a divorce?"

Timofei Sharovatov folded his arms across his chest and nodded.

"And neither will the Church?" Her voice was like ice cracking.

"Correct."

Everything was going awry, a crooked wheel veering off course. Elizaveta closed her eyes to detangle her muddled thoughts. *Angel of God, help me be smart.*

"Then I request a separation from this swine that fouls my personal chest. Please. Every day, I live in fear that he'll kill me." She leaned on her cane, distrustful of her trembling legs.

"If you were granted a separation, how would you support yourself?" Karpov asked. "You'd become a burden on the village."

Timofei Sharovatov shook his head, refusing to be sidetracked by subjective arguments. "The peace mediator told me that the court can only approve separations that have the husband's consent. Do you give your consent for a separation, Ermak Vorontsov?"

Ermak stopped his knuckle-cracking long enough to bellow, "Under no circumstances! I need her labor. Without her, the fieldwork will suffer."

Her words burst forth like a flame. "How much help will I be in the field with this knee?"

Ermak's arm lashed out to point at his wife. "Listen how she talks! She shows no respect for me or for my family that takes care of her."

Elizaveta bit her tongue until she tasted blood. She had known Ermak would lose his temper, allowing the judges to discern who was the villain and who was the victim. She had promised herself, sworn to herself, that she'd keep her anger reined in. But she'd failed.

Constantin Sipko advised Elizaveta, "Look past the few bad knocks you've taken, for the sake of your children."

Elizaveta shivered with cold panic. "For the sake of the children? My children are grown. They don't need a father. And they certainly don't need a father who beats their mother until she's crippled."

Demian Osokin stated, "We must keep in mind that the husband overstepped his bounds when he defiled her possessions."

The judges agreed that particular transgression deserved punishment. The logical choice was flogging.

Reflexively, Elizaveta glanced at her husband. His eyes burned like the pits of Hell. All about the room, the indistinct faces of her neighbors closed in, ever closer, threatening to suffocate her.

"But don't you see? If you flog him, he'll beat me more. He'll whip me the way you're going to whip him."

"That's the court's decision. Take it or leave it."

Elizaveta pictured the public humiliation of Ermak lying prostrate on a bench on the town square and receiving twenty lashes on his naked back and buttocks. The supposed deterrent to future misbehavior would only provoke further violence. Besides, nothing would be gained if Ermak were flogged. She'd been denied her divorce. The ground had crumbled beneath her.

"Then I'll leave it. I thought this court was supposed to administer justice. But I see you couldn't care less about the welfare of myself, my children, or my future grandchildren."

In a parody of justice, the court fined Ermak a bottle of vodka plus two rubles as admonishment for his impetuous behavior of defiling her dowry chest.

"LEAN ON ME." Katya took her hobbling sister's arm as they walked from the tavern. The sweltering heat lay like a wet blanket over the village.

"I was a fool to expect anything from a group of men who believe it's their

God-given right to beat their wives. After all, haven't we heard since childhood that a husband's fist leaves no bruise?"

"Liza, maybe if you'd be a little nicer to Ermak. Sometimes your words are so blunt."

"My words are blunt? I suffer every single day at the hands of that son of Satan."

"I understand how you feel. I really do."

"You can't understand how I feel! To understand, you'd have to go through what I've been through. And may God spare you that!"

"I may not know everything—"

Anger so vicious came upon Elizaveta that it overpowered all rationality. "Listen to me. I swear to you, I will find a life free of that monster. I swear by almighty God and all the saints." Her clenched fist pounded her good thigh. "Someday I'll meet violence with violence!"

Katya flinched. "Be careful, Liza. Don't damage your own soul. Don't forget the Lord God."

When Elizaveta stopped walking, so did her sister. Elizaveta twisted toward Katya. Her voice was a fearsome snarl. "Who has forgotten who?"

CHAPTER 48

Elizaveta

1865

The peasant throws it on the ground.
The master collects it in his pocket.
What am I?

Snot.

THE VORONTSOVS WERE at the Sunday service, but Elizaveta was too angry at them and at God to attend. She stared at the sheepskin stretched across the boards of the door, keeping the winds at bay. If only she could walk out that door and never return.

Her life was a shambles. She was an exhausted, worn-out woman, stripped of hope like laundry that had been wrung dry of all its water. She was in physical pain and doubted her knee would ever fully heal. She agonized continuously that she might get pregnant. Or that she and Feodor would be discovered. She was an adulteress, guilty of a sin so heinous that the flames of Hell awaited her.

We mustn't fool ourselves into thinking what we want today will be enough tomorrow.

But she'd done it anyway. She'd thought that occasionally seeing Feodor and loving him would be enough. But it wasn't. She wanted to whisper in his ear in public. She ached to climb onto their sleeping bench at the end of a long day and collapse next to him. She longed to grow old beside him. And now her hopes for a divorce had no more substance than a fart in the wind.

"Mamasha, I'm home!" Anna burst through the door carrying a feathery plant the size of a rooster's tail. After setting the ceramic pot on the floor, Anna flung her arms around Elizaveta's neck and smothered her cheeks with kisses. "I loved being with Mademoiselle Elena, but I missed you so much!"

As Elizaveta dislodged the arm that threatened to choke to her, she wondered what had possessed Anna to bring that leafy weed into the izba. Why was it in a pot rather than in the ground?

Anna pulled back and bounced on her tiptoes. "Platoshka's bringing in my things."

As though on cue, Platon appeared at the doorway, hind end first, tugging a bulky wooden chest across the threshold. Once inside, he turned, stretched his arms out behind him, and tried to haul the trunk as though it were a wagon. Deciding that his initial attempt to walk backward was easier, he once again reversed his position. The chest was much too heavy for a boy his age to pull, shove, tow, or push. But that didn't dissuade him. Platon, as always, was undaunted by the seemingly insurmountable. Sometimes he was successful and sometimes he wasn't, but rarely did he ask for help.

Anna lent a hand to her young cousin. Laboring together, the two of them budged the cumbersome trunk across the rough boards to position it beside Elizaveta's bench at the table. Winded, Platon sank onto the rounded top. His hand cupped his bicep as he flexed and extended his elbow.

Elizaveta's fingers went to her dropped chin. Such a large and expensive chest! Not a splinter-ridden homemade box like all the village women had, but a beautifully painted store-bought chest, its latch and corners made of metal.

Anna's elation knew no bounds. "Mademoiselle Elena gave me all of this to thank me for my help!"

Platon sprang from the lid. "Open it! Open it!" Suddenly he took half a step back and put his nose in the air, sniffing like a cotton-tailed rabbit that picked up the scent of danger. His nose crinkled as he extended his neck toward his cousin. "Anna, is that you?"

"It's called cologne." She thrust her upturned hand under each of their noses.

Platon and his godmother exchanged quizzical looks as Anna explained this particular cologne had a French name, but she couldn't remember it.

Using both arms, Anna opened the heavy top and gingerly laid it back. Lying on top was a shelf clock, its width and height almost equal to the chest's opening. Anna picked up the clock by its long sides and scuffed her feet in a circle until she could set the timekeeper on the table.

"Dasha polished it for me, both the wood and the metal." Anna gave her mother and Platon a moment to admire the mahogany case and cracked porcelain face. She then unhooked the shiny brass latch and swung open the bottom half of the timepiece. Her fine-boned hand reached into the bowels of the case and emerged with a thin piece of metal, which she displayed between her index and middle finger.

"This is a *key*."

After they scrutinized the instrument, Anna inserted it into one of the two round apertures in the clock's face. In half-turn increments, she rotated the key.

"See how these heavy things go up?" She pointed to two heavy cylindrical objects. "They're called *weights*."

Platon put his nose into the hollow of the clock and examined the top, bottom, and sides for other loose or moving pieces.

"Then you take this—it's a *pendulum*—and you swing it like this." Task accomplished, Anna closed the door and secured the latch.

The three tilted back their heads to observe the apparatus. For two minutes, their gaze locked on the big hand as it tiptoed forward.

"Why would the Maximovs give you something so valuable?" Elizaveta asked.

"They have lots of them. One in every room. This was an extra."

"In every room?" Elizaveta was dumbfounded. Why did rich people attach so much importance to clocks? They weren't needed. A peasant worked until dark, ate, then slept. If a more specific accounting of time was needed, that's what the church bell was for.

"And the men carry a tiny one in their pockets." Anna's head rocked up and down to validate the accuracy of her statement.

Her mother muttered half under her breath, "My, my, don't the gentry overburden themselves with keeping track of time."

Anna's eyes widened as she thought of something else. "Also in their pockets, the men carry little pieces of cloth." She held her hands so her extended fingers made a square the size of a stool's seat. "When they need to blow their nose, they take out the cloth, put their snot into it, then fold it up, and put it back into their pocket."

Elizaveta ran the peculiar scenario through her mind. "Anna, are you sure?"

"I saw it."

Although skeptical, Elizaveta had no choice but to believe her daughter. Anna, unlike Platon, didn't have an unbridled imagination.

"Look what else." From her treasure chest, Anna removed a child's book, replete with illustrations.

Platon took custody of the faded book with the same care a bishop would bestow on the Holy Scripture. He turned it over and examined it from all sides—the front, the back, the spine, each of the edges, and the front a second time.

"Mademoiselle Elena taught me to read some words." Anna's index finger traced the title. "*The Golden Cockerel and Other Fairy Tales*." She looked expectantly at her mother, but received no praise for her accomplishment.

Elizaveta's shoulders slumped as she watched Platon turn the pages of the book. *Of all the useless things! Why couldn't the girl have brought home something functional, like a flour sifter or some matches?* Elizaveta's eyes slid back to the chest. "What else is in there?"

"Lots and lots of beautiful clothes." Anna removed the top garment from the chest, so her mother could feel the silky material. Platon glanced at the shiny blouse with its blush-of-rose tint, then reburied his nose in what he had already claimed as his book.

Anna reached into the pocket of her jumper. "Look here." She withdrew a translucent comb. "Makes your hair look pretty."

Platon gave the object a fleeting look and retreated to his sleeping bench with his book. Anna's mother had equal interest in the comb. To her way of thinking, fingers did a perfectly good job of detangling hair.

"Oh, something else I saw!" Anna squealed. "Besides spoons, they also have little pitchforks for stabbing food."

Elizaveta was losing patience with Anna's giddiness. "Why did you bring that plant in the izba?"

"It's called a *fern*, and it can get real big." Anna reached a flattened hand in the air over her head.

"What do you do with it?" her mother asked.

"You water it. And you look at it."

Elizaveta paused, absorbing the explanation. "What for?"

"It's pretty."

"Take it outside."

"Outside? Why?" Anna's face sagged. "The Maximovs have lots of them in their house."

"Because it's silly, and there's no room for it in here." Elizaveta's attention was drawn to Platon.

Clenched in his hand were the four twisted ends of a square of linen. The resulting gunnysack was thrown over his shoulder. "Good-bye, Auntie Elizaveta. Good-bye, Anna."

Elizaveta's hands went to her hips. "Where are you going?"

"To Moscow. First, the church school. Then gymnasium. And then university."

Elizaveta's forefinger motioned the boy to her. She placed a hand on each shoulder and spun him around. An inspection of the contents of his improvised knapsack revealed a single item, *The Golden Cockerel and Other Fairy Tales*. She rotated the child back to face her. "Don't you think you're a little young to be heading off to Moscow alone?"

"Don't trip over the boat by the gate." Anna giggled into a fringed shawl of the softest weave with red, yellow, and bronze flowers.

Elizaveta's impatience deepened. "Boat?"

"Uh-huh. Monsieur Sergei and Monsieur Anton made it when they were children."

"What are you going to do with a boat?"

Anna cocked her head to one side and her hip the opposite direction. Surely, her stance said, her mother knew what a person did with a boat.

Elizaveta saw no purpose in dwelling on another completely useless object, so she returned to Platon's trip to Moscow. She told him in no uncertain terms that going to school was out of the question.

"Not fair!" Platon's lower lip stuck out.

Elizaveta calmly intertwined her fingers atop the table. "I don't recall any promise about life being fair."

A temper tantrum ensued, and Elizaveta sent him to his sleeping bench. She rose and started pickling a batch of cabbage.

"Mama, wasn't Mademoiselle Elena nice to give us all these things?" Anna draped the shawl about her shoulders.

"Don't be deceived. The Maximovs gathered their rubles and fancy clothes and clocks from the sweat off our backs."

"But they were very kind to me. They really were."

"Get it through your head. Count Maximov cares not a fig about any of us. He'd sell us to the Devil if he could make a few rubles."

Anna's eyes grew to astonished circles. "Mama, I've never heard you say such mean things about the Count."

"It's a lesson I learned when I was your age." The girl's excessive tenderheartedness tested Elizaveta's forbearance more than the antics of Ilya, Gerasim, Serafima, and Platon combined. Elizaveta occasionally forced herself to acknowledge the truth, which was that she had never warmed to Anna as she should have. She had been too distracted by her own troubles even to name the child.

She and Anna were as different as night and day. Elizaveta was headstrong and pragmatic, while Anna was sensitive and sentimental. As Grandmama Anafreva had said many times, when Elizaveta made up her mind, she might be in error, but she was never in doubt. Anna, on the other hand, was constantly biting her lip with insecurity.

Anna's voice filtered into Elizaveta's thoughts. "What did you say?" Elizaveta asked.

Anna repeated, "Do you think this would be good to wear to the circle dances?" At her waist she held a taupe skirt of fine broadcloth.

Elizaveta paused with the cleaver raised to shoulder height, ready to split the head of cabbage. In slow motion, she lowered the utensil. "Circle dances? What are you talking about?"

"I'll be fifteen next week. There's no reason I can't go to the circle dances."

Elizaveta couldn't find her voice. Through her memory skidded visions of her own peers at their dances—their rowdy games, their suggestive riddles. And now it was time for her youngest child, delicate Anna, to step forth into that risky world of boys and kisses.

Elizaveta lifted the cleaver and drove it full force through the head of cabbage. "The Maximovs' clothes might be a little too fancy to wear to the dances on the square. You should save them for Church."

"But these'll be special dances. Serafima told me the boys from Darovoe plan to come."

"Boys from the village up the river?" She watched Anna hold the skirt to her waist and turn in circles, the material billowing more fully and more gracefully than any homespun to have ever come off a loom.

Platon jumped down from his bench, his disappointment over his foiled trip to Moscow already put behind him. "Anna, guess what! I'm learning how to whistle. Look." He puffed out his cheeks like a bellows.

At that same moment, Elizaveta sucked her cheeks inward in frustration over her inability to halt her children's race toward adulthood and her powerlessness to control her own life.

"What's going on?" Platon dashed to the window.

Elizaveta swiveled about. Villagers were sprinting past the izba toward the square. She grabbed her walking stick and hobbled after them.

CHAPTER 49

Elizaveta
1865

I am not a ploughman, nor a
    cabinetmaker,
nor am I a blacksmith or a carpenter,
yet I am the foremost worker in
    the village.
Who am I?

A horse.

THE HORSES! THE village boys who were hired as daytime shepherds for the communally pastured horses had arrived to find the midnight shepherds bound and gagged. Every horse was gone.

A posse was formed. All the men of prime age gathered at the town square, outfitted with ropes, shovels, sticks, hayforks, axes, and kitchen knives to wage war against a gang of thieves who would be armed to the hilt.

The Zhemchuzhnikovs volunteered their two wagons to transport the men, but the sole horse remaining in the village was an old mare giving birth in the Sipkos' barn. Word of the catastrophe had been sent to the Count.

On the other side of the river sped two empty wagons down Maximov's road. Each driver popped his whip over four horses. Two additional horses were tied behind each wagon.

While Maximov's wagons clattered across the bridge, deep male voices swore to avenge the crime with a bloodthirsty brand of justice. Weapons swinging impatiently, the men whipped themselves into a state of frenzy as they talked about cutting off the thieves' heads and shoving them between their legs.

Timofei Sharovatov described his style of vengeance. "After we rout them from their lair, we'll skin them and pull out their veins one by one."

Matvei Vorobev showed his sons the best way to tie the thief's hands and feet with rope. "Then toss him over the limb of a tree."

One of the Naryshkins elaborated, "With a stick, tighten the knots until his limbs are all broken."

Vorobev added, "Even better—raise and drop the swine to the ground, raise and drop, raise and drop, until his backbone snaps."

Ermak whittled deep notches in a long stick and described in the blackest colors how he'd ram it up the rectum of any thief he caught.

Maximov's wagons and horses arrived. The men with their arsenal of assorted weapons leapt into the wagon beds while women loaded baskets of food and wiped tears onto their aprons. The young boys and old men, yearning to be either older or younger, wished them Godspeed.

Yegorka and a herdsman, themselves too old to accompany the posse, put the Zhemchuzhnikov brothers in charge of Maximov's possessions. Curses and vows of revenge hung in the air as the men headed toward Efremov in the province of Tula, an area notorious for horse thieves.

Elizaveta scuffed back to her izba, a headache forming behind the furrows between her eyebrows. Her hand was on her gate when she felt in her heart the tug of the bent willow and heard the quiet sigh of the river. Her emotions were as twisted as a bramble of berries, and she needed to sort them out in privacy. She turned her back on the Vorontsovs and sought comfort in the familiar cove.

Seated half-hidden under the bent willow's flaccid branches, Elizaveta pushed her legs out in front of her and massaged her aching knee. With the men's departure, a broody silence descended on the village. Not a sound broke the solitude except the water lapping against the shore.

Fear gnawed at her belly. Stolen horses were rarely recovered. If the Vorontsov men didn't retrieve their animal, Sidor would immediately borrow money to replace it. The family couldn't go further in debt. Yet there'd be no alternative except to replace the horse.

And then there was her trembling, unspeakable dread that the men could be killed. Ilya. Gerasim. Feodor. Katya's Pavel. Yulia's Demian. Virtually all the men in the village who were in the prime of their lives. God alone knew which, if any, would return.

THE HUSHED VILLAGE waited and prayed through that day, and the next, and then the next, and then yet another . . . At sunset on the tenth day, families poured from their izbas at the approach of hoofbeats. Ermak, Ilya, Gerasim, and Onufrii were smothered with arms and kisses.

Everyone clustered around the wooden table as the men recounted their pursuit. Yes, all the horses were recovered. Yes, the crime was avenged, in ways the men didn't want to describe in front of the children.

No, not all the men made it back alive. Maximov's wagon was delivering the dead to their families. Evstafii Karpov had been shot and killed. Avdotya's brother, Timofei, was stabbed in the stomach and died on the way back.

"Couldn't recover Zhemchuzhnikov's body," Ermak said. "Trampled to death by the crazed horses."

Elizaveta sat motionless, her body prickled with fear. Her throat clamped down, threatening to suffocate her. With brutal determination, she kept quiet. Someone would ask the inevitable question.

"Which Zhemchuzhnikov?"

Time hung suspended until a voice responded.

"Feodor."

CHAPTER 50

Maximov

1865

What flies faster than a bullet?
Thought.

HIS EYES ALL but concealed behind bloated lids, Anton stepped squarely in the center of the dusty canvas of the old Maximov family portrait.

"Shit."

As he extracted his foot from his great-grandfather's chest, he was already envisioning Stepan's conniption fit.

Why was the painting lying on the upper landing of the staircase? He ran a finger along one edge of the deep-colored rectangle on the otherwise faded wallpaper. Perhaps he had knocked it free from its velvet tie when he stumbled up the stairs last night—or rather, in the predawn hours this morning.

Something rustled at the foot of the stairs. Anton squinted. "You're home?" His mouth barely had enough room for his thick tongue.

"Mother and I came back early," Elena replied. "She sank into a melancholia. She's in her room."

"Where's Father?"

"He stayed in St. Petersburg another week or so. He'll be back before Christmas."

The Maximovs and the Rusakovs had made a joint six-week trip to St. Petersburg, so Sophia and Stepan could visit their children and grandchildren while Yustina and Vladimir added the final touches to their new apartment.

Anton resumed his descent. The stairs were difficult to maneuver as they swam about erratically.

Upon reaching the foyer, he greeted his sister with a glancing kiss on her forehead. He caught sight of himself in the wall mirror. His eyes looked like two piss holes in the snow. His face, at one time chiseled and angled, was habitually puffy and flaccid.

In the dining room, he placed a hand on the samovar. Cold. "Gennady! Bring me some tea. With biscuits and jam." His voice was as gummy as molasses.

He dumped his body into a chair and grappled for presence of mind. Elbows propped on the table, he let his upturned palms cradle his forehead while his fingers disappeared into his dark curls. The play of sunlight through the tall windows impaled his skull like a rusty bolt.

Elena's uneven footsteps entered the room. One of her legs hadn't mended properly, leaving her with a limp that she refused to let slow her down.

"Mother's in an awful state," Elena said as she settled into the chair across the table from Anton. "How foolish of us to travel with her during the winter. But she was so insistent on seeing her new grandbaby."

Old Gennady creaked as he bent over the table to place a china plate domed with steaming biscuits, followed by a cut-glass saucer of gooseberry preserves and a matching saucer with balls of butter and a silver butter knife. A strong yeasty scent filled Anton's nostrils. Quite the converse, he assumed, of the deplorable food in the vermin-infested, smutty-walled post inns where his mother and Elena had stayed during their return trip from St. Petersburg.

Anton broke open a biscuit and lifted the butter dish. His weak grip put the saucer at a lopsided angle, and the knife slid toward the saucer's edge. Anton overcompensated and knocked over his glass of rowanberry cider. Chagrined, he again cradled his aching head in the palm of his hand while the servants sopped up the mess.

After a new tablecloth had been laid out, Anton adjusted the slits of his eyes toward his sister. "So you and Mother came back alone?"

"No. Vladimir came home early, so he could meet with a potential purchaser for their estate. Yustina stayed in the capital, deciding on the wallpaper and drapes."

"Yustina remained with Father?"

Elena nodded.

He mumbled, "While the cat's away . . ."

"Pardon?"

"Nothing." As he reached for another biscuit, his hand refused to stop trembling. Feeling Elena's stare, he strove for a breezy tone. "How are things in St. Petersburg?"

He gave half an ear to Elena's descriptions of their brand-new nephew as well as the current typhus epidemic plaguing the capital. When she moved on to featherbrained Sergei's latest promotion in the Guards, Anton lost all interest and entertained his mind with thoughts of crawling back into bed.

Finally Elena excused herself from the table, saying she needed to check on her cows. "I'll ask them if they missed me while I was gone." She gave him a wink and a smile. "And maybe I'll practice target shooting to see if I remember how to fire a pistol." She filled her chest with a deep, satisfied breath. "How refreshing to be back on Petrovo."

Two hours later, Anton was jolted awake from his nap on the divan by an uproar in the foyer, reminiscent of the commotion nine months earlier when injured Elena had been carried into the house. This time, however, it was a young girl. Yegorka carried the unconscious child to Matriusha's former room next to the kitchen, old Gennady urging him to hurry. Dasha kept pace alongside with a towel to keep blood off the wood floor.

"Why didn't you bring her in the rear door?" Matriusha's disgruntled voice had been reincarnated in Dasha.

Yegorka laid the girl on the bed. Elena and Dasha removed her coat and shirt, then deftly wrapped her bleeding upper arm with towels. The girl appeared to be seven or eight years old. Her face and lips were blanched the color of the bed's linens. Anton eased onto a ladderback chair against the far wall, trying to make sense of the scene before him. His head felt as if it were about to rip open.

"What's wrong with her other arm?" Dasha asked. "It's all shriveled up. And only half as long as it should be."

Everyone except Anton bent forward for a closer look. His stomach pitched in circles. Saliva pooled in his mouth. He swallowed and took deep breaths. When was the last time he was this hungover?

Elena finished wrapping the wounded arm, snugged the blanket around the girl, and stepped away from the bed. Her composure abruptly shattered.

"I shot her."

Elena's gasping words knocked the stupor out of Anton.

Gennady whispered, "You shot her?"

"Target practice. Aiming at an elm tree." She gulped back tears. "My first shot."

Anton looked at the small bump under the wool blanket. How in the world had Elena managed to hit such a scrawny little thing?

"What if she dies?" Elena's hand went to her throat. "Or what if I've crippled her good arm?"

The pocket-sized room grew airless. Anton's mouth formed an oval as his chest heaved.

Gennady glanced about for Anton and, finding him incapacitated, put a thin, old arm around Elena's shoulders. "She'll be fine. Completely fine. See, the blood's already stopped."

Elena's hand rose from her throat to wrap across her forehead. "Do any of you know who she is?"

"Looks like the one whose mother . . . in the stable . . ." Yegorka rolled his eyes toward the ceiling.

Anton's breath caught. *Zhanna's suicide? This is my daughter?*

"We must notify the family," Elena said.

"Oh, no," Yegorka said. "Seleznyov gave her up to the nuns' orphanage."

"The orphanage? Why would he send her to the orphanage?"

"Why keep a deformed child?"

Elena was as incredulous as Yegorka was befuddled. "You're saying the Seleznyovs refused to keep their grandchild because of her crippled arm?"

Yegorka's nod was matter-of-fact. "What use would she be, either in the izba or in the fields? She'd be another mouth to feed, one that couldn't earn its keep. And one that no one would marry. The kid is a bastard."

Anton bolted from the room as vomit gathered at the back of his throat.

CHAPTER 51

Elizaveta

1865

In summer it's merry,
in autumn it's lavish,
in winter it's warm.
What is it?

A tree.

EVDOKIM SELEZNYOV, WHO never allowed a mercenary opportunity to slip through his fingers, exercised his legal right as a free rural inhabitant to own a business. He uncloaked his clandestine tavern and turned it into a legitimate enterprise.

However, the aged shopkeeper didn't have the fortitude to completely dismantle his covert dealings. He expanded his inventory to include salt, matches, sewing needles, and a few other staples that the villagers previously had to acquire in Sukhanovo. The sale of such items was forbidden in drinking establishments, so these goods were stashed in the family's izba, out of sight of the government inspectors.

Elizaveta waited at the counter while Seleznyov retrieved some contraband salt for her. Platon stood transfixed beside one of the tables, around which a half dozen men were seated. The boy's tongue was trapped between his lips as he hung on the words of Feodor's younger brother reading aloud from a newspaper. Once Elizaveta had her sack of salt in hand, she walked past the table of men and, without slowing down, tapped Platon on the shoulder. "Come along."

But Platon was engrossed in the newsprint's essay on Alexander II easing censorship of the press.

"I said, come along." It baffled her that the eight-year-old was spellbound by events that not only were beyond his comprehension but held no significance for the villagers.

As she and Platon headed home in the fresh dusting of snow, Elizaveta was weighted down with the leaden sorrow that had accompanied her every step for the past half year. A loneliness like no other had wound itself through every part of her being, an unbearable longing for what she and Feodor once had and what could have been. For half of her childhood and the entirety of her adult life, she'd clung to her unstoppable resolve to someday be with Feodor. Now she stared into an empty future, as lonely and endless as the road that stretched across the windblown fields.

She realized Platon was asking a question for the second time. "Does Anna have typhus?"

"What?"

"In the newspaper. Typhus is in St. Petersburg and Moscow. And now it's come to Tambov. Is Anna sick with typhus?"

Anna had been grappling with an on-again, off-again upset stomach for a couple of weeks. "Probably just worms. I think typhus puts little spots on your skin."

Platon heaved a sigh of relief. He tipped his face up to the falling snow. Large velvety flakes landed on his cheeks. "You have to wonder where they come from, don't you?"

"Where what comes from? Worms? Or spots?" Elizaveta looked at her god-child and saw the flakes form tiny specks of water on his upturned cheeks. "Or snowflakes?"

"Those." Platon flung his arm straight up and pointed skyward. "Don't you wonder where they've been and where they're going?"

Elizaveta didn't have to look up to hear the raucous cries of the geese. "Of course. Many times I've wondered where those birds are in such a noisy hurry to go." It was a lie, but Feodor had often warned her to not stifle Platon's innate curiosity.

Platon sidestepped an ice-crusted puddle. "Do people in Africa walk with their feet up?"

"What?"

"Africa is on the underside of the world, so do people there walk upside down?"

Elizaveta had no understanding of how people walked on a round Earth. In truth, she was skeptical about the rumor that the world was round. "You'll have to go there someday and see for yourself."

"Me? Africa? When fish learn to fly." Such a journey was beyond even Platon's vivid imagination.

They arrived home to find Vera alone in the izba. Layers of shawls were draped across her shoulders and lap while she embroidered a new window curtain.

Elizaveta mindlessly put away the salt and skimmed the fatty surface from a pot of cooling soup. As she set aside the grease for later use, the door burst open.

"Papa's hurt!"

She spun around to see Ilya and Gerasim entering the izba with Ermak hanging limply between them. Each son had a shoulder under one of their father's arms and an arm around his waist. Ermak's feet dragged on the floor behind him. Blood dripping from his scalp left a trail on the boards.

Ilya and Gerasim laid their father on a sleeping bench. After Elizaveta removed his wet boots and outer clothes, his mother covered him with extra sheepskin blankets.

Between gasps from his panting chest, Ilya explained that he, Gerasim, and Ermak had been in Maximov's forest scrounging firewood when they heard a single gunshot. Fearful they'd been caught, they peered about but saw nothing. A woman screamed, but still they saw no one. The aspen they'd been chopping could no longer brace itself and tumbled over. As Ermak's eyes scanned the forest, he didn't see the falling tree.

Vera dabbed the blood from her son's face and beard. The gash started a hand's width above his ear and traveled down and forward to his temple. Elizaveta lifted his head so Vera could wrap linen around his skull. Ilya felt the length of each limb for broken bones.

Vera spent the rest of the day either in the rocking chair beside the sleeping bench or kneeling in front of St. Nicholas the Wonderworker, beseeching him to work his miracles.

CHAPTER 52

Maximov

1865

I climb in the window
like a white cat.
What am I?

A sunbeam.

WHEN ANTON WOKE at eight o'clock rather than his usual noon, he pieced together the previous day. He'd been as pickled as a herring and sick as a dog. His sister and mother were home. He had a daughter. And the person he held dearest had needed him, but he'd failed in his inviolable duty to her. It fell to a tottering old servant to console her.

Self-disdain curdled in his gut.

He should have wrapped his arms around Elena and allowed her to sob on his shoulder. He should have stroked her hair and murmured reassuring phrases. My God, how many times had he done it for his mother! But yesterday, he'd been paralyzed with drink, and the realization penetrated his heart like a dagger.

Anton pulled the blankets over his head. It was unfathomable that, at thirty-one years of age, he was still financially dependent on his father. He was neck-deep in debt. He wasn't received by any respectable families, even in a backwater town like Sukhanovo. His relationship with four out of the five members of his family lay between superficial and antagonistic. His prospects were nil for a wife and children, except for yesterday's thunderbolt surprise. He had flitted around like a bird without a perch, and now his future was void of respect and meaning.

Anton lowered the blanket and studied the slit of sunlight between the closed drapes. It was the tail end of another year. Yet he had no idea where the year had gone. It had vanished into the debris that was his life, a life that once held so much promise.

"Face up to it, you idiot jackass," he muttered. "You held your future in the hollow of your hand. And then dribbled it out between your fingers."

He was worthless to himself and to everyone else.

Or was he?

Yustina had raised a valid point during their staircase discussion when she'd visited the housebound Elena. His father was getting old. None of Roeglin's replacements had worked out, and once the serfs were freed, Stepan had taken over the steward's duties himself.

What the estate needed now wasn't more fences or crop rotations. It needed to chart a new course. It needed someone who understood the peasants' way of thinking. Someone who could drag and cajole honest labor from them. Someone who had grown up with them, playing knucklebones, splashing in the river, and dallying with their sisters. Someone to help the poor devils realize that their subversive displays were useless. Someone who could help them grab hold of the opportunities offered by emancipation.

What would it be like to get out of bed with a purpose? Anton had no feel for the land, but he used to have a working knowledge of the distillery. With Feodor Zhemchuzhnikov dead, someone needed to take over the reins.

Anton had always been keen on the interplay of structure and function. Perhaps he could repair, even improve, the neglected carriage house and barns. That would sharpen his intellect, which had grown dull as a knife about to permanently lose its edge.

All in all, these were champion ideas.

He gave an audible gasp. *Champion ideas?* Had he actually used his father's pet expression?

It would also be a "champion idea" to be honorable and repay his gambling debts. How in Christ's name would he accomplish that?

His gaze confronted the crystal decanter perched on the burled wood of his bureau. Every particle of his being throbbed with disdain for the amber liquid.

He had learned the hard way that he couldn't piecemeal his way to sobriety. Just as a snake sheds its skin, he had to completely throw off his old life. By God, this go-round wouldn't be a mere brush with sobriety. This time he'd see it through.

Anton tossed aside the blankets, strode to the chest, and seized the decanter. He crossed the room and yanked open the drapes. The window, etched with hoarfrost, was iced shut. He thumped the sash with the heel of his hand, but it wouldn't budge. He wasn't even capable of carrying out the melodramatic gesture of dumping the vile liquid out the window and watching it melt a hole in the snow! As a weak alternative, he emptied the decanter into the chamber pot.

While descending the staircase, he pondered how long he'd have to be sober before his pecker once again rose to the occasion. Would it ever? Had he squandered that also?

He found the peasant girl propped up in Matriusha's former bed while Elena removed the bloodstained bandage. He put an arm around his sister's shoulders, squeezed her to him, and kissed the top of her head. A quizzical smile played at her lips. A flush of self-reproach crept up his neck that she had already forgiven yesterday's abysmal behavior.

Beneath the bandage was a hole in the girl's upper arm that resembled a sliced strawberry. Thankfully, the damage to the underlying muscle appeared slight.

Anton's eyes moved upward to the child's hair, and he instantly recognized his own curls. He also noted Zhanna's dark eyebrows and high Slavic cheekbones. Except for her deformed arm, the girl was destined to be a beauty.

Unless his life took an unexpected and dramatic turn, this peasant would be his only child. What obligations did he have toward his bastard daughter?

While Elena applied a fresh dressing, she recounted that late yesterday afternoon, she had gone to the Holy Trinity Women's Community to notify the Sisters of the girl's accident and explain that she was being nursed by the Maximovs. She was told the girl's name was Anastasia.

"I told them that her arm was in a sling and, with the other one being useless, we would tend to her for the next few days."

"That's a champion idea." Good God, he'd said it again! "If you ladies will excuse me, I'll have a quick breakfast, then head to the distillery."

Elena's stare was mystified.

The shuttered distillery stood as a silent witness to the past, its dense quiet offering both loneliness and comfort. Anton lit a fire and allowed the small room to rekindle his youthful captivation with how grain, water, and yeast entered one end of the labyrinth and exited the other end as quality vodka.

The wooden barrels, the soot-encrusted window, the lingering scent of wood smoke . . . The lackluster mosaic roused deep-rooted recollections of nippy autumn days of sitting cross-legged atop the woodpile, lapping up Cockeyes's riddles. The steam from the boiler pots had allowed him to feel snug and secure, shielded from the vampiric clinging of his mother.

He was tempted to spend the rest of the day in simple reverie, closeted inside the brick walls. Instead, he brushed the cobwebs off the serpentine coils and probed the alterations Zhemchuzhnikov had made over the years.

With unwelcome insistence, his thoughts kept returning to Cockeyes, particularly how the worn-down guy was getting along in St. Petersburg. If, indeed, he had ever made it to St. Petersburg. Anton's shoulders slumped forward under a heavy load of shame.

CHAPTER 53

Elizaveta

1865

On the yearly holiday
a nifty young chap
stretches it tight
and shoves in deep.
What is it?

A boot.

WIND WAS WHISTLING through chinks in the walls when Elizaveta rose the morning following Ermak's injury. Everyone else was still asleep.

Elizaveta looked down at her husband. He was breathing, but his face was as pale as chalk. The shadows cast by the early light hollowed his cheeks.

Her fingers curled and her nails dug deep into her palms. Oh, the vicious irony if Ermak were to die and she were to be free at last. But Feodor was gone.

She turned away from the man she despised with her whole heart and soul. As she stoked the fire in the stove, Anna climbed off her sleeping bench. Elizaveta swiveled from the stove, watching as Anna reached up toward the shelf clock. The earliest rays of the sun through the window outlined the profile of her willowy body through her well-worn sleep shirt.

"How's Papa?" Anna asked as she inserted the clock's key.

Elizaveta didn't respond. She was straining to see her daughter's silhouette. Anna obliged by standing still while she rotated the key round and round.

"Anna?" Elizaveta whispered as she took a step toward her daughter.

Anna replaced the key and turned toward her mother. "Yes, Mama?"

Elizaveta took three more steps until she stood in front of Anna. She looked down at her daughter's stomach, then up at the dark circles under her eyes.

"Anna?"

Anna bit her lower lip.

"When did you have your last bleeding?"

Anna's blue eyes looked askance. Her teeth tugged at her lip.

Elizaveta took hold of the thin shoulders. Anna trembled like a captured bird. "When?" Elizaveta shook the girl's shoulders. "Tell me."

"After the harvest."

With all the power she could muster, Elizaveta flung the flat of her hand against the crimson stain on her daughter's face. Wearing her nightshirt and hastily thrown-on boots and sheepskin coat, Elizaveta hauled Anna to the privacy of the bathhouse.

Elizaveta was smacked by the image of dejected Zhanna outside the Maximovs' hunting lodge. Had Anton Stepanovich taken advantage of Anna during her stay at the estate house?

But no, Anna was wailing about a boy from the upstream village of Darovoe who had been at the summer dances on Raikovo's square. Something about a promise to marry her.

"Promised to marry you?" Elizaveta pressed Anna further. Had he given her some tangible piece of evidence to validate his pledge?

"He said he wanted to give me his grandmother's cross that she wore every day until she died."

"He *wanted* to give you a cross? That's nothing! Absolutely nothing!" What kind of fool was her daughter that she would risk everything based on a hollow promise?

Sickening impressions ricocheted inside her head. Anna and the boy lying together in a world of winking stars. The earthy scent of grass and night damp. A soft night breeze sifting through the ripened barley. The boy kissing Anna's bow-shaped mouth, caressing her young breasts, coaxing her to raise her skirt.

She shook Anna's thin shoulders. "Stay here."

Elizaveta retrieved a hidden bottle. It contained the liquid remedy for an unwanted child. Two years ago, Elizaveta purchased it from a midwife in Sukhanovo. Just in case she ever needed it.

Elizaveta watched Anna dutifully take a swallow of the concoction, the sight making her ill, like a thousand vultures pecking away at her insides. She told the girl to get dressed and muck out the cow's stall.

The next morning, Anna, as pale as a slice of potato, reported that her belly hurt. But there was no bleeding.

"Take another swallow. A big one."

Anna complied, tears clinging to her eyelashes.

Elizaveta was close to tears herself. Only by calling upon every morsel of her determination could she go through her day pretending to be worried about Ermak when her real agony was over her daughter. She was powerless to help Ermak. He either would recover or he wouldn't. But Anna's predicament was something over which she had at least some control.

Elizaveta moved distractedly about the izba. If the midwife's potion didn't work, Anna would be cruelly censured by the entire village. They'd shear her braid and hang a horse collar around her neck, then parade her past every izba. Worst of all, she'd be shunned as a marriage partner. A woman faced with spinsterhood faced no life at all.

The public shaming wouldn't stop with Anna. The village's tongues would wag. Hadn't Ermak and Elizaveta Vorontsov taught their children the commandments of God?

She collapsed onto a bench and placed a cool palm across her throbbing forehead. Why in Heaven's name had the boy selected Anna out of all the girls in the village? Her blue eyes and hair the color of ripened flax stood out as an oddity among the brown-eyed brunettes. She was small-boned and flat-chested. Not to mention that cursed mark on her face.

Elizaveta crossed her forearms prone atop the table and rested her cheek on them while she continued to brood. The childhood ridicule Anna endured because of her Devil's mark would be nothing compared with the harassment her bastard child would suffer. When the child became an adult, the assembly could deny his right to a communal land allotment. No father would allow his daughter to marry someone without a grain field allotment. In this tiny village, a person could never unburden himself of past sins.

She heard the rustle of straw. Her head jerked up just as Ermak's leg moved under the blanket. Vera was at her son's side in less than a heartbeat.

"Ermak. Can you hear me?" Cupping his chin in her palm, Vera gently rocked his head back and forth. "Ermak. Wake up."

Everyone crowded around the bench, bidding Ermak to open his eyes. A moan came from deep in his chest.

"Oh, precious Savior, he's coming around." Vera crossed and recrossed herself.

The man made no further movement, but hope had come to the izba.

Late that afternoon while her father lay on his sleeping bench, his eyes closed and phlegm gurgling in his throat, Anna reported to her mother that she had belly cramps, but nothing else.

Elizaveta moved to the next stage of her plan.

"YOU RAISED A whore!" His face purple with rage, her father-in-law ranted a few more foul phrases before he sat down to catch his breath.

Sidor, Vera, Elizaveta, and Anna were seated in the seclusion of the tiny bathhouse, its air keen with frost. Anna chewed her lower lip while tears rolled down her cheeks.

Elizaveta kept her voice conciliatory. "Obviously Anna realizes how wrong she was—"

"Speak up! I can't hear you," Sidor bellowed.

"Anna realizes how wrong she was."

"I hope to God she does!"

Anna fell forward and wept into her skirt.

Elizaveta's tone remained submissive. "What do you have to say, Mother?"

Vera's old, watery eyes shifted from her daughter-in-law to her granddaughter. "Can't say I'm surprised, considering the retching."

Sidor pulled his elbow back, then thrust his arm forward its entire length, his pointed finger quivering. "What that girl has done to the good name of Vorontsov!"

"I realize that, Father."

"As if I don't have enough troubles on my mind! Our emancipation is a farce. We owe Maximov rubles for the land we've tilled for generations. And—"

"All that is true, but let's worry about that later."

Sidor bowed his bald head and kneaded it with his fingers. His speech calmed from deafening to booming. "Christ above, you know that no one will marry a girl with a physical failing or unholy behavior. Unless, of course, the girl has a large dowry. Which your daughter doesn't. But she *is* tainted with a deformity *and* immorality. You can't expect Ermak to be able to marry off damaged goods."

"Maybe we could take care of this, so no one finds out."

Sidor's bushy eyebrows dropped.

Elizaveta swallowed. "I've heard there are ways not to have a baby even after one has started. There's a midwife in Sukhanovo who knows how." She held her breath.

Sidor sucked air into his lungs. "All I can say is, I'm glad Ermak can't hear this. That his daughter is a whore and his wife is a murderer."

CHAPTER 54

Maximov

1865

In our grain, there's a good sprout.
What is it?

A child.

DURING ANASTASIA'S SECOND evening at the estate house, Anton sat beside her bed and read aloud *Emelya and the Magic Pike*, a story she'd never heard. The following evening, as the sun cast the last of its shadows, Anastasia said she enjoyed the story very much. Would he read it to her again?

Anton obliged. Every time he bellowed, "By the pike's command; by my own request!" he heard his father's voice from a quarter of a century ago.

He found it peculiar that a seven-year-old wasn't familiar with the classic children's story. She was able to decipher a few written words but couldn't master an entire book. Apparently nurturing young intellects wasn't among the nuns' priorities. Anastasia was undeniably polite, but how in that forlorn hermitage was she going to acquire Hilda's "underpinning of society"? The child might be half peasant, but she was also half gentry. Who would teach her poise and dancing and the art of flirting without being obvious?

The girl grew homesick on her third day of forced bed rest, so Elena had Yegorka drive her and Anastasia for an afternoon visit at the orphanage. That evening after Anastasia fell asleep, Elena told Anton she had learned that the nuns were an autonomous group of three dozen or so women who had taken vows of celibacy and dedication to God. Because the monastery wasn't formally connected with the Church, the Sisters were an independent lot who possessed the unremitting determination and discipline required to be self-supporting.

The Holy Trinity Women's Community had a small endowment, and the Sisters received an occasional cash donation. However, the bulk of their overhead was covered with income generated by the nuns' own hands, largely from working the monastery's acreage. Hand-thrown pottery brought in a few rubles. Sheep, goats, and chickens provided the orphans with meat and eggs.

Anton knew nothing about the stucco buildings on the cliff overlooking the river and, until three days ago, had cared even less. He viewed monasteries as remnants of feudal times best left behind with other macabre medieval relics such as thumbscrews and beds of nails. However, out of politeness, he asked, "How many children live there?"

"Twenty-five or so."

"The nuns outnumber the children? Seems like it should be the opposite."

"The Sisters do all they can, taking into account the workload they shoulder and the number of hours they dedicate to God. Their purpose isn't to perform works of charity but rather to seek the meaning of life through fasting, meditation, and prayer."

Elena took Anastasia on daily visits to the orphanage, accompanied by donations of clothing, old furniture, and two fully serviceable wheelbarrows. In the evenings, Anton read various fairy tales to the child. Elena and Anastasia shared a love of singing, and Anton, Gennady, and Dasha clapped wildly at their duets.

At the end of a week, Elena returned the girl to the permanent care of the nuns. Anton shifted from foot to foot under the portico as Yegorka opened the carriage door for Anastasia. With the intent of giving the girl a quick good-bye, Anton put an arm around her shoulders. However, Anastasia wrapped her arms around his neck, and he found himself squatting on his haunches, clutching the tiny thing to his chest.

"You must come visit us." He stroked the dark curls that cascaded down her back. "And we'll visit you, too."

As he watched the sledge glide along the snow tracks toward the bridge, Anton felt a massive hesitation to admit the girl into his heart. Except for Elena, he trusted no one. How could he, when the disquiet constantly gnawed at him that Sophia's affection toward Anton-the-child lay outside the boundaries of maternal? When, in turn, he had concealed his own vile, unbidden physical responses?

"DO YOU THINK Mother even realized that a seven-year-old lived here for a week?" Elena asked at the evening meal.

Anton rolled his eyes. Sophia hadn't left her room since returning from St. Petersburg.

His sister picked up her soup spoon. "I notice you're not having any wine."

He stared at the fork quivering in his hand, the hand that would normally be reaching for a glass. Unable to stop the tremors, he set the fork on his plate. Its clang bounced around the room. Placing both forearms against the table's edge to steady himself, he gazed at Elena's round, loving face.

"I've stopped drinking."

She set down her spoon, placed her hands on her lap napkin, and leaned back against her chair. "I know."

"Last week."

Her head dipped in a slight nod. Her expression was so kind, so understanding, so full of desire to help him that his stony bearing cracked. "I've never done anything this difficult." His throat was tight, his words raspy. "I don't want a drink. I need a drink. Constantly. I think of nothing else."

She slid the palm of her hand across the tablecloth toward him. "How can I help you?"

"I got myself into this predicament. I have to see myself clear of it." He clenched a fist in front of his mouth. "I've fouled up so many things. Oh, Pigeon, please, you must stand by me." He grasped his upper lip between his thumb and forefinger. It struck him that this was the first time he had laid his heart open to anyone.

"Of course, Antoshka. Anything you require. Say the word, and we'll play billiards or saddle up the horses or whatever will help your mind find peace."

Although forthright honesty had much to its credit, he'd had enough for his first attempt at it. He managed a paltry half smile. "Maybe mucking out the stalls would be a good diversion." When he received her return smile, he patted her extended hand. "I know you love me, and I'll take you up on your offer. But for right now, let's talk about something else."

Elena withdrew her hand from the table and picked up her fork. "Well, in that case, I have something to tell you."

"Oh?"

"I'm joining the Holy Trinity Women's Community."

The wind was knocked out of Anton's chest as though she'd dropped a load of hay on him.

She poked at her spinach cups with creamed peas while he sat like a deaf-mute. "I thought you'd have something to say about my decision. I'm certain you disapprove."

"You're . . . you're . . . you're jesting, right?"

"I've already spoken with the Abbess."

"And?"

"She's accepted me on a probationary basis. How do you think Mother and Father will react?"

"Mother won't give you any trouble. Hell, she'll probably go with you."

Elena withdrew into herself, and he gave himself a mental tongue-lashing. Moments ago, she had showered him with unconditional love and support, and now he was responding like a pompous oaf. "I apologize. This is an overwhelming shock. Whatever possessed you to make such a sacrifice?"

"To me, it's not a sacrifice. It will be my life's work."

"And work you will!" Anton's fork jabbed the air toward his sister. Appalled yet again by his unintentional mimicry of his father, he pitched the fork onto his plate. Now it was his turn to reach partway across the tablecloth. He looked into a face so still, it could have been cut with a chisel. "Pigeon, you have a title and the land to go with it. You can marry well and have a family. You don't have to work like a peasant. Why would you want to endure a pauper's existence with four dozen other women?"

She replied, "I know it's hard for you to understand, but being around the simple needs of Anna Vorontsova and now Anastasia has taught me that I have something to offer children, a way to be of service to others."

"Yes, of course, serving others is always virtuous. But you don't have to enter a monastery to be charitable. You're only twenty-one years old. Why not wait a little while and see if you change your mind? Why would you throw away the life your inheritance can afford you?"

Elena stopped fiddling with her spinach cups and set down her fork. She crossed her arms around her waist and leaned against the back of her chair. "I don't at all feel I'm throwing away my life. If and when I receive an inheritance, I'll keep the money with Father's broker and donate the income from it to the Community. I have no intention of touching the principal."

"Don't you see? That's why those nuns want you to join their monastery. They think you're bringing the Maximov wealth with you."

Her face tightened. "I already informed the Abbess that I have very little money of my own and that Mother and Father are both healthy and expected to live many more years. And that we are not a wealthy family."

Anton's fingertips tapped his tea glass. "But why would you choose to live like a hermit?"

"Antoshka," she bent forward, "I already do."

AS SOON AS he closed the door to his bedroom, Anton thumped his forehead with his fist. How could he not have seen it coming?

How the donated items she made to the monastery kept growing. How, when she broke her legs, she chose Matriusha's windowless cubbyhole as her bedroom. How she personally tended to her cattle. How she eschewed balls, fine clothes, and jewelry. How she was well liked by all, yet had no close friends. Elena would meld wonderfully into the humility, simplicity, and collective self-sufficiency of the Sisters and the Community. The monastic life would be perfect for his little Pigeon, who had never quite fit in with the rest of the world.

The lamp cast a dark image of his profile on the wall. He had a sudden glimpse of the future. If Elena were to leave, only he and his parents would remain to wander around the shadowy vacuum of the estate house.

CHAPTER 55

Maximov

1865

Who is richest of all?
The one who is satisfied
with his circumstances.

THE ENVELOPE WAS addressed to Count Stepan Stepanovich Maximov and Family. The penmanship, small and precise, was familiar.

December 3, 1865

To the dear Maximov family,
It has been almost seven years since August and I ventured forth from Petrovo to Saratov. Our employer has treated us fairly, and we made a good life for ourselves. The years have passed joyfully.

I felt it imperative to let you know that August left this world last month. He succumbed to a case of lockjaw. I am certain, Count Maximov, that he would want you to know, as he held you in the highest regard. He valued your honesty and lauded your enthusiasm for the land.

My employer has encouraged me to continue my tenure on the estate. However, now that I am alone and increasing in years, I hope to obtain a more secure position at a boarding school.

With fondest memories of our time with you,
Hilda Roeglin

Anton hadn't given August Roeglin more than a fleeting thought since the steward left Petrovo. But today's news spawned a soft ache as he remembered the couple's bashful initial game of hide-and-seek. Once the romance took hold, Roeglin had never failed to treat stocky Hilda as the enticing love of his life, showering her with unmitigated devotion, which she reciprocated in equal measure.

Devotion. Something Anton didn't stand a chance of ever experiencing. Could he recall witnessing it in his parents? If he tried hard enough, he could exhume a couple of moth-eaten images that suggested a caring attachment: His parents having tea at the small iron table on the terrace, his father's hand covering his mother's. Both of them laughing as their three eldest children played vulture-and-chickens. The family on countless sleigh rides through the frozen forest. Huddled together under heaps of blankets. Bounding over drifts. Harness bells jangling.

For several long moments, Anton stood immobile, his eyelids pressed together in self-disgust. Regardless of how much or how little devotion his parents bestowed on each other, it was infinitely more than he had shown the mother of his child.

WHEN STEPAN WALKED through the mahogany door the following day, his mouth sagged like a yoke burdened with buckets that were too heavy. He tossed a cursory greeting to his son and daughter and the servants, then ordered the bathhouse be fired up so he could steam the travel dirt from his pores. His pinched face swiveled upward as he took measure of the long staircase.

As Anton watched his father drag himself up the banister, he wondered if perhaps it were time to extend an olive branch to the man. Although Stepan was no saint, Anton acknowledged that his own compulsions, and yes, even defiance, had exacted a toll on his father.

For the next two hours, Anton tried out various phrases to express his sentiments. He strove for a tone that contained a sincere desire for reconciliation yet was not mawkishly effusive. Try as he might, the man with the glib tongue couldn't produce the appropriate words.

That evening when Anton and Elena entered the study, Stepan was wrapped in a soft-gray dressing gown, entrenched in the tumbledown relic of his red brocade chair. Normally fastidious in his grooming, he had the slate-gray stubble of a three-day beard. His grim lips were as thin as a kopek, and his horseshoe of remaining hair jutted every which way.

Stepan immediately began grousing how the post inns, abysmal to begin with, had deteriorated over recent years. "They were bereft of decent food. The mattresses crawled with vermin and were as hard and lumpy as sacks of potatoes. By the time I got Yustina home, she was so drained, she was the color of stale porridge."

Stepan went on to say that when the rail line opened between Kozlov and Tambov, the family would be able to travel the whole distance via train. "Picture it: going from Tambov to Kozlov, changing trains, continuing to Moscow, then boarding the Moscow–St. Petersburg line. The trip will be made in a third the time and in twice the comfort. Should be anytime now."

Anton pulled back his head and stared at his father's permanent frown lines and thin, ragged hair. *Should be anytime now?* How clouded was his father's mind? The Tambov–Kozlov Railway wouldn't be operational for a couple of years.

"You look tired, Papa," Elena said.

Stepan yawned. "I am, Pigeon. Bring me a blanket. It's chilly in here."

Stepan was already dozing, open-mouthed, when Elena returned to the study. Across her father's shoulders she tucked an old down quilt that had been worked by the hands of Stepan's mother.

As Anton left the study, he glanced at the feeble gray man who only vaguely resembled the imposing pomeshchik of Petrovo. *Maybe*, Anton pondered, *Victor Rusakov was correct.* The looming decisions about the estate were hugely consequential, and his father's strength was waning.

Tomorrow, Anton vowed. Tomorrow he'd take the first steps toward building a rapport with his father.

The next day, however, Stepan's lassitude was unmistakably more than simply travel fatigue. He ached from head to toe and was seized with bouts of chills and nausea. He craved sleep, which gave Anton a convenient excuse to avoid the sick room.

The following morning, Stepan bordered on delirium. A.A. Gabrichevsky's physician was summoned. The medical man apologized for being slow to arrive at Petrovo, but he had stopped on the way to tend to Yustina Rusakova.

Following the examination, Anton, Elena, and Sophia met him at the bottom of the stairs. Gennady and Dasha stood to one side. The doctor said that Stepan's symptoms were the same as Yustina's. She had already developed the characteristic red spots. Stepan was sure to get them in a day or two. "They brought typhus fever back with them."

From the corner of his eye, Anton saw his mother swoon. In an instant, the butler stepped up and supported Sophia with an arm around her waist. Gennady's ripe old voice was low and comforting. "Come along, Madame, up to your room where you can lie down."

The physician explained that the disease bestowed its most poisonous effects on older people. "Scrub the house with aromatic vinegar to expel any lingering bad air. I'll return tomorrow to let more blood. Meanwhile, laudanum will offer some relief."

Anton went upstairs and stood before the door to his father's bedroom. He lifted his hand to knock, but couldn't force his knuckles to rap the wood. *Later*, he told himself. It would be pointless to go in now. The laudanum would be taking effect.

Anton's gaze remained fixed on the dark mahogany of the door. His mind's eye pictured seven-year-old Styopanka sleeping on the other side of this very door while Napoleon occupied what was left of burnt-out Moscow. Anton contemplated the changes that had occurred since young Stepan played within these walls.

Stepan had lived the majority of his life before any thought was given to emancipating the serfs or abolishing the liquor tax farm. He had grown up prior to talk of trial by jury or connecting Moscow to the rest of Russia via iron tracks. Maybe it was asking too much of an aging man to fit into a world overhauled by the Great Reforms. After all, an oak can't turn into a willow simply because the wind suddenly picked up.

Anton lingered a moment longer, not staring at the door but through it. He watched Stepan lead his lovely bride across their bedchamber. Anton's chin dropped to his chest as a suffocating wave of sadness crashed over him.

In his own bedroom, Anton lit the lamp that now occupied the site where the decanter used to faithfully wait for him. Right now, he'd sell his soul to have a single swallow of liquid relief. He flung himself onto his back on his bed, clenched his hands together, and held them against his lips as he groped for the strength to stay in his room rather than go downstairs in search of a bottle. His knuckles grew wet. Tears?

Well, he thought, *it's only natural*. Many a son would cry when faced with the possible death of his father, even if the relationship had never been close. A question crossed his mind: When was the last time the two of them had embraced? Probably well before that harebrained Maximov Ball when Anton had caught Stepan and Yustina in their little tryst under the porte-cochere. He recalled another incident from that evening—his father tapping him on the shoulder while he danced with Sophia, rescuing him from his mother's clutches.

Anton had to commend his father—he never belittled his unbalanced wife. Nor did he speak unkindly of her behind her back. Of course, Stepan would on occasion lose his temper, but his anger never turned physical. All told, his father was quite tolerant, to the point of being benevolent, with Sophia.

He'd been tolerant with the peasants, too. Purchasing grain during shortages. Bailing Zhemchuzhnikov out of jail. Lending the villagers his valuable animals to chase the horse thieves. Not to mention buying every mushroom and berry the ragged children peddled. And all those countless sprinklings of holy water Stepan had secured from Diakonov for the peasants' horses, livestock, grain, and bees. Which was a pittance compared with the tens of thousands of rubles that had gone into maintaining the church building.

What about tolerance with his children? Stepan hadn't seemed tolerant at the time, but maybe he was. Just look at how he had put up with their incessant and irrational supplications, Vaska the goat not the least of them.

Although Anton was loath to admit it, Stepan had been heroically patient with Anton himself. His arm went to his forehead as his mind harked back to his expulsion from the Cadet's College. Of course, it all turned out just as well. He wasn't suited for a military career. But perhaps there might have been a more decorous way to leave the College than being ejected for bedding a professor's wife. His father could have—and probably should have—flayed him alive.

And how had he repaid Stepan? By submerging himself in self-absorbed behavior that time and again inflicted pain on the family.

Anton rolled off the bed and paced the room.

Father. What kind of father did Anastasia have? Had Anastasia's father gotten down on all fours and allowed her to make reins out of his hair? Had Anastasia's father ever cuddled her on his lap and shared tidbits of poppy seed pie? Had Anastasia's father taught her how to spin a top or build ice castles or paddle a canoe?

His self-deprecating ruminations were interrupted by a rap on his door. Dasha handed him a folded and sealed piece of stationery. The handwriting was ragged and infirm.

Anton,
I must talk to you. Come without delay. Tell no one.
Yustina Ivanovna Rusakova

CHAPTER 56

Maximov

1865

Who flees and gives chase
like two wrestlers wrestling?
Life and death.

AS VICTOR LED Anton up the staircase, he said that his mother seemed a bit stronger today.

"However," Victor whispered before knocking on the fluted casing of the bedroom door, "the physician said Mother might be recovering or it could be a final rally before the end."

Yustina's bedroom was tainted with the sour smell of sickness. Vladimir was sitting beside her bed, a situation quite dissimilar from Petrovo, where Stepan's spouse had taken to her own bed and required as much attention as the patient.

Despite her hollow-eyed appearance, the petite woman smiled when she saw him. "How good of you to come by. Help me sit up, Vladimir, so I can speak with Anton."

After a mountain of pillows was positioned behind her back, she requested her husband bring her a little toast with butter and some juice. "And close the door, so Anton and I can chat without disruption."

When they were alone, her haggard eyes settled on him. Her voice lost its levity. "Listen close. I haven't the strength to repeat myself. But you must realize this isn't the babbling of a sick, old woman."

Wary, Anton took the chair still warm from Vladimir. "You have my full attention."

"I know you have your opinions about your father and myself. Whatever you think is irrelevant to me. The truth is, I love your father. Not with the consuming, tempestuous love of twenty-year-olds, but with an undemanding, transcendent love. I would do anything for Stepan, and he for me. We're asking the same of you."

She sounded in control of her faculties, but her message was far too effusive for Anton's sentiments. And the last sentence triggered a protective reflex.

"You didn't know your grandfather well. You were a child when his mind became affected. But did you know that *his* father died in the lunatic hospital?"

"N-no."

"Runs in the family. I can't say if you'll get it. But it's taken hold of your father."

"You're saying he's going senile?"

Her nod was the mere closing and reopening of her eyelids. Her voice was weak but unequivocal. "In St. Petersburg, he wanted to visit Sergei. Couldn't tell the driver how to get to his apartment."

"That's understandable. A strange city and all."

Yustina's cracked lips fell silent for a full minute. When she spoke, her voice shattered, like thin ice under a carriage wheel. "Couldn't remember his son's name."

"He couldn't remember Sergei's name?"

Yustina's eyelids fell like heavy curtains. "Stepan made arrangements."

"Arrangements for what?"

"Gave him my word—I would help him. But I'm too sick. Must be done now." Her eyes slid open. "You must do it."

Anton tilted his head away from her. Despite Yustina's opening comment, this certainly sounded like the babbling of an old woman.

She brought forth an ashen hand from beneath the coverlet. Both her eyes and a brittle finger directed him to the bureau on the far wall. "A note."

Anton's gaze shifted across the room.

Yustina's finger remained fixed on the bureau. "Middle."

Anton pressed the heels of his hands against his knees and rose. As if he were a third party to all of this, he watched his hand slide open the middle drawer. The faint smell of lilac wafted out. His fingers fumbled under Yustina's handkerchiefs and brushed across an envelope. His thumb and forefinger picked it up by a corner. It was sealed. He straightened and, with his back still toward the bed, loosened the wax. The solitary sheet of ivory paper was dated November 1864 and contained his father's writing.

> *Yustina, my oldest and dearest friend,*
> *I may be leaving you, but please never doubt that you've been in my heart for the whole of my life and that you have my unending gratitude for the noble and selfless act you agreed to perform when the need arises. As we discussed:*

1. The cure is in the storeroom, where we keep extra on hand for illness.

2. More bottles are hidden in the hunting lodge, on the top shelf above Anton's stash of liquor.

                                        My undying love to you,
                                                Stepan

Clutching the note in one hand and the envelope in the other, Anton dropped his arms to his sides and turned back toward the bed. "The cure?"

"Laudanum."

Horror sank its claws into Anton's spine.

"He can't bear the thought of burdening his children. Because of his father. Incontinent. Drooling. Fits of rage. You know Stepan has no understanding of irrationality."

Yes, Anton plainly knew his father had no tolerance for excessive emotions, particularly his wife's. But still, this must be a vulgar joke. Lightheaded, he leaned against the bureau. "He wants to . . . to kill himself?"

"His illness is a godsend." Her voice was spent and desiccated. "His death will surprise no one."

"What are you saying?"

"A final act of kindness." Tears gathered in her red-rimmed eyes.

Anton's mouth went dry as sand. "You're asking me to kill my own father?" His feet scuffed across the deep-piled carpet. He stood over her and shook the ivory stationery. "Based on what a single piece of paper says?"

"Under the bottles in the hunting lodge. A note like that one."

"No!" Anton glanced at the closed door and lowered his voice. "My father made a suicide pact with you and now you expect me to carry it out?"

"Wants this for his family." Her pallid eyelids closed. She placed a frail hand on her breastbone and took in several deep breaths between her colorless lips. When she opened her eyes, they bored into his. "If not enough laudanum, finish him off."

"Finish him off?"

"I'd smother him."

He stared at her. *She's delirious!*

The stairway floorboards creaked. Yustina's speech became clipped. "He wants to die."

"Hell, he might die anyway."

"And if he doesn't?"

Anton squeezed his eyes shut. Thunderous words assaulted him. *Do it, you spineless bastard. Reach inside and find the gumption.*

The words certainly weren't Yustina's. Then he realized they were his own, echoing from the past. From the day he ended Vaska's suffering.

CHAPTER 57

Elizaveta

1865

She sits on a spoon,
dangling her feet.
What is she?

Noodles.

A BLIZZARD AND then a sprain in the horse's ankle postponed Anna's trip to Sukhanovo for ten days. The midwife chastised Elizaveta; waiting so long meant the procedure would be gruesome and the recovery agonizing.

After the midwife inflicted her torture, Anna lay as still and pale as death on her straw pallet for a full week before she was able to sit up and prop her back against the rough wall. At that point, Elizaveta put an end to helping Anna eat and drink. She handed her daughter a bowl and spoon and left her to her own devices to get the noodles and broth past her ashen lips.

Elizaveta wanted to offer soothing, motherly words. But she refrained. Her daughter needed to learn a lesson from all of this. Once Anna was back on her feet, Elizaveta planned to tell her how the Vorontsovs had spent their very last rubles to pay the midwife. It was best she hear it from her mother. Elizaveta could well imagine the Vorontsovs shrieking their bitter accusations. *"Our pockets are empty, thanks to you! And no way to acquire even so much as a kopek until next summer when the grain is harvested!"*

Although Anna was recovering and there would be no bastard in the Vorontsov family, a problem still lingered. It was only a matter of time before the tale leaked out of the Vorontsov izba and the wind carried whispers throughout the village.

Meanwhile, death tugged steadily at Ermak. His sunken eyes were open but sightless. His throaty noises were without meaning, as were the random movements of his limbs. He could swallow broth only if someone propped him up and dribbled it into his mouth. His breath smelled of rot.

The family was convinced he would recover. Elizaveta wasn't so sure. A couple of spoonfuls of soup couldn't keep his body from melting away, and his pasty skin was as cold as a dead fish. His vacuous stare and lack of purposeful response to either touch or voice told Elizaveta that his head was as empty as his heart had always been.

Which provoked another worry to rear up. If Ermak were to die, would the Vorontsovs kick her out? After Stanislav died, they wasted no time sending his wife back to her birth family. Of course, Elizaveta was younger and still had years of stamina. So maybe the Vorontsovs would think she was worth keeping.

Only one reason could persuade her to continue living with such cold-blooded people. She didn't want to be separated from her sons. The Vorontsovs would keep Ilya and Gerasim. Not only were the two youths of their son's loins, but they were also able-bodied men.

And there was the question of whether the Anafrevs would welcome her return. Uncle Artamon's wife was dead. Elizaveta hardly knew his three grown sons, each of whom had brought a hale and hearty woman into the izba. The Anafrevs had no need of a woman who stood at the brink of her declining years.

While Anna grappled with her noodles, Elizaveta cleaned Ermak of his feces and smeared a protective layer of lard on the festering sores made by his waste. She dropped the filthy rag into the bucket of murky water. After wrapping him in the rags that served as a diaper, she flung the brown water to a spot just outside the door where dozens of previous pails of water had created a circle of melted snow. As she watched the liquid disappear into the ground, she yearned to disappear out of her own bone-weary life.

Elizaveta sank into the rocking chair. She was alone with Ermak and Anna while the rest of the family was at Count Maximov's funeral. As a favor to her exhausted self, she decided to rebraid her hair, then take a long steam bath. The bathhouse was still warm from the morning's baths.

While she plaited her hair, she thought about the memorial service occurring at the other end of town. A memory surfaced.

Count Maximov said if ever we need anything, we should ask him.

That's what Anna told the family after she had returned the dog with the broken leg. And when Elena Stepanovna Maximova busted her legs, she supposedly made an identical offer to Anna.

Wait, Elizaveta thought. *The Count is dead.* But the Count's son, Anton Stepanovich, had been there when Anna returned the dog. Would he honor the Count's pledge?

Elizaveta reflected on the potential chain of events. The Count's funeral had been postponed to allow his son and daughter to travel from St. Petersburg. And cousins had arrived from Moscow. Would one of Maximov's children be willing to take Anna with them to St. Petersburg as a servant? Or maybe the Moscow cousins would take her? Anna was too weak to travel now, but she was gaining strength. How long would the mourners stay on the estate? Was there any possibility that all the right pieces might fall into place?

When news of Anna's pregnancy began to circulate, the villagers would first chastise Ermak and Elizaveta for their daughter's actions, then value the Vorontsovs' good sense for sending her away. The public shaming would be severe but temporary.

A ray of hope descended on Elizaveta, like the sound of the river's ice cracking with the long-awaited approach of spring.

She cocked her head. Someone was knocking.

As she walked toward the door, she glanced at Ermak and his swollen knuckles. "You black-hearted beast," she snarled through gritted teeth.

She jerked open the door and was greeted with a chilling one-eyed stare.

CHAPTER 58

Elizaveta

1865

I am a flattie, a little board.
At the edges is a little border,
and in the middle is a little hole.
What am I?

An ear.

VARLAAM GORBUNOV REACHED for her hand and lifted it to his lips, the same as he had on that long-ago day by the river. "My sweet Elizaveta."

She stood dumbfounded, unsure if she wanted to say, *What?* or *Why?* or *Go away.* When at last she pulled back her hand, she stammered, "Where did you come from?"

"From God, from Whom everything comes." Gorbunov clasped his hands in front of him and tilted his head like a kindly grandfather gazing at a beloved child. "May I come in?"

"I . . . I suppose so."

He walked past her and hung his snow-floured great coat on a peg. The hollows of his cheeks had deepened. Otherwise, he was unchanged: the opaque eye that gave the impression of being turned inside out, the forked apostolic beard, the silver cross hanging from his thin neck, the voice of docile timbre that evoked the listener's trust.

Gorbunov abruptly turned and embraced Elizaveta, placing his lips next to her ear. "My poor woman. Such hardships."

She stepped back.

He extended his long-fingered hand toward the table. "May I sit down?"

He paused as he walked past Ermak. After making the sign of the Cross three times, he grasped the prone man's shoulder. "Don't lose faith, my friend. Even in your deepest slumber, turn to God. In Him, all things are possible."

He repeated the sign of the Cross as he passed Anna sitting on her sleeping bench. He continued to the table, each lengthy stride accompanied by the flapping of his robe like the rhythmic wings of a raptor.

Elizaveta took a seat across the table, beyond Gorbunov's reach. He placed his fur turban on the bench beside him and tucked his stringy hair behind first one ear, then the other.

Elizaveta's eyes went wide. His ears! Those telltale wolflike ears! *If this fool sees Platon, he'll instantly know the child is his.*

Might he want to take the boy with him? Who wouldn't want their own flesh and blood, particularly a child as lovable as Platoshka?

Was she was jumping to harebrained conclusions? Possibly. But possibly not. She had to get rid of Gorbunov before the family returned and he recognized his son.

"I can see your thoughts are burdened, my child." He lifted his open palms toward the rafters. "That's why God sent me here. When I arrived this morning, the first thing I did was call upon my dear friend, Fredek Sharovatov. The last time I was here, he was so kind as to allow me to sleep in his barn. But I found he and his wife are with God now, as are Avdotya and Timofei. Such losses for us mortals." He shook his head. "Then I happened upon your Uncle Artamon. A delight to see his family. He told me about your husband's dreadful accident. And now I see you also have a sick daughter."

"Yes, she's been ill. Perhaps you'll come back sometime to pray for her?"

"I shall pray for her right now."

"She's sleeping." How had such stupid words sprung from her mouth? The girl was sitting on her sleeping bench. "I mean she just woke up, and we were about to take a steam bath, when you arrived."

"Why are you in such a hurry to be rid of me?" His good eye grew blacker.

She realized he was too intelligent for her to outsmart. "I have many chores before my family returns." His eyebrows lifted, so she added, "Besides bathing Anna and tending to my husband, I need to get a meal on the table."

"I remember many, many enjoyable meals while I was in Petrovo. The village was most generous, never failing to fill my kasha bowl."

Beneath the table, the tips of Elizaveta's fingers drummed on her good knee. The scoundrel was hinting at an invitation for a meal. "And where have you been since you left Petrovo?"

"God's ministry has taken me many places. Along the Volga and the Don I've helped the blind to see. I've witnessed cripples brought to their feet in the Ukraine. All over Russia, I've seen despair and grief replaced by showers of blessings."

"Aren't you afraid of typhus as you wander about? The Count died of typhus, you know."

"How can I be afraid when I never walk alone?"

"Have you a place to sleep while in Petrovo?"

"Not yet. But something will manifest. Besides, I won't be staying long in this village."

"Oh?"

He tilted his head sadly. "Once again, you are eager to be rid of me."

"I was merely wondering if you'll have time to visit all the people you know."

"I saw many already. On their way to the church. Your family included."

"My family? You mean the Anafrevs or the Vorontsovs?"

"I already told you. I saw the Anafrevs. You weren't listening. You're distracted by your problems."

"That's true. I am."

"And I also saw the Vorontsovs. And your young nephew Platon—such a little scamp. He'd be eight years of age, correct?" Gorbunov's good eye gleamed, shrewd and fiendish.

Her breath caught. *He knows! That's why he's come to Petrovo—to collect Platon!*

Placing his forearms on the table, Gorbunov leaned toward her. "Platon will be a leader among men one day, assuming he doesn't wander from God's plan."

"And what plan is that?"

"Who knows? For it to be revealed, we must listen." He dropped his chin and rolled his eyeball upward to stay focused on her. "It is your responsibility, Elizaveta, to keep Platon's soul open to God."

The pent-up air left her chest. The fool had no intention of taking the child with him. Along with reassurance came her old cynicism. The rambling bum probably has so many bastards scattered over Russia, he can't count them all.

"I swear to you, I will take excellent care of Platon. Now I must get on with my chores." She rose from the bench. As she had hoped, he stood and picked up his hat.

"Go along to your bath, Anna. I'll join you in a moment." Elizaveta gave her arm to her daughter to grasp as she struggled to rise from the sleeping bench. Relying on her mother's old walking stick, Anna scuffled from the izba.

Elizaveta removed Gorbunov's coat from the peg and held it out to him. She wouldn't allow him to leave it a second time.

"I pray your tragedies haven't caused you to lose faith. You were close to doing so the last time we talked. You and your loved ones will be in my prayers."

"We're grateful." She opened the door and the biting cold swirled in.

He stepped outside, then spun back toward her. "We were talking so earnestly, I neglected to mention that I bring greetings to you from someone you know." He pulled his hat over the peaks of his ears.

Elizaveta already had the door half-shut. She pressed her shivering lips together, annoyed at the devious ways he postponed his departures.

"While I was traveling through the town of Efremov, God sent across my path someone from Petrovo."

Someone from Petrovo? *That's ridiculous*, she thought. No one ever left Petrovo. Unless they were conscripted into the military. Perhaps he'd seen her little brother, lost to them a decade earlier?

Gorbunov supplied the name. "Feodor Zhemchuzhnikov."

"Feodor Zhemchuzhnikov?" Her voice was flat, dismissive. "Feodor Zhem-chuzhnikov is dead."

"Oh, no. He's alive."

"No. Horses trampled him to death."

"Horses trampled him horribly, but not to death. He survived, even though he was thought to be dead. A local family took him in. It was days before he woke up and weeks before he could remember his name. Like a modern-day Lazarus, he held tight to God's hand. Now his mind grows clearer a little at a time, and with two canes, he can walk."

Elizaveta stood as though turned to stone while her emotions tumbled riot-ously. "You're sure?"

"Quite sure. He even speaks well enough that he dictated a letter to me to give to his brother, assuring him that he'll soon be strong enough to make the journey home." Gorbunov patted the pocket of his coat. A piece of paper crackled.

Elizaveta's gaze dropped to his pocket. In it were words from her beloved!

He lifted her hand to his lips. "Good day, Elizaveta. Keep in mind what I told you on your sick bed. In the end, God's will always triumphs."

Elizaveta slumped against the closed door. Mouth hanging slack, she sucked in air, trying to steady the spinning room. She staggered across to Nicholas the Wonderworker and fell to her knees.

"Please bring him home soon," she beseeched the Wonderworker. "Please! It's such a long distance. Give him the strength. I beg you to intervene with the Blessed Virgin. And with God himself."

Behind her came a sound like eggshells being pulverized. She turned to see Ermak's arm lying atop his sheepskin, his bony fingers reflexively opening and closing into a fist, creaking with each flexion. Opening. Closing. Opening. Closing. Like the lethal talons of a hawk.

Elizaveta rose and walked over to him. Chest heaving and head erect, she cast her eyes down at the face she knew so well and despised. His unseeing gaze remained fixed on the rafters while his fingers continued to extend and flex and rasp.

She put her hands over her ears. She couldn't stand that noise! *Crack*—a boot in the middle of her back. *Crack*—a skillet smashing her knee. *Crack*—her unborn son and her father going to their graves.

A poisonous rage flared in her.

"Shut up," she screamed at her deaf husband. "Shut up before I—"

Before I what? Kill you?

CHAPTER 59

Elizaveta

1865

If I stood up,
I'd reach the sky.
What am I?

A road.

ELIZAVETA'S HANDS SLID from her ears to her mouth. Holy Savior, what was she saying?

Could she do it? Physically, yes she could. He was a feeble invalid. After years of arduous labor, she was as strong as a draught horse. But did she have the fortitude to exact the ultimate reprisal for the sins he'd committed?

She was alone in the izba. The family would think Ermak had simply been called to the afterlife.

She paced to and fro, her thoughts snarled. Would it be a sin? Of course it would be a sin. It was murder.

But in order to be murdered, the person has to be alive. Was Ermak truly alive? Could his stupor be called *living*?

His hand lay still now, its withered skin draped over veins and sinews. His ash-gray mouth hung slack, and his breath grew more fetid by the day. His own mother could squeeze his hand and whisper loving words in his ear, and he didn't show an inkling of understanding.

Was he alive? It was an ethical question Elizaveta couldn't answer. But this much she knew: She'd seen lots of sick and injured animals, and no amount of feeding, tending, or praying could keep them alive once their bodies wasted away. It always ended in death.

Gorbunov said Feodor had taken days to wake up and weeks to remember his name. But Ermak had been injured weeks ago, not days, and he was still as lifeless as the boards he was lying on.

Feodor. She breathed his name. Feodor was coming home. When he arrived, would she be bound to a merciless brute, cowering in fear of another beating? Or would she be free of tyranny, free to . . . Free to what? Because of the ties through their godparents, the Church would still forbid them to marry.

However, they were now free rural inhabitants, weren't they? Couldn't she and Feodor leave Petrovo? Perhaps meet up with Anna in the city? But how would they earn a living? Maybe she and Anna could work in a sewing shop. With Feodor's experience in Maximov's distillery, could he get a factory job working with machines?

Or perhaps Anton Stepanovich would hire Feodor. He could live in one of the empty cottages behind the manor house where the house serfs lived before they left Petrovo. Even if she and Feodor couldn't marry, they would still be able to see one another.

It was all so confusing. But at least there were choices, something she had never possessed in all of her life until this moment.

Voices from the road filtered into the izba. She stopped breathing and inclined her ear. The voices moved past. Anna's shelf clock chimed twice.

If she was going to do it, she needed to do it quickly and then join Anna in the bathhouse. When the two of them returned to the izba, there Ermak would be. Dead. Or maybe the family, when they returned from the church, would find him first. Either way would be fine.

As Elizaveta pulled the curtain closed, she felt St. Nicholas's gaze scorching her back.

Her fingertips dug into the taut curls of Ermak's sheepskin blanket. Was she capable of doing it?

She reached down and massaged her knee. It still refused to fully bend. After a long day of walking through the fields, its aching kept her awake at night. What if next time Ermak used that skillet to hit her head instead of her knee?

Or what if the worst of her fears came true, and he went after Platoshka when she wasn't present to protect him? And soon there'd be grandchildren for him to terrorize.

She picked up Anna's sheepskin and layered it over Ermak's. Jutting twisted and isolated atop the sheepskins was her little finger.

Across her mind flashed an image of another hand, one with burn scars created when Ermak thrust Gerasim's hand into the boiling soup.

Her stomach went sour with a wild hatred. "It may be murder, you bastard," she hissed, "but you're proof that not everyone deserves to live. If Hell awaits me, then I'll meet up with you. And the two of us will have a reunion with Stanislav."

Her palms moist with sweat, she lowered the double layer of blankets over Ermak's face and pressed them tight to the bench along both sides of his head. Phlegm-choked gasps curdled beneath the sheepskins. His head pitched side to side. His arms flailed beneath his blanket.

Elizaveta's muscles strained. She was losing her grip. She flung the length of her body atop the sheepskins.

His legs kicked and his body writhed. His strength shocked her. Could she continue to hold him?

An arm came out from the side of the sheepskin. Fingers grasped the empty air, trying to seize something, anything. The arm fought to stay alive.

Die, vermin!

His body gave a monstrous jerk and pitched her off, tumbling her and the sheepskins to the floor. He screeched, the frantic, piercing yowl of a wounded animal.

What if a passerby hears him!

Elizaveta leapt to her feet. Ermak's bulging eyes screamed hatred and fear. She slammed her chest across his face and thrust an arm under the wooden bench for leverage. She pulled upward on the bench with all her might, pressing her body tightly against his face. As he strained for breath, his teeth scraped against her shirt, like the mouth of a flailing fish. Open, close. Open, close.

She felt him weaken. The frenzy slowly subsided. At long last, the movement below her ceased.

How long did it take a person to die? How long should she lie here? What if the family arrived home right now? Or Anna came in from the bathhouse? Was he dead?

About to burst, she counted to ten with anguishing slowness. Then she counted it four more times. The stench of his decay filled her nose and strangled her throat.

She put her feet on the floor and straightened her back. She held her hand below his nose. No breath. No movement in his chest. The flat of her hand tapped his cheeks. No response. She slapped harder.

Her tormentor was dead.

The blood pounded in her head as she flattened Ermak's shirt over his stomach as smooth and proper as if he were going to church. She picked up the blankets and tucked them around his skeletal shoulders. Her finger poked his protruding tongue into his mouth. His tongue and lips were blue, but that shouldn't arouse any suspicion. Dead people, like dead animals, were often blue.

Elizaveta slid open the curtain and joined her daughter in the bathhouse.

THE BATHHOUSE WAS thick with steam when a primal howl came from the izba. Onufrii's wife came and broke the news to Elizaveta and Anna. Once inside the izba, Elizaveta beat her chest and wailed with the rest of them. Tears simply wouldn't come, so she rubbed her eyes to make them red.

Everyone in the family was accounted for except one person. "Where's . . . where's Platon?"

"After the funeral, he joined up with some boys," Ilya said between his sobs.

"I . . . ," Elizaveta blubbered, "I need to tell him myself."

She was weak with emotion and her knee ached, but she willed her legs into galloping, ungainly strides down the road. Her mind spun wildly.

Sin.

Hell.

Freedom.

Her felt boots crunched the road's hard-packed snow as she headed to the one place she could be alone with her thoughts.

When she reached the ice-slicked path to the river, her feet slipped out from under her, and she skidded on her rump down to the willow. She secured her sheepskin coat between her skirt and the snow, then settled her shoulder blades around the trunk of the old, bent tree.

The day was frosty, but the sun was bright and the wind was still. Children's shrieks echoed off the air's ice crystals. Upriver, a group of boys were making an ice slide down a high bank. It reflected the sun like polished glass. Frozen white plumes burst from their shouting lips.

One of the boys waved at her. Platon. She waved back and watched him take a running start and glide spread-armed down the slope and onto the solid river. She hoped he was having too much fun to come talk to her. What she had to tell him could wait.

She bent her good knee up to her chest and wrapped her arms around her calf. Her neck arched, and her head dropped back against the willow.

As she squinted into the flawless blue sky, it seemed impossible that moments ago she had committed the most heinous sin possible. What happened to murderers if they were caught? Were they hanged? Sent to Siberia?

How might she get caught? Who could have seen her?

No one.

Beneath her pounding anxiety, Elizaveta felt an uncanny sense of abiding peace. No longer would she succumb to her husband's barbaric fury. Never again would she cower before the insane monster.

Gradually her erratic heart slowed, and her clenched jaw slackened. She straightened her neck and looked at the brilliance of the river's shimmering ice and, strangely, felt uplifted. The river was contained in banks of its own making. It maneuvered around obstacles. For so long, she had been held hostage. But no more! Like the river, she would surge past obstacles. Never again would she allow herself to be tossed about by Ermak, the Vorontsovs, Count Maximov, the village assembly, the Church, the weather, fate.

She gave her head a violent shake. As worthy as those lofty goals were, she needed to put her thoughts on more pragmatic matters—solving the problem of Anna.

Did banishing Anna from Petrovo genuinely have the girl's best interest at heart? Or was it based on her own selfish motives of avoiding lifelong condemnation by her neighbors?

Did sending Anna to Moscow or St. Petersburg imply she was a bad mother? Or, on the contrary, did it mean she was giving her daughter opportunities beyond the prison walls of Petrovo? The city would toughen Anna. She'd learn how to survive. And she'd have the chance to marry and raise a family, something Petrovo would never offer.

Time collapsed, and Elizaveta saw Anna as the little girl who wouldn't steal the mother hen's eggs. The softhearted child who righted upside-down beetles that were clutching the air with their frantic legs. Delicate Anna, who wouldn't squash mosquitoes, because she felt how much it hurt their wings. To this day, the girl would rather be the calf than the butcher.

It was her daughter's fragile reticence that had gotten her into trouble. Anna couldn't say no to the boy's advances and stand by it. She was the essence of vulnerability, a hapless victim of her own naiveté. And perhaps also the victim of her mother's lack of tenderness and guidance.

"Auntie Elizaveta, what are you doing? It's too cold to be sitting here."

Elizaveta reached up and brushed the snow off her godchild's trousers. "Yes, Platoshka, it is cold. But I need to tell you something."

"Tell me what?"

"I'll tell you if you walk home with me."

"Is it something good? Or bad?"

"I'll tell you closer to home."

"I was thinking. I was thinking about winter. Why . . ." His voice trailed off, then resumed with deep consternation. "Why does February never come before January?"

Of all the quandaries weighing on Auntie Elizaveta, that wasn't one of them. "A difficult question, and I don't know the answer." She extended her hand. "The dark will soon be here. Help your old Auntie up. The cold hurts her knee."

As winter's weak light ebbed from the sky, they started down the road that would take Elizaveta's youngest child away from her. *Farewell, my little Anna. I will pray for you every day.*

Her gaze rose to where the road met the far horizon. There she imagined a man returning to her. His words warmed her soul.

I've always known His will is for us to be together.

Yes, somehow they'd find a way to unite their two lives into one.

She glanced at the sprouting boy walking beside her. "Tomorrow is St. Spiridon's Day, the shortest day of the year. Did you know that?"

"It is?"

"Yes."

"So the days will get longer?"

"That's right."

More questions tumbled forth. "Why do days get colder after the shortest day of the year? And why do they get hotter after the longest day?"

"I don't know, Platoshka. I doubt anyone knows. But I'm sure you'll figure it out someday."

THE END

Reading Group

GUIDE

1. Do you think Stepan and Yustina were having an affair? Why or why not?

2. Do you think Anton killed his father? Why or why not?

3. Would you say that Anton was "abused" as a child? Or were his mother's actions merely "inappropriate"?

4. Sophia suffered from what was believed to be incurable melancholia. Based on today's medical knowledge, what possible mental or emotional conditions might have affected her? Would these be treatable today?

5. Stepan was obsessed with his crop rotations. What benefits would these rotations have provided?

6. Put yourself in Elizaveta's shoes. Given the chance, would you be tempted to kill your abusive husband? Do you think you could actually do it?

7. Did Varlaam Gorbunov truly believe himself to be a holy man? Or was he merely a shyster?

8. On the family trees, note the number of deceased children. Contrast the number of deceased children in the nobility's families versus the number in the peasants' families. Do similar trends occur today?

9. It was common for a peasant family to have children born yearly, one right after another. But then a three- to four-year gap would occur, which was followed by another string of births. Why do you think this pattern occurred?

10. Discuss the following quote as it pertains to your beliefs. Might you feel differently if you lived in nineteenth-century Petrovo?

   > "Although everyone knew certain children accidentally died due
   > to drowning or suffocation, it was accepted that those occasional
   > mishaps were in the best interest of the family and the village.

Such was the case when a child was born so deformed, it would be a perpetual drain on the household and would never contribute to the welfare of the community. Likewise, a mother might understandably end a starving baby's life when a famine plunged the entire family into destitution."

11. What are the differences between serfs and slaves?

12. How did the emancipation of Russia's serfs differ from the emancipation of American slaves?

13. The ending left open several options for a sequel. What characters and storyline would you like to see included in a sequel?